# THE

# BODY

# BELOW

# NOVELS BY DANIEL HECHT

*The Body Below*
*On Brassard's Farm*
*The Babel Effect*

THE CREE BLACK SERIES
*City of Masks*
*Land of Echoes*
*Bones of the Barbary Coast*

THE MO FORD SERIES
*Skull Session*
*Puppets (prequel)*

# THE
# BODY
# BELOW

DANIEL HECHT

**BLACK
STONE**
PUBLISHING

Printed in the United States of America

First edition: 2023
ISBN 978-1-5385-1967-7
Fiction / Thrillers / General

Version 1

Blackstone Publishing
31 Mistletoe Rd.
Ashland, OR 97520

www.BlackstonePublishing.com

The truth will set you free. But not until it is finished with you.

—David Foster Wallace

Murder in the murderer is no such ruinous thought as poets and romancers will have it; it does not unsettle him, or fright him from his ordinary notice of trifles: it is an act quite easy to be contemplated, but in its sequel, it turns out to be a horrible jangle and confounding of all relations.

—Ralph Waldo Emerson

# CHAPTER 1

# CONN

I have been taking long swims in Vermont's lakes for the last ten years because it keeps me fit and, more important, keeps me sane. Ultimately—literally—it is what has kept me alive.

Ordinarily, being a free swimmer in a Vermont woodland lake is a joyful experience. That elemental merger with water and air, the self-mastery required to sustain hours of exertion, the joy of arcing down and challenging the deep: These are good for you. Eventually you slouch out, shedding water, exhausted, muscles pumped, heroic. You've absorbed the powers of earth and water and air. You've been another kind of animal and you return to your humdrum human life bearing a good secret about yourself, a private and sure knowledge. You're emboldened by your hours spent skimming just above the mysterious, the unseen.

And yet the fear of the deep is always imminent. With eyes open under water, I see my own shadow raying away into the haze, giving the illusion of great depth and triggering an instinctive warning: *Hidden things lurk below*. I know better, rationally, but that hardwired panic nerve always fires when something startles me as I swim.

Of course there are no monsters in these shallow freshwater lakes. Aside from the occasional reckless speedboat, the worst danger I face is forest debris that has washed off the hillsides. These snags can inflict a vicious scratch or damage a swimmer's eye.

I usually swim four to six miles, crossing from one rocky or mucky shore to another and then back, with no way to anticipate where I might encounter flood-dragged branches or other obstacles. By long habit, I swim with eyes open, above and below the surface, yet these clutching things almost always surprise me. They materialize suddenly, startling me and sometimes scraping my skin as I flail away.

Once something caught just the waistband of my suit, barely touching my skin, as neatly as Celine might hook a finger there when we're making mischief at the beach. I was a hundred yards from any shore, and my body felt it as an intentional gesture by some *thing* that had been waiting for me beneath the surface. I scrabbled away before turning to peer back underwater. Just the witch's claw of a tree limb, clutching up from the bottom. A freakish, low-odds accident of timing and position. Still, it took me several minutes to regain control of my breathing.

The day I kicked the blue-white, bloated thing, I was swimming in Richfield Reservoir. Many Vermont lakes are diamond-clear, their water electric on the skin and sweet on the tongue, but Richfield is not, and I had avoided swimming there for a few years. It's a narrow lake, and the water is cloudy with suspended silt. I was there only out of desperation—it was just a few miles from my office, the sun was dropping behind the mountains, and I figured I'd better swim while I still had some light. I badly needed my ritual ablution, so impatience won out over the will to drive another twenty miles for better water.

The reservoir is fed by a river that winds through miles of wetlands before it enters the lake proper, two basins joined by a narrow waist between bedrock cliffs, three miles long in all. There's a public beach in the upper basin, and about midway a boat launch ramp angles into the water. The larger basin ends abruptly at an earthen dam built in the 1930s.

It's hardly a remote spot—Route 16A runs along one side, a two-lane carrying a sparse but steady stream of traffic during the day. But there are no houses on the lake, and the shoreline is a lovely meander of craggy, lichen-crusted rocks and leaning white birches. Forested hills rise beyond the shore trees.

I had learned never to swim there on weekends, when I'd likely have to dive under the cleaving hulls of reckless speedboats. I'd swim only in the early mornings, or evenings, or when light rain discouraged boaters. Anyway, I preferred the solitude then: just the loons and me.

It was a chilly early July evening after two days of rain, the air thickening with mist that slid down the hills. There were no boats, and almost no traffic along the road. I started at the gravel beach and swam with a purposeful crawl that would bring me to the dam in about forty minutes. At the narrows, I switched to a sidestroke so I'd have a better chance of avoiding branches that might have washed downstream and slowed there. I kept my eyes open, dipping my head under at intervals to scout for obstacles. Beneath the surface, the water didn't permit a long view, just eight or ten feet of greenish glow, lit by the sky's fading light.

Halfway through the narrows, I paused to tread water and admire my lake's-eye view of the cliffs on each side: rugged bedrock topped by white birch trees bright against deepening forest shadow. That was when my foot struck something heavy and solid. I flailed in panic and tucked my head under to look down. A large, pale mass was pivoting slowly away from my kick—an irregularly swollen shape, blue-white, the color of a cataracted eye tinted olive by the silt.

I *clawed* through the water to escape it.

The contact was momentary, but the sensation was disturbingly familiar. You're at the beach with friends, sharking around in the water, and your limbs collide. Or you're goofing with your girlfriend in deeper water and your foot kicks her thigh, and because you're both weightless, you're sent away a bit and so is she.

There's a particular quality of density and resilience to human flesh.

That's the sensation my foot remembered. The image stuck with me, too: that pale, bulbous object spinning away in slo-mo and vanishing into the murk. Those bulges within the milky shroud, round here, creased and bunched there: grotesque and unnatural. It was in view for at most three seconds. When I looked back above water there was no sign of it. Apparently it had neutral buoyancy and had been hovering four or five feet beneath the surface, just where my pedaling foot could strike it.

My nerves screamed alarm. Only after I'd done a hundred feet of fast crawl did reason return.

It had rained for two days, I reminded myself. In these hills, a downpour can turn streams into torrents that leap their banks, cutting through fields and yards and carrying things away. I had dodged aluminum lawn chairs and soccer balls in Richfield Reservoir, and once I swam past a half-submerged doghouse placidly making its way toward the dam. I'd stopped swimming there after gouging my thigh on an eight-inch rusty nail protruding from an old barn timber that lazed below the surface. Six stitches and a Pavlovian aversion had kept me away.

Reason told me that the bulbous thing was one of those huge plastic bags sold to contain lawn trimmings and raked leaves. It had no doubt washed off some upriver backyard and drifted down into the lake. Along the way, it had soaked up water and achieved neutral buoyancy.

By the time I'd swum another half mile, that rationale began to soothe me. Just another underwater startle. Still, on my return between the cliffs, I swam close to the right side, away from where I'd hit the awful hovering thing. Irrationally, the idea of being immersed in the same water revolted me.

But I didn't see it. It didn't pursue me, and I didn't encounter any other terrors. In near darkness, I made it to the gravel beach, splashed out, found my towel and jeans and shirt, and walked shivering up to my car. By then a cool fog had layered above the lake, full of the lush scent of wet summer forest.

I got home as Celine was setting the table, and she had started heating a pot of water for the pasta carbonara I planned to make.

I relished the warmth of the kitchen. In the electric light, the skin of my arms showed mottled purple from the cold.

"Ahoy," Celine said. She smiled as she brought down the salad bowl from the cabinet. "How was it?"

I almost mentioned the thing, but then decided it would only sully a nice time together. I told her that the swim was good, that I was frozen and starving and glad to return to the pleasures of the harbor.

I *was* glad to return—to her, to home. I was soothed by chopping vegetables, stirring the sauce, minding the boil. We had a pleasant dinner, with all the candles lit and the logs of my cabin's walls giving back a golden glow. A good antidote for my moment of revulsion and horror.

Celine is a lovely conversational companion and a lovely woman to look at. She is fairly tall—her eyebrows level with my lips and thus convenient for kissing—with almost-black hair cut to chin length. I consider myself a connoisseur of noses, and hers is one of the best: long and sculpted, implicit of strength and intelligence.

The authority of her nose is betrayed by lips that are sensual and, somehow, vulnerable. That paradox is both beguiling and appropriate. As head of the guidance department of Richfield Unified School District, she deals with kids gone adrift and parents at a loss or abusive. She has developed a toughness to match her naturally empathic nature.

She is also an avid, responsive lover. But that night, when we went upstairs to the loft's big bed, even with wine softening the edges of my unease, I couldn't reciprocate her attentions. When I stroked her thigh, my body recalled the similar resilience of the thing in the lake. Celine was warm and very much alive, but a sickening unease had begun to grow in me. It spread like an infection from the lingering sensation in my foot and the image of that pale bundle tumbling behind me, away and down into deeper water.

By midnight, Celine got sick of my uneasy wakefulness. She switched on the beside lamp and demanded to know what had upset me. I told her about the thing I'd kicked and admitted that I didn't understand why the encounter had stuck with me.

She put the pieces together in short order. She decided I had subconsciously conflated the thing in the water with the woman who disappeared from Waterbury the week before.

I had been following the story as part of my job at the *Richfield Herald*, checking press releases from the State Police but not doing any reporting on it. Waterbury was too far from the *Herald*'s main circulation area to warrant assigning a reporter or any more column inches than I gave the topic. Celine had followed it, too, at first just through my shop talk and then in the local news. She is perpetually curious about why people do what they do and where life leads them. And, she grudgingly admits, she shares the universal fascination with morbid things.

It began with a press release from the Vermont State Police, who were seeking information about Gertrude Carlson, known as Trudy, a Waterbury-area resident and single mom who had gone missing. Apparently the Washington County Sheriff's Department received a call from neighbors and went to Carlson's mobile home to find her two children alone and scared after two days and one night without an adult in the house.

This triggered a missing-persons investigation. The girls were in state custody pending their mother's return or the identification of relatives, and the State Police requested that anyone with knowledge of Trudy Carlson's whereabouts contact their confidential tip line.

A few days later, new developments painted an increasingly grim picture. The State Police located her car, parked off a logging road about a mile from Pendleton Pond, a lake a few miles from Waterbury. They searched the area and found an abandoned tent containing items that indicated it was Carlson's campsite. Unspecified circumstances at the site, along with details about her personal life, suggested foul play.

Waterbury is thirty miles from Richfield, and there was nothing connecting the disappearance to our area, so I didn't do any reporting on it. I just continued reading the State Police press releases as they crossed my desk.

New information emerged every few days. Dogs brought to the campsite caught a scent that led them half a mile to the shore of

Pendleton Pond. State Police officers searched the shoreline and came up with the theory that someone had killed Carlson and had disposed of her body in the lake.

After their dive teams found nothing, the police announced plans to drain the "pond"—misnamed, now, because it's actually a substantial body of water, over six miles long. They had just begun the three-day process when I kicked my mysterious thing in the Richfield Reservoir.

Celine's take on it was that the ongoing case of the missing woman had infiltrated my thoughts, and that I had conflated it with my encounter. The awful image of a corpse in a lake had merged with my startle reflex to forge an unwarranted connection between the two events. In that narrative, I had touched a dead body during my swim and had swum back through the same water that rinsed its decomposing skin.

But it was not rational, she insisted. The missing woman had camped out thirty miles away. The dogs had tracked her to a different lake's edge. The police didn't even know for sure that she was dead! My theory that it was a big plastic bag full of lawn debris made a lot more sense.

Ultimately, I had to agree. We were both groggy—me especially, after a long work day, a four-mile fast swim, and my adrenalized startle.

"Serene Celine," I mumbled. "So rational. Persuasive. Study any psychology in college?" She had a PhD in psychology from the University of Chicago.

"Are you uncomfortable having me apply my astute insight to your internal processes?"

"Do you always answer questions with questions?"

"Would it bother you if I did?"

We laughed and I said, "Okay. Cease and desist." We had our signals down pretty well, and she was okay with me telling her I'd had enough of shrink mode for now. Anyway, she had done a good job, therapeutically speaking. We were both asleep within minutes.

# CHAPTER 2

# CONN

They finished draining Pendleton Pond two days after I kicked the underwater thing. Photos showed the basin as an expanse of dimpled mud interspersed with shoals of gravel and rotten tree stumps. Here and there were silt-mounded foundations left over from the tiny village of Pelton, abandoned when they dammed the outflow of the original pond ninety years earlier. I made a mental note to myself: underwater ghost village, good material for a feature article.

They didn't find a corpse. Police planned to pursue other avenues of investigation.

Just as I forwarded the item to design, my phone light began blinking. The caller ID told me who it was.

"Hey, Mace," I said.

"Conn. I just heard something, and I thought you should be the first to know." His tone told me it wasn't something I'd like to hear. "The woman missing, up in Waterbury? Gertrude Carlson, Trudy? That's not her real name. Not her birth name, anyway. Her real name is Laurel Whitman. Sorry, man. I thought I'd . . . I should be the one. To tell you."

After a stunned moment, my shoulders hit the back of my chair. Laurel Whitman was my sister.

I hadn't recognized the name Gertrude or Trudy Carlson because Laurel had gone through several names in the last fourteen years. Her last name changed according to her husband of the moment, but I had no idea why she'd change her first name, too.

Mace broke the silence. "How're you doing?"

"I don't know. You?"

"Well. Lot of water under that bridge. But."

Another silence as I sifted through my feelings: a mix of disbelief, loss, and shame. I had drifted away from my sister—hadn't seen her in almost five years. From what I knew of her affairs, I was not surprised that something bad had happened to her, because she lived a messy, careening life among others who shared her habits.

For the most part, hers was a tawdry, pathetic story: divorces, drinking, arrests for possession of controlled substances, a stream of edgy misogynistic boyfriends, two kids by a deadbeat dad long gone. Midnight appearances on my doorstep with black eyes, bruises, suitcases, and, later, a baby. And when she went back to her own place, something often left with her: a CD player, a sterling silver tray, anything she could pawn. It was my efforts to goad, plead, or shame her into making better choices that led to six or seven years of complete estrangement. She told me I had no right to claim any moral high ground. Also to fuck off and leave her alone.

At that time—just after the birth of her second kid—I told her I'd do just that. I'd had it. My last round of paying for rehab, and then co-signing a loan for a car that her husband of the moment totaled within a week, had forced me to look at what our relationship was doing for both of us. I was enabling her and she was dragging me down. And, as she'd pointed out, I had only recently come through my own rocky and morally compromised patch. My balance was still precarious. I told her that when she got her shit together, she should look me up.

As it turned out, after those years of total disconnect, she did. We cautiously began talking on the phone. When I felt I had finally gotten reliably sober, I invited her for dinner at my house, and I visited her and the kids at her place once. She looked better, but I was not impressed with her boyfriend or the bongs, bottles, and takeout wrappers that cluttered their living room. We managed to smile at each other, one of the kids experimentally sat on my lap. But our earlier conflicts, when we were both deeper in the shit, had taken their toll: We kept a safe distance. The fact that I'd been reading the press releases for two weeks without realizing this Gertrude Carlson was my sister was a good measure of that distance.

Mace broke the silence: "I guess I'm surprised at how hard it's hitting me. After all these years. After all the crap we went through."

Mason King was a deputy in the Richfield County Sheriff's Department and my friend since childhood—one of very few who didn't drop me when I limped back from Washington in shame. He had also been Laurel's first husband. I had enthusiastically encouraged the match, twenty years ago, and it was partly her poor treatment of Mace that awakened me to her real character.

"So," I said, "State Police called you guys? For help with the missing-persons investigation?"

"Yeah. Not that we can do much. But they're looking for connections wherever they can find them. Now that they know she's originally from over this way, they'll want to have our department's help locally. And you and I are 'connections'—they'll probably want to talk to us."

"I'd be of no use."

He went silent again, and I could hear a phone wheedling in his office. "I'm still keeping my fingers crossed," he said. "That she's okay and has just, I don't know—"

"Run away from the obligation to take care of her kids?" I felt a flash of anger at her. If she had, it wouldn't be the first time she had abdicated responsibility. She hadn't helped care for my father in his fading years— an emotional burden I could have used some help carrying.

"Something like that. But the cop grapevine is pretty sure she's been murdered, Conn. I don't know the details, but aside from evidence at the campsite, the Major Crime people say there are indications in her social situation. Boyfriend issues." He stopped again and seemed to choke up.

Mace was a big guy, thickening as he approached middle age, with sandy hair, round cheeks, a close-cut cop's mustache. I could visualize his face as we talked: a friendly mug that gave away his feelings by how expressionless it became when something upset him. I knew because over the years I had seen him doing his job as I covered car wrecks, drownings, and house fires—always holding his face impassive. A solid guy, married, two kids. But Laurel's affairs and dumping him and the mess her life turned into: Those had hurt him, and some of the pain had lingered.

At last he said, "Laurel. You know? God damn it."

That about summed it up. Not much I could add.

After we disconnected, I'm sure Mace stared at his phone for a time just as I did. A backwash of emotion hit me. I had been thinking of giving her a call—why hadn't I? We'd left it at "Let's get together soon, yeah?" One of those vague stepping-stone commitments that sat unresolved, like a problematic email that languishes in your inbox. If I'd acted on it, we might have moved on to a real friendship. Whether she was alive or dead, this latest episode of Laurel's dire straits awakened concern and dismay, followed quickly by guilt: Was there really nothing more I could have done, back when her life fell apart? Couldn't I have tried to be a better brother during the last few years?

But mainly I felt sorrow for her squandered life. A sense of loss. Loss and a twinge of, what, emptiness? Loneliness?

Several lights on my phone had begun blinking, but I put a clipboard over it so I could process things a bit longer. As her nearest living relative—we had cousins in Wisconsin, but I was pretty sure she'd severed those ties—I had a right to ask the police for more information. Also, there were her kids. I was no kind of candidate for adoptive father, but I figured I should contact Child Services and take some role in helping them.

I started by calling Richfield County Sheriff Paula Levinson. I knew Paula not only as Mason's boss, but from my work: a capable, personable woman who ran an effective department. She invited me to meet at her office at two o'clock.

I drove over, parked, went in, shook hands with Paula and two of her deputies, Lane Hudson and Jerry Penkowski. Jerry and I had gone to high school together; he had been in a few classes with Laurel, too.

Knowing people helps. Having grown up in an area makes it easier to cover human interest stories and local news. Paula and the others knew me as a buddy of one of their own and a longtime community member, and they knew I'd covered some sensitive stories while I was at the *Washington Post*. I figured they'd be willing to trust me with more information than they'd give another reporter. In any case, I was there only as next of kin. Whatever they might tell me wasn't material for a story.

We settled at a meeting table in Paula's office. Lane brought a skinny case folder with him. A window gave a view of a row of cruisers and, beyond, pedestrians passing on the sidewalk. From the door I could hear robotic-sounding voices as calls came in to the dispatcher.

"You must be very upset, Conn," Paula said. "Are you two close?"

I told them about our years of estrangement, using some euphemisms that put a happier spin on the degree of our reconciliation. All three nodded, a bit embarrassed for me.

"But if she doesn't show up, I guess I'm the one who has to handle her affairs, whatever that entails. And probably deal with the kids. The father is a deadbeat, I don't know if anybody knows where he is. I should learn all I can."

Jerry told me the basics. It was mainly in the hands of the State Police, he said, but he and Lane had helped out with legwork—talking to neighbors in the Maple Meadow neighborhood, and to her boss and coworkers at Martinson's, Waterbury's supermarket, where she managed the bakery section. Everyone called her Trudy. They had identified a couple of her friends, who in turn told them that, yes, she'd had some problems recently.

"Boyfriend issues," Jerry explained. "Apparently she was trying to scrape one off the bottom of her shoe, and another suitor was in the picture. Nobody knows who the new guy is, but we got a name for the old one. Anthony Shapiro. Upright citizen—three DUIs, lost his license a couple of times, a cocaine bust a few years ago—"

"And 'unavailable for comment,'" Paula put in.

"Ah," I said. That is, they couldn't locate him. His taking to his heels would put him at the top of any list of suspects.

Jerry went on, reading from his file: "Bar fights . . . um, some burglary, bad checks—"

"Sounds like my sister's type," I told them.

Jerry explained the accumulation of suggestive data. Coworkers confirmed that she had been planning a camping trip, a few days in the woods while her kids spent a week at a summer camp. She found subs for her shifts at the store. Yes, she had seemed somewhat uneasy—distressed, under pressure—for the last few weeks.

My mind rebelled against the implications. "They don't think maybe Laurel and this guy, they just ran off together and—"

"I'm sorry, Connor," Paula said. "I'm sure they'll keep that possibility in mind, and it's true that without a body they're reluctant to call it homicide at this point. But that's how they're treating it. There's just too much that doesn't fit another scenario."

"Can you elaborate on the, um, the 'indications of foul play'? At the tent site?"

"Well, the blood on the—" Jerry began.

Paula coughed discreetly, and they shot each other glances. Jerry went quiet.

"I'm sorry, Connor," Paula said.

I wasn't sure whether they were protecting my feelings or the confidentiality of their information. But I didn't really need more. "Where does it go now? Given that Pendleton Pond didn't . . . pan out?"

"Again, it's the States' responsibility," Lane said. "Captain Welles, head of the Major Crime Unit, is in charge. We'll liaise and do what we can. It's a matter of chasing down every connection. They're looking at boyfriends, Shapiro foremost, but it's difficult because it's, you know, she . . ."

Lane petered out, trying to be tactful about that which had little potential for tact.

I let him off the hook: "Because she had a lot of boyfriends and they were all losers."

Lane nodded, apologetic. "So it means a lot of legwork. Talking to neighbors, friends, everybody and anybody. But yeah—legwork."

We were all silent for a moment.

"Have you talked to the DCF yet?" Paula asked. DCF meant Department for Children and Families, which would have taken custody of the kids.

"No. I truly just heard about this an hour ago. I'll call today."

Paula nodded. I stood up, figuring we were done for now.

"Um, Connor," Paula said. "You're going to get into the spotlight here. Being her brother. And . . ."

I gave her an attempt at a grateful smile. I knew what she meant. I had a well-known checkered past that included bad drugs, bad company, and dubious behavior that might suggest me as a suspect. At the least, it offered juicy background gossip for some zealous colleague at another paper.

I thanked them and drove back to the *Herald* offices, exhausted.

My phone was blinking when I stepped back into my cubicle. The woman on the other end introduced herself as Vickie Landauer, from the DCF, who first asked me if I had heard about Laurel's disappearance. I told her that I just had.

"I'm very sorry. You must be terribly concerned. I sincerely hope it all turns out all right."

"Thank you."

"Mr. Whitman, the reason I'm calling is that I am the case manager assigned to oversee your nieces' transition. Your sister's absolutely lovely daughters are safe in a foster care situation pending our attempt to locate their next of kin. It took us a while because they . . . well, they couldn't remember your name at first. We informed Captain Welles at the State Police."

"My sister and I were kind of estranged for a while."

"I understand. Well, the way our department works is that children who can't live in their parental home become wards of the state. Our goal is to place them in happy, safe situations as close to their home community as possible. Ideally, that's with family—kin care. If that's not possible, they are placed in stranger care—one of our licensed foster homes. That's where Maddie and Julie are now."

I knew a little about the process from my reporting, more from hearing Celine talk about her work with troubled families in the school district.

"I should go see them," I said. "But I really don't know them. I don't know where I'd even start! I don't know what they've been told about their mother. Can you tell me?"

"Only that we and the police are as concerned as they are, we're doing everything we can to make sure she comes back soon."

"How are they holding up?"

She sighed. "Maddie is quite mature for an eleven-year-old. She's managing it with a sort of stoical attitude. Julie is nine and not as . . . steady. Their foster parents are good people and are experienced with situations like this." She paused and I heard her shuffling papers on her desk. "Mr. Whitman, the girls have told us that they don't know their father. Anyway, the police tell us he's got quite a criminal record, so he wouldn't be a candidate for kin sheltering. That leaves you as next of kin. We wanted to explore your thoughts on serving as their shelter. Their guardian."

I gave her the rundown: unmarried, working full-time, living in a log cabin with, basically, one room, never spent time with kids in my life. It sounded wrong, like a dodge. And too dismal: In fact, my cabin was a nice home, my life had taken on a pleasing order and wholeness—at least until the news about Laurel. I told her I would certainly consider taking them on in some way if it turned out that Laurel was, in fact, never coming back.

"Okay." She was jotting things down. "And can you see having a presence in their lives in the interim? Keeping dislocated children con- nected—that's the main thing, Mr. Whitman. Connection and continuity."

Connection and continuity: exactly what I couldn't offer. I had no more role in their lives, or their mother's life, than their deadbeat father. But I knew what I was supposed to say.

"I'd like to get to know them. I'll do whatever I can."

We left it there. She gave me instructions on how to set up a visit, and we disconnected.

The whole thing was catching up to me, and I felt justified in signing out of the office a bit early. There's a demoralization of the spirit that comes with glimpses of the dark side of human beings. You wonder what we are. Sometimes you wonder if being one is worth it. Or if there's any cure. I figured I'd pull out of it—in DC, back when I was somebody, I had done so after various scandals and some foul politics and a sex-trafficking nightmare.

But it takes a while. And it's worse when it's someone you know. Knew. Loved, love, something like that.

# CHAPTER 3
# CONN

Celine saw it in me the moment I got home. When I told her that the missing woman was my sister, she held me briefly, then sat with me as I gave her more details. She had never met Laurel—Trudy—but over the last two years I had told her bits of the calamitous saga.

I said I was surprised by the strength of my reaction to the news.

"She was your sister. Whatever she did or didn't do, that's reason enough to be upset. To grieve."

"I don't even know if I should grieve! Maybe she's all right and is just being an irresponsible shit again. The people she worked with said there was a new boyfriend in the picture. Maybe she ran off with the new Romeo."

"In which case maybe she'll be back."

"Part of me is just saying 'I don't need this crap! Laurel's a grown-up, she should deal. Not my problem!'"

"Sure. Sounds like an easy way through," Celine said drily. More gently, she noted that while it was less painful to resent than to grieve, neither was a happy prospect. I should wait until I knew more before berating myself for these feelings—they were likely to get more complex and more difficult later.

I couldn't argue with that point.

Celine uncorked a bottle of wine and poured a glass for each of us. At first I thought I wanted music, but I couldn't find the right ambience. Van Morrison, no. Bach cello sonatas, no. Gipsy Kings, no. Buena Vista Social Club? From baroque to bluegrass, nothing worked. Cheery music would be inappropriate, minor-key music too sad. Anything from the eighties or nineties would bring back memories from before Laurel's life nose-dived, right now a recipe for heartbreak. So we had a quiet dinner.

My house is a log cabin, built by my father as a getaway when I was a kid. Thirty-five years later, the wood of the interior walls and rafters has aged to a warm yellow. It has a spacious one-room ground floor, with just a counter and stools dividing the main living space from the kitchen. It's half open to the peak and half covered by a loft where I set up a bedroom and an office. After my father died and I returned from DC, I fixed it up for year-round living. The decor is an eclectic mix—modern appliances, contemporary couch, good stereo system, but braided rugs on the floor and old wooden chairs my father had restored. I had positioned standing lamps at strategic spots, but I'd also kept the original lighting, a dozen antique tin sconces nailed to the walls. Their candles gave the place a warm luster, augmented on winter nights by the fire in the woodstove.

After dinner, we sat on the couch and sipped our wine. The momentum of my distress slowed. We talked through the obligations that came with being next of kin. I should schedule a time to visit the kids soon. I would need to look into Laurel's legal affairs—did she own or lease her mobile home, did she have a will—and make plans for the disposition of her things. I should contact the State Police, introduce myself. Later, if she were conclusively proved dead, I'd need to deal with her possessions—whatever that entailed.

It helped to reduce the issue to a bunch of tasks. Check 'em off the list, be done with it. Having consigned tomorrow's duties to tomorrow, we did the dishes and snuffed the candles.

My steadier footing lasted until we started upstairs. At the bottom, I had hung a little gallery of family photos: my mother and father, myself as a child, various dogs. Mason and me at around twelve, grimy and proud after stacking six cords of firewood, another with fish we'd caught. My first car.

And photos of Laurel—a gap-toothed girl holding up a blue ribbon awarded for some summer-camp triumph, a high-school portrait, a shot of her with Mason at their wedding, glowing. At the sight of her smiling, freckled, trusting face, I burst into tears.

Celine said nothing, offered no analysis. Just a reassuring hand on the small of my back as we headed upstairs. Not just a PhD in psychology, but a compassionate woman who, astonishingly, loved me. Sometimes simple companionship is the best medicine.

# CHAPTER 4

# CONN

The next day I called my boss and said I'd need a couple of days off—urgent family matters. No problem, she said: Dennis would fill in for me on the new dog ordinances in Marshfield and the zoning tussle in Williamstown. These I wouldn't miss, but I was sorry to postpone my interview with Martha Oatley, who was having her one-hundredth birthday. Centenarians: You have to catch them while you can, no matter how vigorous they seem. But my sister was haunting me. And the side of my foot, where I'd kicked the thing in the reservoir, was making me ill.

The State Police headquarters are located in Waterbury, not far from Pendleton Pond and Laurel's home. The head of the Major Crime Unit, Captain Welles, was someone I hadn't met. From his accent, I knew he was not a native Vermonter, and he had a military sort of brusqueness, a style reinforced by his jarhead haircut, at-arms posture, and over-firm handshake. We met in his office, not an interview room, but his attitude made me feel more like a suspect than a helpful family member.

It went sour fast.

"So you're a reporter at the *Herald*. We've been putting out press releases about Gertrude Carlson being missing for almost two weeks. Mind telling me why it took so long for you to contact us?"

"I didn't recognize the name. I didn't know she'd changed her first name."

"Any idea why she would? Or would choose that name? A relative, maybe, some beloved aunt—?"

"No idea. Look, to be honest, I wasn't even sure of her last name! Carlson—that was the name of her second husband, but that was a long time ago. I'd have thought she'd've gone back to Whitman again."

The look he gave me was a mix of skepticism and accusation. "You really were not in communication with your sister. At all."

"No. We had a falling-out, I guess you could say, some years ago. We keep meaning to get together, but we just—"

"So, would you characterize your relationship as rancorous?"

*Ah*, I thought. I leaned back in my chair to appraise him. I had started to hurt—over my sister's life, I still wasn't letting myself admit she was dead—and I wasn't up for taking shit off this guy.

"You have to take a course in interviewing skills to make detective, let alone head of a Major Crime division, right?" I asked. "But I haven't seen one such skill yet. I can explain what they are, if—"

"It's my job to locate your sister, alive or dead. I'm starting out with an open mind. Is there some reason that should bother you?"

"Let your subject complete his sentences. He might incriminate himself even more if you let him talk."

His mouth tipped in a tight grin. "Just giving you an experimental poke, see if you squirm. I got the gist of the relationship from Sheriff Levinson. I don't expect I'll finesse a famous investigative journalist."

That was a jab, too. I wasn't happy that he'd googled me and knew the unsavory details of my past. Still, I liked him a little better. Also I realized he had a brain. We rebooted.

Welles gave me a summary of events. Apparently Laurel's daughters got dropped off by the mother of a friend who had also been at camp. The girls assured her they were accustomed to coming home to an empty place—after school, Laurel was usually at work and both girls had keys. Their cell calls went to her answering service, but they were reluctant to call around to figure out where she might be. When night came, they just stuck it out and eventually fell asleep. It wasn't until the next day that they got worried enough to call their neighbors.

Welles had been pacing as he spoke, but now he squared his shoulders and faced me. "Here's where we're at. In public, we're going to keep calling it a missing-persons case, and we'll keep open minds about that. But in here, we're effectively treating it as a homicide. We were denied a search warrant for her house on the basis of the homicide assumption, so we requested a warrant for evidence of child endangerment. That one we got, and the girls gave us the key. Child Services and one of my investigators are over there now."

That sounded reasonable. Without a body, and given that the house wasn't considered the scene of a murder, the only crime they knew of for sure involved the kids.

"I don't know how I can help," I told him.

He didn't respond, but his gaze was unrelenting. His mental video camera was on, recording me. The man had learned to make good use of silence. I spread my hands, a gesture of helplessness, and waited him out.

"You're wrong about not being able to help."

"How so?"

"We know even less than you do. She's got a mobile home full of her things. Photos, furniture, books, souvenirs, clothes—we don't know where any of it came from. The food in the fridge—is broccoli something she liked, or is it some other party's taste? If so, whose? We're looking at boyfriends or drug suppliers, of course, but if this turns into a whodunit, we'll need perspective. You might recognize a face in a photo, or see something that rings a bell. A knickknack—from back when, or did someone give it to her recently? See what I'm saying?"

"You want me to go over there?"

"Sooner the better. That means tomorrow morning. We'll get the key from Child Services."

Over the years, I had come to trust the powers of forensics, of police ingenuity. I had no doubt that they'd locate her alive, or find her body, soon. Also that if and when death was confirmed, I'd be the one to deal with her possessions. I had the day off. Had to do it sometime.

We arranged to go to Laurel's house in the morning. He read me some names of past boyfriends, none of whom I knew. I gave him the names of our relatives in Wisconsin, on the off chance she'd landed on a doorstep out there, and then headed out to my car.

If I've learned anything from my late-acquired appreciation of fitness, it's that you have to keep at it. After talking to Welles, I went for an early afternoon swim at Lake Elmore. It's a much longer drive than Richfield Reservoir, but I'd never swim there again, and Elmore has beautiful water that makes your skin come alive. The shore is lined with houses and docks, gorgeous wooded hills rising behind. The Worcester Range runs just to the west, and a CCC-era trail starts at the lake and winds up Mount Elmore to a rickety fire tower at the top. Lovely country, a fine lake.

I swam from the state park beach to the line of buoys that wards boaters from the dam and spillway. I fell into a hypnotizing fast crawl, glad for the clear water—no narrow juncture with bloated submarine horrors. As always, I swam with my eyes open, but Elmore is both clear and deep, so there are never snags and thus less primal paranoia. I swam the full length twice to get in my miles, and on the way back I chose a backstroke so that I could stare at the sky and absorb some of its calm and clarity.

*The water is good,* I kept telling myself. *It heals you. The water washes you clean. There are no monsters here.*

No monsters except for the persistent, dull thud along the side of my right foot.

I got home as muscle fatigue began to catch up with me—the whole-body stiffening that follows a good swim, like a boiling egg firming up. When I saw that Celine was there, the world righted itself a bit. I told her about my meeting with Captain Welles and our plans to go through Laurel's house tomorrow.

"Sounds like a smart man," she told me. "Find the truth through the person—the personality. He's right that you might have something to offer."

"It's been too long, babe. Just too long."

"We'll see. In any case, you'll find out what you'll be up against if you have to deal with her stuff."

I balled up my wet towel and pitched it into the laundry alcove. "Something to look forward to," I said.

After dinner, it occurred to me that Mason was another person who could offer perspective on Laurel's house and possessions—they'd been married for six years. I didn't think Captain Welles would object to having a sheriff's deputy join our walk-through, so I called Mace.

Mason didn't want to do it any more than I did, but I twisted his arm hard.

"I don't know, Conn. Jody and I have a lot of work to get ready for the party this weekend. Tomorrow, I've got a meeting at eleven thirty, then traffic duty until—"

"Welles said nine. We'll make it quick." No answer. "Mace. This isn't going to be any fun for me. I could use your company. We'll get it over with, get you back in time."

He still sounded dubious. "I take it you had a talk with Dudley Do-Right today?"

"Yeah. Seems like a guy who . . . plays by the rules. We got on okay, though."

"He's new to the area. Fifteen years in the Army, fifteen with the Mass State Police, transferred up here last year. Hasn't endeared himself to his colleagues. Something of a macho approach, I gather."

"Worked with him?"

Mace sighed. "Not yet. But it looks like I'm going to."

He knew that if Anthony Shapiro didn't pan out—or the husband, or some boyfriend, or drug supplier—his status as former spouse might bring him into it.

He agreed to pick me up at eight thirty in a County car so we could drive to Waterbury together. Knowing he'd be there calmed me a little. I thanked him, and we got off the line. It was a difficult time, but I knew I had a lot to be grateful for, and Mace ranked near the top of my list. Even more than Celine, he could understand—share—my contorted sense of loss.

Once I explained that Mason was Laurel's long-ago ex, Welles had no problem with his coming along. We met at the Waterbury State Police headquarters, then took Welles's car to Maple Meadow Mobile Home Community. It was just off a rural road only ten minutes away.

While Mace and Welles made cop small talk in the front seat, I kept quiet. I was thinking ahead to what I knew I'd see: a trailer reflecting the lifestyle of its inhabitant, reflecting the causes of our estrangement. In the living room, a shag rug with tobacco and marijuana crumbs in it, couch with cigarette burns on the arms, wastebaskets full of beer cans and fast-food wrappers. Kitchen: dishes piled in the sink, burned food crusted on the stove top. Bedroom: rock-band posters taped to the walls, a rented black-dyed-wood monstrosity of a bed, more butt-burns on the Formica bedside table. That smell of stale booze and cigarettes with an overlay of unvacuumed mildew.

That was the decor I'd seen when she lived with Husband Two, before we'd parted ways, and the time I'd visited her place five years ago.

Maple Meadow consisted of a central avenue coming off the town road, with shorter streets branching to left and right. They were lined with single- and double-wides set in small, well-tended yards, many separated by hedges. Plastic kids' wading pools, bicycles tossed beside front steps, bird feeders on posts, only one dead snowmobile: a friendly little neighborhood. At the end of the main avenue, a bunch of kids played soccer in the street.

Laurel's home was a vinyl-sided double-wide with a yard big enough for a spreading maple tree and a small Quonset shed. Welles handed us latex gloves and waited until we tugged them on before he unlocked the door.

*Here goes*, I thought. Mace went expressionless. Welles had to urge us inside.

Mace tagged along behind me as if reluctant to see how his ex had lived, and I couldn't blame him. What indications of personal disintegration or decadence might we see? Would she still have something from when they were married? The place could be an emotional minefield for him.

But it looked like a normal house. Clean and orderly and without the smell of smoke, unwashed dishes, or the body odor of drunk boyfriends. The living room included a potted fern, robust but starting to sag, and the covers of the throw pillows on the couch looked hand-embroidered. No overflowing ashtrays, no candles shaped like hands with fuck-you fingers raised or skulls, no beer cans.

"Anything?" Welles prodded.

Mace and I shook our heads.

"Conn would know more than me," Mace said. This was hitting him hard: His voice had a slight quaver. "Laurel and I were together only six years, ended fourteen years ago. Conn'll have a better perspective. Longer view. And he saw her after we broke up, something I never did except in court."

"It's a lot better than the last place I saw," I said. "I mean, from a housekeeping perspective."

This sounded irrelevant and Welles gave no indication he'd heard me.

"What does the warrant allow you to look at?" I asked.

"Not much. Overt signs of child endangerment such as drug use or physical abuse. Indications of criminal activity. Indications of neglect— we've also worked the neighborhood on that—her general circumstances, the kids' health and behavior. Personally, I'm looking for indications she intended to disappear. Or not."

I led the way into the kitchen. On the table, empty cereal boxes, an empty milk jug, cornflake-rimmed bowls, and a scraped-clean peanut butter jar told us how the kids had fed themselves in their time alone. There were a few dishes in the sink, but it was basically clean, by no means the crack-squat mess I'd imagined. It was an ordinary kitchen. Spices in a rack. Kids' drawings held to the fridge by ladybug magnets. A calendar with dentist's appointments and summer activities penciled in.

Among other knickknacks on the windowsill over the sink, I spotted a three-inch tin model of the Empire State Building I'd gotten her during a vacation trip to the Big Apple.

"Yeah, this," I said. I picked it up, looked it over, felt a twinge near my heart. The price tag was still stuck to the bottom—$1.98, a price from another century. "Got it when we were ten or twelve."

Welles nodded.

Overall, it seemed an ordinary lower-middle-income kitchen: small breakfast table and four Walmart hoop-backed wooden chairs, Sears fridge and stove, a too-vivid pattern on the linoleum.

"I was serious about looking at the refrigerator," Welles said. "The search people didn't find anything of relevance. But you might."

He swung open the door, releasing the smell of rotten vegetables. The rot made sense: Laurel had been gone for almost two weeks.

Looking through the contents of a stranger's refrigerator: I quelled my resentment at Welles for foisting the task on us and did my best to see it with a reporter's eye. It seemed reasonably well-stocked. Yogurt, salad dressing. Eggs, butter in the bin, wilted celery and browning lettuce in the crisper . . . What revelations could hide here?

"She eat meat?" Welles asked, over my shoulder.

"Used to," I said. "I don't know." But his point was interesting. I noticed jars of walnuts and almonds—something I kept in my own fridge since I got clean and started eating right. But reading anything into Laurel's dietary preferences would be meaningless.

Mason just shrugged.

The freezer was the same: ordinary things. Enough frozen meals for a working mom to feed hungry kids fast. Frozen pizzas, pre-fried chicken pieces, peas, strawberries, blueberries.

"The kids said they didn't cook anything because Mom didn't want them using the stove when she wasn't home," Welles noted.

We went back through the living room and into a hallway where I saw something that surprised me. She'd put up a collection of photos a lot like mine: Mom and Pop, some aunts and uncles, several shots of me at various ages. Half a dozen shots of babies and toddlers, presumably her daughters, a couple of birthday-party scenes. A few showed groups of men and women I didn't recognize, with mountain or lake views behind them, mementos of hiking trips. A couple were clearly selfies, taken at arm's length with a small tent in the near background and forested hills far behind.

Surprisingly, she had also kept a photo of herself and Mace at their engagement party: two radiant young people wearing rented fancy clothes.

I hadn't thought of Laurel as the nostalgic type, not enough to keep photos of me or Mace. I'd assumed she'd be even better than I was at cutting off the past, at burning bridges. The investigative nerve in my psyche twitched: My avalanche of a sister had kept these photos, had gone to the trouble of buying frames, and had mounted them in a neat display. However bad it had gotten, she had cherished a few tokens of the sane life she'd once lived.

"Something caught you there," Welles said. He was observing Mace and me as closely as he was the house.

I explained that I was surprised Laurel had kept family photos. I told him the names of those I knew, told him which faces and settings I didn't. Mace didn't know any more than I did about the more recent faces.

We continued the tour. Bathroom: reasonably clean, nothing un-usual in the medicine cabinet or drawers, kids' toys on the edge of the tub along with two colorful washcloths. A tiny laundry room with stacked washer and dryer, a canvas basket with clothes ready to be washed.

All in all, beneath the surface messes the girls had made in their time alone, this was a clean, orderly household. Functional, *coherent*. Needs of daily life holding together. Past and present holding together. Held together by a person holding together.

It was not the home of a negligent, drug-addicted loser.

*Find the truth through the person,* Celine had said.

My anxiety mounted as we moved on to the bedrooms. Bedrooms are where intimate lives are lived, places that casual company doesn't see, redoubts where people's secrets reside and are likely to speak. We went into Laurel's first. It did have the heavy-beamed bedstead, bedding rumpled—and two extra pillows, butterfly-patterned, showing where the girls had slept for what must have been a harrowing night. Clothes were draped on the back of chairs and on the wicker hamper. But here again were photos, Mom and Pop most prominently, along with framed drawings done by her daughters. No rock star posters. On the bureau, a jewelry box, a couple of perfume bottles, and a tray holding lipsticks and mascara. No coke-dusted mirrors or ashtrays full of roaches.

My sense of being an intruder, a voyeur, deepened.

"Huh. Amazing," Mason said. He picked up a vase containing a bunch of dried flowers. "I gave her this. Long time ago. I guess she liked it, after all." The blown-glass rose from its base in an iridescent-blue column ending in a tulip-shaped opening. I remembered it, too, from some anniversary or birthday—he had been proud of finding something he knew would please his young wife. And here it was, miraculously unbroken or pawned by some boyfriend.

"What does it tell you that she kept this souvenir, Mr. King? And that photo of you on the wall?" Welles asked.

Mace shrugged. "Beats me. I wouldn't think she'd be that sentimental. Memory of happier times? I'm not a psychologist."

Welles, expression inscrutable, made a note on his iPad.

At the window, Laurel had set up a desk just like mine at the cabin, a hollow-core door laid across two metal filing cabinets. On it, an inkjet printer sat among a scattering of papers—shopping list, kids' drawings, pay stubs from the grocery store—a couple of paperbacks, some pens. A computer cord and adapter snaked from the outlet, but no computer was in evidence.

"What do you make of the missing laptop?" I asked. "Think she took it camping?"

"Possibly. But it wasn't found at the campsite, so someone stole it, either from here or from there. That's unfortunate, but it's suggestive."

"Of?"

"If somebody took it from here, it wasn't for its resale value—they'd have taken the cord and adapter. So it was to get access to its contents. Or prevent *us* from getting access." Welles's mouth turned down, unhappy with the implications: It suggested a deeper, more tangled story here.

I tugged at the handle of one of the file cabinets, but it wouldn't open.

"Locked," Welles said. "Both of them. We haven't been able to find a key."

"If she's dead, I'll need to deal with her stuff, with the kids. Can't we just jimmy them and see if she's got a will, or guardianship provisions?"

"No. There's a whole domain of law dealing with locked containers. Except in rare circumstances, it's viewed as a severe breach of constitutional rights. Trust me, I learned this the hard way. Your sister is not a suspect, and we're not even a hundred percent sure she's dead. So it'll have to wait until we have better probable cause." Welles didn't look any happier about it than I was.

I was frustrated but couldn't argue. In fact, I rather appreciated his playing by the rules. Would I had done the same back in my high-flying DC days.

We opened the bedroom closet to find clothes on hangers, a shoe bag on the door with a range of footwear pouched in it, sweaters and jackets dumped on a shelf full of folded blankets and sheets.

Mace looked in, then took an impatient turn and came back. "Do we really have to do this? I mean, every last thing? Jesus, you've searched the place, you've got photos, fingerprints, DNA—"

"Hardly anything that elaborate. We looked for basic indications of child neglect, that's it. I expect we'll be back here soon enough and will conduct a complete forensic investigation at that time."

"So what do you want with Conn and me? Fuck's sake! This is just—"

"Stick it out for another few minutes," Welles ordered.

We looked into the girls' room: a bunk bed, toys and clothes, things cuddly and colorful. Messier than Laurel's room. In the bureau drawers, folded T-shirts and undies and jeans, socks neatly paired. On a shelf, My Little Ponies in parade formation. Throughout, lots of pink and lavender miscellany. It occurred to me that there was nothing in this room that came from me, their uncle, not a toy or curio or fucking anything.

Mace had been quiet for a while. Probably he was sharing my feelings: This was an ordinary house, and seeing it both abandoned and exposed to the scrutiny of strangers struck us with its pathos.

I felt sleazy: a guy walking around in someone's house and getting his jollies by imagining whether any of it had creepy implications. Walk through my house—what's the "meaning" of that stupid rubber pig Celine won tossing darts at balloons at the Tunbridge Fair? What's its sinister implication? We're all guilty of living individual lives, mysterious to anyone but our most loved ones. The things you'd find might be private jokes, random items that conjured important memories, knickknacks kept ironically for their poor taste. Wasn't Laurel entitled to the same?

Welles roused us. "Is there anything that seems significant to you? Anything seem out of the ordinary for Trudy, Laurel, as you knew her?"

Mace and I looked at each other.

"We didn't really know her," I said.

On the way out, passing her photo gallery again, I was struck by the shots of mountain and lakeside campsites. Laurel had not been a big outdoorsy type, not even as a kid. She and Mason had done some camping when they'd first married, but she'd never gotten into it as much as he had. Whatever else these photos suggested, to me they revealed a changing person. Her tent camping near Pendleton Pond might have been her last outing, but it was certainly not her first.

We left the house and Welles locked the door behind us. "Impressions?" he asked.

"Not the house of someone who voluntarily left her children alone for two days and still hasn't come back," I said. "Whose kitchen calendar shows dentist's appointments for next week."

Mason, expressionless, nodded his head.

"That's where Child Services ended up, too," Welles said. "I agree."

We finished with a tour of the vinyl-covered Quonset shed. It was big enough to use as a snug one-car garage, but Laurel had just stored stuff there: lawnmower, snow shovels, leaf rake, an adult's mountain bike and two smaller ones, a plastic wading pool. Four snow tires. A pair of snowshoes, dangling from the superstructure. Coils of garden hose. Farther in, a dusty tricycle, a child's car seat. A set of metal shelves with a few cardboard boxes on it.

"The boxes are full of kids' clothes," Welles said. "Outgrown, I suppose." He lifted a mostly empty sack of birdseed, looked it over, set it down. "So, Mr. Whitman, any insights?"

I thought about it, and yes, something possibly anomalous registered. "This bicycle. Disc brakes, front shocks, and rear swing-arm shock. Looks brand-new. I've just been looking at bikes to replace my old beater. I'd guess this one would cost about two grand. Would a woman working at a grocery store, two kids to support, be able to spend that much?"

Welles nodded noncommittally and made a note on his pad. "How about you, Deputy King? Anything strike you here?"

Mace's shoulders twitched at being addressed, and it was clear he didn't like Welles's probing. "Yeah. What strikes me is that it's just like every other yard shed I've ever been in."

Welles nodded again as he pretended to inspect the lawn mower. "You know, you seemed very uncomfortable back in the house. Your divorce—acrimonious? If you went to court, I assume—"

"My wife was sleeping around. I divorced her. Get off me."

"You the type to bear a grudge, Mr. King?"

Mace rocked back as he processed that, his impassive face taking on an expression I had rarely seen, a mix of anger and pain kinking his mouth. "Listen, Sherlock. I don't work for your outfit and you're not in my chain of command. So I can tell you to fuck off. So fuck off."

Mace was a big man, taller than Welles, and he held Welles's eyes for a couple extra beats, getting the point across. Then he turned and went out into the yard.

"Another one of your experimental pokes?" I asked.

Welles kept his mouth tight. "We are looking for your sister's killer," he bit off. "For the shadow of her killer. The echo."

"I'm done now," I told him.

I flipped aside the zippered door and went into the yard. Mace was striding in circles over near the driveway.

Mace and I drove back to Richfield, each in our own funk.

When I'd asked what was next with the investigation, Welles gave me the answer I'd expected: boyfriends—in particular Anthony Shapiro, the most recent one, but they'd look at all of them. Billy Carlson, her ex-husband and father of her girls, was out of the picture, doing a long stretch in a Colorado prison for interstate meth transport. Welles didn't expect anything of evidentiary value from the earlier cursory inspection of the house. The only crime committed there was child abandonment, no doubt involuntary. The photos the Child Services people had taken would show a well-tended, appropriately kid-centered home.

Mace broke the silence bitterly: "I'd just as soon have skipped that, Conn."

"Sorry. It was . . . sorry. It helped to have you along."

"Sergeant Fulsome—social skills need a little work. Fucker."

"He did the same thing with me. He's just trying to do his job. Isn't that what you guys do?"

"You know what we do? We serve papers in civil cases. We go to car crashes and try to keep people alive. Manage traffic for road construction. Put the hairy eyeball on noisy teenage parties. If it's a serious crime, we take control of the scene and wait for the States. And you know what? We're *nice* to people when we do it."

"I know, Mace. I've been there with you."

Five minutes of silence later, he took his hand off the steering wheel and held it up to show me shaking fingers. "Shit, look at this! Man, I don't need to have it all come back at me. I mean, her house, it wasn't all that different from when we were together," Mace said. "A house. A home, whatever."

"Well, it was very different from where she lived after you guys got divorced. Trust me, you wouldn't believe the—"

"Jesus, Conn! What, I need to hear precisely how fucked up she got? Could we both just shut up now?"

Good advice. We abided by it for the rest of the drive.

# CHAPTER 5

# CONN

It was almost noon by the time I got home. I was feeling uncomfortable in my own skin and realized my body was itching for my daily ablution. I drove out to Mirror Lake, the clearest water within fifty miles, and swam several times around and across it. I worked it hard, pushed my limits, trying to purge the day from my system. But a single question loomed and grew until it obscured the silky water and the forested hills: Whether I should tell someone about the thing I kicked in the Richfield Reservoir. Whether it might have any connection.

Whether it had been my sister.

Celine was spending the night at her own place, so I had the cabin to myself. As always, I missed her. Even if one of us was at work in the office, the other downstairs, when she was there it was like the house had a heart, a pulse quietly and steadily beating. But that night I didn't mind some time alone.

I still couldn't imagine what kind of music I could listen to, so as night came on I left the house quiet, a silence punctuated only by the faint voices of neighbors calling kids and the hoots of barred owls in the woods. I sat on the couch and took notes on a yellow pad.

I began with the proverbial one true thing:

*I wish my sister had not fucked up her life. I wish she wasn't gone or dead.*

I wrote it and then looked at it for a long moment before I went on.

*Seeing my face among her photographs, at first I felt good about it. Then it hurt.*

*I wish somebody hadn't done something bad to her. Or that she hadn't felt like she had to run away from her life.*

I read what I'd just written and realized I'd used the grammar and diction of a twelve-year-old. Celine would have a psychoanalytic field day with this—all kinds of resonances with a much younger me and the dynamics of sibling relationships.

I blew out a breath and tried to find a more practical state of mind.

*Not the house of a screwed-up person. Just the house of a competent single mom raising two kids and keeping things together. She has come a long way back from where she was eight, ten years ago. She has changed, has been changing.*

*Even changing her name. Why? Gertrude, Trudy—any significance?*

*She was trying to get rid of a boyfriend. She had probably outgrown him—outgrown his type. She supposedly had a new one, maybe a better choice for the future she envisioned.*

*The mountain bike in the shed—Trek something, looks brand-new, disc brakes and shocks, probably worth $2,000. She works at a supermarket, section manager, probably makes fifteen bucks an hour. Where'd the money come from? Drugs? A suitor? Sugar daddy?*

*Into hiking and camping out—all those photos. Snowshoes in the garage. The bike. All very different from before. Brain-dead druggies and boozers can't climb Mount Mansfield.*

*Jars of walnuts and almonds in the fridge. Frozen blueberries
in the freezer. Health-conscious food.*

∿

I scanned my memory for more impressions of the house and kept
coming back to two selfies Laurel had taken, mountain scenes with a
tent in the near background. The light blue of the waterproof tent fly.
That pretty, pale, pale blue tent fly.

I started to feel sick to my stomach. It was too far-fetched. I couldn't
imagine trying to explain to Captain Welles. There was only one person
to bounce it off.

Mace's phone rang a couple of times before I thought to check my
watch. I saw with a shock that it was after eleven, and the man— not
to mention Jody and the kids— would be in bed or trying to get there.
Also, their big police party was tomorrow, and they'd no doubt have
been working overtime to prepare. But just as I was about to cut the
connection, I heard a fumbling at the other end.

A rasping croak: "Conn. What's going on?"

"Did I wake you up?"

"Like it matters." Mace yawned.

"Sorry. I need to ask you how crazy something is."

"This about Laurel?" In the background, I heard Jody's voice: *Who
is it, honey?*

"I hope not," I said.

I heard him take a deep breath and exhale, half a sigh and half a
groan. "Spill it. I gotta get some sleep."

"I ran into something when I was swimming in the Richfield Reservoir. A few days ago."

"The reservoir? I thought you didn't swim there anymore."

"I don't, not for years. But I was desperate and didn't want to drive
for another half hour—"

"What do you mean 'ran into'? Anyway, what's this have to—"

"I kicked something in the water."

He paused as he tried to make the connection. "Conn . . . man, I've had two more beers than usual because it's been a really tough day, and—"

"It was a big thing. I hit it with my foot. Underwater, I saw it tumbling away and it was like something wrapped up in a bluish white . . . shroud. Like the tent fly on Laurel's tent. In the photos she had. I only saw it for a few seconds, but it completely creeped me out. The way it felt on my foot, like somebody's thigh or shoulder or something. It was like a person bent over and wrapped up tightly."

Mace didn't say anything for a few breaths' worth of wordlessness.

Eventually I broke the silence: "I know, it sounds weird, that's why I'm calling you and not Welles. I mean, should I report it?"

"You just did. I'm an officer of the law, right?"

"I mean officially. Does this rise to the level of a valid 'tip'? Would Welles think I was crazy?"

I heard rummaging noises at Mason's end. "Lemme write this down. When was this?"

"Tuesday. When they were draining Pendleton Pond. Around sunset."

"Where in the lake?"

"In the narrow part. The cliffs at the waist of the lake there."

"And it was all below the surface, not floating?"

"Yeah. It just . . . hovered. Four or five feet from the surface. Neutral buoyancy. Or it could've been tied to the bottom, I guess."

He blew out several whistling breaths as he took notes and thought it over. "Okay. It's pushing midnight on Saturday and nobody's gonna do anything about it tonight, if ever, so I'm gonna call Welles in the morning. If I can get him. Maybe he'll think it's nuts, but I don't think so. My guess is the States are dead-ended until they find the boyfriend. All that shit of bringing us to Laurel's house? Like we'll see *what*? Grasping at straws. I'll call him. Leave it up to him to do something about it. Or not."

"Thanks, Mace. I mean it. Thanks."

"Anytime," he said sourly.

# CHAPTER 6

# CONN

Mason and Jody's July party was the year's biggest social event for the region's first responders, attended by police, fire, and rescue personnel from a dozen departments. I went every year because it was fun and served as a useful networking opportunity for a local news reporter. The shindig would go on into evening as people spent a few hours, left when they had to, and were replaced by a continuous stream of new arrivals. They'd share war stories, play horseshoes, and drink; cops and firefighters would over-indulge and spouses would do the driving. When Celine and I arrived, the street was lined with cars, including a few marked cruisers. After almost twenty-two years on the job, Mason was popular among his colleagues.

My sister's disappearance had thrown me off-kilter, and I wasn't really up for making small talk. But I wanted to check in with Mason to see if he'd called Welles, and what the response had been. I was also hoping to get material for one of my weekly "Around Here" columns—an informal portrait of our first-responder community when they let their hair down.

On the way to the Kings' backyard, Celine and I passed through a group playing basketball on the blacktop in front of the garage. I introduced her to those I knew and noted with pride the appreciative glances the men gave Celine. Without intent or effort, she was striking: summer dress and sandals, tan from working in the garden, a graceful stride. She waved greetings with her good hand and kept the other curled around her little purse, held discreetly at her waist.

We continued between garage and house to find the backyard full of a happy-looking melee, probably thirty north country people making the most of good weather while they had it. At the far end, Mason stood at the grill, Red Sox hat on backward, turning meats in a haze of smoke. Pairs and trios stood in conversation around the grass or sat on folding chairs, sipping from beer cans or plastic cups of wine or punch. On the right, four horse-shoe players were in place behind stakes, watched by a cluster of spouses and a few smaller kids. Other kids darted out from under tables or scuttled around the edges of the yard, little Katy King among them. The clink and clang of horseshoes provided counterpoint to a subdued boombox on the patio: Elton John. We started making our way back toward Mason.

"It's been a long time since we've seen them socially," Celine whispered.

"Not since New Year's. Some catching up to do for sure. But not today. Jody and Mace'll be running their asses off."

"Do you think there'll be . . . awkwardness? About Laurel? Do the police guys know she's Mason's ex? Do they know she's your sister?"

"If they didn't before they came, they'll know by now. You're looking at the grapevine in action."

I was right. The glances and nods I received seemed wary, uncomfortable, from people uncertain what courtesies or sympathies were called for. Small-town life: You know your neighbors and they know you—sometimes all too well.

Sheriff Paula Levinson was talking to Will Patchen, Richfield's chief of police, and she waved us over. We shook hands.

"Hey, Will," I said. "I almost didn't recognize you, out of uniform and all."

He made a half-pout, half-smile. "Tell me about it."

"How's it going, Conn?" Paula asked.

I had worried about this question and decided I'd keep it simple: "Day by day," I told her. Weak smile, ambiguous shrug: I was a guy keeping a stiff upper lip and sticking to a wait-and-see holding pattern.

She was about to respond when a clang and a cry came from the horseshoe court. A shoe had bounced off the stake and bounded into the shin of an onlooker. The woman turned to limp a couple of steps away, grimacing and swearing in vehement nonsense syllables: *"Fut-a-but-a-wutz!"* A mom, I deduced, staying proper. Sure enough, a little girl came to comfort her and inspect her shin.

"It's a combat sport," Jody said, appearing behind us. She had come out of the patio door carrying bags of potato chips. "Hey, kids," she said, meaning Celine and me.

"Beautiful day," Celine told her. "You have a crystal ball for the weather?"

"I wish." Jody's eyes caught mine, wary. She had dark smudges under her eyes and looked every bit the weary hostess. "Sorry about your loss, Conn."

"Well, I'm still holding out hope that she'll show up alive."

"Of course." Jody bobbed her head noncommittally and continued on to the refreshment table. Celine and I followed to help replenish the chip bowls and clean up the debris of paper plates and plastic cups. Then somebody called for Jody, an urgent question about potato salad.

"No rest for the wicked," she said as she left us. "But I'm gonna take a break and shoot some hoops pretty soon. Conn, we'll need another player, hint hint, no pressure."

I was grateful that Jody, at least, wasn't walking on eggshells around me. Celine and I continued back to say hello to Mason, arriving just as a big flare went up, fat catching fire below the gas flame. Mace moved some burgers aside and sprayed it down with a bottle he had at the ready.

"Should've cleaned this fucker before the season," he muttered. "Hi, Celine," he added.

Mason's face was red from the heat of the grill, and he looked exhausted. We complimented him on the size of the crowd, the abundance of goodies and booze, and made small talk that was somewhat forced. Celine carried it with grace, but for Mace and me there was an elephant in the room. He seemed put out with me. I thought to apologize again for dragging him to Laurel's house, but even that would have been uncomfortable. Or maybe it was my late-night call, roping him into it yet again. After a couple of minutes of his mostly ignoring me, I squeezed his shoulder and went away to make the rounds. Celine stayed on to load buns with dogs and burgers as Mace forked them onto a platter.

I recognized many of the partyers from prior gatherings or from my work, and probably most of them recognized me, if only from reading my columns. To give my hands something to do, I grabbed a cold beer from the bucket and started saying hello.

It didn't take long to realize that this wasn't going to be easy. How many strategies are there? Bill Delacorte, Richfield fire chief, chose the brisk and blithe route, studiously avoiding the topic of Laurel as if he didn't know about my connection. Linda Billingsley, Richfield police dispatcher, went the other way, offering sympathy—too much of it. "We're praying for your sister," she told me, eyes wet and sincere, "and for you, too, Conn." Others just got uncomfortable. Faces that had been laughing a moment before went neutral or somber when I approached them, glances ricocheted quickly from my eyes.

"Twenty-one!" someone cried from the horseshoe game. Supporters of the victors cheered and clapped. I looked over to see the woman who had scored the last ringer pump the air and take a beer from someone's hand. Francine something—a Richfield cop.

Celine carried a piled-high tray to the serving table, and a crowd converged. Back at the grill, Mason observed the rush, shrugged wearily, put on some more burgers.

I joined Celine, slipping my arm around her waist, grateful when her hand took mine. We greeted those we knew as they came to load their plates. I tried to project a posture that was appropriately somber and concerned but implied I was holding up and still able to have an okay time. It felt bogus.

"We don't have to stay super long," Celine whispered in my ear.

Then Jody was there again, this time with a pair of six-packs still in their collars. "Okay, Conn. Let's go up front and hit the hoop."

I was grateful for the command. Lingering at the table had started to feel too much like standing in a receiving line at a funeral.

"Mace seems pissed at me," I told Jody as we headed to the front. "I'm really sorry I—"

"He is pissed. So am I. He'll get over it."

"How about you?"

"Hey, she wasn't my ex. And you know me—farmer's daughter. You do what you have to do. Need to butcher a hog, chop heads off chickens, I'm your gal. I'll get over it, too."

From her tone, I wasn't sure whether she was letting me off the hook or simply reminding me of her bone-deep pragmatism. I wondered what Mace had told her about my late-night call, about the thing in the lake. I hoped he hadn't burdened her with the details. We walked between house and garage without saying any more.

When Celine and I first got together, Mason had hopes for some bonding between the two women. They were certainly friendly, but no real closeness had emerged despite our occasional get-togethers. I had thought that might change when Celine helped smooth over some friction with the Kings' kids at school. Katy and Marshall were Jody's kids from her first marriage, to a Marine killed in Iraq, and were the only kids of color at Richfield elementary. Vermont being the whitest state in the union, some of their woodchuck peers took a while "to get over their lack of experience with Black people," as Celine kindly put it. Celine had worked to pull together consensus on behavioral standards to be implemented throughout the district, and had arranged workshops that would help teachers and parents foster a culture of broader understanding. It had helped.

But they were very different women—Jody was a local, raised on a dairy farm, Celine a Chicago girl whose parents had been educators. Jody saw Celine's efforts on her kids' behalf as her simply doing her job, her duty. On one hand, I appreciated Jody's approach. It was an older

Yankee ethic that I agreed with, like Thoreau's when he said, "Rescue the drowning and tie your shoestrings." Moral acts shouldn't be lauded as heroic but rather taken in stride as the ordinary obligations of citizenship. On the other hand, while it was indeed Celine's job, she had also been motivated by genuine personal concern for Katy and Marshall.

A powerful duty ethic informs not just a day's work, but relationships with people and with the past. I doubted Mace got much sympathy from Jody for the hard stuff he dealt with at his job. Working at the farm and garden store, keeping a respectable house, cooking, being a stand-up sheriff's deputy's wife, wrangling two kids—Jody worked hard, with discipline and a levelheaded competence that I admired. For her, reasonably enough, family and the present would take priority. Mace's long-ago ex, alive or dead, was to be relegated to the past.

The players were shooting bull, not balls, when we came around the garage, and the adults were glad to take the beers off Jody's hands.

After a beer break, Jody told me to "show us that swimmer's bod." The sun hit hard on the asphalt, so I stripped and tossed my shirt to the sidelines among the others. We agreed to play to twenty-one. After a few beer-lubricated comments, the observers made small bets and the game was on.

Jody wore a Celtics jersey and an elastic compression brace on her elbow, making her look very much the basketball jock. On the court, she was what we would have called a "physical" player, back in high school— one whose imposing presence made up for middling skills. She had a rangy build, and she stayed sturdy from working at Richfield Farm and Garden store, where her job entailed slinging sacks of grain and dog food as often as taking inventory or running the register. Her family background was more like Mason's: farming and blue-collar work, and hunting or off-road four-wheeling or motorcycling for fun—Vermont woodchuck tastes. In basketball, she liked to occupy the center of the Kings' driveway, legs braced wide, hard to budge whether you were defending or trying to shoot, and she wasn't hesitant to throw a hard hip check.

There were four on each team. On my side were two Richfield municipal cops and Mia, a teenage girl whose slight physique was offset by a mean eye for the hoop. On Jody's side were a sheriff's deputy, a Richfield fireman, and Marshall King, their fourteen-year-old son, to balance out the youth contingent.

Stu, one of the Richfield cops, shot a ball that racketed off the hoop. Jody's long arm snagged it and flipped it back to one of her guys, who dribbled forward and took a shot, easily skirting my inept defense. The backboard whacked, the chain net rattled, onlookers cheered.

"Up one!" Jody said. "Keep it up, guys!"

"I haven't touched a basketball in twenty years," I reminded my team.

"Really? We'd never guess," Mia said.

Jody's team quickly took the lead, due largely to my lame playing. Marshall proved to be pretty clumsy, too, but the others were fit, capable players. We closed the gap nine to seven, and then Mia, our sharpshooter, landed a long toss that gave us two more points.

No time for high-fives. Jody got the ball, tossed up a bad shot that was recovered by one of her teammates, who passed to Marshall who passed it again. One of my guys, Ron, intercepted the ball and took off toward the hoop. Marshall boldly leaped in front of him. Ron jumped to shoot over Marshall's waving arms. The ball got through the hoop, but as Ron came down his elbow hit Marshall's cheek. Marshall staggered back, a hand to his face. Play stopped.

"Oh, man, I'm so sorry!" Ron said. He went to Marshall, who was fighting back tears, and gently took his hand away from the injured cheekbone. A red mark stood out clearly on his brown skin.

Jody came to inspect it, too, then called to the bystanders for some ice. A mother took off for the backyard to grab some from the beer bucket.

"I'm so sorry!" Ron repeated. "It's going to be fine. Just a bruise. You okay, Marsh? You did a great job of blocking, man. I got lucky."

Marshall nodded, still suppressing tears and pushing his mother's hands away. "I'm fine, Mom. Jesus!"

Jody scrutinized Marshall, then gave Ron a hard once-over. Mia did some nervous dribbling as we waited for the ice. I stayed back, glad I hadn't been the shooter.

It was a hot day. The sun bounced off the garage, heat rose from the asphalt. I thought of Celine's permission to leave early if I needed to. But we had appearances to maintain, and maybe later I could catch up with Mace, if we could find a moment of privacy. The basketballers were sweating, some a little drunk but still very much into the game. After another cold beer all around and a few minutes of ice on Marshall's bruise, we continued.

We were up by one point. That fact energized Jody's team, and Ron started playing a more cautious game. They caught up to us, then pulled a point ahead as we were approaching twenty-one. You have to win by two points in pickup basketball, and we were all into it by then. Eighteen to seventeen, we were behind when I actually scored, to everyone's amazement. Then Stu had the ball and made a bad pass. Ron reflexively intercepted, dribbled in for a shot, and was taken by surprise when Jody tossed an aggressive hip check that upended him completely. Ron landed on his elbow as the ball bounded into the lawn. The onlookers gasped.

It was an intentional foul. Jody helped Ron to his feet, apologizing profusely if not very sincerely. They exchanged a look: Jody, gray-haired, stolid, Ron at once in pain, offended, and apologetic.

Ron took a turn around the driveway, rolling his shoulders, trying to get his parts working again. Ill at ease after the foul, Mia missed our free throw. Jody's team went on to win, twenty-one to eighteen.

Returning to the backyard, I circulated again with no greater satisfaction. So many police—I'm sure Laurel was a frequent topic of conversation, but I didn't hear whatever was being said because it dried up when I approached any group. Clearly, I wasn't going to get any material for the article I'd envisioned.

I thought to snag Mace, but the grill was unmanned and I didn't see him in the crowd. So I grabbed a hamburger and nibbled at it, feeling out of place and suppressing an urge to cozy up to Celine, my touchstone. She was deep in conversation with Wendy Patterson, a woman I had interviewed for an article about kids with special needs in the school system. Celine had arranged tutoring for her son Rowan, a smart but highly dyslexic kid who was now in eighth grade. I was glad to see them laughing together, suggesting that Rowan was doing well.

I needed a bathroom visit anyway. I finished my burger, went to the patio, and slid aside the screen door.

The Kings' house was a big, 1970s two-story Cape, gray with red shutters beside the windows. Inside, the decor was respectable and coordinated—a colonial-style dining table with six matching chairs, a living room ensemble of couch and plump armchairs. Mace and Jody kept it neater than I'd have expected, given two kids in school.

I stopped as I was cutting through the dining room. The big mirror over the buffet cabinet had a halo of circular cracks at its center, fracturing my reflection. Given how well the Kings kept up the place, I could only assume the damage was recent. As I stood there, I heard voices from the stairwell: Mace and Jody, upstairs. I couldn't make out their words, only the jagged tone.

Clearly, they were arguing—not something they'd want overheard.

I didn't want to interrupt, didn't want to spy, so I retreated quickly back outside. I felt for both of them and blamed myself for putting too much of it on Mason's shoulders.

Celine drove us back to the cabin. I was exhausted by my efforts to schmooze, which had felt artificial and forced throughout.

"Well," I said, "as Woody Allen said, 'That was Kafkaesque.'"

Celine laughed ruefully. "I'm sorry it was so uncomfortable. Nobody knows how to react to you. Can't blame them. It would be easier if there were some certainty about what happened to Laurel."

"I know."

"How was basketball?"

"Marshall got hurt, Jody fouled one of my team in retaliation. It made things tense. And I suck at basketball."

Celine nodded. "She's definitely out of sorts—she looked exhausted. Mason is pretty frayed, and it's no doubt wearing thin for her."

"I never got a chance to hang with Mace. What'd he have to say?"

"Just that he wishes he hadn't gone with you to Laurel's house. That the whole thing is hitting him harder than he'd have thought. That man was totally beat, Conn. Apparently the kids are acting out because he's been . . . remote. Jody's peeved with him, they've been fighting, she's basically telling him to 'man up.' Marshall threw a soccer ball at a mirror last night, broke it. Portrait of a family under some stress."

I could only agree. "Did Mace tell you whether he'd contacted Captain Welles?"

"He said he'd left a message and would try again later. Also asked me not to say anything to Jody about your underwater encounter. He wants to keep his family out of the whole thing as much as possible."

I was glad to learn he hadn't told Jody the substance of my late-night call. We listened to the hum of the tires and watched the flow of trees passing, bright with late-afternoon sun. A deer crossed the road far ahead, followed by a timorous faun. Celine slowed in case others followed.

"We should get together with them," Celine said decisively. "Melt the edges a little. If we can have a halfway good time and not mention Laurel, I'm sure they'll both calm down. Life does go on, right? You could use a reminder, too."

She took my hand and gave me one of those focused smiles that you feel like sunlight on your face. She was right, and I was grateful. I steadied a bit.

# CHAPTER 7

# CONN

Still, the party underlined the stress that came with uncertainty, and that evening Celine and I got into what passes for an argument with us.

I'd been trying to think of what I would say to Laurel's daughters about where their mother was. From there, I began asking myself *who* my sister was. I made a comment to Celine about that—which vision of her was the "real" Laurel. The spunky, pesky, smart little girl? The optimistic, idealistic young bride? The irresponsible, sleep-around druggie? The keeping-it-together mom who lived in the house I'd just visited?

We'd had a long-running discussion about what constitutes "truth." It was a central issue in both of our professions, but we came to it from very different angles.

My past mistakes as a journalist had made me extremely scrupulous about strict adherence to factuality. Something is true, or it's not. Verify it, or forget about it.

In Celine's profession, she had explained, truth is more subjective. If you're talking to a patient or client, your first obligation is to accept their narrative as "true." You can probe the story for nuances that might be therapeutically useful, and you can suggest alternate interpretations: "Do you really believe your mother didn't love you? Is it possible she was just not very good at expressing her emotions?" But you can't simply challenge the narrative—can't say, "You're wrong," or "That's not what happened."

We both learned our perspectives in grad school, and we had generally agreed on a truce about the topic. But I was in a lousy place and some comment of Celine's set me off.

We were taking a brisk walk in the lingering evening twilight—with two fingers missing from her left hand, she can't swim well, so I often join her for her walks and runs. My cabin is about four miles from downtown Richfield, in the woods just off a dirt road, not really "country"—there are other houses every hundred yards or so—but suburban, by Vermont standards. The road, Whimsy Falls Road, wanders up into the hills through forest and eventually over the ridge into farm country.

"So," I summarized, "you're saying there's subjective truth and there's objective truth, and even if they're different, they're both equally true?"

"Essentially, yes."

"I just can't buy that."

"We've been over this, Conn. But that's how we have to work in my field."

I needed to push back. "That situation you've been telling me about. The kid who blames her problems on parental abuse. What about that?"

Celine abided by the laws regarding client confidentiality, but sometimes she talked to me about her job. Of course she never named names, and she fudged details if it might be too obvious who she was talking about.

Throughout the prior school term, her department had been dealing with a difficult problem. A girl from one of the smaller towns in the district started showing signs of emotional distress: plummeting grades, social conflicts, even self-inflicted bruises and scratches. One of Celine's staff spoke to her and learned that she had been seeing a psychiatrist, and during her sessions she had recalled memories of her parents sexually and physically abusing her throughout her childhood. There were overtones of Satanism.

When this first came up, Celine and I were both surprised. We had thought "satanic ritual abuse" was thing of the past—a relic of the 1980s, when dozens of reports made the news and it became a subject of hot debate. Deeply buried memories of subterranean ritual chambers beneath suburban ranch houses, altars, scarlet robes, incest, rape, sacrifice, babies born and murdered—a gruesome litany of claimed aberrant behavior.

In one well-publicized case, local police—in an area where many held literalist religious views—took a teenage girl's claims seriously: rape by her father and other men in the satanic coven, forced termination of the pregnancies, grisly rites with the aborted fetuses. The police interviewed the parents, who denied everything. The parents were well-known and respected, but the police were not satisfied and got search warrants for the family's house and land. They tore the place apart trying to find satanic paraphernalia, dug into the basement floor and walls to find the hidden sacrificial chamber. They brought dogs to sniff out the burial places of all the sacrificed babies, and dug scores of holes in the yard.

They found nothing. And after many similar cases throughout the country, skepticism and resistance grew. Ultimately, it was all debunked, the theory of sequestered memory largely discredited. But at the height of it, parents lost their jobs. Some were threatened, some attacked. Many divorced, many had to relocate to escape the local stigma. All had their hearts broken. Volumes have been written about repressed memory, dissociated identity disorder, false memory syndrome; whole encyclopedias could be filled with studies and dissertations exploring it.

In the case Celine had dealt with, the girl claimed she had been raped by her father, and had two near-term babies that her mother delivered by Cesarean section. The parents ritually murdered the babies and buried them in the yard. Her story certainly rang the school's alarm bells, but not for its credibility—she was fifteen years old and no one had ever noticed indications of pregnancy. Celine's department worked with the police, social services agencies, and consulting psychiatrists. When they finally persuaded a judge to require a medical exam, doctors determined that the girl had no internal or external abdominal scarring whatever, and was, in fact, a virgin. As they'd suspected from the start, what they had was a very troubled child and a psychiatrist guilty of confabulation and countertransference—projecting her own mental state onto her patient.

The degree to which I pushed this point during what was supposed to be a pleasant walk was a measure of how off-balance I was: "Okay. Here's a kid who truly believes her father raped her and her mother cut open her belly and so on. The parents say they didn't. All the material and medical evidence supports the parents' claims. The parents either did, or did not, do what the girl says. What's true?"

"The girl believes her story. It's true for her. That's where we have to begin unraveling it if we want to help her."

"Great," I said. "But the parents believe theirs, too. One or the other is factually true, Celine! You can't have it both ways!"

"Well. In most cases, it's been demonstrated that the 'victims' of this stuff were coached by psychiatrists, who projected their own traumas or morbid fantasies onto the child's story. They encouraged imagining events, they rewarded unsavory 'revelations' with approval and affirmation. That's what we found in this case."

"So . . . now there's another truth? The girl's psychiatrist's narrative versus the opinion of your people? 'I truly believed it! I didn't project anything!'" I started counting the variations of truth on my fingers, which irritated Celine.

Our walking tempo had picked up, an unconscious response to the growing tension between us.

"If it can be proven that the psychiatrist did indeed lead a patient, they're legally liable for malpractice. There *is* a process by which—"

"So their truth was not true?"

Celine was puffing—the hill gets steep there—and didn't answer.

I should have left it, but I didn't: "I'm just saying, there is such a thing as objective truth. The father did, or did not, rape the girl. They are mutually exclusive propositions. Events flowing from those determinations are crucial to the lives of all concerned. It's important to verify one or the other."

"Okay, Conn. I get the point. Look, the definition of 'truth' has been puzzled over since time immemorial. We're not going to solve it this minute."

"I mean, the parents do, or do not, go to prison. The—"

"I want to enjoy my walk now." She picked up her tempo so that she pulled ahead of me. But I'd pushed too many buttons, and her decision to cut it off didn't stick. She slowed again, panting. "Look, you want me to be honest with you, or would you like me to humor you?"

I realized I had let myself in for stuff I wasn't ready to face. "Honest."

"Okay. Some of your vehemence is coming from contrition for your own past misrepresentations of facts. As a journalist. More immediately, it's from the lack of resolution about your sister. She's either dead or is not dead. She was either a criminally negligent mom, or she was a good mom. She had either been on a one-way crash-and-burn trajectory, or she had pulled out of that dive. That's the logic, right?"

"More or less, yeah."

"Okay, so now the next step. I completely, totally understand the need for clarity, for certainty, okay? And at some point the investigation will get there. But the simplicity of the true-false construct dooms you to pain, Conn. Because you'll ask yourself whether you were, or were not, to some degree responsible for Laurel's problems, by doing something or failing to do something. In that case, you should either feel guilty, or you should not feel guilty. You should beat yourself up forever, or you should forgive yourself."

She waited for me to respond, but there was nothing I could say. She had it right.

"So this is where I get to explain why my profession has its axioms about what's 'true.' For questions like that, you aren't going to find a clean divide between true or false, this or that. The best you'll do is live in a . . . no-man's-land of ambiguity and ambivalence. The healthiest approach would be for you to work on constructively managing your uncertainty, not trying to pin down which was absolutely, unequivocally 'true.' Create a narrative—yes, I get it, another 'truth!'—that allows you to cope and to live life again!"

She pulled ahead of me again, striding quickly. I trailed for a full minute, but caught up with her when she stopped at the spot where the falls become visible through the trees uphill—a thin silver streak, bounding in vigorous arcs down through the woods. A magical place. We stopped to look at it, panting steam in the cool, water-scented air that slid down the cleft.

I stood next to her, feeling shy and awkward. "God, it's beautiful," I whispered. An apology, a thanks.

"I'm going to say something as your lover now, okay?" she said, preparing me. "Not your shrink. Because I'm not your shrink."

"Okay," I said. "Please."

"You did your best with your sister. Maybe you didn't do a great job, but you didn't single-handedly fuck up, either. Takes two to tango. You did your best for where you were at, at the time. I'm sure you and she would have come back toward each other again. But something bad happened to her before you could! And *that is not your fault*. If she's dead, it's because *somebody else* deprived you of each other. And you can't go forward blaming yourself. You have to work at letting that go."

Tears streaked her cheeks. I put my arm around her, and we gazed up at the silvery falls. I felt overwhelmed by love for her, by the beauty of the woods, the falls, the night.

She had given me a degree of exoneration. With the guilt stepping back a little, a new set of feelings descended on me. I moved closer to Welles's mindset: somewhere out there was whoever had hurt Laurel, had killed her, and we had to find that person. I felt the first taste of anger, of outrage, of hatred for that person.

# CHAPTER 8

# CONN

On Monday morning, Captain Welles called me to say Mace had reported the thing I'd kicked in the reservoir, and he wanted to talk to me about it.

I had to wrap up a couple of stories at the *Herald*, so I didn't get to Waterbury until around five. Welles had already spent eight hours on the job, yet he looked as if he'd just started his day: clean-shaven face, crisply creased trousers, a uniform shirt so smooth it looked starched.

"Take long swims often, do you?"

"Four or five days a week, weather permitting. Early May through end of September, sometimes October. I wear a wetsuit to extend the season."

"So you're quite the 'enthusiast.' Ever swim in Pendleton Pond?"

"Yes. It's a good swim, one of my favorites. And you're wasting your time with that line of inquiry."

Half of his mouth smiled. "That's what they all say."

Before I could come up with a sarcastic reply, he turned and took a large piece of paper from the broad document shelf behind him—a topographical map of the Richfield Reservoir and nearby hills.

"I'm a method man, Mr. Whitman. Get used to it." He weighted the corners of the map with items from his desk and smoothed it from side to side. "Let's talk about the object you say you kicked. Your impression was that it was loose. Not attached to anything."

"That's what I assumed, just because of how it tumbled away. But I guess it could have been on a rope, tied to a weight."

"And you saw it briefly, underwater. What color was it?"

"Blue—a light blue. The light wasn't good, but it seemed like the same pale blue as the tent fly in those camping photos at my sister's house."

Welles bit his lips. "Fact is, your sister's tent was missing its fly. The pale blue you describe is also consistent with the color scheme of the rest of the tent."

All I could do was blow out a breath.

He handed me a pencil. "Show me the route of your swim. Then show me where you kicked the underwater object."

I had never seen an overhead view of the reservoir, but it was easy to locate familiar places from the shore contours. I drew a line from the gravel beach at the north end to the dam at the south end. "That's approximate. In the wide sections, I probably stray twenty yards either side of that line. Where I kicked the thing—about here."

"Can you do better than 'about'?"

I thought back. I had paused at the narrows, treading water as I admired the granite cliffs and the white birches. The bedrock reared high above the surface, and I found the exact place easily in the map's topographical elevation lines.

"Right here." I pointed to a spot just west of the center of the channel, where the cliff walls were highest.

"Sort of a gorge, it looks like."

"Almost."

"How deep?"

"The cliffs are about twenty, thirty feet, but I don't know about below water. When I was a kid, everybody said it was bottomless there, even though the rest of the lake's pretty shallow. High-school kids used to jump off the cliff, but then one got killed doing it—hit the rocks on the way down. I've never seen anyone doing it."

"Is there a path along the lake at that point?"

"I assume so. Used to be, on the side nearest the road. I've seen kids fishing there when I swim. Not on the cliffs, down at water level—the flat rocks just south of the narrows." I put a finger on the map's ragged contour.

"And the current—stronger right there?"

"Virtually none. The water moves north to south, but you can't feel it."

He turned away to stare out the window. If he'd had a riding crop, he'd have switched it against his thigh as he thought. After a moment he came back to study the map again. "Route 16A is not that far from the shore. Can you see the road from there? Could passing cars see a person on the lakeshore at that point?"

"Definitely not. There's a strip of woodland about two hundred feet wide between the lake and the road, big trees and saplings and low growth. At the boat launch, where the access road comes down, yeah, there are places where you might see cars pass. But just barely."

He made a note on his iPad, then gave me a look that was not without sympathy. "We'll start tomorrow. It would be helpful if you joined the shore search. Pin down the exact path of your swim and the point of contact."

I never wanted to see the place again. But I agreed to join the team.

I was about to leave, but he beckoned me to wait as he pecked a number on his phone. "Marlene. Can you bring me the list on the Carlson case? I've got Conn Whitman here, and I'd like him to look it over." To me, he said, "Detective Selanski is the case officer assigned to lead the investigation. With me—we're going to tag-team this."

A half a minute later, Detective Selanski appeared in the doorway. When Welles introduced us, she didn't shake my hand but made a point of looking me up and down with a critical eye. She was about forty, with short, dark hair, a weathered face, and the slim muscularity of a marathon runner. Her blue blazer bulged over a sidearm holster.

"Here you go," she said, handing me a single page of spreadsheet printout. "Have a look, have a ball."

I scanned the names—Tony Shapiro and six others. None of them rang a bell.

"Sorry," I said.

"Aside from Tony, we're particularly curious about this guy." Standing at my shoulder, too close, she put her finger on the name Jesse Nadeau. "An oldie but goodie."

She had a quirky style I couldn't quite figure out. I translated the comment to mean that he wasn't a recent boyfriend but that they thought he had potential as a suspect.

"What's so good?"

Selanski leaned a shoulder against the doorframe as she ticked off his attributes on her fingers: "Well, Jesse had a line of merchandise that he brought in from the Big Apple. Got caught, spent twelve years in penitentiaries. Seems your sister, after they had their fling or thing or whatever, was one of the people who testified against him at trial. Seems Jesse got out about three months ago. Seems he went off everybody's radar since then. Now, I'm no Einstein, but . . ."

She trailed off, holding up a hand with five fingers extended. I got the message: He could have a motive—revenge—and Laurel's disappearance not long after his release was suggestive. She continued looking at me with a grin that mixed sardonic amusement and provocation.

"Don't know him? Didn't know him back in your misspent youth? Um, he's around your same vintage, and his product was some of the same shit you enjoyed so much in DC."

"I don't know any of these guys. I'd tell you if I did." I assumed "my vintage" meant about my same age. Her bringing up my past pissed me off, and I brandished the paper at her. She didn't take it back, just folded her arms across her chest.

"You hang onto that," she said. "See if anything comes to you. Maybe dawn will break over Marblehead. Funny, how memory works, right?"

The reservoir search started early. A convoy of vehicles had already pulled up in the boat launch parking lot when I arrived at six thirty: a large van that I presumed would serve as headquarters, five State Police cruisers including members of the K-9 corps, a van for a four-person underwater search team and their equipment, towing a motorboat on a trailer. A couple of Sheriff's Department deputies were there to help with the shore search. Mace hadn't been assigned to this detail, and I envied him.

I didn't see Selanski anywhere and was relieved. I wasn't in the mood for more insinuations or goading.

The day was dull, foggy, too warm for this early in the morning, and a slow drizzle brought up the scent of the reservoir's muddy shores. I joined the group in the HQ van, where Welles had put up his map and was working over a search plan with the various teams. He introduced me as "the witness."

The plan was simple: Start with the dogs. If they pick up sign, dive in the gorge channel and start searching the nearby shore. The slight current of the lake headed toward the overflow chute at the dam, so both water and shore teams would focus on the larger basin, working their way south.

I pointed out the general direction. Those who joined the canine team, six of us, tagged along behind the dogs and their handlers, single file. Welles was correct that a path ran through the forest of sumacs, chest-high ferns, and blackberry brambles toward the gorge, a ribbon of dirt beaten by generations of kids hoping to get lucky with fish or love over on the shore rocks.

I got soaked to the skin before we were fifty feet in: the rain, the water on the dense foliage. I hadn't dressed right. I hadn't screwed my head on right. Numb, dumb, soggy inside and out.

Within a hundred feet we were out of view of the parking lot and boat ramp. From the pace of our walk and the voices of the handlers, it was clear the dogs were getting excited. I tried to drop behind, but Welles urged me to the front of the group so I could indicate the point of contact.

After a couple hundred yards, the undergrowth gave way to low shelves of granite that angled off into the water. And there it was, ahead of us: the waist of the lake, the narrows, the gorge. Just north, a little ridge transected the lake, rising steeply to the cliffs and falling just as fast a hundred yards farther on, a notch carved by the river a hundred thousand years earlier. Even in the drizzle, with the glistening police raincoats all around me, the cliffs of the far shore, topped by birches standing crisp white in the misted air, struck me as beautiful. The water was too murky for my taste, but I'd swum through that granite gateway scores of times and had always loved the view.

"Whitman?" Welles's voice startled me out of my thoughts.

Everybody was looking at me. The dogs were focused, noses down, snuffling eagerly right and left, at the water's edge.

"Yeah, they've picked up something," the K-9 team leader said. "Definitely."

Welles prompted me with his eyes.

"Diagonally out from here. Like fifty feet from here, north and a little closer to the cliff on this side."

A buzzing that had started up subliminally grew louder and within another minute a motorboat carrying two divers came around from the southern shoreline, cruising unhurriedly and leaving a minimal wake. Back at the motor, a third member of the team stopped the skiff just south of the spot Welles indicated. The men in wet suits hoisted themselves onto the gunnels on each side and simultaneously flipped themselves backward into the water. They spent a moment at the surface, adjusting their gear, before kicking down and out of view.

Nobody said anything. The K-9 handlers stilled the dogs, who obediently sat and, like everyone else, watched the trails of bubbles weaving along the rain-dimpled surface. Eight people standing in the drizzle, silent, paradoxically hoping yet hoping not.

The rain intensified; the humidity of the day seemed suffocating. Seeing the men submerge had brought back the horror. I'd been in that same water, at that same spot. Now the scent of the shore mud struck me as foul, the stink of decay. A visual memory bloomed in my eye, the blue-white bulbous *thing* spinning away.

"I'd like to leave now," I told Welles. "I've done all I can. Nothing I can do from here on in."

Welles didn't answer because just then one of the divers surfaced, well toward the center of the narrows. A quickening ran through the shore group as he pulled back his face mask and took out his regulator.

*Celine would ask: What are you feeling? And I'd say, I hope there's nothing there. And she'd ask, Why? And I'd say, Because then I could think my sister was still alive. And that I hadn't kicked a dead body and I wouldn't have to see anything really really horrible today.*

The diver was just reporting general conditions. "It's only about twenty feet deep, but visibility is poor. Too much suspended silt. We'd do better if the sun was out. So far, all I see is some snagged branches, some boulders."

The shore group calmed, but for only a moment, because thirty feet from the first diver, another head broke the surface. He left his face mask on, just yanked out his regulator.

"Got something," he called.

The woman on the boat started it up and guided it slowly toward the spot. The shore crew moved north among tangling bushes and tripping rocks to the closest point. Numb, not thinking, I joined them.

The second diver had found a rope and the rope led to a heavy object on the bottom. The two went down again and came up to report that it was an anchor. They couldn't bring it up because it was stuck among rocks at the bottom. The woman in the boat passed down a crowbar, and in another few minutes the divers jointly struggled up with it. They toppled the thing into the boat and disappeared underwater again.

Welles turned back to me. "So. If there is or was a body there, how'd it get there?"

I shrugged. "Somebody could have come in a boat. Or somebody carried it from the boat launch to here, then up to the cliff top. Threw it in." I pointed out the steep hill between our position and the broken-granite edge just north of us. It would be a hard climb through the shoulder-deep scrub, especially carrying something heavy.

"Is there a path straight from the road to the top of the cliff?" Welles asked.

"I'm not sure. I mean, maybe. I think I remember, back in high school, yeah, a sort of a path."

"That would seem a more likely route to get a body from a vehicle to the cliff's edge, don't you think? All downhill from the road."

I followed his eyes. The forested ridge continued past the cliffs, sloping up until it leveled out near Route 16A. "You're probably right," I told him dully.

Welles turned to the others. "Let's get the dogs going on the hill there," he ordered. "Up to the cliff top."

The handlers urged their animals away from the shoreline and toward the wall of vegetation. The dogs took interest immediately, each finding their way quickly into the thicket, their handlers struggling to keep up. We watched them labor up the hill, slipping and tangling. It was only a hundred feet or so. Within three minutes they reached the highest point, almost directly above the spot where I'd kicked the thing. The dogs tugged in circles at the end of their leashes and then settled on their haunches at the very edge.

The team leader nodded and tossed Welles a thumbs-up: Yes, there was scent sign. Welles radioed back to base camp to ask for more officers.

The divers were down for at least fifteen minutes. We could see their bubble trails meandering far up the channel on our side, then back down closer to the middle, then up again and back under the far-side cliffs. Eventually the bubbles headed our way and the divers clambered onto shore where we stood. They pulled off their flippers and shrugged out of their tanks and vests.

"That's it," one of them said. "Nothing else in this area except you could get rich collecting all the lures snagged down there."

The boat idled over, close enough to shore that we could see the anchor. It had a bifurcated, spade-shaped head attached to a shaft that was linked to the rope by a short length of chain. The divers said the split spade had wedged itself hard into a cleft in the bedrock. Their team leader compared it to the anchor for her fourteen-foot skiff, showing that it was considerably larger—heavier than you'd expect for the boats people usually took out on a little lake like this.

The rope was about ten feet long, that indestructible, braided plastic-weave marine rope. The cut was frayed, obviously the result of repeated abrasion. According to the divers, neither anchor nor rope were silted enough to have been there for long—they'd been dropped this summer, they thought, definitely no earlier than last summer.

The dog team headed along the ridge and up toward Route 16A, calling back to Welles on walkie-talkies: Yes, there was a faint footpath worn into the low growth, and yes, the dogs took great interest in the path. Two state troopers took the dog team's place at the cliff top, bending to inspect and photograph the ground there. Welles ordered a shore search, a boat search with nets and poles, and more dives, and he sent a couple of officers to the dam to check the debris-catching bars at the outflow.

I told him I had to go to work. I have a job, I said, I can't be away from it forever. Got to do my job, don't I? As I left, the group of men and women, black and glistening as harbor seals in their raincoats and wet suits, began to spread out among ferns and bushes to inspect the shore.

I stayed numb as I drove. A boat anchor: It didn't mean anything. Hundreds of water skiers and fishers came to the reservoir every summer. It could have been there for years. I'd encountered someone's lost anchor on the shore of Peacham Pond a few summers back, almost the same kind.

I stopped at home to change clothes before heading to the *Herald* offices. The house felt too empty, *I* felt too empty, and I wished Celine was with me. I took a quick shower and while I was toweling myself off, I realized I was avoiding looking in the bathroom mirror. I don't think I was afraid of seeing a bad man or a sad man or an angry man or even a man coming undone. I was just hollow. I was afraid I'd look and see nothing at all.

# CHAPTER 9

# CONN

I wasn't ready for a visit to Laurel's daughters. I didn't know them, I wasn't in great shape to talk about their mother, and there were so many uncertainties. The search at the reservoir had left me queasy and unsettled, and I was sure the kids would sense it. But I had to bite the bullet, and sooner rather than later. Vickie Landauer of Child Services arranged it with the foster parents, and told me that visits like this were supervised—she would be joining me to "facilitate."

I told her I'd take all the help I could get.

Just after lunchtime we met at the commuter parking lot outside Richmond, planning to drive in one car to the foster home. I joined her in her car, and we sat for a time as she helped me formulate an approach. Our windows were open and a light breeze blew through, bringing with it the rushing sound of cars on the interstate.

"To be honest," I told her, "I don't know how to handle this. I don't know the girls. I've never spent much time around *any* kids! Last kids I dealt with were fucking *product,* children damaged from a human-trafficking operation. Sorry about my language. It was . . . I was not at my best on that assignment."

Vickie was in her late twenties, plump, with a ready smile, dressed in gray slacks and a blouse with ruffles down the front. She struck me as a person comfortable in her own skin, and her professionalism was apparent as she did a good job of calming me.

"Let's set some simple expectations," she suggested.

"Okay."

"First, we'll say from the start that it's going to be a short visit. It's better to leave as planned than to stall out and let things get awkward. I'll be the one to check the time."

"Okay. Thanks."

She turned in her seat to face me. "Simple messages—I love you, I love your mom. Simple questions—open-ended questions that give them choices about how to answer. What do they like to do, what have they been doing. *Do not* ask about summer camp or coming home to an empty house, don't try to get, like, 'clues' about their mom. And don't overdo it emotionally—don't expect some big bonding to happen this first time."

"Okay."

"I know you're a reporter, but are you familiar with trauma-informed interviewing techniques?"

"I've certainly interviewed people who were dealing with trauma. I don't know about 'techniques,' though."

She checked her watch. "Not to worry. It boils down to trust. Be honest—be yourself. Empower them by respecting their choices about what to talk about—or not."

"Got it."

She started the car and began the drive into downtown Richmond.

"This is your mom and me when I was eight and she was about six," I said.

Celine had suggested this approach: Bring photos that established my connection to Laurel. I had gone through the family archives and selected ten that showed us together, or both of us with our parents. Happy occasions, or moments that revealed trust and affection.

The photo I handed them showed Laurel and me trying to fix her bike, which had thrown its chain and which I, the elder, felt proud to know how to fix. Watching studiously, Laurel wore shorts and T-shirt, her brown hair loose around her face and shot with summer gold.

Maddie and Julie and I were sitting cross-legged on the carpet. The girls took the photos from me carefully, as if they were important heirlooms.

"She was pretty," Julie said. At nine, she was the younger sister, more tentative and yet more edgy and direct.

"Yeah, your mom is very pretty. I've always been proud of her." I had rehearsed using the present tense. And maybe it was still valid. Around these two, I wanted badly to believe it.

Vickie Landauer looked on, invisible yet keenly observant. The foster mother, Elaine Clarke, leaned forward in her overstuffed chair, stolid, heavy, dubious of me in a protective way. We were in the Clarkes' living room in their ranch house, scrupulously neat and with a determinedly neutral decor in which to receive foster charges from the state. In the kitchen, Elaine's biological son, Ben, explained something at length to another foster charge, Anderson. We'd been introduced on the way in, and I'd seen immediately that Ben was on the autism spectrum, a handsome boy with taut facial features and high attention to detail. Anderson was a badly overweight kid who had been there for some months and, according to Vickie, was "just beginning to settle in." He shook my hand with a moist, flaccid grip that betrayed a life of sad insecurities.

"Here's another. Your mom and I had this sort of competition thing, where we'd try to outdo each other's Halloween costume?"

The photo showed me wearing a can of beer made of cardboard and lots of paint and Scotch tape, eye holes cut into the Budweiser logo. I was about twelve, Laurel ten. She wore a blond wig topped by a tiara, and a scarlet gown improvised from old curtains. My mother's artful makeup job and Laurel's affected hauteur made her look older.

"She was Buttercup," I explained. "That's the heroine of a movie that was very popular that year, *The Princess Bride*? My costume fell apart after about an hour of trick-or-treating."

The girls didn't comment. They just studied. Maddie, I noted, also watched her sister.

Julie was small, with a serious face, a delicate line of jaw, given to quick, uncertain glances. Maddie was rounder, with plump cheeks, darker hair, five inches taller than her sister. I could see traces of Laurel in both of them—the profile of nose and those smart hazel eyes. Celine had told me a lot about daughters becoming the female authority figures in homes with alcohol- or drug-dependent moms. Looking at Maddie now, I suspected she had often served as ballast in their household, daughter as mom, before Laurel got herself together.

"Cool," Julie said noncommittally.

I brought out more photos: Laurel and me at the Champlain Valley fair, a family outing we looked forward to all year. Sugar-frenzied from cotton candy, grinning and drunk on the whirl of carnival lights, we looked like twins. Another showed me looking on as Laurel balanced on a slack rope setup my father had installed in our yard. Laurel proved much better at it than I did. Lacking the discipline to practice, I focused on learning entertaining pratfalls.

"Do you love Mom?" Julie asked.

Our observers shifted in their seats.

"I do. I love her very much."

The girls moved uncertainly, not much believing it, wanting to.

"What else?" Maddie asked, keeping things in safe territory. She gestured at my remaining photos.

I handed them over. In the kitchen, Ben began to whine, a high keening like a muffled telephone buzzing through a wall. Elaine leaped up and went to sort things out between him and Anderson. The girls exchanged a glance, then went back to examining photos.

Anderson had done something that Ben objected to, and Elaine started interrogating them. Vickie gave me a look.

"So," I said, "I have a question for you girls." I didn't think this one would violate Vickie's rules.

"What," Julie said.

"Your mom—I keep calling her 'Laurel,' but she changed her name to Gertrude, and people called her Trudy. When I first met you guys, she was still Laurel. Why'd she change her name?"

Clearly, they had established a language between them—glances, slight postural shifts.

Maddie took the lead on this one: "She said she'd tell us when we were older, when we'd get it better." They exchanged a glance, a tiny upturn at the corner of Julie's lips.

I deduced it was "a Mom thing"—one of those inexplicable things they loved about her, a little tease or mystery she was setting out for them.

"I thought Gertrude was a stupid name," Julie said. "But I like the way Trudy sounds."

"So . . . what did you guys call her?"

"Mom," they both said. Of course.

We labored on. The voices from the kitchen rose and then someone stomped off through the house. I heard Elaine speaking in subdued disciplinary tones to whichever kid had remained. Vickie Landauer caught my eyes, suggesting that we'd done what we could this first time around. We'd been there for about an hour. I nodded.

"Well," Vickie announced. "I have to be getting back to the office, and your uncle is riding with me, so we'll have to say goodbye for now. You girls are the greatest."

"Are you going to come see us again?" Julie asked me. She had curled in on herself, a self-protective posture.

"I sure will, if you want me to."

"Sure," Maddie said. The pragmatist, the Stoic. She glanced at the kitchen doorway and I sensed that friction between the boys was a common source of uneasiness here. Unsmiling, she stood up and spread her arms for the obligatory hug she knew I'd offer.

"Is Mom dead?" Julie asked.

I opened my mouth, shut it, tried again. "I hope not. I don't think so. We're all looking for her."

I gathered Maddie into my arms and she held me lightly, her frizzy hair tickling my chin. Julie came into it, too, her skinny body desperate against my side, her grip harder.

"I'll do my best to find her. She loves you and I love you, too. I'll be a better uncle, I promise."

And then it was time to go. They watched us as we left, standing in the living room, Maddie with one arm around Julie's waist, her left hand holding Julie's hand.

I spent Wednesday in my cubicle at the *Herald*, waiting for an update from Welles, doing routine work, and trying to focus on my next "Around Here" feature.

I wrote twenty-six of these a year, covering noteworthy regional individuals, landmarks, historical events, and curiosities. When I started the column, a couple of years after joining the *Herald,* I rather randomly started with the supposed Druid ruins on Spruce Mountain. Back in the day, Mason and I used to go up there, scouting the woods and convincing ourselves that some marks on boulders were runes, or arrays of stones, the remains of ancient henges. Laurel came along once and had the good sense to ridicule us: "Look! A Druid beer can!" We threw sticks at her, but Mace and I had to laugh and began doing it, too: "A Druid stump!" "Oh my God, Druid deer scat!"

Twenty-five years later, I hiked up to our old Druid hunting grounds to do research for that first "Around Here" article. I interviewed historians, hikers, and even a couple of self-proclaimed modern-day Druids. Of course there was nothing to it, but I ended the piece on a slightly ambiguous note, leaving some small hope for the wishful thinkers.

"The Druids of Spruce Mountain" begat a deluge of mail—a lot of people had been wondering about it as long as I had—that launched the column as a regular feature.

Next I did a piece on a collapsing covered bridge near Cabot, two hundred years old, describing its mortise-and-tenon construction and relating stories of people who had known the bridge when they were kids. "I stole my first kiss in that bridge!" one eighty-year-old farmer told me. Inspired citizens started a fund that eventually paid for its restoration, and three years later I reported on the ribbon-cutting that opened the lovingly rebuilt structure.

I relished the license the column gave me to dig beneath the surface of daily life in our region. It quickly became the *Herald*'s most popular feature, so my publisher gave me free rein. I didn't have tight length restrictions and could inject some literary flourish into the prose.

Ordinarily, the writing came easily, but today I couldn't make any headway. My idea for a piece on the Kings' first-responder fiesta was obviously not going to happen for me this time around. So I looked over my notes for a piece I'd been nibbling at, about a murder—or execution, or accident—in a town I'd lived in as a kid. Celine had found the story thought-provoking, but now it struck me as too dark, too autobiographical. Anyway, members of the dead man's family still lived in the area and might find it upsetting.

But what, then? I couldn't decide on my next topic. My thoughts were slippery, elusive. I flashed back to the reservoir search, and felt again the impact of the thing against my foot. I thought about Maddie and Julie, suspended in a limbo of uncertainty, waiting out their days in that sterile and dissonant household. Waiting for what?

"I'll do my best to find her," I'd told them. With that in mind, I conjured some journalistic discipline: listing resources I had that might lead to Anthony Shapiro or whoever else might be involved.

I did have several. The *Herald* had gone digital ten years before, and its files would be a good repository of information. And I had working relationships with people in the various town police departments, the attorney general's Trial and Investigative Unit, sheriffs' offices. More promising, I thought, were the hundreds of individual contacts I'd made through my reporting. I doubted that Welles fully understood the complex skein of roots that bound our region together, and how much might be learned there.

When the phone light began blinking, Welles's name on the readout, I snatched the receiver.

"What'd you find?"

"Nothing but the anchor. We're doing forensics on it, but I doubt we'll learn much. It's a common brand, sold as a stock accessory with a lot of boats. The rope is Chinese-made and can be bought in any hardware store. In any case, we have no proof it's related to the thing you kicked or that the thing you kicked has anything to do with your sister."

My pulse had picked up when I answered, and I realized I needed to slow down.

"Still," Welles went on, "we find it interesting that Mr. Shapiro owns a 1990 Chris Craft Bowrider. A boat big enough to need an anchor that size."

"What! Can you—"

"Based on that fact, we've requested a warrant to search the Shapiro property, including the boat. But, again, the whole issue could be irrelevant."

"So what's next?"

"We drain the reservoir. We keep sifting through your sister's life. And looking for Mr. Shapiro. I've got two of my staff assigned full-time to it, with assistance from other units."

"Okay."

"One more thing. We have a tip line, right? Don't get your hopes up, but we've gotten several calls from good citizens who say they've seen your sister. Alive."

"Oh, man." My legs and pectoral muscles twitched in a single, clenching tic.

"Yeah, that's what I said. I like clarity. Some left their names, some didn't. I'd dismiss the reports, you always get some, but a few of the details don't seem entirely off the wall. I thought you should know."

"Where? What—"

"I'm going to wait before we share that information, Mr. Whitman. We'll check out the reports."

The monstrous uncertainty swelled again, that awful dissonance of mixed hopes and fears. I could only imagine what the girls were going through.

"To put it in perspective," Welles added sourly, "we've also gotten plenty of calls naming the killer. Apparently about a dozen people murdered her, none of whom were on our radar at all. We're checking them, too."

I slotted that into the mix. Of course a story like this would draw pranksters and nutcases and anyone with a grudge against a neighbor or just hungry for attention. Shapiro himself, or his buddies, could be calling in to muddy the waters.

I hadn't had a craving for hard liquor for years, but I did that evening. Something to dull me out, stop the twitches in my legs that started when Welles called, indicative of a level of tension I hadn't fully been aware of.

I'd kept a short leash on booze for years, and I didn't indulge the yearning. Swimming was a better fix anyway. After work I drove up to Molly's Falls Pond, a gorgeous L-shaped lake that starts near Route 2 but then angles sharply off into sparsely populated, pine-forested land.

I parked in the pullover, got my suit and towel from the trunk, made my way to the water's edge. And sat, staring out at an avenue of blue water between green hills. I just sat. A windless day. The water bounced back the color of the sky and mirrored the meandering shoreline—a jagged zigzag line of trees, upside down and standing, neat as a design on a Navajo blanket. From far up the lake, the whickering laughter of loons.

I couldn't swim. It wasn't going to do the job. Instead I called Celine and told her that her fiancé was coming unglued and would love to see her. Needed to be with her.

Sometimes water seems too cold. What I needed was warmth, and I knew of only one place I could find the sort I needed. One person: Celine.

# CHAPTER 10

# CELINE

The fact is that Conn and I didn't know each other that well yet, even after two years together. But after his encounter in the lake, events brought us closer to each other. And, paradoxically, made us start keeping secrets. Throughout, I had to learn some basic psychology they didn't teach us at the University of Chicago.

As Conn put it: Murder puts you right up against some serious shit.

When we first met, I was a comparative newcomer—an immigrant from suburban Chicago and a Vermont resident for less than three years. Richfield proved a steep learning curve for a city dweller: a town of six thousand residents, with a business district of two- and three-story buildings, their redbrick walls capped by high cornices and with windowsills of Vermont granite. Awnings sheltered the storefronts, cranked down every morning and up again at closing time; artfully chalked sidewalk signs advertised computer repairs, deals on haircuts, and specials on local beers. Beyond the town center, tree-shaded neighborhoods of nineteenth-century wooden houses lapped up the sides of the valley, and a district of granite-carving sheds and lumber yards lined the river. On the edge of town lay a strip of car dealerships and convenience stores, eventually giving way to farmland, forested hills, and scattered villages threaded together by narrow two-lane roads.

Coming from a modern urban environment, I didn't really understand how Conn saw his home turf, what he meant by "the village." Trying to explain, he said that when he was a child in the 1980s, the area was "still in the 1940s." Even when he returned, after almost twenty years away—college, grad school, seven years at the *Washington Post*—he still found traces of that older world. And it enchanted him. Here, he said, the small towns retain features of older social orders—of the tribe, the clan. There are local legends and myths and intricate webs of blood relationships spanning centuries. People are more intimately connected, and do things in ways come down through generations. For better or worse.

He wrote a popular column for the *Richfield Herald*, exploring this landscape. After the disappearance of his sister, he began re-working a particular story that he'd never finished. Reading his other articles had helped me understand the region, but for some reason this one really got it across to me.

His working title was "Chief," and he began the tale by stating, "Killing people is sometimes acceptable—sometimes necessary."

That got my attention. He told the story, then let me read his notes.

When Conn was around eight, his family lived for a time in a house in one of Richfield's outlying towns, right on Route 170, a narrow two-lane that served as the area's main north—south thoroughfare. Truly, almost *on* it, according to Conn—the front wall of the house was only seven feet from the pavement.

This is still common up here. Two centuries ago, people built close to what were then dirt tracks carrying only horse and foot travelers. Over the years, cars appeared, traffic increased, and roads got paved and widened, inching ever closer to front porches. Conn's parents rented the house on Route 170 knowing that some years earlier a truck loaded with saw-logs had lost control and had entered the living room uninvited. Everybody survived, even the house, which forever after served as a cautionary tale and source of humorous allusion.

Conn recalled the noise of traffic passing, each car sending a shock wave of displaced air that thrummed the walls. Car traffic dwindled at night, but that's when the heavy trucks came on, and then it was the floors that shook.

Despite the noise, Conn says he loved his life there. He liked being at the center of town, close to school, friends' houses, and the river.

Especially interesting to him was the gas station across the road, Burton's Mobil. It was a narrow pullover, with two pumps backed up by a one-story, badly modernized building containing a single repair bay and an office with a big plate-glass window. Battered cars and pickup trucks packed the lot, along with barrels of used engine oil, piles of worn-out tires, and rusting engine parts. The illuminated plastic sign provided by Mobil had lost one face during a windstorm, so if you were heading south, you could tell that this crowded lot and dirty white building constituted a gas station. Heading north, you saw a tiny automotive junkyard and a big sign showing some electrical components but no message.

Conn's second-floor bedroom window overlooked the road, and his homework desk offered a direct view of Burton's. Cars came and went as people got their gas. Lance Burton and his sons labored under cars on the lift, or on the lot, using jacks and wheel ramps to get at defunct transmissions and busted tie rods. To Conn, the chatter of the air compressor and the Bronx cheers of pneumatic tools seemed the sound of things happening, of industriousness, of high tech.

Burton's was the only gas station in the village, so it was a busy place. Lance and his sons worked at the lift, manned the pumps, or lay in the lot with straining legs sticking out from beneath cars. A radio blared in the lift bay, country music full of static. Intermittent squawking voices came through Burton's police-band scanner because he was the town constable—the part-time policeman hired to be first responder to accidents or disturbances of the peace nearby. Women from town came by often, with car problems that apparently could be dealt with only by Lance's personal attention. At night, when they shut down the repair bay and turned off the sign, Burton and his sons and men from town would sit in the fluorescent-lit office, bright through the big window, or on lawn chairs in front, drinking hard, talking, playing poker. At intervals, the scanner crackled with staccato voices.

Living directly across from the station had its advantages. Conn filled his bike tires at their air hose and occasionally asked to borrow a

screwdriver or wrench. Preoccupied, the Burtons always lent it, handing it to him with grease-blackened hands. Their negligent trust made
him feel grown-up and respected.

Lance Burton was handsome, with sculpted facial features that resembled Clark Gable's except that he wore them easily, ruggedly—no pomaded
hair or pencil mustache. He had tan skin smudged with black smears, light
brown hair, and a muscular build earned by daily struggles with recalcitrant
car parts. Women took note, Conn learned through overheard conversations, and he was popular in bedrooms around town. None of his sons had
comparable charisma, and Conn didn't think any of them had the same
mother. Burton senior was in his late forties but came across as younger;
his sons ranged from early to late twenties. One was skeletally skinny, back
hunched with scoliosis, a cigarette always wedged in the corner of his mouth.
The other two had builds like Burton's: of medium height, with corded
forearms and capable shoulders, they impressed and intimidated Conn.

Burton was not "respectable." He wore grease-grimed coveralls, and
he was usually lying on his back under some decomposing hulk that he
was doing his best to help some neighbor keep running. He slept with
too many women, and he got drunk every night.

But he held unmistakable sway. As constable, Burton had more immediate power than the sheriff, who would have to drive a half hour
from Montpelier to deal with any trouble, or the mayor. He helped the
townspeople by certifying their rust buckets as safe by state inspection
standards. He knew everyone, talked to everyone, and as constable was
responsible for everyone. On the desk in his office, along with papers
and car parts, he kept a .45 revolver. His womanizing gave him trouble,
but it also enhanced his prestige.

As Conn saw it, Burton was a traditional village headman. He provided essential services, he commanded a small army of loyal retainers,
he was legally empowered to dispense justice. He sired children by many
women. He was seldom roused to anger, but the few times Conn saw
it from his window it was quick, muscular, and unforgiving. His de-
meanor was that of a work-weary yet pleasure-loving chieftain who saw
to the needs of his tribe with gruff humor and authority.

In summer, lying in his bed with the window open, Conn eaves-dropped on conversations across the street, making out bits and pieces of gossip and profanity.

He also listened to the scanner. He was listening the night Burton got a call about a domestic disturbance that had turned violent, far up one of the hill roads. It was around ten at night, and all the men were drunk—slurring, laughing at one another's burps and bad jokes, knocking over bottles when they stood to visit the station's bathroom or the bushes.

When the call came, Lance and one of the men piled into a pickup and sped away, and two of his sons followed in a separate car. Conn fell asleep and didn't learn the rest of the story until a few days later.

He could only recount it as understood through the filter of news-paper reports, village grapevine, and later-acquired adult knowledge, but he believed his sense of it was accurate.

Lance and his posse drove five miles up dirt roads to the house of Charlene Fecteau and her husband, Don. It wasn't the first time they'd made the trip.

An angry snake lived in Don Fecteau's heart. He beat Charlene and their kids, and Burton had arrested him half a dozen times for it. Des-perate, in fear for her life, Charlene would call for help, but the next day would refuse to press charges, every time. The community knew how it worked: Charlene pleaded for Don's release because she blamed his violence on her own failings. She loved him, feared him, needed his income. And there were the kids to think of.

In my trade, we refer to this type of forgiveness of intimate partner violence as the social-cognitive pattern, based on low self-esteem and self-attribution. Burton might not have known the terminology, but he understood what it entailed and how hard it was to break out of.

Conn's notes said Fecteau reneged on agreements and threatened anyone who disputed him. He fought with neighbors over property bor-ders, he poached deer, he brought strange and hostile complaints to town meetings. He had gotten off a charge of assault against someone he was feuding with, escaping punishment only through technicalities. His ex-plosiveness scared people, and he used it to get what he wanted. Conn's father told Conn—all the parents told their kids—to stay away from Fecteau. The man created instability that constituted a real danger to the village. It had gone on for years the night Constable Burton got that call.

Lance and his deputies pulled up at the house. They went into the shabby mess of a kitchen to find a badly bruised wife and three crying kids. Don Fecteau was raging drunk and told Burton to get the fuck out and fuck himself and fuck shit all. Burton took him by the arm and said they should talk together in the living room, out of hearing of wife and children. They'd been in there for about one minute when Burton killed Fecteau with his .45, a single shot under the chin.

Nowadays, Conn stressed, it's hard to get the feeling of that time—there's 911 to call now, the roads have street signs, and people have put floodlights over their barnyards and driveways. But this was the 1980s, and as Conn put it, the area had one foot in 1940 and one in the Bronze Age. An isolated, falling-down farmhouse on a dark hilltop, a dangerously volatile man: Burton had made too many late-night, adrenaline-sweating trips up that hill.

Was Burton just drunk, angry, sick of being called away from his evening's entertainments? Was it simply a testosterone-fueled contest for dominance? Or was he doing his duty as village headman by administering justice, resolving with finality a long-running problem?

In court, Charlene claimed that Burton murdered her husband without provocation, but Burton said Don had pulled out his rifle and threatened to kill him and everyone else present. He'd shot him in self-defense and to protect the others. His two sons and their drinking companion corroborated Burton's account. Fecteau's history spoke for itself. A jury of Burton's peers acquitted him, and he resumed his job as mechanic and as constable. As chief.

Conn said that he believed Lance simply executed Fecteau, and that the jury believed it, too. They let him off because they agreed it was a necessary act—a headman's duty. Conn holds a passionate belief in due process, but he is certain that Burton kept the town safer by doing it, and he may well have saved the lives of Fecteau's wife and kids.

Sometimes it's necessary and acceptable to kill someone.

The old village: Lance Burton's story got it across to me. It helped me understand Conn. It also marked the beginning of my drift into secrets, uncertainties, and compromises.

I had worked in the Richfield area for almost three years when Conn told me the tale. But I hadn't really seen my new home until I caught Conn's sense of it. On one level it was a charming sensibility—neighbors helped widows get up firewood, general-store proprietors let charge accounts run long if a customer was out of a job—but, as Burton's story illustrated, some hard questions came with it.

If I was at all susceptible to Burton's outlook, it's because in my work I frequently deal with abusive parents and their damaged kids. Too often, police and social services agencies can't do anything, and the hurting can go on for years. Damaging families are factories that turn out people who do damage in their turn. It makes me sad and makes me angry, and it frustrates me that my staff and I can't always fix it.

After hearing the story, I had to honestly ask myself: When is it necessary to cut through the overlay of laws and professional standards to serve more fundamental human interests? When can you betray those modern inventions—so recent in our history, thin as a coat of paint on a whale—if that betrayal protects the real people and complex relationships that make up a village, that verb of a community Conn lives in?

Yes: Murder puts you up against some hard questions.

Conn and I met while he was writing a feature on local schools for the *Richfield Herald*, where he worked as chief local news reporter and was their most famous, and famously disgraced, journalist. He wanted to interview me because I was head of the guidance department of the Richfield Unified School District. Though I was fairly new, I came to know a lot of kids and their parents and their circumstances in a very intimate way. That's the perspective Conn sought—an inside view, from my angle, of the regional community he loved.

I had been a widow for less than four years and had mangled my hand in a car accident—I viewed myself as disfigured—so I wasn't in the relationship "marketplace." But I was crushingly lonely. As Conn interviewed me, I was struck by his slim muscularity and a way of moving that suggested robust but understated fitness. Paradoxically, his face was etched with lines revealing emotional wear and tear, making it hard for me to guess his age. He wore a heavy Harris tweed jacket, the kind I associated with Irish farmers cutting peat. With his tie and khakis, his outfit struck me as a rugged variant of business casual—a deft balance for a reporter who was just as likely to interview a dairy farmer in his pasture as a school administrator in her office.

Though it made me feel disloyal to my dead husband, I couldn't deny that I found him attractive or that our slight awkwardness resulted from a buzz of sexual interest. It was the first time since Richard's death, and I was surprised that I could still experience such a thing. We started dating, cautiously, after we ran into each other some months later.

At our age, "girlfriend" and "boyfriend" sound juvenile, "lover" sounds sort of clandestine and limited in scope. So we started using "fiancé" to describe what we were to each other. It didn't imply firm plans for the future, just served as a workaround convenient for both of us. I often stayed at Conn's cabin, but I kept my own apartment in town and stayed there when work demanded it or one of us needed time alone. We were both determinedly independent, both holding back for different reasons, and our arrangement worked well enough.

I attributed Conn's caution to a lingering distrust of himself. From the start, he had been candid about his flaming downfall from the *Washington Post.* How could he not be? His debacle had gotten abundant national press ten years earlier. He had retreated to his old hometown only because he had nowhere else to turn. He hid out at his father's cabin, staying drunk and pondering suicide. But then he started swimming, which, as he said, helped "wash off the blood and scum of Washington." He gave up whiskey, started eating right, and eventually rejoined mankind.

Conn likes to say I helped him come back, but it's not true; really, he had completed his bootstrapping by the time we met. Still, I don't mind the gratitude he expresses.

Once I asked him: "Remind me. How did I rescue you?" I was tired after a long day's work and was fishing for compliments. We were sitting on the couch in the big room of his cabin, winding down, and he had lit candles and set a fire burning in the woodstove. The log walls glowed, golden—everything was warm in the house and between us.

For a moment, he thought about how to answer. "Well, there I was, drowning—drowned, really. And then you came along."

"Yeah, and I did . . . what?" I persisted, coy, wanting affirmation.

He leaned and gave me a long, deep kiss. "Mouth-to-mouth resuscitation," he said. "And compressing my chest—getting my heart going again. Basic CPR, really."

It was a weak joke, especially for a wordsmith, but we laughed. He had gotten my heart kicking over again, too. We were still new together and had a lot to learn about each other.

Of course, this was before he encountered the thing in the lake, when it was easier to laugh.

Neither of us had any idea what was coming at us. How could we? Few people have had to face the twin ironies that love can beget murder and, sometimes, murder beget love, in a damning daisy chain that has wound through the history of the human family forever.

# CHAPTER 11

# CELINE

I had been planning to stay at my own apartment that night to catch up on time-sensitive school-district budget work. But when Conn called, his voice revealed just how shaky he was—the shore search and his visit to his nieces had unsettled him. I told him I'd join him for dinner, but that I'd have to get back to my spreadsheets, not his bedsheets, afterward.

Conn had been working up a repertoire of Italian cuisine, and when I arrived at his place I helped with the lasagna. He told me about his morning with the police at the reservoir. I could only imagine the hovering sense of imminent horror he'd felt. Between kitchen tasks, I kneaded the taut strands of tension in his shoulders. When we got the lasagna into the oven, I insisted we take a walk in the long summer twilight.

We linked elbows and strolled along the dirt road that runs at the valley's bottom.

"Now," I told Conn, "we are going to talk about how beautiful it is tonight, how delicious dinner is going to be, where we should go if we ever take a real vacation. We can even talk about whether my car needs new ball joints. But we are not going to talk about Laurel or school budget cuts."

The woods were darkening, and in the tall grass by the side of the road fireflies blinked their first tentative flashes. We passed a neighbor's house, windows alight, and waved to the teenager who was practicing some fancy footwork with a soccer ball in the driveway.

"Right?" I prompted, when he'd taken too long to agree.

"Okay," Conn said. "I'll try."

We walked on into the deeper shadow of some tall pines, our shoulders touching occasionally.

"Can I ask you something?" he said.

"Maybe. But is it dark and overwhelming and—"

"I don't know. That's part of the question. I want to know how you think of Richard. What it's like, now that you're with me. Six years after."

Richard, my husband, died three years and three months before I met Conn. He had been spending his monthly weekend with the Illinois National Guard and the helicopter he'd been riding in crashed, killing him and five others. It was the worst day of my life. I knew why Conn was asking, and I debated whether the topic was a violation of my prohibition against dark things. I decided it wouldn't necessarily be.

"What's it like?" I mused. "Well, I think of him often. But I try not to think of that day, or that period. If I do, I try to think of our lives together, not the accident. Not the aftermath."

"So you think of the good times."

"Yes. I mean, it wasn't all good times, of course. But I don't think about emotional impasses and arguments and all that."

Actually, those did linger and I was daily tempted to castigate myself for every unkind word I'd spoken to Richard, every careless act. I suspected this was something all widows felt, and I wondered how others managed it. How did Jody fold memories of her Marine husband into her current life, her marriage to Mason? Of course, she'd had longer to recover from his death, and she had two children who surely resembled him—in a sense, caring for them probably offered a way to continue to love him. And, of course, to continue inflicting the inadvertent unkindness and carelessness we all impose on those we love, to regret later. The daisy chain again.

I lied to Conn because I did not want to give him justification for pondering all the ways he could have done better with Laurel. He was really asking for strategies for thinking of her, and yes, I had some advice.

"I kept it all away, even the good things, for a long time. Because at first when I let myself feel the love, I'd feel the hurt again. And I just . . . couldn't. But little by little I am letting myself love him again. The hurt is worth it, Conn. It's part of becoming complete again. I wish I'd learned that earlier."

He nodded deeply.

I hadn't answered the other part of his question—how being with Conn affected my feelings about Richard. Had Conn healed some of the injury? Very much so. But did I still hold back due to that irrational sense of disloyalty to Richard? Yes. He held parts of himself back from me, too. When our reciprocal reservations came up—rarely—we agreed that we shouldn't try to "work on" them. In every relationship, people hold some things back. And it's not necessarily a bad thing.

Anyway, as Conn said, extensive dissections of relationships tend to turn into autopsies.

Our mostly unspoken agreement was that it was best to just let the barriers erode. Rub up against each other long enough and strong enough until they wore away. It's wise to be patient with these things. I loved him for never pressing too hard on the subject of Richard.

But I had to tell him one thing: "Connor. Your being in my life has allowed me to tolerate remembering the good things. To love him again. If I could do that for you . . . with Laurel . . ."

It was getting dark enough that I couldn't really see his expression—he had to put his wrist up to his face to check his watch.

"We better get back," he said. "The lasagna is just about ready."

Conn's question about Richard awakened memories which, incredibly, set off my phantom limb sensations. It was as if I went back in time to that day, when I still had those two fingers. Setting the table, I dropped silverware because I inadvertently tried to use the nonexistent fingers when gripping things. When I shut my eyes, my proprioceptive sense assured me they were there. When I opened my eyes, they told me my left hand was incomplete—I had a thumb and two fingers and then a knuckly ridge of scarring, just skin over bone, where the ring and little fingers had been.

It was fascinating. Close eyes: fingers. Open eyes: no fingers. Coming right after talking about Richard, it reminded me how complex and mysterious the human mind is. All of our research, even with fMRIs and CAT scans, has barely touched the subject. After the accidents—Richard's and, only hours later, mine—I had reviewed my brain scans with the neurologist, but though I looked very hard I hadn't seen Richard in them anywhere.

Conn noticed me standing there, wiggling my fingers, alternately shutting my eyes, then opening them. I was chuckling as I did it. When I told him what I was doing, he said, "Cool!" Then he took my wretchedly incomplete hand and looked at it with honest curiosity. "Do you think they could feel it if I kissed them? You'd have to close your eyes."

"Okay."

I shut my eyes. I felt him lift my hand to his face, felt his breath warm on my palm, and then heard the tiny sound of two kisses in midair, one for each missing finger.

"Did you feel it?"

I was going to say "No," but then I thought maybe I *had* felt just a brush, a tiny sparkle like electricity. Or maybe I had just felt his kindness, his intentional acceptance of my worst injury and by implication the other injuries that had come with it. I loved him intensely at that moment.

I opened my eyes, and my fingers vanished again. "Conn! I think I did!"

We both laughed, pleased at the thought. Over dinner, we joked about whether this could be the basis of a groundbreaking scholarly thesis on the phantom limb phenomenon. It was a pleasant, relatively unburdened interlude except for one moment when the dark waters momentarily breached the dam.

"I am letting myself love her," Conn said, out of nowhere. "But it's not just grief that comes with it. It's different. Something 'happened' to Richard, no one to blame, only the gods to be angry with. But somebody *did* this to Lauren. Someone made this grief happen. You see what I mean? When I let myself love her, that comes with. That mix of feelings."

"What's in the mix?"

He looked truly wretched, and his hands made frustrated gestures. "This . . . *anger*. Outrage. This sense of how *wrong* it is. It's . . . toxic."

I didn't have an answer to that except to hold him.

Later, Conn withdrew into somber thoughts, the dark whirlpool drawing him in, and against my will I began pondering one of the awful ironies of the day Richard died.

After I identified his body at the medical examiner's office, I drove homeward and head-on into an overpass abutment—a flaming nightmare that disemboweled my car and should have killed me. Whether I was suicidal or just exhausted and inattentive is a question I can't answer. Richard and I had worn our wedding rings on our left hands. How strange, how appropriate, that my ring finger had been severed on the very day our marriage was severed by his death. I had lost my husband, and I had lost not only the wedding ring but even the finger I wore it on. I was vulnerable to the cruel symbolism implicit: that I'd never marry again, that the capacity to do so had been removed from me.

So those two little kisses Conn gave me—if my devotion needed any sealing, that did it. That night, the love I felt for him was as great as any I'd ever felt for anyone. I told him so, and I said I'd changed my mind about the spreadsheets-not-bedsheets provision. That got him laughing. We went upstairs, and it was another hour before I reluctantly headed back to my place.

# CHAPTER 12

# CELINE

I was in the throes of creating a new budget for the school district's special-ed and guidance departments. In May, half the district's towns had voted down their school budgets, rebelling against rising taxes, so each department in the system had to come up with ways to trim costs. Conn had covered the issue for the *Herald* over the years, and he knew what I had to do. He also knew I was no fun to be around when I did it.

It was as horrible this time as it had been the first. Do you cut staff and put skilled, devoted people out of jobs while imposing an impossible workload on your remaining staff and leaving kids without support they need? Impose salary cuts across the board? Try to foist the hurt off onto the art programs? A new vote was to be held soon, and we had to get meticulously detailed, multimillion-dollar budgets developed fast, even if they might just be voted down again.

I worked on the spreadsheets until the numbers swam in my vision. I got ready for bed, even opened the book I'd been reading, but found myself too restless. Instead I turned on my computer again, then went online and accessed my school files. I had dealt with the Shapiro family off and on during my time in my job.

If I remembered correctly, Anthony Shapiro—Laurel's boyfriend, or former boyfriend, the foremost suspect—was the father of Gracie Shapiro, an eighth grader at Wilson Middle School. She had come to our attention due to absences, listlessness in class, and a plea from her mother. Her mother blamed her faltering academic and social life on strife at home. I wasn't her case manager, so I met Gracie only once: a thin, pale, uneasy girl who to my eye desperately wanted to both hide and to open up to somebody. The first time, I said hello, reminded my staff member Lily of a meeting later, and was about to leave when Gracie asked me "What happened to your hand?"

Her candor, or social naivete, charmed me. "It's kind of personal," I said. "But I'll tell you when we get to know each other better." I was tricking her into telling us her more about herself—a trading of secrets. It worked. I never fulfilled my half of this bargain, but Lily said it broke the ice.

When I went into the school system's server to review our files on Gracie, it seemed reasonable. I told myself I simply wanted to figure out how we could help this kid and her family. My extra attention was completely justifiable. Her father's prolonged absence, newspaper articles about his affair with Laurel and suspicion of murder, and police visits to her house had to be amplifying her difficulties. She would be savaged by her peers at school when the fall semester began. Best to give it some consideration in advance.

But part of me knew it was the first step on a slippery slope that led to a division between agendas. I was drifting into Conn's world, the super- or pre-legal world of the old village. I wanted to learn more about Gracie's father, who was quite probably Laurel's murderer. What had we learned about him or the Shapiros' family dynamics during our work with Gracie?

I wouldn't be betraying confidentiality, I told myself, if I didn't discuss anything outside the guidance office. How could there be anything wrong with trying to find out a murderer in our midst?

The next day, I kept up the inner mantra that I was acting entirely out of concern for Gracie, for the family's well-being. But I began to admit my other motives. They didn't seem unjustified. I wanted my life, our life—Conn's and mine—to calm down. I wanted Conn to move past this, and the only way out was through—"through" meaning Conn's achieving a more accepting, coping state of mind.

And *I* needed to stay afloat. I had spent years with the memory of Richard's mangled body springing to mind, years of remembering every unkind or careless word between us and my monstrous frustration at being unable to retract even one word. Dead is so far away. I'd been much better since being with Conn, but now it all seemed to be coming back at me. I needed to act, to ward off the sorrow and guilt.

At first, my review of the meeting notes with Gracie and her mother, Irene, seemed to reveal nothing we didn't already know. But thinking about it later—trying to sleep—a single letter in my staffer's notes kept coming back to me. Among other domestic stressors noted in Lily Stanforth's meeting notes was "friction re Tony's other relationships." The S—the plural—bothered me.

Lily was the guidance counselor working with Gracie. Her notes said that in one of their meetings, Irene Shapiro had spoken candidly about Anthony's extramarital relationships and the damage they inflicted on herself and the kids. Irene was sure that if she and Tony could just straighten out their marriage, Gracie would get back on track.

I wanted to know whether the plural of "relationships" was meant literally or had any real importance. Did the police know about girlfriends other than Laurel? Might Tony be hiding out with one of them?

I called Lily to explore it further. Summer, seven weeks off work: Public school staff either take on temporary jobs or simply try to decompress and catch up with their own lives. I knew Lily was a passionate gardener and felt lucky to catch her on the phone that morning.

We talked briefly about small things—her voice told me she knew this wasn't a social call—and then I brought up my topic.

"Lily, you've been reading the newspapers—about the murdered woman and Anthony Shapiro being a suspect? And his being missing for the last few weeks?"

"God yes. Poor Gracie! As if she didn't have enough to deal with already!"

"I was thinking the same thing. I'm worried about her re-entry this fall."

"Me, too."

"I'm planning to make contact with her mother before the semester begins, and I had a question for you about them—Gracie and her mom."

"Sure."

"Can you tell me more about what Mrs. Shapiro said about her husband's extramarital affairs?"

"Yes. A sordid tale. The father's drug busts and DUIs, police knocking at the door, had been a long-running problem, but then there's harassment by dad's sleazy girlfriends. On top of which comes his possible murder of Trudy Carlson, more police, statewide press . . . We've got a distraught mother and frightened kids. Celine, I'm thinking this is one of those times when we have to adjust expectations. We don't know how this will turn out—like, forensically. Legally. And therapeutically, it's beyond the scope of what a school guidance-department conference can address. They'll need some real counseling."

"What's the girlfriend-harassment business about? I didn't see that in your notes."

She took a moment to reply, and I sensed she was assessing the implications of my question.

"I believe I mentioned that there was friction between them and Irene. But that was to be expected, and in any case the issue wasn't particularly on the agenda. We knew Tony didn't stay at home, and that the family was in turmoil as a result. That's what I focused on. It didn't help that at least one of his old girlfriends seemed to think she had some claim on the man and could come at his wife. But in my best assessment, following up on that would have diverted our conversation and was outside the intended scope of our interview." Lily's tone had become defensive, formal, but I barely registered it.

"They did? Girlfriends, what, accosted Irene? Attacked her?"

"One did. I don't know the details, but it was physical as well as verbal and it frightened Irene. But our meetings were about Gracie, only secondarily about her mother's emotional state. She didn't tell me whether Gracie knew about the incidents or was affected by them. I used my best judgment as to what was germane to Gracie's well-being and her academic success, and that's what I focused on."

Lily apparently felt that I was criticizing her record-keeping or judgment. Then a revelation hit me, something that should have been obvious: It was budget-cutting time. How vulnerable Lily must feel, when I held her employment future in my spreadsheets! An unexpected call from your boss in the middle of summer. She must have heard the axe whistling in the air—*I'm sorry to have to tell you this, Lily*—from the moment she answered the phone. And then I appeared to be finding fault with her work.

I let go of the Shapiro family and segued to my progress forging a new departmental budget. By the way, I told her, this call had absolutely nothing to do with her job performance or employment future. I considered her an invaluable member of the team, and her job was secure no matter what.

She puffed out a breath of relief. "Thanks, Celine."

I considered probing the issue further, but then decided that I had pushed it as hard as I could without some warning flag popping for her.

Anyway, her focus had been elsewhere during their meetings—on Gracie—as it should have been. The rest of this conversation would have to be with Irene Shapiro.

I could imagine how Irene felt. The papers and TV news told the world that her husband had disappeared; in every story about the missing Trudy Carlson, a.k.a. Laurel Whitman, the police named Anthony as a "person of interest"—which everybody knew meant "suspect"—because he'd been romantically involved with the victim. Among all the other fears and pains, the fact of his betrayal, publicly broadcast, would trigger shame and a sense of inadequacy. People might express sympathy, but Irene would believe that the world was secretly asking: *Why couldn't you hold on to your husband? Why can't you hold your family*

*together?* Self-blaming in the classical pattern, she probably asked herself the same thing.

The police had undoubtedly probed Anthony's discontents, and Irene's, but all in relation to Laurel. If what Conn said about Captain Welles's "method man" approach was true, they probably still had one eye askance at Irene—betrayed wife kills husband's lover. Under the circumstances, I doubted she would want to advertise the fact of his other infidelities. Her admissions to Lily were confidential, and in any case were peripheral, intended to help find therapeutic strategies for Gracie.

*It's all about Gracie*, I kept telling myself, even as I used a blatant subterfuge to make contact with Irene and wring information from her.

Gracie had an older brother, Mark, and a quick search of the school's database told me that he played in the RHS Gladiators' summer soccer league. With Tony absent, I was sure Irene would bring Mark to games and probably stay on as the sole parental cheerleader. I pulled up the Gladiators' schedule on the school's website, then made a point of going for a jog near the field on the day of their game with the Montpelier Solons. I would swing by the game and accidentally encounter Irene.

It was all about Gracie.

Anyway, I told myself, I have always loved soccer. That much was true. The geometry of it pleases my eye: the manicured green crisply cut with white lines and arcs, juxtaposed against the continuous kaleidoscopic rearrangement of the players in their colorful uniforms. There are a thousand acts of heroism in the tireless energy of the racing players, deft dribbling and passing, feints and trickery, desperate sprints and mighty headers, all played to gales of joy or woe voiced from the stands.

I ran a couple of miles and was appropriately sweated up as I came in from the bike path. I spotted Irene immediately—a worn, gray-clothed woman holding her arms around herself as if she were cold on this hot day, sitting alone, high at one end of the bleachers. The scoreboard showed a one-to-one game. The Gladiators were controlling the ball as

I approached, but I didn't know Mark and so couldn't recognize him among his purple-clad teammates.

I climbed the stairs in the Gladiators' section, sat on the plank seat, watched until a penalty call suspended play. Then I pretended to notice Irene for the first time. I caught her eye, smiled, waved, saw her look of confusion—we had only met once—and then recognition. I moved over to sit next to her.

"I'm Celine—we met at a guidance conference about Gracie?"

"I remember." She barely flashed me a glance, then looked out to the field. The side of her eyes seemed wide and scared.

"Got a kid in the game?"

"Mark. Gracie's brother. He's a sophomore."

"Which one is he?"

She shook her head. "He got yellow-carded for mouthing off to the ref. Coach has him on the bench to cool down."

I made a sympathetic noise, then figured I should explain my appearance: "I was just finishing a jog and then saw a game was on. I love soccer."

"I don't. Like baseball better."

We watched as the Gladiators' striker took a long free kick that the Solons' goalie easily snagged. The Montpelier parents cheered approval.

Irene shrugged.

"This has got to be a tough summer for all of you. How is Gracie?"

"I don't know. She doesn't tell me much."

"She's a strong young woman. She's going to come out of this just fine."

Irene didn't respond. From the side, her eyes looked glazed, those of a rabbit trying to be invisible. We watched as the tide of play swept back toward the Gladiators' goal, then slowed, then stopped as a missed pass went out of bounds. A big Montpelier kid jogged to the sideline, took the ball from the ref, and tossed it back into play. We didn't say anything for a while as the purple and green mingled and skirmished.

"Irene. Would it be helpful to talk with me about it? Before the next term begins? If I knew more about how she's coping, we could maybe come up with a plan to make her re-entry a bit easier."

"I guess." Irene gave me a longer glance, her face revealing a mix of distrust and need. "Don't see how, given we don't know what else will happen. Between now and fall."

"True." I looked out to the field. "Still, it's a good idea to start thinking about it."

A Solon kid headed the ball expertly and the offense moved quickly to capitalize on the reversal, converging on the Gladiators' goal. Half the crowd stood, suddenly quiet as the scoring attempt approached. The Solon forward ran to the rolling ball, the goalie shifted, and then the Solon kid swiped a short lateral pass rather than kicking. A teammate was there to make the kick, well-placed in the high right corner. The Gladiator goalie had anticipated it wrong and was nowhere near it. The crowd howled and whistled, the green players postured, and the purple players slumped. The scoreboard ticked another point, and then the ball went back to the center circle for the Gladiator kickoff.

I waited until the action resumed. "How about you? How are you holding up?"

Irene turned toward me fully this time, anger adding to the blend of emotions on her face. "How do you think?"

She looked older than when I'd seen her only a few months before. She was about my age, I guessed, but her face had gone gaunt, her hair uneven, with split ends needing a trim. She wore jeans washed to a dull blue-gray, grass-stained running shoes, and a gray sweatshirt that was too large. My heart panged as I wondered if it was Tony's.

"I'm doing shitty," she said.

"Understandably."

"They asked me if they could search the house, a 'consent search.' I told them *hell no*, Tony will turn up with his tail between his legs soon enough. But they said they're going to come back with a warrant. Not enough they have to come by and talk to me, cop cars in our driveway so the neighborhood has to know everything, now they want to tear the whole place apart. For what? Like there's some 'evidence' sitting around the house that I wouldn't know about? I keep a clean house. He didn't kill that Trudy Carlson woman."

"I can't imagine how awful it must be," I said. My platitudes were making me sick.

She dropped her voice, anger and shame turning her voice to a hiss: "I'm a good wife. I work hard at my job and I bust my ass to make a good home. I gave him two great kids. I've never let him down, never. And this is what I get back. And everybody has to know about it."

The game receded as her intensity mounted. "I still fuck him whenever he wants. But it's not enough."

"It's not about your failings!" I whispered back. "It's about his!"

"But I'm the one who has to pay for it. Me and the kids, that's who pays. At least all his other shit didn't get statewide coverage. The sluts really don't help."

"Lily Stanforth said one of his girlfriends harassed you."

Her eyes flared and she turned away again. "Good to know everybody has to hear about that, too."

"No. Just Lily and me. It's confidential. Our concern is whether Gracie witnessed that. And what she saw."

"She saw a lard-ass woodchuck practically break down our door. Who said Tony had promised to divorce me and marry her and he was hers now. I told her no, he was Trudy Carlson's now, go have it out with *her*, get out of my house. I had my broom and I shoved it at her? And she grabbed it? What Gracie saw was her mother and this freak, this fucking *goon*, wrestling in the hallway. That's what Gracie heard. That's what Gracie saw. Okay?"

"Oh, Irene." I wanted to touch her, console her, but knew she'd see it as condescending. "Did you report it to the police?"

"This was before all the other shit began, the murder stuff, and I didn't want the kids seeing cops in the living room. I didn't need that little drama to appear in the police blotter in all the papers. Little did I know."

"Who the hell is this woman? How dare she?"

"Penny something. Or maybe that's her going rate. Cheap at twice the price! Kind of fucking name is 'Penny'?"

"You should report her. Get a restraining order. But they'd need a last name."

"You know who's gonna 'restrain' her? *I'll* fucking restrain her. Bet on that. Coming into *my house*! She works where Tony works, Big Lots. I might just swing by one of these days. I've had enough of cops. Do my own 'restraining.'" Irene's words had started out fierce but had diminished to a muttered, self-directed monologue. Her eyes had dulled and she was flagging as exhaustion overtook anger. She had used herself up in the last three minutes. She hugged her arms again and began rocking forward and back on the bleacher seat.

The crowd roared at something, but it seemed very far away. Neither of us had followed the game.

After a time I checked my watch and said, "I should get going. But if you think of anything I can do to help you or your family, will you call me? Just call the main switchboard at school, ask for Celine Gabrielli. Please?"

For a moment she kept her eyes on the game as an injured Gladiator limped off the field and another bounded in from the bench. Then she nodded, one grudging dip of her chin. Pleading now, she said, "Could I just watch the game? My son is coming in. I'd like to watch my son play now. Is that okay?"

I felt dirty as I drove away. My sympathy for her and Gracie was genuine, almost overwhelming. But I had intentionally finessed information from a woman in deep despair and confusion. I had ingratiated myself with her to gain her trust, and I had manipulated her.

My first thought was to tell Conn about Penny, but then realized he'd be appalled at my violation of basic professional standards. Worse, at my misuse of the tiny gram of trust that Irene Shapiro had granted me.

But this Penny sounded like an angry and unstable person, and if she could threaten Tony's wife, she might do even worse to another of Tony's girlfriends—Laurel. Or maybe Tony had made his choice and was shacked up with Penny now. I couldn't let the facts get overlooked just because I felt bad about my relatively minor breach of ethics. The community came first, didn't it?

Fortunately, I had other ways I might get Penny into the investigation. Start with Mason. He'd relay the information to Welles, just as he had told him about Conn's bulbous monstrosity in the reservoir. I knew Mason well enough to trust that he wouldn't tell Conn where the information had come from, if I made him promise.

But how could I avoid having the police come right back to Irene with questions about Penny? She'd know I'd betrayed her confidence. I'd have to think about that, ask Mace if he had any ideas.

And I truly did think about Gracie during that drive. I thought: *I hope your father isn't a murderer. I hope he comes home and has learned some lesson that allows him to be a good parent for you.*

# CHAPTER 13

# CONN

Friday afternoon, I was working in my cubicle at the *Herald* when the front desk informed me that a Detective Selanski was in the lobby and wanted to see me. I wasn't thrilled at the prospect of seeing her, but the police had been draining the reservoir and I wanted to hear any news she might have for me. I told the receptionist to send her on back.

I met her in the corridor and led her to the conference room, a small glass-walled chamber with a view of the newsroom. It was a fishbowl but fairly soundproof—we could talk without being overheard.

I shut the door, gestured to a chair, and sat down at the head of the table. "You know, sometimes people call first to set up a time to meet. To what do I owe the pleasure?"

She didn't answer. Instead, she took a leisurely turn through the room, inspecting the conference phone and video screen, checking out the newsroom through the plate glass. Heads turned as reporters and copy staff took note of the badge on her belt and the bulge in her blazer. Selanski gave them a crinkle-fingered wave.

She returned to my end of the room, half sat on the corner of the table, and crossed her arms, still looking around with interest. "This is so cool! The proverbial free press in action. Just like the movies!"

I waited, looking up at her, determined not to let her get under my skin.

"Yeah, so, updates for you. All the news that's fit to print, as they say."

"Okay."

"I had some nice chats with your relatives. Out in Wisconsin. Nobody has heard from Laurel in years."

"I know. I called them myself."

"Your cousin Terry, in Milwaukee? Said last time was like ten years ago, when she called asking to borrow money. He sent her three hundred bucks, but when she called for another installment and he expressed some reluctance, she hung up on him."

She seemed to find the story amusing. I didn't.

"You came here to tell me that?"

"Well, in other news, we finished draining the reservoir about two hours ago. We found nada. Zip. No corpses, clothes, anything. Dogs didn't pick up sign anywhere but the cliffs."

I felt a mix of relief that my sister might not be dead and that paradoxical dismay—the frustration of the desire for closure.

"Captain Welles told me you'd gotten a search warrant for the Shapiro house. What about that?"

"Yup. Got 'er done this morning." She got up to patrol the room again, catlike. "Nothing much in the house except one sad, angry wife, bless her poor soul. But Tony's boat was there, parked on a trailer under a tarp. Guess what? No anchor or rope aboard. We ask the wife about that. Seems Tony is a good citizen about transmitting aquatic weeds from lake to lake, takes the anchor and rope out and hoses them down between boat rides—it was probably in his truck. We were bummed that we couldn't make an easy match with the rope or anchor from the reservoir. But we got fiber samples from those things, where you tie ropes, what are they called . . ." She made shapes with her hands.

"Cleats."

"Yeah, cleats! Which microscopic analysis might match. The forensic lab is on that."

Someone knocked at the door, and I turned to see Patrick hovering at the glass, looking rumpled and apologetic as always. He put his head in and nodded hello to Selanski.

"Hey, Conn. Sorry to butt in. Boss wants to see you when you get a minute." I gave him a thumbs-up and he backed out, shut the door.

When he was gone, Selanski came to sit on the edge of the table again, her wandering gaze focused now on me. I made a point of checking my watch.

"On the chasing-down-people front, we've now identified and talked to most of the wholesome, hikey-bikey friends in those photos of hers. Nobody's ringing our chimes. We've eliminated a couple of boyfriends from the suspect list. One's been up in the state correctional facility in St. Albans for a couple years. Another was in Florida at his sister's wedding in the time period when Laurel went missing. Talked to the Florida relatives myself and had them send me photos of the event."

"What about the other one, the one Laurel testified against?" I couldn't remember the name.

"Ah, Jesse Nadeau. I can't find hide nor hair. Actually, I was hoping you'd have something for me. He went to your high school, a few years ahead of you. You sure the name doesn't ring a bell?"

"There were three hundred and fifty hundred kids at that school, from a large rural district. It was twenty-five years ago."

She shrugged, skeptical, disappointed, then continued: Anthony Shapiro was still at the top of the suspect list. On the basis of the anchorless boat, they'd put out an interstate APB—Shapiro was known to have contacts in New York and Maryland—but no one had seen him or his truck. Irene Shapiro gave Selanski access to their credit-card accounts, which showed no recent activity except hers. However, Tony had withdrawn five hundred dollars from an ATM a few days before Laurel was reported missing. Welles thought he might have squirreled away cash from past drug dealing and could probably stay invisible for quite a while.

Selanski continued to study me, a speculative look. With the fluorescent ceiling light directly above her, I could see a scar on her left cheek, a thin ridge running from her nostril almost to her jaw. It gave her face a subtle asymmetry, amplifying the sense of a sardonic personality.

"If that's it, I gotta go see my boss. Thanks for the update. Any reason why you didn't just give me a phone call?"

She clapped her hands, startling me. "Right! Jeez, I am such a space cadet. Thanks for reminding me."

She reached into her blazer pocket and came out with a plastic envelope containing two glass vials with long-stemmed swabs built into the cap. She set them on the table and put on a pair of nitrile gloves.

"Yeah, I know, I should have done this last time, but I figured I'd riled you up enough for one session. Now, though, we really should button down the evidence, confirm the DNA on trace is for sure Laurel's. Trudy's. You don't have a problem with it, do you? We don't want to bother the little girls with this."

I gave her a look that I hoped would convey my dislike as I opened my mouth. She swabbed the inside of my cheeks with firm strokes, then put the swabs in the vials, screwed on the lids, and slipped them into the envelope.

She went to the door but turned back, her smile slightly tipped awry by the scar. "Great to see you again, Mr. Whitman. Better go see your boss."

I didn't feel any trepidation at being summoned by Ricky Thurston, publisher of the *Herald*. I was secure in my role at the paper, and Ricky and I knew each other well. She was a tall woman in her midfifties, slim, given to wearing conservative grays and beiges defied by one splash of vivid color, often a silk scarf wrapped once and flung over her shoulder. She carried herself with a dignity of the special variety that I associated with senior press people, a feisty form of grace. I admired her greatly, and we sometimes had after-work drinks together, comparing notes on journalism and life as colleagues, almost friends. And I owed her: She had overlooked my disgrace in Washington to hire me, a risky gamble.

Also, I had a kind of special status at the paper. Ricky gave me more credit than was due for saving the *Herald* from bankruptcy.

I had been mustering along at the bottom of the reportorial food chain, doing what I was paid—not much—to do. But between my daily reporting and "Around Here," I had become something of a scholar of life in north-central Vermont. Ten years in, I had my finger on the pulse of local politics and business and society and schools and sports and the trajectories of many individuals' personal lives. I conducted probably five hundred interviews each year, and came to know Richfield and the surrounding area better, quite possibly, than anyone else.

Meanwhile, the newspaper industry was going down in flames. Big papers were folding up throughout the country, and small-town dailies had it even worse. People weren't buying them because they got their world and national news on the radio, TV, cable, the internet. The *Herald* was no exception to the trend, and when I came on board it had already begun the downward spiral. They'd begun laying off staff, even the veteran cooking-feature writer and the curmudgeonly but rock-solid reporter who worked the statehouse beat.

But Ricky read the tea leaves sooner and better than most. She restructured, boosting local news coverage because that's the one thing the other streams didn't provide. Also, a paper makes its money from display advertising, not subscriptions, so lots of local coverage means lots of good relationships with the people who buy ads. Readership rebounded. Ad revenue bounced with it.

I was the one with those good relationships, so lowly Conn Whitman segued into a position of importance. Ricky felt that my "adroit nurturing" of so many connections, my lively writing, my eye for a good story, had helped save the paper; among the other reporters, I was seen as something of a small-time rainmaker. When she offered me an editorial position, I declined, saying I wanted to stay feet on the street, finger on the pulse. I liked my close-up view of the community's moving parts.

Ricky was behind her desk when I knocked on her door. She swiveled in her chair and set aside her reading glasses with a smile.

"Con-nor," she said. She liked to pronounce my name with an Irish accent.

"Hey, boss."

I went in and shut the door behind me. Despite her being top dog, Ricky's office was a utilitarian space only about twice the size of my cubicle, with a view through venetian blinds of the parking lot. I took a chair in front of her desk and she put one leg over the arm of her chair. Her posture signaled casual, but the look she gave me was one of hard appraisal.

"Connor, you look like hell. We need to figure out what to do with this situation."

She didn't have to spell it out. I had told her early on about Trudy Carlson being my sister, in part because it gave me a conflict of interest that precluded my covering the story when events moved our way. Patrick had taken on the job.

Her concern was justified. It wasn't just the extra days off I'd been taking. I was writing lackluster prose when one of my strengths was supposed to be an animated tone. I was providing thin content when I was known for digging up intriguing details, was missing deadlines on small stuff when I was a stickler for timeliness. When I looked in the mirror, I saw tired smudges under my eyes and bristles on my face that I'd missed while shaving.

"I agree," I told her. "Any ideas?"

She tipped her head equivocally, thinking about it. She frowned at her computer as it chimed to signal an incoming email. "You need more time off?"

"I have mixed feelings about that. I need to stay engaged in . . . normal life. But yeah, I could use some time. Maybe just cut my hours? Give over business or sports to someone else for the duration?"

"And what's the duration?"

A rhetorical question. I had no idea of what the end point might be. If Laurel was confirmed dead, I would need time to deal with her burial and house and possessions and kids. If not, if this limbo dragged on, I'd live with the preoccupation that was paralyzing me now. But I couldn't abdicate my job responsibilities forever.

"Ricky, you are wiser than I, and I defer entirely to your judgment."

She chuckled and looked out the window, rattling her fingernails on the desk. Her computer chimed again and another light began blinking on her phone.

"We can't do without 'Around Here.' Think you can keep up with it?"

"Wouldn't miss it."

"Town-council stuff needs a steady hand. You've been following the issues, so you should stick with that."

"Definitely." There were eighteen incorporated towns in our main readership area, each with its own town council, each with its own civic wrangles and dramas, all with nuanced histories.

She turned to look at me, a frank appraisal mingled with sympathy. "Not to get preachy, but I think the real measure of duration is emotional, Conn. Whatever obligations the situation might impose on you, or not, it'll become manageable only when you can handle it personally. Emotionally. You can always jigger practical matters so they fit your schedule, but you can't finesse your preoccupation and stress. Make sense?"

I nodded.

Another couple of phone lights had come on and now the whole panel was ablaze with blinking red.

"Let's plan to bring you to half time for the next two weeks, then take another look at where things stand," she said. Lifting the receiver, she looked at me with wry affection. "Take care, Connor."

# CHAPTER 14

# CONN

I was glad to let go of some responsibilities at work. But that talk with Welles had stayed with me: those anonymous tips that Laurel was still alive, the others naming her killer. That *ad hoc dissidium*—disagreement as to fact—buzzed in my brain. Grieve for her. Don't give up on her. Assume she's alive and figure out why she's hiding out, where she's hiding out. Or assume she's dead and hunt for her killer.

The stress of it was exacerbated by a phone call I made to Maddie and Julie on Friday. I knew I wasn't up to seeing them but I wanted to stay on their radar as family. Feeling useless, I asked about their day, asked if they'd like to go for a hike or swim sometime, or shopping in Burlington. Or whatever they liked. Maddie was unruffled and unimpressed, again, a flat affect that worried me—a kid accustomed to managing adult emotions, keeping them from worrying.

When it was Julie's turn to talk, she came across as scared and overwhelmed despite my lame attempts to sound reassuring.

"Maddie says Mom's dead," Julie said, very quietly, very close to the phone.

Maddie, in the background: "I did not! I said the police think she probably is."

"What do you think, Uncle Conn?"

"I don't believe that. I refuse to believe it."

"Then where is she?"

"We're going to find out. In the meantime, I'm here and I'm going to come see you again soon. We are a family. Please don't forget that."

When I disconnected, I felt that my every word had been inadequate. And yet what else could I say? The hollow, the vacuum, of uncertainty was painful and frustrating. I understood Celine's point about learning to manage uncertainty, but it's agonizing for a loved one. And it wasn't just me, it was two kids in a very scary and sad place.

That night, after some sleepless hours, I did something I hadn't in years: I went for a midnight swim. I needed to consult my private oracle, the water. I also needed to recover my sense of these beautiful lakes as benevolent, nurturing, clean, not as watery graves for dead things and painful memories. I needed to put in some miles of water to leave the swollen white-blue thing behind.

Celine woke when I got out of bed and turned on the lamp to dress. When I told her where I was going, her sleep-puffed face showed concern, so I reassured her that I would do nothing rash, that's not where I was at. She shouldn't worry.

Celine. Celine: She didn't say anything. She just took my hands and held them against her cheek for a moment. Reminding me of what mattered.

It took me an hour to get to Lake Willoughby—the glow of headlight-lit trees flowing toward me as I forged through a wilderness of night, my car alone on the road. Route 5 runs along one side of Willoughby, but the lake is almost entirely surrounded by state forest, without houses. It's about five miles long, a glacial slash between high cliffs that plunge as deep below the surface as they rise above, and the water is more of an electrical medium than it is a fluid. Cold plasma, energy I needed.

I found a narrow pullover among the trees, then walked through forest to a rocky shore spot I had launched from before. I was at the lower end of the lake, and from my starting place its waters stretched out of view as a channel or corridor between steep hills. In the distance, the surface of the lake merged imperceptibly with the night sky and its spray of stars.

It had been a sunny day, so the shore rocks still retained heat and the shallow water was comfortably warm. But farther out, as I came beneath Mount Pisgah's cliffs, I began to feel the chill radiating up from the lake's deepest waters. The cold would demand a fast pace, so I began a crisp, quick crawl, stabbing the surface hard with bladed hands. I hadn't made up my mind about how far I'd swim. Longer-distance swimmers need at least a little blubber to stay warm, and I had lost weight in the last week—I wasn't sure I could do the full ten-mile round trip. Still, I hammered at it. When my mouth broke the surface I didn't inhale so much as *pop* air into my lungs, and underwater my lips exploded bubbles. My lungs were like pistons, like guns.

It was a dead calm night. It seemed I was the only human being on the planet. I'd swum hard for half an hour before I saw the headlights of a single car meandering along Route 5, a mile away. Then I was alone again with just the water, the sky, my thoughts.

My thoughts were the problem. For the last few weeks they had been all over the place, trying to find strategies or mental postures or excuses that made me more comfortable or more complacent or more something, but they had refused to calm or order themselves. My brain was a Christmas snow-globe paperweight, shook up, the swirling flakes never settling.

Exterminating thoughts was my errand. They had led me only to confusion. So now I denied them and ignored them as I sliced the water. My body knew how to do this. Clean entry, quick stroke, one-to-four syncopated flutter kick, no splashes, no sound. I left only the small wake of water displaced by one man's body. I was a knife slipping through the skin of the lake's dark surface.

You lose any sense of time during even a daylit swim of any length. The rhythm of your stroke hypnotizes you, and the undulating massage of water along your body flows like a song, mesmerizing. At night, determinedly fleeing your own mind, time marked only by the almost imperceptible swing of the stars along their arc, you enter an egoless place. I was no longer making these strokes, I *was* the strokes. I wasn't feeling the water, I *was* the water.

I awoke to my surroundings only when I saw a glimmer of light ahead and realized I had come around the eastern curve of the lake. I was seeing a few late-lit windows of the hamlet of Westmore. That meant I had swum four miles and had four miles of return swim. By now, the water had given my skin a surface burn of cold over a deeper numbing. Much as I wanted to, I didn't turn over and gaze at the galaxy. I just reversed direction and sliced through it again, with increased urgency and growing anxiety about my ability to make it back.

I began to tire when I still had about two miles to go. The clarity of emptiness had a flaw, too, and my thoughts returned like mice to chew at it. Pendleton Pond, Richfield Reservoir, the monstrous *thing* in the water: between them, a hidden logic or pattern that I couldn't make out. I couldn't concentrate on it, because about the time the moon came over the lake and lit the cliff faces, my calf muscles cramped into agonizing fists, hard as bone. I had to tread water and massage them, trying to break the clench. But before they released, the cold drove me on. I began to vary my stroke every few minutes to use different muscles, ease the cramping. I hadn't had a close encounter with the limits of my own endurance for years, but here was one, full-fledged and potentially fatal. The deep water had a gravity I could feel, a suction or vacuum, pulling me down to its cold and quiet.

*No,* I made myself think, *your body is scared but you can always manage this. Doesn't matter how deep the water is as long as your mouth can reach the surface.*

At last I felt the water warming, and then I was clambering and slipping and cutting myself on the rocks in the shallows. I had lost my land animal's instincts. When I finally stood, I teetered, uncertain of balance, and though I placed one foot in front of the other, I could still feel my legs flurrying in the flutter kick and the two-beat hump of my back muscles.

That's when I let a thought return. It was this: *The first thing I need is to* know. *I need to know if she's alive or dead. Only then can I start sorting out the rest of it. That's the starting place.*

Having a starting place helped. I drove back slowly, in a dreamlike state: the pouring-forward headlight wash always opening a channel of summer-dense forest ahead and always sealing it dark behind me, the center line on the two-lane weaving sinuously, moonlight bursting wide and startling where farm pastures opened, then shuttering when the trees closed around again. Eventually: my driveway, the cabin, a moment of post-headlight blindness and the in-rush of the sounds of insects and frogs in the summer night. Then the food-scented interior air of home, the stairs, the warm bed, and Celine's hand reaching to find mine beneath the covers.

# CHAPTER 15

# CELINE

When Conn told me he was going to visit the "finder" out in Marsh-field, I was dismayed as much as surprised. His midnight swim and now his resort to a supposed psychic to find out if his sister was indeed dead told me just how desperate this man was. I reluctantly agreed that certainty about Laurel's fate would help deal with Laurel's daughters, and might help him start on a path to managing the situation emotionally. But the investigation was largely stalled, offering no quick resolution. And if his rational skepticism had unraveled to the extent that a psychic would help, I had to be concerned about his stability.

On the other hand, Conn's fuzzy-logic, oblique-seeming thought processes had served him well on innumerable occasions. When he left to visit Estelle D'Ambrosio, I feared for him—but I was also curious as to what that conversation might be like, and what Conn would garner from it.

I had been mulling over Irene's revelation of the other girlfriend's assault for some days, and when Conn left I used his absence to call Mason, to ask him whether Penny struck him as worthy of interest in the investigation.

When the line connected, I heard vehicles rushing past in the background, and I remembered that Mace often had traffic duty on Saturdays.

"Celine," he said.

"That would be me. Where are you?"

"I'm spending the taxpayers' hard-earned money by sitting here in a two-ton vehicle for the sole purpose of holding up a set of flashing blue lights. On I-91, where they're replacing the bridge."

"How've you been? Conn says it's been hard on you."

Mace paused and in the silence I heard a crackling voice, his police radio. Not something that needed to involve him, apparently. "Ask my wife," he said.

"What do you mean?"

"Ah, we're having a hard time. Because I'm pretty fucked up."

"How so?"

"Laurel and I had some good years. Some really good times, and as much as I'd like to, I just . . . I just refuse to deny that. But I can't talk to Jody about that part of the whole equation. Lingering memories of first wives don't make for constructive marital discussions with second wives. Huh. Why am I telling *you* this? You're the PhD. I'll get over it."

"Have you talked to Conn? I think he's in a similar place. It would be good for you guys to share notes on what you're feeling."

"Sounds like you're worried about him."

"You know where he is today? He's visiting a psychic out in Marshfield."

My phone went quiet for a while except for the whoosh of traffic flowing past Mason's cruiser.

"That must be Estelle D'Ambrosio? I'd think she'd be dead by now. She was old back in the day."

"Well, he's looking for her, anyway."

"Jeezum. Okay. He and I should get together, I guess. We haven't been fishing this year. Or maybe do some target practice out at the camp. Think he'd go for that—the six-pack afternoon guys are supposed to do?" Mace sounded wearier and more sarcastic than I'd ever heard. "Talk about them Red Sox?"

"So, Mason. I'm calling for a specific reason, and it's . . . touchy. Tricky. You up for it?"

"I don't know. I've had a lot of that recently."

I told him about my talk with Irene Shapiro, Penny's monstrous intrusion into her home, her self-righteous claim upon Anthony. "Under the circumstances, do you think Penny is someone the police should—"

"Celine, Jesus! Of course!"

"That's what I thought, but there's a problem. I violated some professional ethics, Mace. I used some . . . subterfuge to get Irene to tell me about it. She's on the edge, her family is a mess, and none of them can take any more intrusion by police. Also, I don't want her to know I've reported this to anyone. She'd feel betrayed, she'd pull away from any counseling at all, which she *needs*. And she basically told me, 'No more cops.' And I'd have . . . consequences at work."

"What's Penny's last name?"

"I don't know. I know she works where Tony worked. Big Lots, over on the strip."

Mason chewed on it for a moment. "I think this Penny person is definitely worth looking at. I assume Welles's people talked to Tony's coworkers, but if they didn't pick up on Penny, they must not have dug too deep. Or the coworkers suddenly got that proverbial reticence around cops."

"They haven't told Conn or me anything about it. But then, there's no reason they would."

Mason was quiet for a moment as his scanner crackled with mechanical-sounding voices. "Sorry, Celine—I'm coming up blank on how to protect the source of the information. There's the tip line, but then the States'd go to Irene and she'd have that on her plate, and she'd know who told them, even if you called in anonymously."

"What, then?"

"Celine, you know what I'm doing? I'm sitting on my ass, parked next to some traffic cones and a bulldozer. Says something about my crime-solving expertise, doesn't it?"

"How about snooping around Penny, maybe find someone else who suggests her as a suspect, or something else incriminating? So it doesn't come from me."

"Huh. Who's doing the snooping?"

It was my turn to be quiet for a time. "Mace. I don't want Conn to know about this, either. And I truly cannot do it myself. I'd lose my job."

I heard him whisper *Fuck!* to himself, away from the phone, as he understood my request. "I don't know. Let me think about it, okay? It'd be handy to have a last name, I could do a records search at least."

"Thank you, Mace," I said. "I'll try to find out her last name. And listen—do you think it would help make things easier with Jody if I got together with her? Talk about the grieving process, give her a chance to tell about, I don't know, whatever she's feeling, to another woman?"

"I don't think so. She's got her own way of handling stuff. She's sick of this whole thing. You bringing it up again would just make it worse. I think it's on me—to get the fuck *over* stuff."

I wanted to say something to ease him, put a damper on his self-castigation, but suddenly he swore again and then said quickly, "Look, I gotta go ticket some fucker speeding in a work zone. Talk again, yeah?"

And the line disconnected.

Conn's place really did need some new lawn furniture—his metal and mesh chairs were rusting at the joints. It was Saturday, and he was off looking for the psychic. I thought I'd surprise him by buying new chairs for the table on the cabin's front lawn. My treat.

Uncomfortably, I wondered whether the type of covert mission I planned was coming easier for me.

The Big Lots store was out on Richfield's strip, set in a huge parking lot alongside auto parts stores, burger and pizza franchises, a Walmart, and car dealerships. Heat wrinkled the air above the asphalt. Inside, a row of widely spaced checkout stations spread the length of the building, only two of them with cashiers present. The aisles were spacious, wide

THE BODY BELOW                                            113

enough to move around the couches, dining sets, and lawn furniture the store specialized in. On my way in, I grabbed a shopping cart and ambled past the customer service desk, hoping I'd find Penny's name posted somewhere, but there was nothing.

Back at the yard and garden area, I perused the chairs and found them all hideous—the kind of overlarge, faux-bronze things that would give Conn fits. Then I meandered aimlessly in the fluorescent buzz, hoping for an inspiration, a ruse that would allow me to ask Penny's last name. There were hardly any other customers, and I felt conspicuous, as if my motives were obvious. The air conditioning was so intense that my arms got goosebumps.

Nothing clever came to me, except to hope that she was one of the cashiers on duty, and that she'd be wearing a name tag that included her last name. I picked up a handful of kitchen towels with an attractive pattern, left my cart abandoned deep in the store, and headed to the checkout area.

One of the cashiers was tall, big-boned, heavy, and the other was a tiny grandmotherly woman. I decided on the former.

I was right. She wore a store uniform shirt and a nametag that read *Penny*—but no last name. Penny was truly big, taller than Conn. I felt a stab of compassion for her. Though she was probably in her thirties, she seemed to be trying for a high-school look to counter her plain face and ungainliness: a too-short skirt showing doughy legs, blond hair with a hennaed streak in it drawn back in a pert ponytail, and pink eye shadow with sparkles in it. She chewed gum that gave off a saccharine strawberry scent.

"Hi," I said.

"Hi." Disinterested, she took my towels and scanned their price tags one by one. "Sixteen ninety-two," she told me.

I took my time getting my wallet out of my purse and extracting a credit card. "This is a funny question, but you aren't by any chance Penny Farrell? One of the Farrells from Williamstown?"

She paused in chewing her gum to look at me like I was daft. "No. McKenzie."

"That's so weird! So help me, you look just like my friend Lisa

Farrell's family. It's a big extended family—no Farrells in your family tree?"

"Just McKenzies and Blanchards. You need a bag?" Her eyes were incurious, disengaged, her movements brusque. She handed me the receipt and glanced back into the store as if hoping another customer was imminent.

"No, that's fine." I gathered up my towels, thanked her, and left.

I should have gone home right then. But it was almost six, closing time. I drove my car to the far end of the lot, near the exit, and put on my billed Chicago Cubs cap and sunglasses. Waiting, I took out my cell phone and pretended to text, just another phone-obsessed person.

Before long, the Big Lots staff trickled out. The grandmotherly woman went to a little green car, a couple of young guys found their Mustang. Next came Penny, who went to a worn-looking gray pickup truck, got in, lingered—probably on her phone—as others left the store. At last she started up and pulled out.

Penny had to drive right past me. I noted the details: Chevrolet bowtie on the tailgate, Silverado in raised letters. I jotted its license number on the sales receipt she'd given me. She never even glanced my way. I figured Mace would make good use of these details.

Yes, I had a voice in my head, asking, *Celine, what are you doing?*

I answered, *Helping my beautiful man get to the bottom of this mystery and ease his distress. Solving a murder.*

## CHAPTER 16

# CONN

I met Estelle D'Ambrosio, the finder, three times in my life. The first was when I was a kid, when I visited her with my mother and Laurel, and the second was to interview her for "Around Here." The third visit confirmed for me my sister's fate and my feelings about it.

Estelle was known as a "seer," or "psychic," despite the fact that she never called herself anything but a "finder." For people in the area, she was less an exotic oddity than a community fixture, just like the dowsers people hired to choose locations for their wells or map buried water pipes. People understood that she was born with a gift, that's all.

The first time I met her was when my mother consulted her about a lost item. I was nine or ten, Laurel about seven. I can imagine the drive from our house to her place in Marshfield: "Mom, can she really see the future?" "Is she, like, a witch?" "There's no such thing as magic. It's telepathy, stupid." "No, *clairvoyance*, idiot. Don't you know anything?"

"Kids. Ice it. Now."

Estelle lived right in the village, in a house built around 1850, just like all the others on her street. When we pulled into her driveway, Laurel and I were quivering with curiosity, feeling the imminent proximity of *the beyond*. But the sight of her utterly ordinary front lawn, tidy flower beds, clapboard house with flaking paint, same as all the others, was hardly exotic.

Nor was Estelle a kohl-eyed gypsy, with black skirt and scarlet sash. She was a frumpy woman about the age of Mom's mom: plump, hair gone mostly gray, a potato nose, a faded floral housedress under a kitchen apron. At least her voice was raspy enough for a witch—I remember that.

We stood on her doorstep as my mother explained her errand: She had lost a packet of old family photos that she had intended to send to her brother in Wisconsin. Could Estelle find it for her? Estelle said she'd give it a try and that her fee was five dollars.

Our disappointment deepened when she let us into the house. We passed through a linoleum and Formica kitchen, with appliances from the 1950s, rows of little china pitchers on the window ledges, and the smell of cigarette smoke. Her living room, where she conducted her finding services, was similarly undramatic. Braided rugs, a sagging over-stuffed sofa with lace antimacassars on its arms; a rickety-looking rocking chair, flowered curtains, a crucifix. The scent of lavender sachet and dust—an old-lady smell.

My mother and she made only token small talk. Estelle had the old Vermont accent, one you don't hear much anymore, distinctly the tongue of the backwoods farms: skipping personal pronouns, glottal stops at the back of the throat instead of hard Ts. She came across as brusque, but was in fact simply economical with words in the manner of Vermont's hill people.

Estelle gestured for Laurel and me to sit on the couch, then asked my mother to take a wooden chair at a small table. The table did look a little exotic—antique, three carved legs and pedestal supporting a round marble top. Estelle took the chair on the other side of the table.

She didn't request any information from my mother, nothing about our family, not even where we lived. "How big was the pack of photos?" she asked.

My mother made a squarish shape with her two hands: "About the size of a paperback book. Thin, like this—" She held up thumb and forefinger, about a quarter-inch apart.

"In an envelope? So you could mail 'em?"

"Well, not yet. I had taped a piece of paper around them. I'd gone through our family albums and picked out eight for my brother—he's getting married and wants old family pictures? I was going to mail them in a padded envelope I bought. But I got a phone call, the kids came home from school, and then I had to go shopping for dinner stuff . . . And when I got back to it, maybe two hours later, they were gone. I looked everywhere! My husband helped. We took the house *apart*. I grilled the kids—and anyway, they had come with me to the store. They were just . . . *gone!*"

Estelle fixed a newly penetrating gaze on my mother. When she spoke again, her raspy voice sounded almost masculine, commanding: "Where did you last leave the photos?"

My mother shook her head in frustration. "I don't know . . . I just remember carrying them out of the bedroom."

Estelle's eyes went distant for several seconds. Then she nodded and in a businesslike way said, "On the kitchen counter. Red toaster. Under it."

My mother looked caught up short—it had happened so fast. Laurel and I were disappointed again: Surely, there should have been chanting or incense or special hand gestures. But Estelle was done. She stood up, pulled a change purse out of her apron pocket, and looked expectantly at my mother.

My mother dug in her own purse and came up with a five-dollar bill. Estelle folded it, tucked it away, and snapped the little purse shut. "Thank you," she said. "Glad I could help." This was just a routine transaction in her house, her village. She walked us out to the front yard, where she lit a cigarette and began fussing in the flower beds.

We were dazed as we drove home. I think even my mother had expected more of the hocus-pocus that was surely required to conjure psychic forces.

She started to interrogate us again: "You kids promise, you *swear* you didn't do anything with them? Those old photos are important." Even when we made our oaths, she continued: "You know, lying is worse than losing the photos. If I find out . . ." She left it there, leaving us to imagine terrible punishments. The ride home took forever.

My mother insisted on being the one to look, so despite our eagerness we had to tag along behind her into the kitchen. Laurel and I watched as she lifted the toaster off the counter. And there was the paper-wrapped packet. It had somehow slid between the four no-skid rubber buttons on the bottom of the toaster.

My mother said, "I'll be double-damned!"

Laurel and I were ecstatic.

Some twenty-five years later, remembering that day made me realize that Estelle would be a perfect subject for "Around Here." I interviewed her neighbors, who agreed that she had a gift; people in the community regularly relied on her finding ability. I recorded a dozen tales of her findings and a few anecdotes of "life readings" that people claimed had proven accurate. Finally I interviewed Estelle herself.

I called ahead and told her I didn't need anything located, but would like to write about her for my newspaper. She agreed to see me.

She lived in the same house. The lawn was scruffy, the flower beds had gone to weeds, and the fence was missing pickets; the clapboard walls showed more gray wood than paint.

She must have been in her eighties by then. She had gone rounded and hunched, her face plumped and webbed with fine wrinkles. Inside, the appliances in the kitchen were newer, and instead of vinyl-and-tube kitchen chairs, she had some cheap white plastic lawn chairs. But the same china pitchers stood on the window ledges, now fuzzy with dust, the same curtains hung in the kitchen windows.

She made tea as I coaxed her into reminiscing, and she talked for an hour.

She'd been born on a farm in the Northeast Kingdom, started smoking when she was eleven—thus her raspy voice. Her maiden name was Peterson; her exotic name came from her husband, an Italian granite carver who had worked in Barre. But he died early on, crushed when a hoist failed, and she was already a longtime widow when my mother and Laurel and I had first visited her. Never remarried, never had kids.

She started "knowing things" when she was a little girl. After a while, people started coming to her. She found lost tools, lost cows, lost wedding rings, lost keys, stolen cars, runaway teenagers, misplaced briefcases, a wandering three-year-old kid. It didn't strike her as special because she just "knew" where they were.

Was she ever wrong? "Oh yes. Couple times I got people angry at me, leadin' 'em on a wild-goose chase. But mostly I got it right."

"So, Estelle . . . what does it *feel* like? When you 'know' something. I mean, here you are, making lunch or whatever, and somebody comes to your door and asks you to find something. You must get into a different state of mind, right? What's it like?"

She looked at me with a touch of impatience. "Look out the window and see it's rainin', you know it's rainin'. Look at the kitchen clock and it says three o'clock, you know it's three o'clock. Not one whit different from that."

I continued to push, as gently as I could.

"Louise Martin," I said, "over on West Hill Road? She told me you gave her a 'life reading'—that's what she called it. Said you knew things about her past that nobody could have known. You told her what she'd done when she ran off to California, things she'd never told anyone about, and you knew how she felt about some private aspects of her life." I checked my notebook. "You told her she was in love with a guy who was secretly a crook and that she should marry another man she liked as a friend, because she wanted kids and the crooked guy would end up in jail. All true, she said."

She pursed her lips and when she spoke she seemed almost angry: "Never said I could see inside anybody's head. Never said I could read the future. People come wantin' me to, I tell 'em I can't. But sometimes . . . Louise, I just started talkin' and out it came." She coughed and gave me a severe look as she gestured at my notepad. "Lost things—put that in your newspaper. Just lost things."

My article resulted in blizzard of letters, readers providing more anecdotes about Estelle's findings or wanting to know her phone number.

My savage midnight swim in Lake Willoughby had made it clear to me that *I needed to know.* The uncertainty prevented me from grieving or having any real emotional response, and kept me from relating honestly to two lovely children who deserved answers.

The night after that revelatory swim, as Celine lay asleep next to me, I kept thinking of Estelle. Five years had passed since I'd interviewed her, and she'd have to be into her nineties by now—I considered it unlikely she'd still be alive, given that she'd been a lifelong smoker. But the next day, I drove out to Marshfield.

I felt a pang of disappointment when I saw that her house had been painted and the white picket fence restored, because it probably meant someone else lived there now.

I knocked, waited, knocked again, waited, and I was about to leave when the door opened. And there she was. She had continued to sink into herself, her hair had thinned, her eyes were half lidded by folds of skin.

"Yes?" she rasped.

"I'm hoping you can help me find something," I told her.

She stepped aside to let me in.

We sat at the kitchen table, where I had interviewed her—the living room, visible through the door, was dark, as if she'd pulled the curtains in there. A wheelchair waited near the sink. She looked at me expectantly.

"I'm trying to find my sister," I said. I realized I was shaking.

She sat silent for a long time, her pouched eyes pinning me, disconcerting. Then that subtle transformation came over her, and when she spoke it was less a question than a command: "Where did you last leave her."

She had asked my mother the same thing about the photos. But this was different. I believe Estelle fully knew the weight of her question. It was if I could feel her insight penetrating me, rays through my brain. Despite her disclaimers, she was reading my feelings, my life.

Yes, where did I leave Laurel? It was the right question. I had misplaced my sister. I fought tears, but they flowed anyway. Yes, I had let her go and had lost her and didn't know where she was.

"I don't know. I don't know where I . . . left her."

She didn't look away from my face. Her eyes were just a sharp glint between folds of skin. She said nothing.

"Where is she, Estelle? Please. Can you tell me where she is?"

She winced her eyes shut for a second and her mouth turned down. Then she looked to one side, at the floor, as if despairing of life or reluctant to proceed, then back to me with a face softened and despondent. At that moment she looked not just old but ancient. Still she didn't speak, but her face morphed yet again, taking on that masculine hardness, almost accusatory. She reached across the table and with her index finger tapped my forehead twice, hard as the peck of a raven.

And that's when I knew for certain my sister was dead. The only place I could find her was between my ears.

# CHAPTER 17

# CONN

A lot of pieces slid into place after that. I began to remember where—or at least when and how—I'd lost Laurel.

My flaming downfall from the *Post* has not only been examined in newspapers, on NPR, on Fox News and CNN; it has become a case study in college Ethics in Journalism curricula as an example of how not to do things.

I get out of American University as star graduate, and then I get a plum job and I'm going along, a hotshot rising star with increasingly glamorous assignments, a growing list of celeb contacts. After the Livingston and IRE awards, I won a Worth Bingham Prize for investigative reporting—not the Pulitzer, but I figured that was next. I was on a roll.

The context in which I lived and worked had a kind of bipolar affect. At the office, we maintained a high level of professionalism. Our editors gave the green lights, yellow lights, and red lights. They hired and fired. They made the hard decisions about what did or didn't make it into the paper. They dealt with the legal and financial side of libel, factual accuracy, anonymity of sources, First Amendment rights, the Freedom of Information Act. They worked with the feds on sensitive information that demanded secrecy even as they fought the good fight for government transparency.

The people in the upper strata of traditional newspaper publishing make mistakes, but they sincerely strive to provide the most relevant,

most objective, most accurate news. At the same time, they have to watch
the paper's financial bottom line with extreme vigilance and maddening
moral ambivalence.

God love 'em. Because while we on the reporting side bitched about
their caution and budgetary stinginess, we were secretly glad to have
them taking care of these details while we did what we loved: digging,
taking risks, ferreting out secrets, spying on mankind's covert works,
writing like Hemingway. We were a rowdier, riskier, irreverent bunch.
Competitive, too. There was a lot of idealism among us, and we put an
enormous amount of effort into assuring factual accuracy.

But in that milieu, egos grow, corners can get cut. In my circle, we
drank a lot as we compared war stories and shared gossip and fished
for tips. Late at night, frantically working to make deadline, a little cocaine proved very helpful. Maybe then some oxy to take the edge off,
slow down, get some sleep.

I'd love to blame my downfall on drugs, but that would be bullshit.
What did it was narcissism. My life was about *me*! Of course it was! My
string of successes would continue forever. The Pulitzer? Of course! The
Nobel? Damn right. What did I expect after that, I wonder now—my
face on Mount Rushmore?

When you're full of yourself and your nose is full of coke, your ambition
runs away with you. You succumb to the myth of your own infallibility.

One of the perks of my hotshot aura was that my bosses gave me
a lot of independence. They trusted my judgment about what would
make a great story and let me look for meatier and riskier stories, richer
pay dirt to dig.

My big obsession, at the end: Influential US senator was making
a big push for a number of laws and rules that will "combat America's
moral decay." We must restore the fundamental values, the basic sense
of decency, that this country was founded upon.

I completely agreed with these ideals. But for Senator X, it meant
the following: No abortion, even for pregnancies caused by incestuous
rape. Limited access to birth control. A broader definition of "porn" that
included women nursing kids in public, the nude bodies of sculptures

at museums, or parents' home videos of their naked two-year-old in his wading pool. Draconian penalties for prostitution but not for patronizing prostitutes. Ask him about gay or trans rights, his answer was indignant: "What rights?"

Nationally, his agenda faced a lot of resistance, but he won his seat by solid margins every six years. And in Washington he secured a surprising level of cooperation from his Senate colleagues. Sources told me that much of that disproportionate clout was coerced, extorted, or bought. In the mold of J. Edgar Hoover, he had a hobby of collecting dirty secrets, and he knew how to use them.

I started with that last. I thought, *Wow! I'll bring this guy down by showing the corruption of his political activities.* Forget his moral hypocrisy—that, I took for granted.

Discussed it with my editors, got the green light. Over a period of months, wormed my way deeper into his political and personal lives. Assembled a substantial catalog of rumors about bribes and blackmail.

Then one day I stumbled into an exclusive social circle that gave me much more than I'd anticipated. Turns out this paragon of moral purity maintained a full-time mistress and had a taste for prostitutes and some sexual preferences that put him out at the kinky edge of the bell curve.

Eventually I found the vein—as in ore, as in jugular. Through my coke supplier, I met and got friendly with the pimp who procured for the good senator. We'd drink at high-class bars and trade stories, I'd treat him to a snootful in the men's room, and in exchange he introduced me to some of his "girls."

They really were, as he put it, "high-end." Beautiful women, young, stunningly stylish. Modern-day geishas: accomplished conversationalists with the psychological finesse to make a man believe that every word he spoke was a profound insight. The coke I always had on me did wonders for starting conversations. Before long, I knew which positions the senator liked and how much he spent in an average month. In fact, I learned the same about half a dozen high-rolling politicos of both major parties.

If there was one thing I couldn't stand, it was hypocrisy. The cheatin' and whorin' and embezzlin' evangelist had long been an American cultural fixture, but this guy was doing more than hollering from the pulpit. He was pushing through laws, raising big money for like-minded PACs, and cunningly working the smoke-filled rooms. The more I talked to the women he used, the more I got to like and respect them, and the more I detested his hypocrisy and goddamned gall.

Yes, I liked the women I met. One in particular. Extremely intelligent, exceptionally gorgeous. An accomplished violinist. A sort of shy glance that suggested she had preserved some genuine innocence despite her profession. She said her name was Silk. I felt this was too perfect to be true, but when I insisted that she tell me her real name, she showed me her driver's license, and Silk it was. After a couple of weeks of occasional interviews and a few drinks together, it was clear she was quite taken with me. She loved hearing the adventures of this dashing, prizewinning reporter.

Anyone but a guy so high on himself would have seen where this was heading. One evening we go to dinner, and in the candlelight that elusive gaze and crooked smile capture me. I had just gotten divorced. For a while, I had been half-heartedly trying to get back together with my ex, but now I was falling in love. What a glorious irony it would be to meet my next wife in such a context! We stumble off to a hotel for sex and conversation, then some coke and champagne to fuel still more sex and conversation.

In the morning we walk out the door and in the hall there's a photographer and a couple of reporters and a Senate staffer with a big grin on his face. And a couple of cops. The cops were there for the coke. I'd underestimated my opponent and had fallen for the honey trap. Oldest trick in the book.

So: suspension from the *Post*. When they reviewed my notes on the story, the contamination of my lack of objectivity was visible everywhere. Then they put all my past articles under the microscope to see if others might be tainted by similarly dubious practices. They didn't find any more in the sleaze department, but they found some unacceptable reporting procedures. For one multiple-installment feature, I had sort of invented a person whom I called my chief source. This person was "true" but not "real"—that is, the overall details were true, but I'd conflated various individuals to come up with this representative of the type and spokesman for the facts. I wasn't the first to do this, and I did it primarily to protect my sources—I was looking into a powerful public figure whose vengeance could have been a real risk to people who gave me information—but it was an extreme breach of journalistic ethics.

I also had reported that a crucial meeting had taken place, and though I had claimed an unnamed source, there wasn't one. I got the fact from a tiny act of information burglary when I was left waiting, alone, in an assistant federal prosecutor's office. Thirty seconds was all I needed. I flipped some papers on the desk, pulled open a drawer, riffled through, glimpsed some phone slips. The names and dates brought the whole story together for me. I was back in my seat, sweating with glee, when the prosecutor returned. In the article, I claimed I got the information from a "highly placed source."

Publishers and editors don't like this.

Between my biased and hypocritical vendetta against Senator X, dubious reporting practices, coke, oxycodone, keeping low company, fabrication of a source, and the rest of it, I was cooked. They fired me.

Made the national news. Another press scandal. Played into the hands of those who hate the Fourth Estate's intrusiveness and untrustworthiness and bias.

They opted not to charge me for soliciting prostitution, because I had never paid Silk—it was purely social on my part and a different sort of business arrangement on hers. The oxy got a pass, too—I had a prescription. As for the coke, I got off with a slap on the wrist. The judge bought that I was under stress from my work and my recent divorce. I had lost my way, wouldn't do it again. Six months of substance-abuse therapy and a year of community service work up in Baltimore.

Being news myself wasn't fun. I did a few TV interviews during which the hosts nodded sagely, sadly, as I abased myself and proffered my sincerest apologies to the *Post* and to all my colleagues in the press, whose trust I'd betrayed.

After my year of community service and public contrition, I retreated to Richfield. My father had died, but my sister was there. She was living a wildly unsteady life by then, and I was pissed at her for leaving Pop's care entirely to me in his last months. But I was grasping at straws and still held on to illusions of building upon family loyalties as a foundation for a new life. I was a wreck. Lots of bad habits, not much in the way of money. Whenever I called my former press colleagues, they found reasons to get off the phone quickly. Before the shit hit, I'd been inching toward reconciliation with my ex-wife, but afterward that hope was very dashed.

It was a long fall from grace, but the hard landing did me some good.

Back in Richfield, I stayed drunk for months, scalding my throat with bourbon straight from the bottle. I considered suicide but couldn't quite decide when or how. One night, head-spinning drunk, I jumped into a nearby lake, fully dressed. I had never done much swimming, and that night I put it to the gods to preserve me or end it there and then.

I labored out, gasping, weighted down by wet jeans, truly not caring how fate rolled the dice. After a while I turned over onto my back and stared up at the sky. There between the dark hills, far from houses and streetlamps, no other light competed with the stars. I saw the galaxy up there, that impossible vast band of light against the infinite dark. I hadn't once looked up into the sky when I was in DC, and if I had I'd have seen only the glow of city lights. That night I was drunk enough to see the galaxy as it really was: spinning, just like me. And so beautiful! It was majestic and mysterious and aloof and grand, it was bigger and better than all this crap, impervious to it.

As I floated there, I had an epiphany and it was exactly and entirely this: *Wow!* No fine print. Just a long, slowly exhaled *Wow!*

It was a joyful feeling. I was joyful at that moment.

Joy can save you. And the great cathedral of the Milky Way reminds you that you are a minute and transitory thing. It's a humbling and reassuring insight. That night, even in my bourbon-numbed brain, I saw that the corollary was also true: My troubles were also minute and transitory.

At some point I found myself absent-mindedly paddling back to shore.

That's how I realized I wasn't done living yet. I stumbled on into my life. Over a period of many months, I got dry and clean and started eating right. I also went swimming at night again, just to see the galaxy, and I learned that the water itself did something to me. My swims got longer and longer, and I found that I liked the high of exertion and fitness better than any drug, better even than vanity or self-pity. I spent a year living like a hermit, ashamed to show my face but getting stronger every day. Mason brought me food and offered companionship that kept me sane. Getting the job at the *Herald* was a sympathy hiring: Ricky Thurston, the publisher, had known my mother, and I had played high-school football with the guy who was now editor-in-chief. Connections like that, a decent suit, and a willingness to work for peanuts will get you a job almost anywhere.

Yes, a long way down, a hard landing. But irony is always part of life, and it works both ways. I met Celine thanks to my lowly reporting job at the *Herald*. And I found I actually enjoyed the work—for the stuff itself, not for the prestige it might give me. I re-learned how communities worked, I mean real towns and rural areas, and how the ordinary lives of the people who live in them weave together. Once off my narcissistic high horse, I discovered that the unfamous, "average" people I'd mostly ignored while on my rocket ride were fascinating, complex, skilled, and often courageous. They were full of story and history and engaged in daily lives that weren't so mundane when you saw them up close.

So once the bruises on my ego faded a bit, I found the work restorative. When you're existentially fucked and life doesn't make any sense, there's something reassuring about covering a high-school basketball game or interviewing a dairy farmer about her new cheese-making operation. People in small towns live closer to the historical baseline of human experience—the village, the tribe, the clan. I felt better, learning that. Being part of it.

But how did all this connect to my sister?

It didn't. That was precisely the problem. After my visit to Estelle, that became clear to me. Moving the mental magnifying glass along the timeline of my sorry history and Laurel's, that's the period that leaped into focus. Somewhere right in there, those screwed-up years for both of us, something happened to her. That's where I'd left her, that's where I needed to look for her.

Early on, when I was gaining upward momentum at the *Post* and we spoke on the phone, or got together with Pop at Christmas, I didn't hear anything she said. This problem, that problem, whatever—my other lines, phone and mental, were always buzzing and always my primary focus. For those years I was always dealing with something much, much more important. I was so consumed with my rise to glory, then my dramatic debacle, then my limping recovery, that I let her slip.

Back in Richfield, when my fatally wounded narcissism was still in its death throes and I was drinking and feeling sorry for myself and my phone never rang, I was simply too screwed up to pay attention to Laurel. Looking back, I realized that when she abandoned Mason, when her life began to go to pieces, she had several times tried to talk earnestly with me, to tell me about her state of mind, maybe to ask not just for money but for moral support.

But I didn't listen because I was pissed at her for her treatment of my best friend, and I didn't want to learn more about the tawdry world she lived in. It didn't help that, back when I was still in DC and Pop had gotten referred to inpatient end-of-life care, Laurel told me she was not up for taking any part in caring for him. I paid to get him set up in a hospice facility near DC, where I could visit him. I had to drive back to Richfield a few times to close out his apartment and deal with his stuff—no help from Laurel then, either.

Did taking care of Pop contribute to the failure of my marriage and the rest of it? I don't know. I was angry at Laurel, but I loved the man, and losing him, whether Laurel shared the burden or not, would have contributed to my fatigue, confusion, and bad judgment.

But one result was that I thought of my own downfall as tragic, remotely "noble," while hers was just pathetic, cheap, weak.

When I was in DC, blind to my own failings, I resented her intrusion into my life, scorned her bad taste, derided her lack of self-control, lectured her about sketchy friends—she embarrassed me! After I returned to Richfield, yes, I put her up a few times, yes, I gave her money, picked up behind her, but I did it resentfully. Carelessly.

Estelle was right about where, and how, I lost my sister. She was also right about where I could find her, where my retrospective magnifying glass should hover: that period when I forgot who she was. When I abandoned her.

I was too concerned with my own shit to care for her. "Sometimes simple companionship is the best medicine," Celine says. And that's the part that hurts the most. I couldn't even be a friend to her.

# CHAPTER 18

# CONN

The space between my ears is a wilderness at times, but in this case it seemed to have two relevant locations: memory of Laurel and knowledge of our community. One could help me find the truth through the person, the other might help me figure out the less obvious facts of her social world, the context in which her murder occurred. Captain Welles was a rigorous investigator, but he couldn't know the nerves and capillaries of our region the way I did. It was in that web of connections that Laurel's life course intersected her killer's, that the motivation to kill was born and was realized.

At home, I got a legal pad, went to the screen porch, and sat with the sweet breezes of summer visiting me. I did my "one true sentence" prompt. In this case I started with a question, the key question:

*Who was my sister?*

For no particular reason, my first answer was:

*She was smarter than me.*

Our drive home from Estelle D'Ambrosio's house, after my mother had sought the finder's help, was a good example. In the backseat,

Laurel whispered to me: "Do you believe that lady?" I said, "I don't know." And she said "I do, totally. Mom doesn't because she didn't pay attention." When I asked what she meant, she whispered, "Because she said 'red.'"

Laurel was right. Estelle could have made up anything, taken her five bucks, and never heard from us again. But when she said "red toaster," Laurel had recognized the crucial specification, red, as the difference between guessing and seeing.

When we pulled up at our house, and my mother insisted that she precede us inside, Laurel whispered again: "You know why she wants to be the one to do it? Because she thinks if we do, we'd fake it. We'd run in quick and put them under there from wherever we hid them, so we won't get in trouble!"

This made sense, but I lacked her grasp of either psychology or logic, and I hadn't been observing as closely as she had. In fact, I now realized that watching my little sister's mind at work, over the years, taught me a lot about keeping my eyes peeled. In later years, that principle stood me in good stead as a journalist.

When she was around seven, she once spent an entire afternoon trying to train ants. She knew about Pavlovian conditioning, and when an ant accidentally did what she wanted it to—turn left, say—she rewarded it with a cookie crumb. The problem was that each ant immediately dragged its reward back to the nest. Since all the ants looked alike, she had no way of knowing whether an ant that did what she wanted it to was a "conditioned" ant or a new one. I mentioned that to her, but she stayed at it until sundown, then came in swearing that she'd do the same thing the next day. And I think she did.

At the time, I thought that was incredibly stupid, but now it prompted me to write:

*She could be very persistent.*

A jay squawked and jarred me out of my memories. I stared at my near-empty page for a while, then jotted again.

*She was a more private person than I was.*

Laurel spent more time in her room than I did. She read a lot, things like *The Jungle Book* and *The Chronicles of Narnia,* as well as dozens of other books that I disdained as "girly." She pilfered *To Kill a Mocking-bird* and *The Catcher in the Rye* from my room and read them two years before they were assigned to her in English class.

She had friends, but I can't recall her ever having a "best friend," nothing like Mace and me.

When she began "seeing" boys—in middle school, that meant allowing them to tag along behind as you walked home from school, for weeks, before letting them sit with you at lunch—she didn't tell my parents about her crushes. By contrast, I wanted to drop the names of my loves at any pretext: "Speaking of dogs, Janine has this Rottweiler the size of a horse, literally. She's so weird!" Laurel kept these enthusiasms to herself, but I learned something about her outlook from a scrap of poetry she wrote to some boy: "You don't even know I exist / but I know for certain you do / because you dwell inside my heart /where I can gaze at you throughout each day / and where you will be with me / always." I found it while sneaking around her room looking for loose change that would allow me to buy BBs from Nate's General Store.

*Romantic. Sentimental.*

She listened to Whitney Houston's "I Will Always Love You" ten thousand times, mouthing the words with a moony, martyred look on her face. She must have been fourteen, fifteen. Her heart was drawn to the idea of eternal devotion.

*Devotion? She struck us as eternally devoted to Mace when they got together, too. What happened to change that?*

Sitting on my screen porch, I felt a return of the resentment that began when their marriage started going to pieces. At first I'd felt caught between the two of them, loyalties conflicted. Being Mace's best friend, being her brother, they both called me to tell their grievances and to ask me to intervene. But, hey, I was busy. I didn't need the hassle.

What were those complaints? How did their alienation begin? I couldn't remember. I had been down in DC then, my star was in the ascendant, and I couldn't fully focus on anything but my work and my super-great self.

At first, I figured that all marriages had their ups and downs and that they would get over it. Later—later was too late.

I did remember that when Laurel came of dating age, maybe eighth grade, she was a victim of her own compassion. Her first boyfriend was a gangly kid with a prominent Adam's apple. She thought it would be fun to do homework together, sitting studiously across from each other and holding hands. Then she recruited him to help with a charity gift push for kids with muscular dystrophy. They sat in the school hallway with stacks of solicitation letters, trying to get their buddies to write personal appeals. He was embarrassed and bored but too enamored of Laurel to beg off. Laurel was determined to build their relationship a "mature," "constructive" foundation.

This guy was infatuated with her, but he was a pretty dim bulb, and she got frustrated at his inability to "carry on an adult conversation."

"Men are like that," my father told her. "We're neurologically incapable of it until we're forty."

"It's not funny, Pop!"

Still, for months, she dragged this poor droop to edifying movies, made him read books that were over his head and tried to discuss them with him.

Why didn't she just break up with the loser? I asked her. She had a good bod, I told her, a lot of guys had the serious hots for her—not actually true, yet, just my big brotherly idea of a pep talk.

"He'd be too hurt. I'd rather try to make it work."

*Make it work?* I wondered now. She was what, fifteen? Laurel was a serious sort of person, the kind with a slight, studious frown in her brain. Idealistic.

In my notebook I wrote: *When Mom died, Pop and I really went to pieces. Laurel was just as broken up as we were, but she was the one who stayed brave, steadfast, kept the family together. A sophomore in high school, consoling us, rallying us.* Another paradox. How did this resolute, compassionate girl connect with the young woman who, just a few years later, couldn't be bothered to help with Pop as he was dying?

I scratched my head, baffled, then kept jotting random thoughts as they came to me.

> *She*
> *was more mature than I was. More sensitive.*
> *She*
> *approached relationships seriously. Deliberately.*

Again, I had a hard time reconciling this earlier draft of her with the woman who had slept around, dumped Mace, and embarked on a degenerate lifestyle. What didn't work in her marriage to Mace? What part of the devoted wife role did she discover she couldn't live up to?

Sitting there, listening to the complaining jays in my woods, part of me wanted to ask Mace for more details than I remembered. But, looking back at our last conversation, I figured he didn't want any more of those memories jarred loose, coming back to torment him. Any more than I would, really. Maybe down the road a bit.

# CHAPTER 19

# CONN

In the other compartment between my ears, I had resources within the extended village that constitutes our region, connections that Welles didn't have. People like Dev Cohen. "Oral historians" is too academic a term for their informal function, but Dev's general store was still a nexus of the ley lines of the community in my sister's town, and Dev herself was a trusted resource.

Paradoxically, Dev was not a native Vermonter, and she retained a Brooklyn accent after thirty years here. But she won the hearts of locals with the engaging simpatico of an old-fashioned publican, someone who listened to others' stories and always reciprocated with one of her own. Her wry humor and ready empathy made her easy to talk to. For the first decade of her proprietorship, her store was also the post office, so at one time or another everyone came through to buy stamps or get their mail from the wall of cubbyholes behind Dev's counter.

Later, the post office got its own building and Dev's became just a part-grocery, part-hardware store that also sold hunting and fishing licenses, ammo and lures, and a few locally made handicrafts for passing tourists.

I had interviewed Dev some years before. She was one of three long-time proprietors I profiled in a column on the area's old-fashioned general stores, which were disappearing as modern "convenience" outlets moved in. Dev's store was the real thing, and she was the perfect exemplar of the traditional oral historian and universal confidant.

Dev's General Supplies sat in a gravel parking lot, a flaking clapboard building fronted by a boardwalk with buckling steps to the front door. Inside, the floor had new linoleum and the coolers were fairly recent, and on the shelves candy and chips had replaced some of the staples. But the back was still crammed with motor oil, socket sets, gardening tools, coils of rope, chainsaw parts, and boxes of nails and screws. Near the register, a rack held celebrity gossip magazines, plastic-sealed "men's magazines," advertising weeklies, and newspapers from throughout the state, including the *Herald*.

I was lucky to arrive at a slow time of day. There was just one customer, at the far back, searching through the drawers of fasteners. Dev sat on a stool behind the front counter, a plump woman in her late fifties, wearing a man's shirt over jeans, dark hair in an unflattering perm. She was reading a gossip mag when she saw me come in.

"Hey! You're that guy!" she said enthusiastically.

"And you're the infamous Dev!"

"How've you been? Liked your article, by the way. I got a lot of comments. But I wish I'd done my hair before you took the photo."

We shook hands across the counter.

"What can I get you?"

I glanced at the man in back, still pulling out drawers and sorting through screws.

"I wanted to talk to you about Trudy Carlson." I asked.

She shook her head. "So sad! Those poor kids. I hope she turns up safe and sound."

"Me, too. But what I hear is that the police think she was murdered."

Her eyes caught mine as she winced at this. "Horrible! Just horrible. I liked that girl. Haven't seen her in a while, but she came in with her kids now and then."

"So you knew her. Talk to her much?"

"A little. Seemed like a nice person. Someone who had maybe been around the block one more time than she'd have preferred, but who was sticking it out pretty well. Always insisted the kids be polite—'Girls, say a proper hello to Mrs. Cohen.'"

"I'm her brother, Dev. Her real name was Laurel Whitman." I couldn't think of any way to ease into it.

That rocked her back on her stool and she put down her magazine. "I'm so sorry," she said sincerely.

"Do you know anything about her? Because I don't."

Her sharp eyes caught mine and she assessed me, both interested and dubious. She was not a gossip, she was a listener. She surely heard a lot of rumor, but if she had been the type to injudiciously pass it on, people wouldn't have opened up to her the way they did. She was confessor, confidant, and Library of Congress for an area ten miles in diameter, and discretion was part of the job description.

"What do you mean?"

"We . . . drifted out of touch. The last few years, always meaning to get together, never quite doing it?"

She gave a knowing nod, signaling she knew something about how families worked or didn't. "And you want to figure out what? Who killed her?"

"Anthony Shapiro—do you know him?"

She made a dismissive gesture. "Tony? Tony's no good and has made every mistake a guy can make. But you know where he's at? I mean psychologically?"

The guy at the back came to the counter with a handful of screws and some washers. Dev counted them and rang him up.

"No," I said when he'd left. "But I'd like to find out."

"She showed him the door, oh, going on two years ago. Tony's been making an effort—and look, I've known this kid for twenty years—where he's at is like the song says, 'I'm working my way back to you, babe.' The Four Seasons? Tony, all those years, I've never seen him walk out of here without a twelve-pack. Last time, a month ago? He left with a carton of orange juice, a bag of whole-wheat flour, and a sad face."

I thought about this. Dev and I said nothing as a couple came in and began rustling through the rack of chips and snacks.

"What's that tell you?" I asked.

"Tony didn't kill her," she said quietly. She checked her nails, short-cut and practical. "Tony never hurt his wife or kids, not once— not physically anyway. His curse is, he likes women and they like him. I think he arouses their mothering instincts, *and* he's good in bed, so I'm given to understand. An irresistible combination! Murder is just not in him. As far as your sister goes, Tony wanted a new life and she was gonna be it and he knew he had to earn her back. He even started classes at the community college! He's no dummy—for all the stupid mistakes he's made, he's actually a really bright guy."

She checked on the customers back among the shelves, frowned, and went on quietly, "Of course, what he thought he was gonna do with his current wife and kids, I don't know. But you can bet on this—Tony didn't kill Trudy."

Dev paused and Brooklyn pragmatism came back strongly in her voice: "You know what Tony is? He's *weak*. He's one of these sad sacks who puts up a tough front, who gets into bar fights even though he knows he'll lose. But he wouldn't have the gumption to kill anyone. And he's a little guy, like five-seven. Your sister, into that CrossFit stuff, she could have kicked the crap out of him if it came to a fight."

"CrossFit?"

"The whole-body workout thing. Sometimes she'd come in here with her sweats on, I'd ask her, 'What, now you're running the marathon?' Classes at the gym up on the hill there, behind Agway. Personally, I get my cardio from stressing about my mortgage."

I digested that. "Who should I talk to? About Tony?"

"You could talk to his mother, but I'm sure the gendarmes have gotten what they can out of her. 'My son is a saint!'"

"So why did he run?"

"He ran because he knew with his record they'd think he did it and he panicked. And now he's made it worse for himself."

"Where would he have gone?"

Dev shrugged.

The couple came to the counter with two bags of chips and a box of tampons. Dev rang them up and we waited until they left. She spent a moment looking at the ceiling, and I could sense her sifting through memories, letting her synapses find the connections in her vast repository of data. At last she brought her eyes back to me.

"Between you and me," she began.

"What?"

"Your sister never said anything, but Jocelyn Macey worked with Trudy at Martinson's. She lives out on South Brook Road, comes in here every couple of days. One time I ask Jocelyn how she's doing and she tells me it was a tough day. I ask tough how and she says the store manager at Martinson's gives the girls there some grief."

"'Grief.'"

"As in, uses his leverage as their boss to try to coerce 'favors' or at least forget about uncomfortable moments back in the storeroom. An extremely sleazy individual." Dev said this primly, trying to suppress the full extent of her indignation.

"The police interviewed everyone there," I said. "They'd have taken note if any of the employees had mentioned something like this."

"Oh yeah? Think about it. You're bagging grocs or stocking shelves because you've got such great employment prospects? Tell you what, your boss sees you getting interviewed and you know if you say the wrong thing, you're out of a job. All for a 'he said, she said'? No. The police didn't pick up on that tidbit." Dev's lips puckered with disgust.

"So, what, maybe he had a thing for my sister, and . . . what? He got carried away, or she wouldn't keep quiet about it? Wouldn't murder be something of an overreaction?"

"Huh! For us naked apes, what *wouldn't* be an excuse for murder? Some people anyway. Sad but true, right? What I do know is the guy needs a swift kick in the pants! When Jocelyn was telling me about him, I noticed she had bruises on her wrist, the kind you get when someone grips you too hard? She saw me looking and put her arm so I couldn't see. That piece of shit! But no, Jocelyn never said anything about your sister in this context. Your best bet would be to talk to Jocelyn. Just don't do it at the store."

I appreciated getting Dev's thoughts about Laurel's manager, but I didn't see them as having relevance. Dev's emotional heat was coming from her outrage at sexual coercion. But I was out that way anyway and thought I might try to make contact with Jocelyn Macey. Dev handed me the local phone book, a quarter-inch thick, assuring me that people still had land lines: "Crappy to zero cell service out here." Several Maceys were listed, but no Jocelyn. Dev ran a finger down the names until she found an address that would be about where Jocelyn's house was. She said Jocelyn lived with her mother, who had some kind of disability.

I would have called the corresponding number from my car, but Dev was right about the service: no bars. I headed back toward Richfield, figuring I'd try again later.

*Find the truth through the person*, I reminded myself. What I really needed was to know my sister better. Somewhere in the cycle of her daily life she had encountered the person who murdered her, but I didn't know enough about that life. On the other hand, I'd learned a great deal in just the last few days. I was struck by the fact that she was pursuing a fitness regimen and I felt a bit of pride in her: *Good for you, Laurel.* It also suggested a sibling resemblance—we'd sought similar means to reconstruct ourselves.

The gym where Laurel had worked out was an impressive facility for a town as small as Waterbury. Aside from the room devoted to weights and aerobic machines—four TV screens, mirrors, powerful AC—there were a couple of bright, spacious rooms for specialty exercise classes, a thirty-yard pool, and an annex containing three tennis courts.

I didn't know the woman at the front desk, but I asked about Cross-Fit classes and she told me where to find their main trainer, who was setting up his room for his next class.

Rahjib was short, with brown skin, Valentino eyes, and Rasta hair gathered at his neck so that the dreadlocks fell down his back. He wore workout shorts and a T-shirt and running shoes with no socks. I put him in his late twenties. To me, his easy walk and relaxed smile proved without a doubt the benefits of his regimen—a hip, centered, superbly fit guy. We shook hands and then talked as he laid out mats, plywood boxes, and small traffic cones in different parts of the room. Through the wall I could hear the thumping disco bass of an aerobics class.

"Sure, Trudy's in one of my classes," he said. "Or was, anyway—she's missed the last few weeks. Which surprises me. She's very determined. I was going to check if she'd let her membership lapse."

"You didn't hear?"

"Hear what?"

"The police think she's dead, Rahjib."

He had been placing cones in a slalom pattern, but now he straightened. "Trudy? Jesus! What, a car accident or something?"

"No. They believe she was murdered while she was out camping."

He shook his head as if trying to clear it. "Fuck! I can't believe it! Who'd want to kill her?"

"That's my question, too."

He sat on one of the boxes as if he had gotten suddenly tired. "That's pretty fucked up. You don't think of that shit happening around here. Man. I should read the newspapers sometimes, I guess."

"Ever talk to her?"

"Sure. We've chugged vitamin water together, out at the refreshment counter, before class. Once we get in here, there's no time, I'm just counting down the reps, cracking the whip. No chatter—gasping meaningfully, that's about it." He smiled sadly. "But after class, people might compare notes while stretching, maybe say a few words—'How're the kids?' Or get together out at the counter before hitting the showers."

"Don't take this the wrong way, but is this class any kind of a pickup scene?"

The thought amused him. "I never saw anyone with the energy to try, not after what I put them through. No. Over in the big room, I guess, you know, somebody's on the treadmill next to you and you can get talking. I wouldn't know. I'm not in that game. My wife is one of the tennis coaches here."

He stared at the floor and shook his head again in disbelief. "Man. Trudy." Then he looked up at me. "What's your connection? I mean, you're not with the police."

"I'm her brother."

That knocked him back a bit, and when he checked my eyes again it was with an earnest sympathy. "Sorry, man. You do look a lot like her—I should have seen that right away. Sorry. I wish I could do something for you."

"You said you both did some hydration before your workouts. Did she say anything about herself?"

My question puzzled him a bit, and I realized that he didn't yet know about our estrangement. He was beginning to understand that he had seen her more recently, talked to her, heard about her daily life, more than I had.

"She told me about hassles with her kids—just regular stuff. Laughed about it. Aches and pains from her workouts . . . Crap from her job, the same as I hear from a lot of people."

"Boyfriends?"

"Not that she mentioned. We don't . . . didn't know each other well enough for that stuff."

"What kind of crap from her job?"

"Well, lousy pay. And that thing with her manager putting the moves on her. She laughed about it, but it was one of those things where you knew it wasn't funny and she needed to tell somebody."

It was my turn to be taken aback. When you're fishing and something in the water taps your lure once, you notice. Two tugs, one right after the other, you really pay attention.

"At Martinson's?"

"Yeah. The store manager." He checked his watch and stood to go back to positioning the cones.

"What was that about?"

His expression changed, and he gave me a dubious look. "She didn't tell you about this kind of this stuff?"

I had to tell the estrangement story yet again—sanitizing it, as I did every time. I cringed inwardly as I recited the script and saw a tinge of judgment come into Rahjib's eyes. With it came a reluctance to trust me.

He stalled by checking his watch more pointedly. "I really gotta get set up here. People will be arriving any minute."

"Rahjib. I fucked up my relationship with my sister. We were always going to get back together, but she's dead now and we missed the chance. So please help me. Tell me about the thing with her boss."

"That's about all I know. She didn't like him or the moves he made. When she told me about it, she did that thing where you stick your finger down your throat and pretend to puke? She couldn't afford to quit and said the only reason he hadn't fired her was he was still hoping he'd get lucky. She was pissed enough she was thinking of starting, what do you call it, a dossier on him."

"A dossier?"

"Well, he was harassing all the women. Especially the younger, more financially desperate ones, the ones who wouldn't complain. One time she was particularly ripshit and said she was thinking about collecting their stories and making a complaint or lawsuit or something. I don't know if she went anywhere with it."

"What did you say to that idea?"

Rahjib paused as the door opened and a pair of women came in, wearing sweatpants and tank tops. They tucked their gym bags into the corner and turned to face the wall mirrors as they began tying their hair back.

Rahjib laughed darkly and lowered his voice. "I told her to rip his nuts off next time. And she could have, too. We do a lot of grip and forearm work in here."

"We're ripping nuts off today?" one of the women joked, grinning back at Rahjib in the mirror as she worked elastics over a knob of hair. "Fine with me, but what are the guys going to think?"

A middle-aged man was just coming in, wearing baggy shorts and an oversized T-shirt that failed to conceal a beer belly he had not yet worked off. "What are the guys going to think about what?" he asked.

Clearly, my time with Rahjib was over with.

Rahjib shook my hand and clasped my forearm with his other hand. "Sorry, man. Good luck, okay? I'm really sorry. Wish I could help."

My body was craving a swim by the time I left Rahjib. I thought of detouring to go to Pendleton Pond, but its association with Laurel tainted the idea, and anyway I had left the house without a bathing suit or towel. This was a rarity, a symptom of my mental disarray. I turned toward home with the intent of getting my stuff and heading right out, maybe to Elmore again: water, exertion, immersion in that elemental purity would help straighten me out.

While I trusted Dev's take on Tony's character, I didn't feel any of her certainty that he didn't kill my sister. Tony may have adored my sister, but he could have made a drug-addled or passion-fueled mistake and was now fleeing from remorse and loss as well as the law.

The store manager at Martinson's, the guy who gave the women "a hard time," was another story. Anyway, I realized I needed some groceries. Just a few little items. Why not stop at the Martinson's in Waterbury as long as I was up that way?

You can't judge a book by its cover, can't read a soul from a face. But I wanted a glimpse of this guy. Just to have some image in my head as I thought it over.

I grabbed a shopping cart on my way in, let the automatic door sweep aside for me, and wafted into the air-conditioned cool. It did not seem like a threatening place and the checkout people were doing their jobs in reasonably good spirits. I drifted over near the customer service counter, where the morale-booster boards are usually kept: smiling photos arrayed in hierarchical order with store manager at the top, section managers below that—Laurel's face still there as head of the bakery—and twenty photos of staff without titles. Employee of the Month citations, March of Dimes booster awards, congrats to Shelly on her new baby.

The manager's name was David Laughlin, and his photo showed a face as bland as his name. He looked about fifty, with thinning sandy hair and a snub nose, and from his full cheeks and slight second chin I deduced he was probably chubby. No horns or fangs. If anything, his face looked as if someone had airbrushed obvious indications of personality out of it, leaving the sort of neutral persona I supposed store managers were expected to project.

I cruised the produce section, went to the cheese zone for some mozzarella, picked up some dish detergent, not much lulled by the saccharine instrumental versions of eighties favorites coming over the speakers. I was keeping my eyes open for David Laughlin.

I never saw him. But when I checked out, I ended up by chance in a lane being cashiered by a skinny, eager-to-please young woman with bony wrists and hunched posture, wearing a plastic tag that told me her name was Jocelyn. I almost said something, then caught myself. Not in the store. I had her phone number in my wallet.

# CHAPTER 20

# CONN

Celine stayed at her apartment again that night, leaving me batting around my cabin. On an ordinary Monday night, I'd be out reporting on some summer-league sports event under the lights, or putting final touches on a story for the next edition. But I was largely off duty, and the distraction of work wasn't available. I thought about going for another night swim, but didn't feel up for it. A glance at Netflix offerings made me shudder: murder, betrayal, secrets from the past come back to haunt. No.

I poured a glass of wine and felt a sweet pang as I noticed an imprint of lipstick the dishwasher hadn't quite removed. Celine's. I drank from the same spot, a kiss across the miles between us. I pictured her at her desk, frowning at her budget calculations.

David Laughlin: From Dev's comments and his photo on the employee board at Martinson's, I had a clear and completely prejudicial mental image of him. He had a chunky, graceless build and a small dick that made him compensate by leveraging his supervisory position for little sexual gratifications, little proofs of who's in charge. He wasn't highly intelligent, but was sufficiently clever to calculate odds and angles, enough to get away with furtive gropes and to work his way up the corporate ladder to head honcho at the Waterbury franchise.

But I knew all about the dangers of projection. I erased this profile from my brain and opened my laptop to do a search for him.

The name drew five million hits—engineers, doctors, professors, dentists, teachers, plumbers. After tailoring my search operators, I whittled it down to 250,000 and then 25,000 and finally saw my man's face in the Google lineup. The photo had accompanied an article in the area's weekly advertiser about his becoming the new manager at the Waterbury Martinson's, four years ago. I jotted notes on the basics: married, one kid. University of New Hampshire, a bachelor's degree in business. Managerial positions at various grocery chains in New Hampshire and southern Vermont before he moved to Waterbury.

To my disappointment, this photo made him look like an okay guy, an aging boy-next-door face, with neither Jeffrey Dahmer's good looks nor his caped gaze.

I looked through a few more pages of David Laughlins, then gave it up. I had too much nervous energy for a computer exercise right now. I had ideas for more profitable avenues, one of them being to talk to Jocelyn Macey or other employees at Martinson's.

The other gave me an excuse to call Celine.

"I was just going to call you," she said.

"Oh yeah? Why?"

"Tell you I love you. Complain about work. How are you?"

"Twitchy. Didn't swim today, should have. Now I have the brain-in-the-hamster-wheel problem. I was wondering if you'd do some sleuthing for me."

I thought she'd like the idea—a break from spreadsheets—but she hesitated and then asked dubiously, "Like what?"

"Not about a student. Nothing impinging on confidentiality."

I told her about my conversations with Dev and Rahjib, and gave her the few details I had on David Laughlin. The favor I asked didn't strike me as too outrageous. In her position as head of a certified "vulnerable populations agency," she could request records from Vermont's Criminal Information Center, reporting on arrests, convictions, restraining orders, sex offenses, and traffic violations.

"I mean, does he have a history of sexual harassment? Or some other shady secrets? He's sure moved around a lot—"

"Conn. What would I find if I looked up Connor Whitman?"

"Not a pretty picture, I know. But Rahjib thought Laurel might have been creating a dossier on this guy, laying the foundation for a complaint or lawsuit. I'd like to know if there's some prior history."

"Are we getting sucked too far into this? The police are on this, Conn."

"Not necessarily this guy, though. No reason to look at this angle."

She was quiet in a *listen to yourself* type of pause. She had made it clear that my best approach to staying sane would be managing my own emotions, not finding "hard" answers. I knew she was right, but I'd been pacing with the phone against my ear and at that moment happened to stop at the stairwell photo gallery. And there was my sister's face. A wave of love for her hit me, followed by a wrenching sense of loss. Then that swell of anger with no outlet.

"I'm trying to let myself love her again," I whispered. "I guess this is part of my process with that. Figuring it out—that's . . . who I am."

"I know," she said gently.

Yes, Celine knew who I was. She was deep and good and for some improbable reason loved me. I loved her intensely at that moment and told her so. I told her she shouldn't request the report if it went against her better judgment—my judgment was obviously not in top form.

When we disconnected, I found myself once more very alone in the cabin, still full of a caffeinated sort of energy. I did some push-ups and crunches to try to burn it off, and when that didn't work I had another glass of wine, my max.

I had called Welles for an update earlier in the day, but hadn't been able to reach him. I was curious what the forensics lab had discovered about the rope fibers taken from Tony's boat—did they match the rope found at the reservoir? I also wanted to know if they'd gotten a search warrant for Laurel's house yet. I kept coming back to my impressions of her place—particularly the Trek bike with fancy shock absorbers and disc brakes. Could a woman raising two kids, making grocery-store pay, afford that? I couldn't, not on my salary as a reporter for a small-town daily—my bike was a twelve-year-old, beat-up basic model. Laurel's car, found near

Pendleton Pond, was a seven-year-old Nissan Sentra, hardly a high-roller's vehicle. Where'd the expensive bike come from? Tony? Some other lover?

Or maybe she was a devoted rider and had saved for years to buy it. I didn't know my sister well enough to say.

I festered along for another hour, stress getting the better of me. What about Laurel's daughters? For all I knew, Laurel had a will, or had made guardianship provisions. But I couldn't get to her papers yet. This seemed wrong: I was her next of kin. Why didn't Welles call me back? I deserved to have some clue what I would be in for when I had to take on her affairs.

Of course, I also wanted to look through her files of credit-card bills, purchase receipts, guarantees, manuals, whatever would tell me more about that bike. Had she paid for it? How long ago?

I tried to distract myself by working on my next "Around Here," but when I opened the folder to review any useful bits and pieces, the first thing I saw was my notes for the Lance Burton story, "Chief." I read a few pages into it, thinking about Lance and the way the old village some-times administered justice, trying to quell impulses I knew were foolish.

It was after eleven when I pulled on a dark gray sweatshirt, found my smallest flashlight, then grabbed my own file cabinet keys on the off chance they'd work in Laurel's locks, a small prybar, and a couple of screwdrivers. Then I drove to the cement plant I'd seen about half a mile from Laurel's neighborhood. The looming complex of gray-filmed build-ings and materials elevators was dark except for a few spotlights over doorways, and the front chain-link gate had been locked for the night. But a gravel turnaround and employee parking lot lay between road and fence, with a few cars parked in the tree shadows cast by a lone street-light. I swung in and parked between two of them, just another dusty Subaru among the rest, and got out into the deep night.

Frogs twanged in the woods. No cars passed as I walked between forest and scrub fields along the town road and turned into the Maple Meadow

neighborhood. There were streetlights at wide intervals along the avenues, but the summer foliage cast generous shadows and I felt invisible.
Very few windows were alight: Midnight, sensible people were in bed. I
rehearsed the excuses I'd make if someone caught me snooping around
Laurel's house. Next of kin, I'd say, worried about her kids, wanted to see
if there was a will or any guardianship provisions. It helped that her yard
was fronted by a hedge, reducing the likelihood of anyone seeing me.

When we were kids, my parents had kept a spare key in a fake rock
that they left near our front door. It was made of cement but perfectly
realistic, with a hollow center covered by a metal hatch on the bottom.
I was hoping that Laurel had retained the habit, maybe a way to make
sure the kids could always get into the house.

I shielded the flashlight lens with my fist, leaving just a slot of muted
light, as I scanned the flower bed on the left side of the stairs to her front
door. From the lawn, I couldn't see well enough, so I stepped in among lilies
and peonies and weeds, parting the plants. No rocks at all. I double-checked,
then went over to the right side of the stairs. Nothing. I looked for a key
on ledges or nails but didn't find one. Conscious that I was leaving Conn
Whitman–sized footprints, I brushed soil over my tracks as I backed out.

I repeated the exercise at the back door with the same results. Frustrated, I tried the door. Locked. I went back around to the front and
tried the door there with no better luck. I felt uncomfortably visible as
I took out my wallet and tried the credit card trick in the jamb. But the
gap was too tight.

Actually, I felt a bit relieved. I hadn't relished the idea of creeping
around the dark house. The idea of jimmying her file cabinets was not
much short of crazy.

A dog started barking down the block, and my pulse began ham-
mering. The sheer stupidity of my mission came into sharp focus—my
excuses wouldn't hold up for an instant. Welles and Selanski already
had one eye askance at me. Cloak-and-dagger stuff, I realized, was not
my forte. Somebody said something harsh to the dog, and I heard the
slap of a screen door. In the silence, my nerves screamed at me to leave.

But I had one more errand: the bike. I wanted its model and serial number. The manufacturer would have a database showing where every bike had been shipped. That would lead me to the store that sold this one, and the store would have a record of who bought it. I was fairly sure a retailer would tell me if I walked in with the serial number.

I slipped into the deep shadow at the end of the Quonset shed, paused at the door to listen to the neighborhood, then slid up the zipper and stepped into the darkness. My flashlight blinded me when I first flicked it on.

The place was the same uncrowded jumble of objects, with the exception of the Trek bike, which was not there.

Of course, some stranger could have come in and taken it, maybe an opportunistic neighbor who'd read the newspapers about Trudy Carlson's disappearance. But I didn't think so. Nothing else had been taken—the snowshoes were still there. The kids' bikes were still there.

I took a last look around, then slipped out and zipped down the flap again. I shut off the flashlight and stood for a moment in near-complete darkness. A train wailed in the far distance, giving dimension to the summer night.

Oddly, the thing that most persuaded me the bike was relevant, that its removal had another motive besides greed, was the fact that the door had been re-zipped. If some local kid had thought to make off with something from the missing lady's house, went in, found the nice bike, he'd be dying to get the hell away. He'd grab it and go—why bother zipping the flap behind him? It was an adult's reflex, indicative of surreptitious intent. Like mine.

The neighborhood was dead still. Stymied, I thought again about trying to force my way into the house, maybe prying a window, but decided against it. Within moments I was just another ordinary guy going for a late-night constitutional on a dark road, heat lightning on the horizon, owls in the woods. Rats in my head.

# CHAPTER 21

# CELINE

I finished the departmental budget on Tuesday morning and prescribed myself a personal day at Conn's cabin to let my shoulders down. The weather was glorious, and I was envisioning agreeable conversation in Conn's screened back porch and maybe doing some yardwork together. Later, one of his Italian meals by candlelight. I even brought a bottle of champagne to celebrate my small achievement.

I hadn't made up my mind whether or not to tell him about Penny and her assault on Irene Shapiro, in part because I hadn't solved the quandary of confidentiality. And I hadn't requested a criminal records report on the manager at Martinson's, largely because I still resisted turning his sister's disappearance or death into a forensic exercise. I wanted to keep Conn focused on his own well-being, and I was determined that today we'd have a simulacrum of "normal," enjoying each other, asserting life-affirming rhythms.

The champagne ended up in the fridge pending a more auspicious occasion.

It was just after noon and we were at the counter, sipping coffee and considering lunch, when Conn's phone rang. Our eyes met as Conn snatched it up.

"Hey, Ricky," he said breathlessly.

I couldn't hear her words, only the tone of her voice—measured urgency mixed with compassion.

"Okay," Conn said. "Okay. Thanks for letting me know. No, I'll be fine. Celine's here, we'll, uh, we'll be fine. Thank you."

He disconnected shakily. "That was my boss. Somebody called in a news tip. They've found a body at the stump dump. The police are up there now. Ricky thought I should have a . . . a heads-up on it."

I felt a massive sense of sorrow and disappointment, indicative of how much hope I'd been subconsciously clinging to. When I hugged Conn, his body vibrated in my arms.

The stump dump was where Richfield residents got rid of deadwood, hedge trimmings, or clean demolition debris. Town road crews and contractors also dumped asphalt, concrete, and rocks they dug up during road or water line work. There was a steel swing gate at the bottom of the access road, and you were supposed to go to the Public Works office downtown and pay two dollars to get the key. But they hadn't closed that gate in years and nobody bothered to pay the fee—I knew because I had helped Conn take blowdowns and brush up there. It was only a couple of miles from his house.

"I gotta go," he said. "They'll need somebody to ID the body."

"You want me to come with?"

"Only if you're up for it."

We left our coffee on the counter and hurried out to Conn's old station wagon. We didn't say anything in the five minutes it took to get to the dump access, a dirt road now half-blocked by a State Police cruiser. A trooper got out and came to Conn's window when we pulled up.

"Sorry, sir. The dump is temporarily closed."

"I know. A body's been found. I'm . . . I may know the victim."

"What's your name?"

"Connor Whitman. Is Captain Welles up there? He'll know who I am."

The trooper turned away to speak into his shoulder radio. He nodded, came back to us. "You know your way around in there? Go to the paving dump area. Somebody will show you where to leave your vehicle."

"So I guess this is it," Conn said grimly. Meaning, the great leap into the hard part.

We drove through a meandering clearing of thirty or forty acres, cut into a densely wooded hillside, past signs designating dumping areas. Brush, stumps, and other wood debris were left far uphill, at the end of one arm of the clearing. Our destination was halfway up, where the dump for unusable paving and stony stuff had its own cul-de-sac. People came in their station wagons or pickups, got to the right dumping area, backed up toward the last pile someone had left, then left a pile of their own. In the paving and masonry debris area, this resulted in a helter-skelter landscape of dump-truck-load-sized hillocks of dirt and chunks, with little valleys between, stretching over an area the size of several tennis courts. When heaps encroached too much on the turn-around, a town crew came in with front-end loaders to shove or carry the material up against the steep hillside. Conn said this occurred several times a year, depending on how much had been dumped.

We passed a temporary sand-and-gravel storage area at the bottom and bumped our way up to the next bulge of clearing. State Police and sheriff's cruisers lined the edges of the road; closer, a big crime scene van and the medical examiner's van were parked. A Richfield municipal dump truck and a front-end loader stood off to one side.

A trooper indicated where we should park and told us we'd find Captain Welles in the nearer van.

Conn just sat for a moment after he shut down the car. He drew a deep breath, blew it out, drew in another. "I don't know why I'm so unnerved. I've been expecting something like this every day. I thought I'd . . . resigned myself."

"I'm so sorry, Conn," I told him.

"Think Mace is here?"

"I hope not," I said. We peered around but didn't see him among the small army of police, crime scene technicians, medical examiner's staff, and municipal workers.

We got out. Closer, we could see a cluster of people back among the hillocks, some lifting chunks of rock and carrying them to a cleared

section about fifty feet away, delineated by yellow crime-scene tape. A
pair of police photographers stood on two nearby hillocks, the angle of
their lenses making it obvious where the body lay.

We found Captain Welles outside the largest of the vans. As Conn
had described him, he had a military posture and a crisp uniform shirt
and slacks in State Police dark gray.

"Mr. Whitman," he said to Conn. They shook hands, and Welles
turned to me. "And you are . . . ?"

"Celine Gabrielli. I'm Conn's fiancée."

He didn't look happy to see me—I had put forward my hand to
shake, but he ignored it. Turning back to Conn, he asked, "May I ask
how you knew to come up here?"

"Somebody called the paper with a news tip," Conn said. "I live not
far away. I couldn't just sit there. Is it my sister?"

Welles's mouth twitched. "I can't tell you that for a certainty. We
haven't finished uncovering the body."

"So, it, the, the body was buried?"

Welles told us the basics as he led us past the vans. Around nine
o'clock, a town maintenance crew had begun consolidating the piles. The
front-end loader operator had been moving smaller heaps back against
the steep rubble hillside, pushing and lifting and dumping, when something didn't look right amid the stones and gravel. He got down from
his rig to check it out, saw enough that he knew to stop, and called 911.

"It would appear that someone left the body back among the piles.
They covered it up with rocks and chunks of asphalt. Unfortunately, it
was relocated by the front-loader this morning and we don't know exactly where it was originally deposited. The operator guesses it was about
thirty feet farther this way, which means evidence could now be distrib-
uted over a large area and this scene will take days to process. Indications
of decay suggest the body has been here for some time—days or weeks."

He was watching Conn's reaction. His face was not without sympathy, but more than anything else I sensed an implacable pragmatism
and a calculating intelligence at work.

*Indications of decay.* I realized I'd noticed a faint smell of rot since we got out of the car, and it had grown stronger as we'd moved closer. The moon-suited crew working nearest the body wore face masks. I pitied the operator who had made the discovery.

"I want to see," Conn said.

Welles looked at him appraisingly, considering the proposition.

"Next of kin, Welles. I need to know. I can identify her."

After another hesitation, Welles nodded once. "Touch nothing, leave nothing. No cigarette smoking, no butts. No chewing gum. Go only where I tell you. Don't talk to anybody and don't interfere."

He no doubt welcomed the thought of having someone who could make an immediate identification. Another part of him, I could tell, wanted to observe Conn. Welles hadn't entirely eliminated him as a person of interest.

He led us wide around the locus of the scene to a large mound on the far side, closer to the hill and presumably not a place where we'd disturb evidence. Conn's eyes asked me if I was sure I wanted to do this, and I just took his hand in answer.

Welles noticed the gesture. "This must be hard for you. I'm very sorry. But there's a bright side in that with a body we'll gain a great deal of forensic evidence. Means of death, date of death, maybe hairs, fibers, or DNA from the killer. Items. A weapon. It'll move us all toward closure."

*A bright side.* I marveled at Welles even as he repelled me.

Welles stood with us, and after a moment one of the photographers came to start taking photos from our perspective. We could see two jeans-clad legs, muddy and stained, one stockinged foot and one still wearing a hiking boot. One of the legs was angled sideways at the knee.

"It's probable that the leg damage occurred during relocation this morning," Welles said.

The odor was stronger here, and along with rising nausea I suddenly felt naive and unready. The smell was a biological fact brutally at odds with all the high-minded psychology we'd been trying to disguise the awful fact of death with. In the end, it said inarguably, we are just flesh, just *meat.* Against my will, I was back again in Illinois and there was Richard's body and a comparable dark epiphany.

A group of municipal workers wearing orange vests and hard hats waited on another mound, watching avidly but clumped close together, proximity body language that revealed their discomfort. They'd probably been asked to stand by in case heavy equipment was needed, but the exhumation had clearly gone beyond that phase. Two husky crime-scene men in white suits bent over the body and together lifted off a chunk of broken concrete. They carried it away to be analyzed later, and as they moved off another pair came in to scoop up handfuls of dirt and smaller rocks, which they placed in plastic buckets. Within another few minutes, half the torso lay exposed. It was sunken and shapeless in a blue-checked shirt stained by blood or fluids of decomposition.

"Is the clothing consistent with what your sister would wear?" Welles asked.

"I wouldn't know," Conn admitted bleakly. "Probably. I mean, out camping."

The crime scene techs came and went again, and soon one shoulder and arm were exposed. The body looked collapsed by decay and probably crushing. With only the head left to be revealed, the observers around the scene stepped closer, and the scene went quiet except for the whine of the photographers' cameras.

"You sure you want to see this, Conn?"

"I *don't* want to see it. I just have to. You should leave, though. This is gonna be a hard image to shake."

I just held on to him, needing reassurance as much as offering it.

Finally the larger pieces of debris on the head were gone, and two techs used their fingers to carefully, almost tenderly, remove the last handfuls of dirt. Welles and the photographer left us to go up close for the last of it. They blocked our view, and I was glad.

Welles, holding a paper mask over his lower face, crouched down close to the body. Abruptly he exploded with an exclamation of shock or surprise, a muffled *huff!* followed by something incomprehensible that sounded like swearing.

Conn broke away from me, scuffling down the slope so he could wedge himself between Welles and the medical examiner. He covered his mouth and nose with both hands, bent to look down, and abruptly rocked back on his heels.

Welles straightened, too. "I believe," he said, "that we've concluded our search for Anthony Shapiro."

# CHAPTER 22

# CELINE

Around six that evening, Welles and a female investigator arrived unannounced at Conn's house, pulling up in a big State Police cruiser. By then Conn and I had come home from the dump, showered, put on clean clothes, and gone for a fast walk of a couple of miles. We sought to air our spirits up near Whimsy Falls, trying to expunge death and confusion in the certainty of beautiful things, the vitality of the forest.

When Conn let them in, Welles introduced his companion as Detective Marlene Selanski, the lead investigator on Laurel's disappearance. Conn had told me about her, and he'd described her well: smallish, around forty, a slightly asymmetrical grin, dark hair in a practical cut, with a well-tailored blazer over a white shirt and black slacks.

"Just so you know," Welles said, "we have had body-sniffing dogs search the entire area. There's no other corpse that we know of at this time."

Conn gave a quick nod.

Selanski gazed around, pursing her lips appreciatively. "Nice place," she said. "Rustic chic, would you call it?"

"I don't know that I'd call it any kind of chic," Conn told her. He looked at a loss, as if uncertain of the etiquette required.

"Can we offer you coffee or something?" I asked.

"Nope," Selanski said cheerfully.

"No thanks," Welles said.

"You want to have a seat?" Conn asked.

Welles sat on the couch, but Selanski opted to hover just inside the entry, scanning the room.

Conn took one of the soft chairs and I took the other. Selanski moved into the room and seemed to be studying the artwork on the walls and knickknacks on the shelves. Yes, she had what Conn had called "an edgy vibe."

"I thought I'd catch you up on what we've learned," Welles began. "You know I was expecting Tony to be our bad guy. This complicates things."

"You sure it's him?"

"His photo has been on my desk for two weeks," Welles said. "And his wallet was in his pocket."

"I'm pretty bummed, actually," Selanski added from across the room. "I thought we'd catch Tony, alive I mean, then find Trudy, done deal. No such luck!"

"Is there indication his body was immersed in water for any length of time?" Conn asked.

"The ME says not likely, but that's just a preliminary assessment. Time of death is preliminary, too, pending an autopsy. But looking at decomposition and insect activity, the ME and our entomologist are guessing he died three or four weeks ago."

"Same time as my sister's disappearance."

"Yes. But, again, it's just an educated guess at this time."

"What was the cause of death?"

"Um," Selanski interjected from over near the laundry alcove, "we'd like to keep that to ourselves a bit longer. Again, 'pending the final path report.' Same with murder weapon—don't ask. Anyway, we need a couple more days at the scene. A lot of turf to cover up there." She drifted as she talked, tipping her head to inspect the curios on the mantel above the woodstove.

Conn was getting irritated with her. "Detective Selanski, would you like me to give you a tour of the house?"

"Sure!" she said brightly. It was a provocation.

"Looking for anything specific?"

But Selanski had moved on and now stopped at the stairwell to look at Conn's photo display. She pointed. "That's her, right? Gertrude Carlson, a.k.a. Trudy, a.k.a. Laurel Whitman? She's kinda pretty!" She looked over at us and must have discerned she had pushed Conn too far. "I'm so sorry," she said insincerely. "I don't mean to sound flippant. I keep forgetting I'm in the home of a distressed, grieving relative."

Conn had started to get up, combatively, but changed his mind and settled stiffly back into his chair. Selanski came over and half sat on the back of the couch.

"Where does this leave your investigation into Laurel's whereabouts?" I asked.

"I liked it better when I was ninety-eight percent sure Tony Shapiro killed her," Welles said. "This throws it wide open. For your sister, we'll be looking for the supposed new lover. For Tony, there are connections in his past, drug connections—the whole thing could be about Tony, not about Laurel. She could have been collateral damage in something we don't fully understand yet."

"Lots of possibilities, really," Selanski put in. "If you think about it."

"When will you inform the family?" I asked. I was thinking of Irene, her damaged pride and the sense of public intrusion, and now the complex cocktail of grief that was about to be handed her.

"Tonight. Mrs. Shapiro is our next stop. We'll release information to the media once the family has been informed."

"Point being," Selanski said, "it's not for sharing right away. In fact, nothing that we've told you is for publication. We want to control release to the news media."

"I can't report on it anyway. Conflict of interest."

"Well, don't drop any little hints to your buddies at the *Herald*, either," she said sourly. "We've got an investigation going. We'd like to see if anyone's movements or communications change when the news hits the media."

"Nothing you saw at the stump dump today is for passing on to anybody," Welles said. "I let you in as a courtesy. I hope you will respect that."

"We understand," I told him. Conn nodded.

Welles stood up, and Selanski, taking the signal, rose and headed toward the door.

"Naturally," Welles said, "you've been wondering what happened to your sister. I'd guess that you've also been thinking about what resources you might have in the community that might steer you toward what happened. Or maybe searching your memory for something that might be relevant."

"True," Conn admitted.

"Got any great ideas for us?"

Conn looked a little caught out by the question. "No. But if I come up with any, I'll let you know."

"How about you, Ms. Gabrielli?" Selanski asked. "Being head of the school district's guidance programs, you probably hear all kinds of scuttlebutt. Small towns—everybody knows everybody, right?"

It was my turn to feel exposed. I briefly considered telling them what I'd learned about Penny, but couldn't bring myself to do it. Irene had seen more than her share of betrayal, had more than enough to cope with, especially now.

"I'll certainly keep my ears open," I told her, wondering how much she read into my hesitation.

"And I don't need to say," Welles added, over his shoulder, "that this is a police investigation. Amateur sleuthing on your part will not be helpful."

At that, Selanski pivoted with a dramatic flourish, as if she'd just remembered something important. "You hunt, Mr. Whitman?"

"Did a few times back in high school, not since. I do own a gun, if that's what you're asking. Why?"

She raised a professorial finger. "Well, I have a little math problem for you. It's not hard. Imagine it's deer season, and there's a group of three guys, all experienced hunters, right? Plus they brought along one teenage kid, maybe somebody's flatlander nephew, it's his first time. They're way out in the woods, carefully tracking a bunch of six deer. They're closing in quietly, but just as they're getting almost within range, the kid gets so excited he starts shooting his rifle all over the place. So the math problem is: Three guys plus one kid plus six deer equals what? How many deer do they bag?"

She was talking about the dangers of amateur sleuthing: If the prey hears you coming, it will vanish.

"I get it," Conn said.

She smiled. "Just checking. You can never tell with some people."

"Goodbye," Conn said.

Conn and I waited until their car had left the driveway before saying anything.

"Jesus!" Conn said. "What's your take on our visitors?"

"Detective Selanski really is a charmer, isn't she? Did she say *any-thing* that wasn't snarky and aggressive and accusatory? And that she knew I was in guidance for the school district—they did some research before they came."

"Welles is a smart guy," Conn said thoughtfully. "Finding Tony changes everything. He'll be casting a wide net and he'll be meticulous."

"I thought maybe you'd mention the store manager."

He shook his head. "Not yet. If ever. All I have at this point is two people claiming they heard something nasty about him. I don't know if it's true, or what exactly happened. It doesn't rise to the level where I'd pass it on as relevant. I need to do a little more legwork on David Laughlin."

"In blatant disregard of Ms. Selanski's clever parable?" I asked. We both chuckled, grimly. I didn't like the idea of Conn's involvement, but who was I to complain? I had my own entanglement, one I wasn't ready to reveal. "Why do you think they came here?"

"It'd be nice to think it was some kind of . . . courtesy, an update, but that's not it. I think we were warned to keep our traps shut and noses out of it."

"And take a look at where you live," I added. "Just on general principles, as Selanski might say. In her helpful way."

We went to the kitchen counter and sat on the tall stools there. Evening was coming on, and a gentle breeze moved through the woods and into the windows. I was about to suggest we go out for dinner when we heard the crunch of gravel from the driveway. The stripes of another police vehicle flashed past the window and stopped in front of the house.

Conn groaned.

But it was Mason. He knocked and let himself in before we answered, looking tired and frazzled. "Do they serve beer at this place?"

It was his way of reassuring us: He didn't bring news of any dire discoveries.

"They do," I told him. I got up and grabbed a couple of cans from the refrigerator.

Mason joined us at the counter, a bear of a man in his deputy's uniform and equipment belts. He settled heavily on a stool, giving off the odor of sweat and dust. "I take it you heard?"

"About Tony? Yeah. We were at the dump, actually. And we just had a visit from Captain Welles."

Mason opened his can and took a thirsty swig. "Yeah, I saw him up there, earlier. I just spent a few hours doing traffic control and other support errands at the crime scene. What a fucking mess. The ME had taken the body by the time I got there, but they've taped off an area like eighty feet square. Welles has people going over it on their hands and knees."

"Anything interesting show up?"

Mason took another long swallow, set his can down, shook his head. "I don't know. I didn't see anything. But I heard stuff." He gave Conn an unhappy look.

"Like?"

"Welles and this creepy . . . Nazi lady detective—"

"Selanski."

"Yeah, Selanski. I was outside the HQ van—they'd set up a coffee urn—and Welles and Selanski were having a jam session inside. Riffing, basically, theories about what's going on. Your, uh, your name was mentioned, Conn."

"Terrific." Conn hadn't opened the beer when I'd first given it to him, but he did now.

"They came up with a couple of scenarios where you'd have a motive, or an involvement anyway. Grieving brother discovers the whereabouts of Tony before Welles does. Area native, local news reporter, maybe he has information he doesn't share. So he finds Tony, punishes him, disposes of the body in the stump dump. Conveniently, only two miles from his house."

"That was the vibe I got from the Nazi lady detective. She cruised around in here with a great deal of interest."

"There's more. Did he tell you they'd gotten tips that Laurel has been seen, still alive?"

"Yes. He said he doesn't believe them but is preserving an open mind."

"Well, it was the first I heard about it. They went on about it—'We don't really *know* she's dead.' Which, given Tony, they think opens up a lot of possibilities."

Mason explained: Maybe *Laurel* killed *Tony* at the campsite. Maybe it was *Laurel* who was pulling a vanishing act. Maybe Conn knows where Laurel is and is protecting her, hiding her. Maybe Conn's report of the object in Richfield Reservoir was a smokescreen to throw them off the track. Maybe Conn's fiancée is helping in some way.

"Oh for fuck's sake!" Conn said, unbelieving.

"You know," I said, "I generally don't drink beer? But I think I'll join you lads."

We talked for another half hour. Mason said Welles and Selanski had spun a lot of other theories, but he didn't recognize the names of the people mentioned and so couldn't piece together the implications. Some of them, he inferred, were people she'd hiked with. So far, they didn't know enough to establish any chain of cause and effect, who killed who, why, or when. They didn't know if they were dealing with one murder or two.

"Which is to say, they have doodley-squat on the whole thing," he finished.

Mason drank his beers too fast for my comfort, too needily, and as was his habit he absently tortured the cans afterward, twisting them and eventually flattening them in his big hands. Conn said less and less, internalizing things. Clearly, neither man was handling this well.

Neither was I. Again and again I balked when I thought of mentioning Penny. Despite the closeness of our relationships, I sensed that I wasn't the only one leaving things unsaid, unasked. And the image of that sad forlorn body came back unbidden, cradled in its little crater of rubble—a reminder of mortality and, more difficult, of dimensions of human nature we ordinarily try to avoid pondering.

# CHAPTER 23

# CELINE

I can only explain my actions by saying that this was my first murder. I had never seen a real crime scene, I'd never been even tangentially involved with a victim or perpetrator or surviving family member. I didn't know how investigations really worked, how people responded psychologically or behaved socially. It threw me off-balance in ways I didn't recognize right away, and I made serious mistakes of judgment that I only understood as such after the fact. Conn, too.

After Mason left, Conn and I ended up staying home and eating warmed-up leftovers. The champagne I'd brought cooled its heels, waiting for happier times.

One of the dynamics the situation imposed was that it was hard to think of anything but the murder. We ate, cleaned up, and talked about it as we sat at opposite ends of the couch.

"Welles struck me as an unhappy guy," Conn said. "Probably thought he'd have things easy, moving up here, lowest murder rate in the country. Then he walks into this."

"So what are you thinking?" I wished I'd had a moment alone with Mason, to ask him what he thought I should do.

"I don't know. Looking at the hiking companions seems reasonable, but Selanski told me last time they didn't seem like credible suspects."

"He mentioned a supposed new lover—what's that about?"

He shrugged. "I gather some of her coworkers said there was another guy coming into her life. Not somebody anyone knew."

"But what's the motive? For killing either Laurel or Tony?"

"I don't know about Laurel. Kill Tony because he was in the way? Some jealous moment of . . . craziness?"

"From what you've told me, your sister had moved on. Tony was already mostly out of the picture."

"Maybe she put him up as her prior commitment—to keep the new guy at a distance."

"Like, 'Sorry, I've already got a boyfriend. So bug off.'"

"Yeah, I guess. Except I don't believe it. The killer's got to be somebody from Tony's not-so-distant past. A drug connection. Maybe Tony had debts, or screwed somebody in some way. And Laurel was just collateral damage."

That struck me as much more credible, too. "Except that it happened when Laurel was camping out. Because wherever Tony was killed, *something* happened up there near Pendleton Pond, right? I mean, would she and Tony go there together? And if they did, who would know? How would his enemies find him?"

Conn shrugged. "Followed him? To what turned out to be a great place to murder people and not be seen doing it?" He winced and rubbed his forehead.

"Then why take Tony to the stump dump down here, forty miles away? And why wasn't Laurel's body found with Tony's?"

I was improvising what struck me as "reasonable" responses, but my mind was careening off in a different direction entirely. The internal stress I felt intensified as I realized I couldn't tell Conn my real thoughts.

Penny: Irene had conjured an image of an unstable, dangerous person, determined to possess Tony, feeling so righteous about it she'd confront his wife. My impression at Big Lots supported that. Would such a person kill Laurel, if Tony was still professing attachment to her?

Would such a person kill Tony, if he didn't come around?

Clearly, the State Police should know about her. And yet I couldn't betray my professional, and, yes, personal obligation to preserving Irene's confidentiality. I had given her my word.

I had trapped myself between conflicting imperatives, conflicting secrets. Penny might well have killed two people. I had no real evidence of that, but surely her violent incident with Irene and her involvement with Tony was something the police should know about. Irene's dislike of police was obvious, and I doubted she'd made any effort to reveal details.

The confidentiality of the counseling relationship is often maligned in TV courtroom dramas, but it has much in common with that of the confessional. It is indeed an article of faith, but it has a pragmatic basis. From a practical standpoint, I needed to retain Irene's trust—not so much in me, personally, but in the whole counseling process. Our school-based conferences had been managerial, working on Gracie's academic issues, not therapeutic. But after Tony's murder, Irene and her kids were going to need some outside help. Healing requires candor in talking about the most intimate aspects of a person's life, and that candor won't develop without trust. Irene was already so alone—because she trusted no one.

I'd have to talk to Irene, plead with her to tell the police about Penny, or to give me permission to call them.

"What?" Conn asked.

"What?" He'd startled me, and I'm sure my eyes went wide.

"What are you thinking? The furrowed brow."

I smiled, shook my head, lied. "I'm sorry. Just . . . nothing, really. Long day. I think I'm getting tired."

I tell myself there were lessons to be learned, here, at this juncture. But the exact content of those lessons remains unclear. Don't step on slippery slopes? Don't keep things from your loved ones? Don't stick your nose in when you don't know what you're doing? If I had told Conn about my visit to Irene, I'm sure he would have cautioned me against seeing her again. And a lot of things might have turned out differently.

The conversation I needed to have with Irene was not one for the telephone—it would require a human face, compassion, body language that encouraged trust. So as soon as the State Police released the news about Tony's murder, Thursday, I drove to the Shapiros' address on the edge of Richfield. It was another beautiful day, the kind when the weather is so sweet and innocent, that, given the errand, the natural world seems duplicitous.

The neighborhood had a tired and transitional feel, residences mixed with storage sheds and former granite-cutting workshops, now boarded up. Lovely big trees lined the streets, but the old clapboard buildings were flaking and many had stapled plastic serving as storm windows. The sidewalks were buckled from frost heaves. On the Shapiros' block, an elderly woman tended a flower bed, but otherwise the most active residents were the squirrels, which scampered across the street in front of my car and twined up the trees.

The house was a two-story duplex in a row of identical wooden structures, separated by driveways leading to garages at the rear and, in the case of the Shapiros', a tarped boat on a trailer. As I parked I saw Irene, sitting on the front stoop. She was smoking a rumpled cigarette and looked as if she had been dropped there from a considerable height and had broken on landing. Her face registered no expression when she recognized me.

I came up the walk and stopped in front of her. "Irene. I am so sorry. I am just heartbroken for you and the kids."

"What do you want?"

"I want to remind you that I am available, my staff is available, to you and Gracie and Matt. For whatever we can do for you. Or we can make a referral for some counseling. It doesn't have to wait for the school semester."

She spat a tidbit of tobacco off her lip. "They're at my sister's. In Barre. I wanted them out of here before the cops searched the house. I'm thinking we'll move up there."

"So . . . the police came?"

"That they did. Searched the house. And the yard. And the boat. And my car. Shoulda sold tickets, we had so many neighbors watching. Took me six hours to clean up after."

I wanted to comfort her. I wanted to ask her what, if anything, they'd found, but that wasn't part of my mission. Instead, I sat next to her so that our eyes would be on the same level. Closer, I could smell stale alcohol on her breath. The apartment door behind us was open to a dark exterior that seemed to exhale a dank chill on this fine day.

Irene averted her face from me as she watched the squirrels. In the adjoining yard, three of them were having a spat, chasing after each other, climbing a tree trunk, pausing to chatter and screech. Their claws rattled on the bark. Probably two males feuding over a female, I thought. Or the other way around.

Irene pursed her lips with disdain, pointed her cigarette at them, and said, "*Pshew!*"—a gunshot sound. "Jesus, I hate those little fuckers. Just *rats* with bushy tails!"

We watched the squabble for a moment.

"How're the kids doing?"

She looked at my face and shook her head minutely, side to side, despairing of my stupidity. She struck me as a person consumed by bitterness as much as grief.

"Irene, what's happened to your family is really, really unfortunate and challenging. Please considering getting some counseling! It really can help. To have someone listen. To help figure out—"

"I know the spiel. 'Constructive coping strategies'?" With one hand she mimed a jabbering jaw. Then she lit another cigarette from the first and stubbed out her butt on the sidewalk. One of the squirrels stopped, cocked its head at us, and scolded *zut-zut-zut-zut-zut* before racing on again.

The smoke caught ragged in my throat, but I suppressed the urge to cough. "Listen. What you told me, about that woman, Penny."

She looked at me distrustfully. "What about her?"

"Did you tell the State Police about her?"

"Fuck no! I don't tell those dickheads fuck-all."

"They should know she assaulted you. I think you should tell them."

"After all this, like I give a shit? Like I'm worried about that freak bitch now? Tony's not fucking her anymore, is he? I got a dead husband and screwed-up kids. And no money, given it's over a month with no paycheck from Tony and I'm missing work because of this shit. So fuck her."

I lowered my voice to an urgent whisper. "Irene, listen to me. Please. I'm saying this for a reason. For all we know, she might have had something to do with . . . what happened to Tony. And Trudy."

Her lips seemed to fall into her mouth as she tilted her head and stared dully up, askance, at the sky. I couldn't tell if she was considering the idea or scorning it. Then the squirrels racketed again, claws scrabbling as they spiraled around the trunk.

She scowled and aimed her cigarette at them again. "*Pshew!*" she said, showing recoil in the cigarette. "*Pow!* Little *fuckers!*"

"The police need to know," I said. "You need to call them and tell them. Have them look into her. Maybe it's nothing. Maybe not. They'll figure that out. But they need to hear it from you!"

She came to herself, shook her shoulders, took a deep drag on the cigarette. "I'll think about it," she said, not looking at me. After another long drag and slow, thoughtful exhalation, she bobbed her head and said, "Yeah, okay. You're right. I'll get on it. I definitely will. Are we done now?"

# CHAPTER 24

# CELINE

How could I have been so stupid? Yes, as I drove away from Irene, I was unsettled, some internal gears weren't meshing. But in my naivete, my lack of experience, I never imagined what I'd set in motion. I didn't understand the shock waves that murder sends out, invisible ripples that spread and ramify.

It didn't take long—not even enough time for me to call Mace with Penny's last name. The next afternoon at Conn's place, Friday, both of us taking a day off, a motorcycle pulled up in the driveway. I looked out the kitchen window to see Mace lifting himself off it, in uniform but looking disheveled. He took off his helmet and then stood hesitantly for a moment before coming toward the door.

"Conn," I called. "Mace is here." I registered the concern on Conn's face, always the first reflex: news about Laurel?

Conn met him at the door, and uncharacteristically, Mace pulled him into a bear hug. Over Conn's shoulder, Mace's face looked smudged, and his eyes caught mine meaningfully. I read it as a signal of bad news.

They came into the living room, and Mace saw the questions on our faces. "Not about Laurel," he said. "Have you got a spare beer? I'm off duty. Very off."

Conn went to the fridge and pulled out one can, then another for himself. He looked my way, but I shook my head.

"You don't look so great, Mace," Conn said. "What's going on?"

Mace popped his top, hands shaking, and poured back a good slug before answering. "This has been a not-so-good day." Again his eyes flicked to mine in an entreaty or warning. Then he clumsily made his way around the coffee table and flopped onto the couch.

My anxiety notched up, and I told Conn, "Maybe I will have one." I didn't plan to drink it, but holding the can would help establish connection with Mason, who clearly needed to unburden.

Conn got me a beer and we joined Mace. Mace had mostly finished off his can by the time we sat.

As Mason told it, he had expected a reassuringly routine day, beginning with taking his cruiser to get an oil change at Donny's Citgo, which had the county's routine maintenance contract. He was coming back along the strip when a call came over the radio: An armed robbery was in progress at the Big Lots store, in the Riverside Shopping Center. He was practically right there and so was the first law enforcement to arrive. The dispatcher told him other units were just minutes away.

When he came through the automatic doors, he saw Irene Shapiro at one of the checkout counters, pointing a revolver at the face of the cashier. The other cashiers cowered behind their conveyors, heads down, and beyond them Mace could see customers peering out from behind shelves of merchandise.

He recognized Irene from a couple of encounters. The first was years ago, when he had pulled Tony over for "driving a slalom on a straight stretch of road," and booked him for DUI. Irene had come to the holding cell to shout at her lolling-drunk husband and plead with the sheriff to let this one go. Mace had calmed her, told her what needed to happen, assured her that Tony in the cell was better than Tony on the slab. The second time, some years later, Mace wasn't the arresting officer, but he was involved in the call when Tony got into a bar fight. He was at the bail hearing when Irene showed up, crying her eyes out. Mace was there to escort other fight participants from the dock to the courtroom and back again. But Irene's crying broke his heart, he said, and he went to the bathroom to get some paper towels for her. Desperate for reassurance, she was grateful.

At Big Lots, procedure called for him to draw his weapon and order her to disarm, but the scene was in stasis and Mace thought if he did so, the gesture might catalyze things, Irene would fire. From her appearance, he knew he was looking at a woman on the edge of emotional collapse, filled with rage and desperation and hopelessness. The cashier was backed against her register, cornered, motionless. Mace took a chance on a soft approach.

"Irene!" he called. "Irene Shapiro."

She glanced quickly at him, and didn't seem to recognize him until she scanned his name tag. She snapped her eyes back to the cashier.

"Irene," Mace said. "I'm not going to draw my gun. This is going to be okay. Please put down your weapon and let's talk. Tell me what's going on."

"Fuckin' *talk*," Irene spat. "Tell *Penny* Mac-Freakshow to talk. Tell her to talk about where the fuck she gets off."

The cashier's name was Penny, he said for Conn's benefit, probably thirty years old but with a face like a high-school girl's, with makeup inappropriate for her age—those sparkles in her eye shadow. Her expression was a mix of scorn, defiance, and terror.

"Put it down," Mace said. "Please."

Penny made a noise and Irene stuck the pistol up against her forehead.

"No, I changed my mind. Don't talk, *Penny*. Shut up." Irene raised her voice so that everyone in the front of the store could hear. "Penny here fucked my husband. Penny came to my house and attacked me in front of my kids. Now Penny has *murdered* my husband. So I should do *what*? I should do *what*?"

Just then the town police showed up, two young officers who saw the situation, drew their guns, took shooting stances, and shouted at Irene to put down her weapon.

Mace urged them to stay calm, too: "We can handle this. It's going to be okay. This isn't going to escalate. I know her."

"He wasn't yours to kill, Penny. He wasn't *yours*. You are a cheap piece of trash. A whore. A fucking *horse*, look at you!"

"Irene," Mace called. He took a slow step closer. "If she killed Tony, we'll figure that out. We'll make sure she's punished. You did good, letting us know. Now the ball's in our court. So lower the gun and place it on the counter there. Think of the kids. Don't put them through any more. Please."

Irene's shoulders slumped, Mace said, as though she had abruptly run out of gas or fire or will. I had seen that same deflation myself, revealing the hard limits of her stamina. The gun wavered, and she looked toward Mace uncertainly. The other cops braced themselves.

"I will. I'll give you the gun," she said wearily. But Penny did something wrong—stood up straighter, made a derisive sniff, something—and Irene jerked the gun quickly back to Penny's face. "After this." And she shot Penny at point-blank range. Penny fell backward against her register and then collapsed straight to the floor.

At the explosion, people in the store shrieked and the other two cops fired. Irene spun into the next cashier's station and fell across the bagging counter.

"So, yeah," Mace told Conn and me. "Not such a good day." He crushed his beer can in one big fist. "Got another, Connor?"

"Oh, Mace," I said. As Conn went to the kitchen, Mace met my eyes and the message was clear: We were both complicit. Either of us could have gone to the police before Irene got to Penny.

"Mace," I whispered. "Let me carry this. Not you." I hoped he understood.

Conn came back and handed Mace an open beer can. "Okay. What can we do for you, Mason?"

Mason had to let it out: He had been about eight feet away when the back of Penny's head exploded, so he'd been sprayed by blood. I realized that must account for the smears across his forehead. He'd attempted to care for Penny as the other two policemen went to deal with Irene. Penny had been hit just to the left of the bridge of her nose and the back of her head was not intact. Irene had been hit in the chest and shoulder, and was now in critical condition at the hospital.

"What's the story at work?" Conn asked.

Though Mace hadn't fired, he was relieved of duty until the incident had been reviewed, as were the other cops. He was told his response—failing to draw his weapon—would be under scrutiny, and he was recommended to the shooting-incident counseling his job entitled him to. He had held himself together pretty well during several hours of debriefing and filling out reports, he said, but had started to feel shaky when he was done.

"Have you been home?" I asked. "Does Jody know?"

"Naw. Not yet. You two are my first port of call. I figured I should try to calm down first. Could use some advice on, you know, explaining to Jody and the kids. What happened. So it's not too scary. Or why I am the way I am." Again, his eyes met mine. *And*, he could have said, *I wanted to tell* you *about it, Celine.*

"Well, the news media's going to go apeshit," Conn said. "What a fucking mess. I'm so sorry, Mace."

"I was just getting the damn cruiser's oil changed," Mace mourned. "I guess I should've shot her? But I've never . . . you know, 'fired in the line of duty.' I thought I could defuse it. With a, like, a friendly face. Somebody on her side." His words were turning into mumbles: "Like a, an exit ramp. A way for her to come back down."

"Mace, you did the right thing," I told him. "But right now, I think you're going into shock, okay? You saw a fatal shooting at close range, you're going to feel culpable, you're going to have some trauma. Please take them up on the counseling. Right now, the main thing is, it's over, you're safe, you're with people who love you."

Conn's eyes changed as he just now recognized the smears on Mace's forehead. "How about you take a hot shower?" he suggested. "Relax, get cleaned up. I'll drive you home, we'll put the bike on my trailer." When Mace nodded, Conn went to the bathroom to get towels ready for him.

"We'll talk," I whispered. "But right now, just focus on being okay."

"The freakin' thing is, now we'll have a harder time figuring out if maybe Penny *did* have something to do with it. I mean maybe she—"

"Not your lookout."

"No, Celine, thing is, if she did, maybe only you and I know the connection. Irene yelled all this gibberish, but only you and I know what she meant. Penny's dead, Irene may not live, so we have the same problem we had except now *my* job is on the line. Like, if I tell my boss or Welles, they'll ask why didn't I tell them earlier. And prevent the loss of two lives."

"Just tell them what she said. That should be enough. You don't have to mention what I told you."

Conn bustled out of the bathroom and into the laundry alcove. Mason and I went quiet and waited. I heard the chunk of the dryer door and then Conn emerged with a fluffy towel and a fresh bathmat. He gave us a wan grin and went back to the bathroom.

"Mace!" I whispered. "Your 'job' right now is to stay together and connect with your family and do whatever it takes to get grounded again." This was not the moment, if there would ever be a moment, to tell him about my second meeting with Irene.

His eyes wandered away. "Right. Yeah. Family. Poor Jody. This is not something Jody needs right now." He finished his second beer, and when his eyes came back to mine they had a pleading expression. "Yeah, please, I'd like it. If we could talk. I'd trust you more than whoever they assign. I mean, not just this, I still have all this mental shit from about Laurel."

I took a moment to consider that, and as I hesitated Conn came out of the bathroom. "All set," he called. "My robe is there, too, if you want it. You could take a nap upstairs. Whatever you need, right?"

Mason heaved himself to his feet. "Thank you, buddy. Thank you, Celine. Friends in need indeed." He lurched off to the bathroom, a great big man looking diminished and hangdog.

So there it was: another weave of the paradoxical daisy chain, murder and love, closeness and distance, revelation and concealment. Trying to do good, ending up with disaster. One result was that I felt some obligation to help Mace through what I'd set him up for. He was in shock, feeling guilty for having failed to prevent the shootings, unable to reveal what he viewed as "responsibility" for Penny's death. I was the only one he could open up to.

At some point, when we had a few moments alone, I would have to tell him that his culpability was negligible. I'd tell him I'd carry the burden of responsibility. Whether he knew it or not, I was the one who deserved it.

And that's what I did. It was heavy, but I tried to give myself some forgiveness. I was in the same boat as Mace—we'd been caught between professional obligations and personal values and the exigencies of the moment, and we had made the wrong choices. Or not! Really, neither of us had anything to add to what Irene had told the world in those last moments. Penny had been Tony's lover, had made claims on him, and had accosted Irene. And maybe Penny was, in fact, unhinged enough to have killed Tony, or Laurel, or both. Welles would certainly connect the dots.

For all I knew, Irene would have come to the same suspicion without my suggesting it. I had been trying to do the right thing, just as Mace had been, even if that thing had proven wrong in the moment. But, as easily, it could have proven to be "the right thing": Irene could have called Captain Welles, as I'd pleaded with her to do. She could have suppressed her desire for revenge. Or put down her gun when Mason asked.

And Mason: If he *had* shot Irene, that could have ramified in ways that proved "wrong," too. He would feel just as guilty, as shaken—probably more so. There was no point in either of us excoriating ourselves. Really, the worst we were guilty of was hesitation, indecision.

Of course, such rationalizations are often simply the futile exercise of a guilty conscience.

The problem put distance between me and Conn. I was knotted up inside, and of course he sensed it. Waking in the small hours of the morning, pondering it as Conn snored next to me, going back over my decisions, I tried to be logical. But I found myself facing a similar double-edged blade, or fork in the road. I wanted to be able to tell anything, everything, to Conn, the man I loved. But what would he think? What would confession accomplish except to sow uncertainty and discord between us?

Here it was, again, that accursed daisy chain. The interweaving of love for Conn, my need for his love, love and lies and honesty all spinning together, murder braiding with doing the right thing, betrayal twining with loyalty. Sometimes you reveal too much, sometimes not enough, acting out of love yet causing harm. Laurel had probably lived in that same tangle for much of her life. You can't know it until you've been in the midst of it.

I tried to be rational, to apply my training to my own state of mind. But when I went online to look for texts or examples or advice, I found nothing that fit. Perhaps, it occurred to me, humanity just can't look too closely at the extreme verges of moral nuance and ambiguity. In that zone, we are all hypocrites, no matter what we do.

# CHAPTER 25

# CONN

I ended up driving Mace home that night—too many beers under his belt to take his bike. I hitched my little utility trailer to the Subaru, propped up a double layer of planks, and then Mace and I put our backs into it and rolled the bike up. We secured it with ratchet straps and stood looking at it for a moment as we caught our breath.

"Bike looks great," I told him. Something cheerful to say. He had done a great job of restoring the 1984 Triumph Trident, a classic.

"Thanks. Hard to find parts, though."

He seemed spent, and our conversation during the ten-minute drive to his place was superficial. When we got there, we muscled the bike down and parked it in the Kings' garage next to Jody's little dirt bike. I made a point of entering the house first, wanting to serve as a momentary buffer between an unprepared wife and a man who was coming home from very far away. I called out, heard Jody answer from back in the kitchen.

She gave me a thin smile when she saw me. "Hey, Conn."

Obviously, she hadn't heard about the shooting on the news, which would make this all the harder. But her face changed as Mace came into view, clumping disconsolate down the hallway.

I kissed her cheek quickly. "Kids here?" I asked, and was relieved when she told me that both were at a soccer game. I gave her the hand-to-ear *call me* signal and I saw in her nod that she realized something was seriously amiss.

I left the two of them standing there in the kind of jagged silence that descends when there's too much to say and no easy starting place. I didn't envy either of them.

After dinner, Celine and I sat in the screen porch, looking out to the pine woods and talking about the day's events—mainly, about Mason. We knew he'd need some help to get back on his feet. Aside from the police picnic, it had been many months since we'd seen Mace and Jody socially. We should invite them over for dinner, forbid serious talk, play bocci ball in the yard, enjoy Vermont's fleeting summer while we could. Or drinks and a movie as a foursome, or even some silly fun like bowling. Meanwhile, Mace and I should get together for some guy-type recreation, maybe fishing, give him a chance to unburden.

Mace and I had been inseparable friends throughout most of our childhoods, into high school and beyond—unlikely friends, maybe, because of the difference in our family backgrounds.

My father and mother were blue collar but college-educated, agnostic or downright atheistic, with more urban childhoods. Mace's folks were local natives who had felt no need of more education after high school; his mother was a devout churchgoer. Mr. King had served in the Army, my father had been a peacenik. The Kings hunted with guns while my parents shot only cameras; Mace's folks had a speedboat that they fished or skied from, while we had a prehistoric Old Town canoe that was for paddling quietly so you'd see wildlife. Both families shared the fiercely libertarian outlook typical of Vermonters, but otherwise there wasn't much overlap in political sentiments. I can't remember the Kings and Whitmans ever getting together except for Mace and Laurel's engagement party and wedding.

Mace was every bit as intelligent as I was, but our family cultures guided the expression of our smarts. While I was discovering books and poli-sci, he was learning how to rebuild car engines. For financial reasons, we both went to the state college, but I went on to grad school while he stayed in Richfield and eventually joined the Sheriff's Department.

"How did you get so close?" Celine asked. "Or, more to the point, how did you stay that way?"

When we were kids, it was simply that we had the same ideas about what constituted fun—mostly, knuckleheaded shenanigans. Later, as rebellious teenagers, I turned against my family's ways by leaning wood-chuck—like going hunting with Mace's people, which my mother abhorred—while Mace began quoting poets or Marx at his dinner table, to his father's annoyance. In effect, in our formative years we met in the sociocultural middle. By the time I went off to study journalism, we'd had fifteen years of good times, of surviving harebrained adventures, of sharing candid thoughts about the opposite sex. It built a rock-solid foundation of trust. We knew who the other guy was, and we knew we could count on that guy, no matter what. And when I came back after my train wreck in DC, Mace proved it.

Celine nodded thoughtfully. "So . . . how did Laurel and Mason come about as a couple? Given the family cultures?"

It had seemed both paradoxical and inevitable. Paradoxical because of the differences in style and outlook, inevitable because they'd known each other so long. Laurel saw us together on a daily basis, and we occasionally deigned to let her play with us. Later, in high school, she liked having "two big brothers" in the upper classes. We protected her—symbolically, anyway, there was nothing to protect her from except vicious infighting among the girls, about which we could do nothing. Plus we got our drivers' licenses before she and her friends did, and we chauffeured them around once in a while.

Talking with Celine about it brought back details I'd forgotten.

A few months before we graduated, Mace caught Laurel and her friends smoking dope at our house. Given that his family was pretty strait-laced, and my parents had firmly discouraged it until she was "mature enough to do it thoughtfully," she was afraid he'd tell the school or our parents or the police. But though Mace expressed disapproval, he didn't tell anyone. It would have been hypocritical if he had, given that he and

I occasionally got stoned. But the upshot of his keeping quiet was Laurel's appreciation—she saw it as his being "loyal" to her. She was grateful.

The three of us continued to hang out after Mace and I graduated from high school—the state college was just an hour away, and we were often home. After years of being skinny, Laurel developed curves in junior year and became popular among the boys. When we were home on weekends or holidays, Mace and I spent time at each other's houses or out at the Kings' camp, same as always, and Laurel sometimes joined us. Somehow her being "filled out"—Mace's term—made it more acceptable to include her in fun things. We introduced her to booze and got her drunk for her first time. She had fun with it, hamming it up, exaggerating, getting flirtatious, and we all laughed our asses off.

I had to chuckle at the memory.

"What?" Celine asked.

"I think that's when I first noticed something different in the way Mace looked at her. Something appreciative there."

"Yeah, us filling out seems to have that effect on you guys," she said.

"I teased him about it. 'That's gross, man! You total perv! She's basically your sister!' God, he got red. He didn't used to be able to hide his feelings at all—he didn't get the impassive face thing till he joined the sheriff's. Poor guy was an open book."

We laughed, and I felt some of the tension of the last few days easing off.

"This is good," I told Celine. "I need to remember this stuff. You're not finessing me, are you?"

"Never. Keep going."

After I went off for graduate study in Washington, Mace took a job in Richfield, I don't remember what. Then it was Laurel's turn to go to the state college, which meant she still came home on holidays and some weekends, and often saw Mace when she did. In her second year up there, she met a guy, and that summer she shacked up with him, staying at his apartment in Richfield instead of our family home. I never met him, but our parents disapproved of him, and Laurel told me about one unpleasant experience with him.

Apparently, they had an argument that got physical—Laurel said she hit him first, but the guy clopped her back too hard and more than once. Laurel called me, but I was away at grad school, so I called Mace, who went to talk to the boyfriend. Mace was a big guy, solid all the way through. Laurel was afraid he'd beat up the boyfriend, but he didn't.

"Look," Mace told the boyfriend, "I've known Laurel since she was a kid. She's like my little sister. If you respect her and love her, then show it. If not, break up with her. But you don't hit her. Make up your mind. I mean right now—while I'm standing here."

"I respect her and love her! Jesus! She's the one who punched me first! And it's between me and her, asshole."

As Laurel told it, Mace loomed closer. "Gentlemen are capable of restraint," he said grimly, showing more restraint than I would have managed. "Here on in? You're a gentleman."

"Thank you, Mace," Laurel said. "I think we're okay here." The guy looked relieved. She broke up with him not long after.

And, I suspect, something changed in her relationship with Mace.

"That'll do it," Celine put in. "The damsel-in-distress thing gets them every time." She cleared her throat, hesitated, then asked, "Do you think Laurel was even then making poor choices about relationships? Is it suggestive to you that she got into a serious physical altercation? When she was, what, twenty?"

I shrugged. But Celine had correctly identified the through line of my reminiscence—my desire to find Laurel again. Find the truth through the person. Try to find the place where I'd lost her.

"So, how'd they close the deal?" Celine prompted. "Move from quasi-siblings to married couple?"

This I remembered better, because both of them began consulting me about it. Things progressed by increments.

Laurel didn't complete her degree. After three years of college she moved back to Richfield to take a job selling clothes at a store on Main Street. When Mace started at the sheriff's office, they ran into each other more often and occasionally spent time together. He had always been impressed by Laurel's smarts and her combination of introversion and feistiness, and now her physicality began to get to him. In one phone call he confessed to me, in great discomfort, that her bust swelled her sweaters in a way that made him have to avert his gaze. He said his interest felt disloyal in some way, to both Laurel and me. I don't know if he was asking for forgiveness or for permission.

"But there it was," Celine said. Her grin told me she was enjoying this. I had to laugh, too.

They'd known each other so long that she could be frank with him, rough with him, sarcastic or sweet or impatient with him the way she was with me. All that and eros, too, I admitted, would have made an alluring mix.

"Right, and then there was that . . . incident," I said. It had just come back to me.

"An incident."

"Something they both told me about. I mean, I think it catalyzed their relationship. Moved it decisively off the dime."

One night Laurel was with some coworkers at a bar—not in Richfield, in a smaller town a few miles away—when a fight broke out. It was a divey sort of place, with pool tables at the back, frequented by woodchucks—she and her friends liked the "authentic" ambience there better than the fernier bars downtown. Two guys began tossing words and then fists, and the bartender called the cops.

The first one to arrive was Mace. By then, one of the guys had given up and was on the floor, but the other kept at him, kicking him, even when Mace came through the door and ordered him to stop. The guy was drunk on adrenaline as much as booze, and he threw a punch at Mace. It broke Mace's nose, which instantly spewed blood.

The way Mace told it, he put his hands to his face, and both the guy and he looked at his bloody hands in astonishment. Then Mace tackled him and got him down, kneeling on his back. Just before he put the cuffs on, Mace took the guy's head and smashed it once into the floor. The guy's nose broke—audibly, Laurel said. Mace got him cuffed just as the windows lit up with the strobe of another cop car. Mace bent to yell in the guy's ear: "Okay? Okay? Do you get it?" Which

I understood—basically, *Having someone break your nose really hurts so don't do it again, especially to me.*

Laurel said she was somewhat taken aback by Mace, the way he pretended the guy was still resisting when he smashed his head down. But it was tit for tat, the guy had started the whole thing. And, aside from stupidly walking into a sucker punch, Mace's authority *had* been impressive—he didn't act like it hurt at all, and it took him all of one second to have the guy flat on his face with his hands behind his back.

Laurel went with Mace to the Richfield Hospital and sat with him in the emergency ward, just to keep him company. He was upset with himself for losing it, and she ministered to him, mopping his face with towels and reassuring him that it was understandable, the guy had attacked him, there'd been a lot of adrenaline and testosterone flowing. After a while he sent her home because he'd need to get worked on and debriefed about the incident.

"Wow. So how did it all shake out?"

"Oh, the guy claimed Mace used excessive force, but no one at the bar would corroborate that, certainly not the other fighter, who had some cracked ribs. And Mace's broken nose told its own tale. In the end, Mace didn't face any repercussions."

Celine nodded.

"Yeah, so I think that's where it really began," I told her.

"How so?"

"Well, Mace had to work at his desk for a while because his appearance, with the nose splint and bruising, was unbecoming to an officer making public contact. Laurel worked about a block away and she began stopping in to see him at the sheriff's. And he looked so woebegone. He berated himself, felt sorry for the guy he'd hurt. He apologized to Laurel for letting her see such a thing. She told him she thought he looked cute, like the bandages were the snout of a puppy. Or a teddy bear."

"Small-town love story," Celine said, smiling, staring into the distance.

"After that, it was clear to everybody that they were falling in love. Later, when they began talking about marriage, Laurel told me she worried that they were awfully different. You know her biggest concern? 'We're such an *ironic* family. I'm just never sure the Kings can *get* things the way we mean them.' I told her it wouldn't be a problem—she knew Mace, I knew Mace, she wasn't marrying his tight-ass family. Meanwhile, Mace begged me to put in a good word for the match. And I did. And I meant it."

Celine got up and began straightening up the house, a signal that she was ready for bed. I joined her.

"This is good," I told her again. "This kind of remembering, it's what I need to do. She's . . . starting to take shape for me again."

"It is good. Definitely."

"But you're thinking . . . what?" Clearly, her mind had moved on into thoughts she wasn't sharing with me. I caught up to her, put my arms around her from behind, and was grateful for the burrowing of her shoulders against my chest.

"I just want to know how much we're going to involve ourselves in this," she said. "I understand your need to *do* something, but there's some truth in Selanski's parable, isn't there?"

"Except I am hardly the flatlander nephew. I know these woods better than the other guys!"

"Still, there's always the risk of unintended consequences."

"I know. All too well. I'll be—"

"I mean, it's not deer being hunted here. There's a murderer out there. It's a . . . predator. It could turn on you."

Celine's body went tense as she said that. She was right to bring it up—I hadn't considered the possibility of continuing danger from some unknown person, that any risk could come back at me, at us. As Irene's shooting of Penny showed, the effects of murder could keep reverberating.

"Don't worry. I'll be very careful. I'll be smart. I promise I'll bail if it seems like I'm getting in too deep or anything seems scary in the slightest."

We shut down the house—even locked the door, which I almost never do—and headed upstairs. While we were undressing, she surprised me.

"I've got a couple of criminal records requests to make," she said. "For job applications. I'll throw David Laughlin's name into the mix."

Much later, I woke in the night. It had begun raining, pattering at first and then thrumming on the cabin roof just over our heads. Outside, the woods sighed with it, as if grateful. A soothing sound.

Half-hypnotized, I kept thinking back to Mace's motorcycle, strapped there on the trailer. Maybe it was all the reminiscing I'd been doing, with Celine's skillful prompting, but something nagged at my memory. I thought back to when Mace and I had bought our first bikes and worked on them in his father's garage, out at the King family camp. Warren King had built the little wooden barn and set it up to indulge his late-acquired hobby of restoring antique cars. To his credit, he trusted us in there with some pretty expensive tools, including his spray-paint setup.

Was it that period of my life, or the motorcycle itself? I had ridden during my last year in high school, in freshman year at Johnson State, and only intermittently afterward, but Mace had continued riding. When he married Jody, she bought a bike, too. Road trips hadn't appealed to her, but she'd gotten into motocross, riding a lightweight, agile spider of a Yamaha in dirt-track competitions.

I bought a Honda 450, Mace a Triumph Daytona 500—even back then, he had a thing for the look of the British bikes. We got them cheap and hard-used, and that first summer we did more fixing and custom-izing than riding. I replaced my clunky Honda tank with a teardrop tank and layered it with crimson lacquer, Mace replaced his battered Triumph tank with something sleeker and went for the black look. Then it was time to paint some racy design on the tanks—back then, some-thing like a signature, what a teenager did instead of getting tattoos. He opted for the traditional back-swept red flames; I fudged an array of lightning bolts, a design that never satisfied me.

His current tank sported a bald eagle, wings raised, talons forward, with the whole bulb of tank airbrushed as a richly hued sky of sunbeams and dramatic cumulus clouds. The paint work really was excellent.

I pondered the mental tickle that image prompted. Was it the bird, wings outstretched, or the sky? I still felt the occasional yearning for that feeling of flying that only a responsive bike and a winding road can give. That had to be it, I thought: flying, the sky.

With that thought and the gentle thrumming rain, I drifted to sleep.

# CHAPTER 26

# CONN

I didn't see any immediate risk in poking around David Laughlin, didn't see how he could find out about my activities.

I wanted to talk with Jocelyn Macey, Laurel's coworker who Dev had said complained about Laughlin. When I called her at home on Monday morning, I said I was seeking information about Trudy Carlson. I identified myself as Conn Whitman, reporter for the *Herald*—not Conn Whitman, Trudy Carlson's brother.

As I'd hoped, she was familiar with my articles, but even so she said she wasn't sure she wanted to meet. I assured her that I wouldn't use her name in any article, wouldn't publish anything she said without her prior permission. At last she agreed to meet me at Lupine, a new-agey café in downtown Montpelier. She said we could talk for an hour before she had to get to Waterbury for her shift.

I arrived early so I could think through my interview strategy and have a choice of seating locations. I selected a booth that put me facing the door and would position her with her back to the plate glass that fronted the sidewalk. I wanted an open, public environment, yet I wanted her to feel secure that David Laughlin wouldn't happen by and spot her talking to me.

I saw her before she saw me—a thin girl, tall but a little stooped, coming in hesitantly. She wore a store uniform shirt and black slacks, name tag already clipped to her pocket. About nineteen, I guessed.

I rose to introduce myself and beckoned her to the other side of my booth. I told her I was grateful that she'd made the time for me. We ordered pots of tea, then made small talk for a while. When I complimented the rings she wore, she pointed to one of them and told me she'd recently gotten engaged.

That was a piece of luck for me. I always try to make my interviewee feel sexually safe, assure them I'm neither interested nor available, get that troublesome dynamic out of the picture early on. So I told her I was engaged, too, but joked that maybe I should be calling it something else by now, given that I had been living with my fiancée for over two years. Looking relieved, she showed me his picture on her phone: Gary. He was a smiling, weak-chinned guy whose face glowed with the same country innocence, rapidly becoming a thing of the past, that I saw in hers. He worked on his parents' dairy farm.

Just taking a peek at Gary's face seemed to soothe her. Her flighty hands calmed, and her face became more mobile. I recounted a couple of "Around Here" articles I'd written about her town, mentioning people she might know. She relaxed further, and I got the sense of a sweet, timid girl wanting to do the right thing.

I didn't take out my notebook until the waitress brought our tea.

"I don't know if I can tell you anything useful," she began. "I already told the police, I don't know Trudy that well. Should I call her Laurel? We just worked the same shifts a lot."

"I'm looking at a couple of things that might be different from what they wanted to know. First, I've got a confession to make. I'm her brother. I guess you could say I've got more of a personal investment in talking about her. What I have in mind isn't so much of a 'news' item, but more of a profile—a portrait of her. I hadn't seen much of her in recent years."

That unsettled her even as it caught her interest. "Why not?"

"That's one of the things I'm trying to find out. We had grown apart as adults. I wish we hadn't."

She nodded, puzzled on one level, intuitively getting it as well.

She told me my sister was really good at her job, very professional—uniform always clean, hair done neatly. She didn't criticize her bakery staff when they screwed up, but helped them figure out how to do it better next time. Always patient. When they met in the employee lounge during breaks, Laurel always asked Jocelyn about her mother—"I still live with my mom"—and her boyfriend. "Fiancé," she corrected, blushing.

I circled it for a while, hoping David Laughlin would come up, but she never mentioned him. Eventually I simply had to ask.

"Jocelyn, I had an upsetting conversation with someone who said your manager sexually assaults the female employees, including my sister. He said Laurel had talked about it. Do you know anything about that?"

Her eyes went big, and she turned her head to look around the café. The lunch crowd had thinned and the handful of people who remained were lost in their own conversations. When she looked back at me, the tightness had returned.

"I don't feel good talking about that."

"I'm not going to write about it. Nobody will know but me. He can't hurt you."

"I just don't . . . feel comfortable. Talking about it."

I sipped my tea, giving it some time before I responded, glad I had asked Celine's advice before this interview.

"My fiancée has a PhD in psychology," I said. "She says sexual assault victims have lots of reasons to avoid telling about it. One is the fear of retaliation. Another is that people won't believe the woman, or they'll say she 'wanted it' or 'started it.' Which is really horrible and unfair."

Jocelyn nodded, but still held herself back. She camouflaged her reluctance by working on her tea, dripping in honey, stirring, tasting, frowning.

"She says there's another reason, too. It's not rational, but it's very common. She says women who receive unwanted sexual attentions often feel guilty. Maybe they gave off unintentional signals, they think, they should have known better, it's their own fault. Or they feel like they've been disloyal to their husbands or boyfriends. Or they feel they've been 'soiled' or 'devalued.' But that's completely unfair and untrue! Those are feelings a sincere, decent person has when faced with someone else's lack of integrity."

I looked at her pointedly. "I know you love your fiancé, it's clear in everything you say, the way you look at his picture. You're true to him. He's a very lucky man. Please help me here."

In a tiny voice, she said "I just don't want Gary to think of me in, like, those terms."

Unconsciously, her hands made a sweep along the front of her body. And I knew what she meant: *That he put his hands on me here and here, and he . . .* She and her fiancé were kids, probably had been virgins with each other—or still were. Laughlin's touch had contaminated her body, the sweet intimate gift she wanted to give exclusively to her beloved. My hatred of David Laughlin rose.

"Did Laurel talk about it with you and the others?"

"Yes. She wanted to . . . do something. Said we didn't have to take it. If it had been just her, she'd've made a complaint, but most of us said we couldn't risk it. He fired a lot of girls and we figured that was to show us what could happen. I told Trudy, Laurel, I have to help support my mom. She's diabetic and has problems with walking. I can't lose my job."

"But did your coworkers talk to her about it? I mean, where or when he did things, what he did?"

"I don't see why you're like focusing on this one thing," she said. She was pulling away from me. "Anyway, I mean, it's not all *that* bad, the things he does, it's not so different from what happens at other places. It's just . . . *creepy.*"

I could have added *and humiliating and sadistic and illegal.* But she wasn't defending Laughlin, she was defending her reluctance to talk, and I didn't want to be adversarial.

"Jocelyn, my sister didn't like unfairness. That's who she was. And she was compiling information about your manager because she wanted to have some kind of weapon to use, to make him stop. I want to honor that."

The poor kid wavered, wanting to accommodate me, wanting to escape what had become an excruciating interrogation.

"Did you know about her project? Compiling complaints against him?"

She nodded.

"Do you think he could have found out about it?"

"I don't know. Nobody would ever have told him, but he sometimes went into our day lockers and looked at our stuff. When no one was in the staff room. Gail saw him. Maybe he saw something she wrote down?"

I was starting to detest the guy. I made a note to ask Celine about voyeurism and paranoia as they related to sexual predation. Surely they were linked—"comorbidities," she'd probably call them. How far would such person go to protect himself or maintain control?

"Are there coworkers of yours I should talk to?"

Her eyes widened again. "I don't want to get them in trouble."

"I won't tell them who mentioned their names."

She looked at her watch. Then, looking over toward the counter as if studying the barista at work, she began reciting: "Cheryl Landers. Lydia, I don't know her last name. Rache, um, Rachael Christianson. Jane, she's older, but he, you know." Back to me: "Gail Pelkey, she's the produce manager."

I jotted the names, my hand shaking as rage mounted. I wanted to ask the physical details—how far it had gone. I wanted to ask about the bruise Dev had seen on Jocelyn's wrist. But I had already pushed her hard, and I still had one more line of questioning to pursue.

"I should let you go, but help me on one more thing. Please? My sister—I heard she was seeing someone. Do you know who that was?"

"There was that guy, Tony. The one who . . . they found. I only know what the others said when they gossiped, and I hate that. Gail said he was hung up on Trudy, but she wasn't into him. Anyway, that was like last year."

"Not him. The police told me she was seeing someone new, more recently. Do you—"

"No."

"Never saw him?"

"I'm just a cashier. I don't know what people do back in the store. That wasn't the kind of thing your sister would've told me."

"Who would know?"

"Probably Gail. They're friends. They're more the same age. Gail's a single mom with two kids, same as Trudy. They'd talk and laugh."

I underlined Gail's name on my pad and waited, hoping she'd fill the silence, but this was too uncomfortable and she was eager to be done with it. She checked her watch again, took a last sip of tea, and dabbed her mouth with a napkin.

"I'm really sorry, Mr. Whitman, I have to go," she said. She looked at me imploringly, as if asking permission.

"This has been very helpful, Jocelyn. You've been great. I'm sorry if I upset you."

She stood and opened her purse, then realized we didn't have a bill.

"I got this," I told her. I put a twenty on the table.

"Thank you." She twitched a quick smile and turned toward the door. Then she surprised me by turning back. Her chin was quivering.

"What you said," she whispered. "About feeling disloyal? Or, like, devalued?"

"Yes?"

"That's what he told me, too. Mr. Laughlin. Said I should think about how Gary would feel if I told anybody. Mr. Laughlin would say I started it and that we did, like, worse things than really happened? And Gary wouldn't ever want to touch me again. So I haven't told him."

Despite a powerful physical effort to force her voice out, she spoke so quietly I could hardly hear her. And I was deafened by the blood rushing in my ears, outrage. Before I could reply, she turned and was out the door.

My cell phone rang as I was getting into my car. It was Welles, who said they had gotten some forensics back and wanted to meet to discuss them. At his office. I asked him for details, but he declined to offer any, and his guarded voice gave me no clues as to his intentions for the meeting. My shoulders inched upward as I drove toward Waterbury.

Inside, I was directed back to Welles's office. I came into his door and was disappointed to find Detective Selanski with him.

"Aha!" she said when she saw me.

"Have a seat," Welles said. As I came in, he flipped a big whiteboard so that I couldn't see the markings on it.

I sat down, debating how to manage Selanski's attitude. I decided I wasn't going to give her much leeway.

"So," Welles began, "we have a range of details to cover."

"The wonders of forensic science," Selanski put in. "But not for publication or external discussion. Right?"

"I got it, Detective."

Welles turned out to be a pacer, at least when he was stimulated. "We searched the Shapiro property. Nothing of importance in the house, but his boat proved useful. As I believe Detective Selanski has informed you, there was no anchor aboard, but analysis of the fibers found on the boat prove they came from the anchor rope we retrieved from the reservoir."

"What does that tell you?"

"Lots of possibilities but few certainties. Your suspicious underwater object, finding an anchor and rope in that location, matching the anchor to a boat owned by a suspect linked to your sister, who himself turns up as a murder victim—it's too much to be coincidence. But it's hard to establish a coherent narrative from the facts we have."

"Did the pathologist say whether Tony's body had been immersed?"

"It showed no signs of prolonged contact with water," Selanski said.

"How did he die?"

They exchanged a glance. They had decided on a strategy for this interview and were double-checking as they went along.

"He was stabbed multiple times in the abdomen. One blow penetrated his heart."

"How about the weapon?"

"We recovered it at the dump site," Welles said. He stepped to his desk and came back to hand me a couple of photos. One showed a hunting knife with a blade that was almost five inches long, according to the sizing ruler next to it. A rusty stain filmed the steel.

"Recognize it?" Selanski said. "Didn't happen to lose one, by any chance?"

I ignored her and studied the second photo, a close-up of the area nearest the handle, where the blade broke into serrations. The grooves had trapped more blood, and where the plastic grip met the metal a heavier deposit of dark material had settled. I couldn't see any finger-prints.

"It's been wiped down—quickly, but enough to remove fingerprints," Welles confirmed. "But there's lots of DNA. The blood on the blade is Shapiro's. The material at the handle juncture is blood from two other indi-viduals. One, a very small quantity, we can't match the DNA with anyone in our database. But DNA in the other matches blood found at your sister's tent site, which we confirmed as hers with the sample you provided us."

Welles and Selanski watched me process that. Inside, I felt a some-thing give way, a little wall collapsing. I'd told myself I'd accepted the fact of my sister's death, but each additional confirmation hurt in un-expected ways. Vestiges of hope have a way of lingering.

"I'm sorry, Mr. Whitman," Welles offered.

I took a couple of breaths. "Anything else?"

"For now. But we finally secured the warrant to search your sister's house, including locked container access. We'll go in there tomorrow morning."

"What will you be looking for?"

"Everything," Welles said, mouth setting in a hard line.

"Well, fingerprints of course," Selanski elaborated, cocking one eye-brow at me. "Do they match anyone we know?"

"Former or supposed or aspiring boyfriends," Welles clarified dryly. He shot Selanski a hard glance.

She suppressed her sadistic side bit. "DNA in the sheets, hair in the shower drain? Phone records, papers."

I felt overwhelmed. "I'll need access to her papers. A will, or guard-ianship provisions. If I have to liquidate her assets, I'll need the title for her car, for her house—"

Selanski: "When we're done processing them."

Welles had stopped pacing and was contemplating me, arms crossed over his chest. Making a decision, he stepped to the whiteboard and flipped it. The side he'd initially hidden was marked with a constella-tion of circled factual details, with arrows drawn between. They were the main pieces of the puzzle: anchor, boat, rope, underwater thing,

Tony, Laurel, tent site, dump site, knife, mystery boyfriend, Penny, some others. I was relieved that "Conn Whitman" wasn't one of the nexuses.

"See anything?" Welles asked.

I studied it. "Too much and too little."

Welles nodded. "You might be able to help. We look at this spiderweb and can't put the parts together. But I've been here only a year, Detective Selanksi's up this way from Brattleboro pretty recently. I have to assume there's a ring of details around each of these items. Little planets in orbit around each one. Someone who knows the area better might see some."

Selanski watched my eyes darting around the board, point to point, notes along the arrows, question marks.

I knew what he meant. But the chart suggested no obvious connections or implications, no cause and effect. I debated mentioning David Laughlin, but decided I didn't yet know enough. If Gail Pelkey corroborated what Jocelyn said, I'd tell them about him.

"On the boyfriend front—anything about the supposed new guy? Or the other one, Nadeau?"

"No comment," Selanski said.

"Can you tell me anything about Penny?"

Selanski said, "No comment," but Welles spoke over her: "We're looking into her whereabouts and behavior around the time of your sister's disappearance. She has a history of violent altercations, resulting in several arrests. At one point she was assigned to a psychiatrist, whose diagnosis included obsessive love disorder and obsessive jealousy."

"Where does that put her in your ranking of suspects?"

"It certainly keeps her a contender," Welles said. "We're working on it."

Selanski stood and Welles turned back toward his desk, suggesting that the interview was over.

But Welles turned back to me to clarify: "*We* are working on it. *You* are not. You are a grieving relative and you have our sympathy. But frankly, our main motive in telling you anything has been to reassure you that we're doing our job, and thoroughly. Point being, if I find you are conducting vigilante research into this, I *will* charge you with interfering in a police investigation. Good day, Mr. Whitman."

# CHAPTER 27

# CONN

Welles's warning notwithstanding, I was already in Waterbury. Hey, no sense in burning gasoline on some other day to drop in on Gail Pelkey, the produce manager at Martinson's. The person Jocelyn thought most likely to know more about Laurel.

I entered the supermarket, avoiding the register where Jocelyn was at work, then swinging by the customer service counter. There was the employees' notice board. Another confirmation, another belly-drop: Laurel's photo had been removed, a new face taped in the bakery manager spot. But I found what I wanted next to that one, a photo of Gail Pelkey. She was a strawberry blond, late thirties, looking into the camera with a somewhat forced smile and knowledgeable eyes. I found her attractive, partly because she didn't look like someone a twerp like Laughlin could push around.

But then, it always depended on leverage. Two kids, Jocelyn had said, a single mom providing essential income for her household. A place in the managerial hierarchy she wouldn't want to jeopardize.

Again, I took my time waltzing to canned music through the aisles with a basket over my arm. You always need a few things.

Over in produce, I realized that, of course, unlike the meat and bakery sections, there was no service counter. The angled shelves in the vegetable coolers had misting nozzles that freshened the lettuce and broccoli, requiring staff attention only when restocking was needed. A chunky teenager was trying to consolidate a couple of boxes of oranges, but he was the only staffer in sight.

I cast my eyes over every vegetable and fruit item, trying to figure out a way to meet Gail. I also scanned for security cameras—investigative habits die hard—and found none. Finally, I approached the kid, whose name tag told me his name was Dylan.

"Hi," I said, giving him an appreciative look. "I'm looking for bok choy—are you folks just out of it, or is it something you don't usually stock?"

"'Bok choy'?"

"A Chinese leafy thing, like a cross between, um, fennel root and romaine lettuce."

"Never seen it."

"Well, you folks absolutely must carry it! Is the produce manager around? I'd like to make a recommendation to him—bok choy! I'd buy a ton of it."

"Her. She's a her." He squinted a look at the back of the store, where swinging double doors led to offices and storerooms. "Gail. She's back there." He gestured with an unstacked orange.

I thanked him and headed toward the doors, adopting the role of enthusiastic, well-meaning foodie. I had often played roles before, as a reporter—you gotta get on with the person you're interviewing. True, I never felt particularly proud during or after, but it came easily enough.

Just as I pushed through the gray doors, David Laughlin approached, going the other way.

He wore a blue store jersey, the chain's logo emblazoned in orange across the chest, above nicely creased black trousers. He was puffier than the photos up front showed him, with pouches beneath his eyes, certainly less attractive and wholesome than his Web photos. A preoccupied guy, always multitasking.

Waterbury was outside the *Herald's* main circulation area, and my photo was seldom published along with my articles. But my concern sparked. The last thing I wanted was for this piece of shit to recognize my face.

He blocked my way, wearing an expression of disapproval. "I'm sorry, can I help you?"

I was a foodie with a helpful suggestion for profitable inventory. "I hope so! Are you the produce manager?"

"No. I run this store. Sorry, this area is for personnel only."

"Oh, I didn't mean to . . . the young man out there said I could find the produce manager back here? I have a suggestion for a vegetable I would buy tons of, as would everybody I know."

Up close, I could feel his sleaze—an instinctive sense of hypocrisy that I quashed with difficulty. Laughlin took about one second to compute my presence relative to his agenda, then found the managerial path: "Let's go out to the floor. I'll get Gail for you."

Lightly holding my elbow, he escorted me back through the door and into the aisle, where he pulled out a walkie-talkie. I heard his announcement over the store's speakers: "Gail Pelkey. Customer service requested in produce."

He turned to me. "She'll be with you shortly."

He flashed a perfunctory smile and strode away. Had he sensed something amiss with me? Nothing in his face suggested it, but I regretted that he'd ever seen me.

I hovered for about a minute between a wall of fresh green things and bins of boxed strawberries and blackberries. Then the back doors swung open, and Gail appeared.

She was tall, almost my height, wearing a shapeless store uniform that couldn't disguise a figure that would attract men's attention. Her face diverged from the photo up front: She looked older, with crow's feet around her eyes and a world-weary look in them.

"Hi, I'm Gail. Mr. Laughlin said you had a produce request. We're always happy to accommodate if we can. What can I do for you?"

"Thanks for talking with me. I'm Conn Whitman."

If she recognized the name or was surprised by this random customer introducing himself by name, she didn't show it. When she didn't answer immediately, I gestured toward the back-slanted shelves of vegetables.

"No bok choy?" I grinned to show I didn't mean it as criticism of her job performance.

Scanning the shelves, she said quietly, "I know who you are. I think I know why you're here."

We met at a restaurant in Richmond, a safe twelve miles away, after her shift ended. Again, I got there first and chose a table where she wouldn't be readily seen from the front. She strode in with purpose and swung into the seat opposite me.

"Hello, Conn."

"Thanks for coming, Gail. After a long day. How much time can you give me?"

She checked her watch. "Half an hour. Then I have to pick up the kids." She settled into her seat, met my eyes. "I'm glad you showed up, but I wish Laughlin hadn't seen you."

"Me, too. Were you expecting me?"

"Not exactly. But Laurel told me about you, what you do. With all that's happened, I figured you'd want to know more."

"Did you know that she and I weren't . . . didn't see much of each other?"

She shrugged ambiguously. "She always spoke well of you, if that's what you're asking."

"I'm just saying, I was out of her loop. We were always about to get together and hang out. But."

"I know that one." She took a menu from the wall clip and looked it over, then turned toward the counter. The staff was too busy bracing for the dinner rush and not much concerned with us.

"I had a conversation with another person at Martinson's. I heard about Laughlin. Some pretty coercive crap I'd like to hurt him for. Also heard about Laurel's 'project.'"

"Yeah."

"I don't know anything about the guy. Do you think he could . . . do something to somebody if he felt threatened by them?"

She blew air through her lips, a humorless chuckle. "All I know is rumors and what I've seen at the store. But, yeah, absolutely, I could see him protecting his ass."

"I should tell you I'm not doing this for publication. I'm trying to figure out what happened to my sister. I guess I don't even know the right questions to ask. I'd like to hear anything you can tell me, whatever you remember." I leaned back in my chair, inviting her to follow her own lead.

She said she was now the longest-serving staffer at the store, six years. Laughlin had been there for four of those years, and Laurel had come on not long after his arrival. She and Laurel had hit it off immediately. Both had kids—Gail's were a couple of years older—and were single moms, so they had lots to talk about. Laurel had the determination of a person coming out of a long hard patch, another thing they had in common. One difference was that while Laurel's kids were all hers, the father long gone, Gail had a perpetually fragile custody agreement with a perpetually angry ex.

"See, Laughlin, he's good at finding your weaknesses. When you first meet him, he seems sympathetic, a nice paternal guy looking out for his staff, caring about their personal lives. He's good at this, it works like a charm on the new hires. They talk to him at first and then it's too late, he'll have found the one detail he can use. If you ask me why I don't quit or file a complaint, it's because, A, I need the money and my salary's above average for this area, I'm not going to find an equivalent. And B, I can't be seen as having anything screwy because he'll fuck up my custody arrangement. I need to demonstrate employment continuity. And no scandals."

"He said this?"

"Oh yeah."

"I heard something similar from another staffer. I also heard that he goes into your day lockers. That you saw him."

"Yup. That's our Davey." She looked over at the counter again, frowning.

"Hungry? I'll go up and order something if you want."

Eyes back to me, hard, candid—a person who's beyond lying about herself. "See, when Laughlin came on as manager, I made some mistakes.

My wagon ride has been bumpy. Sometimes fall off of it. Looking for love in all the wrong places, all that."

"Okay."

"He was pretty good-looking four years ago. A good paycheck, college-educated . . . I was between boyfriends, afraid of the future, lonely. Who knows what that white knight will look like? Didn't last long."

"Has he ever tried to exploit that?"

"Not anymore. But it was the beginning. Got the hooks in."

Everybody rides a hard road at some point, and every hard road's a bit different. She was pretty, in a tough way that I admired. Our rapport deepened, and I could see why Laurel had befriended her.

"I had a rocky patch of some years myself," I admitted. "Not so long ago. It's one reason I lost touch with Laurel. I'm lucky that I have a wonderful companion at this point."

We smiled at each other, eye to eye, signals clear.

"How many people work at the store?"

She thought about it. "Must be three, four dozen, if you include baggers and stockers. But not everybody's full-time or on shift at the same time. Probably thirty full-time equivalents."

"So, does Laughlin . . . do his thing with all the women?"

"God, no. He's very selective."

"How so?"

"I think he learns a lot during their job interviews. He learns how . . . desperate someone is. How vulnerable. I wouldn't be surprised if he did research, you know, asking around, Googling people. Finds the hooks, hires the most likely targets, the safest for him. That's why he's never been called on it. Since he first arrived, he's probably done some crappy thing with a dozen or more women. Most of them don't work there anymore. There are five us on the staff now who have experienced his . . . attentions."

I spent a moment trying to imagine how Laurel would react to this, how she'd look into it. "So," I finally said, "Laurel's 'dossier.' What do you know about it?"

"She was dead serious about it. She would have made a good reporter, or cop or spy, the way she interviewed everybody. She even talked to former staff, looked into the stores he managed before he came here. Very systematic. Took notes, typed it up on her computer, looked into legal options."

"Wow."

"Oh yeah. She was on a *crusade*. But she didn't tell me the details, didn't want me exposed."

I was thinking about Laurel's computer, conspicuously missing from her desk and not found at her campsite, and about what might still be found in her papers. And did the expensive bike fit into the picture—a bribe or sweetener from Laughlin?

I was reluctant to interrogate her, but she checked her watch and I knew we didn't have much more time. "I have a couple more questions—you up for my grilling you?"

She smiled. "Shoot."

"Boyfriends. There was Tony Shapiro. Any others that you know about?"

"She was pretty private about that. More than me. I'd tell her my latest tale of woe or high hopes, she was more circumspect. There was a new guy who was into her, but she was more concerned than thrilled with it."

"Any idea who he was? Ever see him?"

"No idea. I saw him a couple of times, but only through the store windows, way out in the parking lot. As if he'd been waiting for her to get off shift. They'd talk."

"Can you describe him?"

She shook her head. "Too far. Through the windows, cars in the way. Tall, I guess. Taller than her anyway, taller than poor Tony. I figured she'd introduce us if it went anywhere."

She checked her watch again, gathered her purse from the floor.

"Was there anyone else she talked to? Not at Martinson's, but maybe another friend? A sponsor at Alcoholics Anonymous, Narcotics Anonymous, or some organization like that?"

"She mentioned somebody who'd helped her. Quoted maxims that had helped. This woman was pretty close to her, I think. God, what was her name? Honestly, I don't know where she was or what organization, or how long ago. Wasn't our local AA, because, uh, I know the people there pretty well."

Again, that rueful smile and the straight-on eye contact.

She stood, I stood, we shook hands, I thanked her.

"Don't take this the wrong way," I said, "but can I have your phone number?"

She laughed. "I got it, Conn. I know it's in case you have more questions about your sister." She found a pen in her purse and jotted a number on a napkin. "Thanks for doing this. And I like you, too."

# CHAPTER 28

# CONN

I got home around four thirty, feeling distinctly rough around the edges. The rain had blown over, and the sun was still well above the hills, making it hot even in my tree-shaded cabin.

Celine knew I'd be needing a swim, and she had plans: "Picnic dinner. You swim, I read and splash about till you get back, we eat at the lake."

I thought it was a brilliant idea. We packed some bread, crackers, cheese, olives, anything quick and easy, then headed out. I decided the right spot would be the dam at Peacham Pond, at the end of the smaller arm of the lake, deep in the woods. We had made love there once, on the flat, stony spillway, just at the edge of the water. A sweet evening full of loon song.

I asked Celine to take the wheel so I could regroup a bit during the drive. I told her about my meeting with Welles and Selanski—the knife, Laurel's DNA.

"So, it's officially a homicide investigation," I finished.

Celine freed a hand from the wheel and squeezed mine. "How're you doing?"

I watched the passing forest, just holding her hand until she had to retrieve it. "I thought I had accepted the fact. Obviously I hadn't, entirely. There were these little pockets of hope." I rubbed my eyes, closed them, leaned back in my seat. "I'm sorry. I am just fuckin' beat."

"A swim will help," she said.

I half-drowsed as we drove in silence through Plainfield, then Marsh-field. We turned onto the Groton Road and rolled past farm and forest land. Five minutes later, Celine brought us onto the pond road, just a narrow tunnel through overhanging trees.

"Welles read me the riot act," I piped up, startling her. "Warned me not to do 'vigilante research.'"

"Can't blame him. What did you say?"

"'Yes, sir. Of course, sir.'"

She sighed, shook her head, grinned.

We turned onto the dam road. Celine slowed and drove carefully, dodging boulders and ruts. We rolled at walking pace for a half mile through thick forest, and then the sky brightened ahead and the lake opened before us. We were in luck: nobody else on the dam. Celine drove its length, a gravel track with steep slopes on both sides. She stopped where the spillway cut through.

"This was a good idea, my beautiful Celine," I said as we unloaded our basket and gear.

The near arm of the lake was still and quiet, too shallow to be safe for motorboats, but we could hear several of them buzzing through the forested spit that separated us from the larger basin. The boat traffic con-cerned me. I liked to swim through the center of the lake to the feeder streams at the far end, about two miles each way. Boaters didn't expect swimmers out that far and were oblivious as they dragged water skiers. I'd have to stick closer to shore, where there'd be more snags and fewer straight lines to really open up in.

We stripped and put on our suits, but I didn't swim right away. Celine was content to sit on the blanket, fold her long legs, and gaze at the scen-ery. I joined her. It was a still day, every shore feature reflected upside down in the water, the blue-gray hump of Hooker Mountain looming behind.

I told her about my talks with Jocelyn Macey and Gail Pelkey. Given David Laughlin's sexual predation, his manipulation, his rummaging through staff lockers, I asked, what else might he be capable of?

Celine frowned, joining me in the David Laughlin non-fan club.

"Well, his playing on the guilt of the young girl is pretty adroit. Shows psychological insight, almost certainly prior experience. But it doesn't prove he did anything worse. Would he kill your sister because she was collecting information, planning a lawsuit? It's possible, I guess. But why would he kill Tony?"

There it was again: the disconnected parts.

"Welles had drawn this chart on his whiteboard, you know, with the facts scattered around on it and arrows between? And I couldn't see logical connections any more than he could."

"Would it make more sense if Laughlin were on there? The missing link?" Celine mused. "By the way, I did the criminal record check on him."

That perked me up—with all the day's preoccupations and revelations, I had forgotten she was going to search. "And?"

"A few traffic tickets over the years. No arrests, no convictions."

"Too bad."

"I also looked into court records. He's been divorced twice, once in New Hampshire about ten years ago and again in Vermont about three years ago. Theoretically, divorce proceedings are public record in Vermont, but it's not hard for one of the parties to petition for them to be sealed. His Vermont proceedings are sealed."

"So . . . some aspect of them was deemed potentially damaging for one or another party if made public?"

"It's not uncommon. Divorces are messy, accusations fly. It's mud wrestling with daggers."

I winced. My divorce hadn't gone there, quite, but only because I'd applied the dagger to myself. "How about his New Hampshire record?"

"Yes. The situation there is similar. Divorce records can be 'scrubbed' of personal identifiers to protect litigants' privacy. There might be work-arounds, though. An entity with a 'direct and tangible interest' could request full access. Also, if you know whose record you're looking for, you could correlate dates and locations and come up with a safe bet who the 'scrubbed' names were."

I thought about that. It seemed hackable, maybe. But what would we be looking for? Even if his wives had brought up his groping his employees, or made accusations of physical abuse, their assertions weren't proof, and anyway it was long leap to murder. His divorce records didn't seem like a line of inquiry likely to produce any meaningful result.

Celine gave my shoulder a shove. "It's getting late. Time to heed the call of the sea, Cap'n."

I began with a breaststroke so I could savor the above-water view while keeping an eye out for snags below the surface. A dive toward the bottom still revealed jagged tree stumps left from before the valley had been dammed, and there were plenty of submerged branches that were slowly working their way toward the dam. But the water felt clean and full of powers, and I started up my mantra: *This is good, this heals. Surrender to this caress, this nurture.*

I switched to a crawl as I neared the bend in the lake where the big basin and populated shore became visible. Underwater, the buzz and rev of motors got louder. As I came fully into the big lake proper, I saw several bounding motorboats trailing skiers and tubers, and to my dismay, three or four Jet Skis, leaping one another's wakes, shooting rooster-tails into the air. Above their cat-quarreling whine, I could faintly hear the shouts and laughter of their drivers. *Just my luck*, I thought, *some family fucking reunion on the one day I come, seeking a dose of tranquility.* They'd be the worst kind of boater, too: unfamiliar with the lake, a bit drunk and prone to high jinks, lacking good judgment. I pitied the loons.

The sound derailed my meditation. My thoughts move back to Laurel's murder: *Laughlin's a bad man, with a strong motive to stop Laurel's potentially career-destroying, bankrupting project.*

Clearly, I needed to keep looking at him. Did he take Laurel's computer? I believed Welles meant every word of his warning against "vigilante investigation." So how to proceed? But what I'd heard from Jocelyn and Gail—surely Welles and Selanski should know about it. I pictured the scrambled whiteboard, added Laughlin, tried to see if connections could be made. None came to mind.

The boaters were really going bananas. I veered toward the left shore, but my tension increased, shoulders knotting as I stuck my head up every few strokes to scout the surface. When I got about a quarter mile into the big basin, the hull of a speedboat veered and came cleaving my way, driver and others facing backward to admire the skier's antics. I stopped, treading water, waved an arm above my head. Nobody saw me. It got closer and closer, and soon I had no choice but to grab a big breath and dive. The hull sliced the water three feet above me, carving a wide silver furrow, and seconds later the twin cuts of skis foamed overhead.

I came up gasping, pissed off. As I looked after them, a woman in the boat saw my head in their wake and pointed me out to the driver. He looked, shrugged, and continued piloting the craft around the perimeter, never letting off the throttle. I flipped them the bird, but nobody noticed.

I headed closer to shore, in water that now seemed acidic with motor noise. Underwater, it sounded like a hive of angry wasps. My adrenaline was cranked and my hope of any healing was eroding. Stubbornly, I stroked for another few minutes until a couple of the Jet Skis came my way, hopping at full throttle. *At least Jet Ski drivers tend to look forward*, I reminded myself. Sure enough, one of the drivers pointed at me, maybe not knowing what I was—a beaver, a bear?—and both angled to come straight at me. I prepared to dive again, but they slowed and veered sharply at the last second, pulling to a stylish halt fifteen feet away. I bobbed in their bow waves.

"Hey, man, you should watch out!" the girl astride the closer ski called. "You could get killed, swimming out here!"

"It's not a fucking highway! I got as much right here as you!"

The boy revved to come closer. "Watch your mouth, asshole," he said. He looked smug, towering above me on his nautical steed. They traded self-satisfied grins and revved up and looped around and away, slashing arcs of water at me.

I got the hint. I wasn't going to get what I needed from the water today. I turned and swam into the shallows, tangling in milfoil and dodging snags as I made my way along the shoreline and back to Celine.

"That was quick," she said as I slouched out of the water. I had only been gone a half hour.

"Ah. Too many boats. No fun." I'd decided not to tell her all the details of my unhappy swim. The woman was already putting up with a lot of misery from me.

She came to me with a look of sympathy and a towel. As she rubbed me down, I stood panting like a big dog after a bath, grateful for her touch. "Time for shore leave, then," she said. "Let's eat."

We settled on the blanket as evening descended. Over on the big basin, boaters headed home for drinks and eats, and the motor noise subsided. We munched, I calmed. There was healing here, after all: Celine was as lovely as the trees, the water, the sky just starting to dim. The air stayed comfortably warm.

We complimented the cheese, the sky, each other, even talked about the Chicago Cubs' chances, until Celine smiled, shook her head in resignation, and punched my shoulder.

"Let's cut to the chase and fucking talk about the murder and what we're going to do about it."

I managed a bitter laugh. "A woman after my own heart."

"So, what do we have? Avenues of investigation, I mean?"

We brainstormed. Tomorrow, Welles's people would be conducting a thorough search of Laurel's house—that could provide some new leads.

Like what?

Celine, looking for the truth through the person: "Okay, Laurel's recovery. Gail Pelkey said she didn't go to AA, not in Waterbury anyway, but had been to some other addiction support service or counselor. How can we find out who, where?"

"In her papers. If and when Welles gives me access."

"In any case, our office has a list of all of 'em. We often make referrals. We could cold-call them all, I suppose."

"But would they reveal whether Laurel was a client? A patient?"

"Not just to anyone. Legally, medical confidentiality privilege survives even after death. But there are exceptions, such as when the information might protect others from harm. I bet a reasonable person would respond to persuasion from the right person or agency."

"Like what agency?"

"Police. Or, dare I say, a school guidance office, seeking information to help Laurel's daughters."

"But what might this person tell us that'd be useful?"

Celine bit her lips. "Something we don't know about Tony? Something scary about Tony's associates? Something about the new boyfriend?"

I could only shrug. "Okay. How about a lawyer? If Laurel had been preparing a civil lawsuit against Laughlin, maybe she consulted an attorney. Somebody with tort experience. Would it be a class action? That would require some specialization, right? How to find her lawyer?"

"Her papers, again. I don't know much about class- action suits, but I'll bet the specialty would limit the number working in Vermont. A short list to chase down. Or maybe a legal-aid organization. But she may have been building toward a criminal case. Would need different advice."

I made a mental note of it, then had another idea. "Okay, so here's a tough one. The girls. Would they know anything about their mother's new boyfriend?"

"That *is* problematic. We need to tread very carefully. Conn, even if they know the guy's name, address, and phone number—grilling two girls who are certainly suspecting the worst by now? No. Your job is to give them an uncle, a family, a living connection to their mother."

"Yeah." I needed to set up another visit soon.

The motors had all gone still. As we lingered in the deepening quiet, a pair of loons came in low over the trees, angling down in shallow parallel glides, wing tips almost touching. Expertly, mirror images, they trailed the lake's still surface with their webbed feet, then lowered and sledded on their streamlined bodies until the water slowed them to a stop. Two long, tapering wakes spread behind them. Elegantly tailored in crisp black and white checks, the male opened his powerful wings and batted them to claim the space. His mate shook herself, then vanished into the water to fish.

I heard Celine's intake of breath, awe that I shared.

"So synchronized," I said. "Like you and me."

She grinned. "As long as they mate for life."

I wasn't sure if they did, but I liked the sentiment. She took my hand and we watched as the male inspected us with his ruby eye, dismissed us as irrelevant, and dove.

"So, Celine. Help me think this through. I think it's probably time I told Welles and Selanski about Laughlin. But I'm a little wary, given their warnings against my poking around. I don't need a hassle from them."

Celine pondered the question. "'Around Here'—have you ever used the column for, what would you call it, an exposé?"

"Once in a blue moon. A corrupt mayor in Williamstown—skimming the treasury, kickbacks from town contracts. A couple of others over the years."

"So, what would your boss say if you pitched an exposé of Laughlin? Or maybe it's bigger, maybe the chain is overly tolerant of sexual misconduct."

"Huh. She'd probably point to a conflict of interest, given that Laurel worked under him. But she might go for it. I could pitch it to her."

Celine was right. If I "stumbled" over a community issue that warranted journalistic attention, I could justify my nibbling around the edges of the investigation. It would be a license to talk to staff at Martinson's, maybe other people who knew Laughlin. Look into his background. The legitimate interests of the free press would provide counterpressure to Welles's prohibition.

By the time we started packing up, the tree shadows had stretched across our spot. Stooping, reaching, Celine was willowy and fine in the sunset-tinged twilight, and I was sorry to see her put on street clothes. She returned my inadvertent ogling with a grin. She readily agreed when I offered to back the car up the length of the dam, always hair-raising given the steep drop on both sides, more harrowing still in the near-dark. At the end, I did a Y turn, turned on the headlights, and we began bumping slowly back toward the town road.

"And as long as we're talking about loons," Celine began.

We hadn't been, but I was willing to listen.

"And nicely synchronized monogamous waterfowl in general. There's going to come a time, soon, when Laurel's daughters will need to leave state custody. They'll go to a permanent foster home or be put up for adoption—and both won't necessarily go to the same place. You will need to consider how you feel about that."

"Which has what to do with loons?"

"The DCF seeks to establish kids in what's called a state of 'legal permanence,' Conn. A married couple will have a better chance of getting approval for adoption, and will do a better parenting job, than a bachelor uncle."

I stopped the car. "You asking me to marry you?"

"Just putting it out there, sweet cheeks. Don't get your hopes up."

"It's not a bad idea," I said. I loved this side of her—pure Chicago. "For entirely practical reasons. Yeah, let me toss it around and I'll have my people get back to you."

It was very dark on that dirt track under the trees. I shut the car down. Without a word, we both got out, retrieved the blanket, and stepped out to find a flat place in the woods. Nicely synchronized, we spread the blanket and disrobed and came against each other in the sweet evening air. She was as smooth and undulating as water, a person made of gliding soft forms. Synchronized, yes. I wanted to tell her what I felt, but I couldn't find any words sufficient.

# CHAPTER 29

# CELINE

Our visit to Peacham Pond stayed with me, a lingering afterglow of many hues, and my thoughts returned to it often the next day. Conn had to put in some hours at the *Herald*, but I was still on summer vacation, and with the budget issue behind me, my shoulders began to come down. I spent the day at his cabin, harvesting some greens for our dinner salad, weeding, pottering with little chores.

I hadn't planned to mention Laurel's kids in the same breath as marriage, but I was glad I had. Not that I wanted to push the issue, but it was a legitimate consideration. Also, I had a philosophy of sorts, imperfectly conceived, that periods of endings should be seized as periods of beginnings. Laurel was dead, and at some point the mystery of her death would be solved: an ending. We needed to plant the seeds of what came next.

We had made a promising list of starting places for more investigation, I thought. I considered calling addiction support services, using the clearinghouse list the school district kept, but decided that would be a long slog, best left until later. I did a quick Web search for Vermont lawyers specializing in class actions and found a few, but again decided I'd wait. Laurel's papers would offer a shorter route to identifying any support counselor or lawyer and they might include a will that would authorize Conn to request information.

Our wish list for those files was growing. Conn had told me that her computer was missing, taken either from her tent or from the house. But she would certainly have saved bills and correspondence, and there was always an off chance she'd have kept some hard copies—I often printed up documents for safekeeping or later review, Conn preferred doing his copyediting with a pen on hard copy. Of course, we also wanted to see if there were provisions for her kids or possessions. Conn figured it would be some days before Welles gave him access to the papers.

So, Laughlin: Sexual predation such as serial assault or harassment was not my field of specialty—I had done my thesis on adolescent development. But some of the details here were highly suggestive. The most chilling element was Laughlin's shrewd assessment of vulnerability and his adept leveraging of it. It implied a lot of forethought, intelligence-gathering, and experience. Without such, he surely would have been caught out by now. The literature noted that sexual predation often involved the perpetrator's acquiring compromising photos, videos, or other items. These served multiple functions: They often served as titillating souvenirs, but more pragmatically they provided tools that made future coercion easier and discouraged accusation.

Was that among Laughlin's habits? Entirely possible, I thought, given his premeditation.

I did some online research, but had limited success because I didn't know the specifics. What exactly did he do—what physical acts, what areas of the body? What specific language did he use while extorting or persuading? If his pathology ran deep, clues could be found in his fixations or fetishes.

I started taking notes for later reference. Jocelyn wouldn't reveal anything, I was pretty sure, but Gail might. Better, a former staffer, especially someone no longer under Laughlin's thumb—again, information we might find in Laurel's papers.

I was roused from my thoughts by the grumble of a motor in the driveway, and a moment later Mason's motorcycle passed the window. I opened the door as he was parking it, and was surprised to see someone on the seat behind him.

"You're just the person I wanted to see," I called to Mace, meaning it.

Conn had chatted with him since the shooting incident, but I had not, despite my promise. I wanted to hear about Irene's condition and hoped fervently that she was improving. And I very much wanted to help him, which would require confessing about my conversation with Irene, letting him off the hook for the full weight of guilt he imposed on himself. I also thought it would be good to compare notes on some of the investigatory ideas Conn and I had been tossing around.

He took off his gloves, fumbled with the clasp of his helmet, got it off, then helped the smaller person with him to do likewise. A shock of curly dark brown hair sprang free, along with the face of Mason's daughter, Katy. She was twelve, small for her age, the proverbial "quiet one," skinny but prettier now that her front teeth had fully come in. I had barely caught a glimpse of her at the police picnic.

"Hi, Aunt Celine," she said shyly. Avoiding looking at me, she busied herself with taking off her little backpack.

"Katy! Gosh, how you've grown! I haven't seen you in ages—I mean, unless that was you at the party, that blurry streak between the picnic tables."

A quick smile. "Yeah. We were playing hide-and-seek tag."

"How is your brother?" I had worried about Marshall since learning about the mirror incident. He was fourteen now, a chunky kid, more outgoing than Katy but moving into his defiant teens.

"Good." Katy ducked her head and leaned slightly against Mason.

Mace's Triumph ticked, cooling, as I hugged them both. Mason returned my hug stiffly.

"This an okay time?" he asked.

"Perfect for me. Conn's at the *Herald*, though."

"I know. We were just out for a drive. I'm still on leave for a bit, figured I'd grab some time with Katy." His eyes told me he needed to talk.

"Want something to eat? We could eat inside . . . or, it's such a nice day, I could bring out some snacks—"

"That'd be great," Mason said. Katy nodded. They perched their helmets on the Triumph's seat as I went in to grab some oranges, Oreos, and a bag of potato chips. Through the window, I saw them walking hand in hand to the round lawn table Conn had set up under one of the big maples. No beer for Mason when he was driving, but I found a couple of bottles of lemonade to bring out.

We sat and peeled oranges as a gentle wind lifted and lowered the branches above us, whispering.

Katy ate tidily, concentrating on her food, flashing quick tentative glances up at me. Mason drank some lemonade but ate only one token potato chip, rubbing Katy's back reassuringly but distractedly with his other hand. He hadn't shaved, and the stubble on his cheeks was coming in gray and black, a patchy look amplified by the faint purple around his eyes.

It wasn't long before he put a big hand on Katy's arm. "Kiddo, how about if you stay here and Aunt Celine and I have a talk? Did you bring your book?"

"Yes." That glance at me again, curious, timid.

Before we walked away, I went around the table and gave her a kiss on the top of her head. "I'll show your father the garden," I told her. "If you want more to eat, just go raid the fridge, okay? And you remember where the bathroom is?"

She bobbed her head.

We ambled around the corner of the cabin to the side yard, where Conn's small vegetable garden took up most of the cleared space. Mason rolled his neck uncomfortably, trying to work out kinks. My own tension was rising as I faced into my confession.

"So what's up, Mason? I've got a couple of things to talk with you about, too. But first, how is Irene?"

"Same, last I heard. Still in a coma."

I felt a dull blow to my chest, deep bruising pain for Irene and her kids. With it came an intensification of my sense of culpability. We walked on, unable to say more.

"And how is Mason?" I ventured after a moment.

"I'm doing for shit, Celine."

"About Irene? Laurel? Both?"

"Laurel, mainly. You heard they found her DNA on the knife that killed Tony, Welles is now officially calling it a homicide?"

"Yes. The confirmation hurts, I know. Even if you told yourself she was dead, part of you refused to believe it. Conn goes through it daily."

He nodded perfunctorily. To my eye, he was displaying stereotypical movements associated with a high degree of emotional lability. He stalked the length of the garden, folding his arms hard and then releasing and swinging them. Then abruptly, he stopped and went immobile, staring out into space. I leaned against the porch railing and waited him out.

"Mace," I called to him softly after a while.

He roused, came back toward me.

"How about the shooting?" I prodded. "Are you seeing the incident counselor?"

He made a dismissive gesture. "That guy, he doesn't get it. It's not so much witnessing the shooting. I mean, yeah, it does come back at me. But it's that I should have been able to prevent it. Irene wouldn't be where she's at, Penny would be alive to tell us something that might help the—"

"Mace."

"What?"

"I need to tell you something. It's something you have to promise not to tell Conn, ever. It's a lot to ask, but we need mutual trust here. Please?"

He nodded, puzzled.

Lowering my voice, I told him about my visits to Irene, possibly planting the seed of suspicion that Penny had killed her husband. Inciting her anger and desire for revenge and providing it with a locus for expression.

"So, whose fault is it, Mace? Yours or mine?"

He rocked his head forward and back on his neck, like a boxer taking a series of punches.

"I was trying to help her, Mace. I urged her to go to the police, tell them about Penny. For all I knew, Penny would come after her and her kids! I was doing what I thought was the right thing for her, for the investigation. But I screwed up."

"She would have put it together," Mace said. "She was pissed off as much as sad, she was half-crazy. You can't blame yourself."

"Yes, that's what I've been telling myself. What I'm saying now is, you need to tell yourself the same thing. You acted with compassion and restraint. That's all you did. It went south, yes. But if there's any blame there, I should carry my share."

His face was immobile, but his eyes caught mine for a moment and I thought I saw a little self-exoneration there. He scuffed at the ground, then turned and walked to the corner of the cabin.

"You doin' okay, kiddo?" he called. He must have gotten a good signal from Katy, because he returned a thumbs-up and came back to me. He sat on the back porch step, hunched forward, elbows on knees, a big wad of a man in a posture of both defeat and defense.

"See, there's this stuff about Laurel," he said, looking at the ground. "I'm going round and round with it, and Jody and the kids are bearing the brunt of my fucked-upness. I gotta straighten out, I know. But I just have this . . . stuff."

"What kind of stuff?"

"When we were married, Laurel and me. I wasn't the perfect husband, Celine. I think, What could I have done differently? Did I cause our breakup? I mean, I did some things . . . Did I push her into . . . where she ended up going?"

I moved closer so I could put a hand on his shoulder. "Oh, man, Mace. That's a long way back."

"I mean it! I have this image of that beautiful girl I married. And then, like, knowing what happened to her? And it's not just guilt, it's this sense of *loss*. I can't talk to Jody about it—it only hurts her."

"We all cherish good memories of past loved ones. I do. You should. You're 'allowed.'"

He lifted his head and I was startled to see his eyes red and rimmed with tears. "Going to her house, with Conn and Welles? It was a perfectly nice house. I realized she was a, a good person. Looked like she was a great mom. I mean, we could have had *that*. Instead of what we, what we—"

"Mason! We all could have 'done better,' if we'd known better at the time. Look, Conn has been raking himself over the coals since she first went missing. Blames himself for absolutely everything. Did he try hard enough? Did he let things slip, did he not pay attention, did he say something, or *not* say something? On and on. He still falls into this emotional quicksand every day."

"What should I do about it? I can't stand this shit anymore, and I can't keep dumping my crappy state of mind on Jody and the kids."

"I think you're doing the right thing. One, you're inspecting it in your head, and that's necessary and healthy. Two, you're talking to me. Even if I don't have great advice, just letting it out helps. The only thing I would add is, bring Jody into the conversation. Tell her. Reassure her that you're working through it. Talk to Conn, too—you guys can compare notes and commiserate."

He leaned back and rubbed his eyes. "Okay," he said to himself, "okay. Okay."

We walked the long way around the cabin on our way back to Katy, taking our time so we could compose ourselves.

"Has Conn told you what we've been thinking? About David Laughlin?"

"No. Haven't talked to him in a few days." He looked at me, miserable. "I've been staying out at our camp, Celine. Just . . . giving my family a break, I'm not fit for human consumption. No cell reception out there. He left a couple of messages, though, I gotta call him back. Who's David Laughlin?"

I told him what Conn had learned from Laurel's CrossFit trainer, Dev Cohen, Jocelyn, and Gail.

His eyebrows went up. "Son of a bitch. And Laurel was laying the groundwork for a lawsuit, or charges?"

"Sound like murder motive to you?"

"Fuck yes! Lawsuit like that, his career would be over. Jail, fines, damages. Guy might do anything! Has Conn told Welles?"

"Not yet. He didn't feel he had enough information. Anyway, Welles is, uh, he disapproves of Conn or me poking around the case."

"Well, he's correct there. Except if Welles's people didn't pick up on that situation when they interviewed Laurel's coworkers, somebody sure should."

"You ever deal with anything like that? Sexual misconduct?"

"A handful of rapes over the years. Some creepers. We had a thing a few years ago where this guy put cameras in the women's room at a gas station he owned. It was a quick-stop place with a deli, mostly female employees. I wasn't involved, though, don't know how it went down."

"That's consistent with certain types of sexual deviance. I've been wondering if this guy Laughlin has a similar habit."

Mace shrugged. "Maybe. But our department doesn't deal with it much. Harassment is mainly an employer-employee thing. The attorney general's office handles that stuff."

"I don't think 'harassment' covers it—more like 'assault.' I'm disturbed by Laughlin's planning and the skill of his manipulation. Not my field of specialty, but it seems deviant, maybe pathological."

"I'm not any kind of detective, Celine. I don't even watch crime shows on TV. Don't like the kids exposed."

"Could a police agency access sealed divorce proceedings? Or compel an addiction counselor or lawyer to reveal confidential communications? Given that the individual is deceased?"

He wagged his head, uncertain. "I dunno. I'm mainly just sitting in a car or at a desk. I deal with stuff on the ground. Anything more, we hand it off to the States, private lawyers, or the AG's office. I could ask, though."

At the back of the cabin, we walked through Conn's airy stand of spruce trees, straight as telephone poles. Mason looked better—renewed a little by talking it out, I thought, probably energized a bit by the "case." Then I thought, *It's pretty sad when a living human being becomes a "case."*

"So, Mace. Tell me about Jody. How is she? You're worried about her worrying about you, and you're both worrying your kids. Makes Conn and me worry about you all!"

I laughed to lighten the moment, but my change of tack caught him by surprise. His face went stiff, and I felt I was overstepping, condescending, by going psychoanalytic on this dear friend.

"Yeah."

"Any ideas what might help fix it?"

"Maybe we need a night out together or something. Eleven years married, you kind of let that stuff slip by the wayside. Kids, jobs, bills, all the crap."

"I think that would be a good idea, Mace." I hooked my bad hand under his arm as we walked, slowing his pace. "I have a shameful secret to tell you. Up for it?"

"I guess."

"After my husband, Richard, died, right, I was completely . . . undone. At a loss. There was no God and no meaning and no love in the world."

"I'm sorry, Celine. Sounds horrible."

"It was. So about two weeks after he died, I got a call from a former girlfriend of his. I'd never met her. But she'd read his obituary and wanted to fucking 'share our grief'! I'm thinking, Share *what*? He was my *husband*! He was your *what*? And how long ago? The crazy part is, I felt *jealous*. I mean it. Jealous of this woman I knew nothing about, for ever having been intimate with Richard, for loving him once upon a time. Jesus, I hate to admit this stuff."

He had closed his eyes and was nodding as if awaiting deserved punishment.

I squeezed his arm. "I guess what I'm getting at is, might some of what Jody feels be that irrational jealousy? From seeing how Laurel's death is affecting you?"

Dully, he admitted, "Maybe."

I came around with my therapeutic coup: "So. I think you already know the solution. Start by having a night out, grown-ups only, candlelight dinner, at some nice restaurant. Remind her she's the one who has your heart. I'll tell you, Mace, speaking as a friend, as a woman? A little romance never hurts. Just that reminder. I guarantee, it'll make things easier between you."

His face remained impassive, but he nodded, and I was grateful that he didn't object to my giving him marital advice. We walked on around the corner of the cabin as he thought about it.

Katy was reading intently when we came around to the front again. She shot her tentative smile my way.

"Well, I guess we should hit the road," Mason said. Katy obediently folded her book and tucked it into her backpack.

"Kiddo, you need to use the bathroom?"

Embarrassed, Katy shook her head.

"Well, I do." Mason headed to the house.

Katy and I stood there, uncertain of each other.

"We have to get together soon," I told her. "All of us. It's been too long!"

She nodded, that tight quick little nod. Very quietly, she said, "Are you going to help my dad? So he's not so sad? He said you would help him by talking to him."

"Your father is a dear friend. We had a great talk, and I think he feels better."

I wasn't sure how much had been said in Katy's hearing and didn't want to ask a question that would tell her more than her parents had.

"Because he's been gone so much," she said to the ground. "He's been out at the camp all the time. Mom's, like, mad at him and she misses him. And she worries about him."

"He'll be back, don't worry." I kissed her on the top of her head again. When I put my arm around her shoulders, I was gratified that she leaned in against me. A child hungry for assurances.

Mason appeared at the cabin door. Katy put on her helmet, Mason double-checked her strap, put on his own. He struck me as more composed as he straddled the bike and then turned to help her climb onto the seat behind him.

"Hold on tight," he ordered. "Remember, always lean with me, not against, right?"

"I will."

"Thank you, Celine. Tell Conn I'll give him a call. I'll think about the Laughlin thing."

I nodded and he fired up the bike. He put it into gear and eased it forward and out the driveway, Katy's arms tight and helmet firmly against his broad back.

# CHAPTER 30

# CELINE

And of course there was Penny.

She had a motive and she fit the psychological profile, and was probably physically capable: She was tall, heavy, big-boned. Irene had called her a "horse." Her attitude at the cash register struck me as surly.

But whether she had means and opportunity was something only Welles could determine. I assumed the investigation would involve tracing her movements around the time of the murders, over a month ago. The police would search out her cell phone calls and emails, and talk to relatives, friends, and coworkers. But I didn't expect to have access to any information they'd come up with.

I had to think they'd also consult Penny's psychiatrist, or at least review her psych profile for details that might guide other lines of inquiry.

On this, I figured I could do pretty well without their help.

Obsessional love: Like most people, I caught my first glimpse of it in middle school. The adolescent brain and body are works in progress, going through rapid changes. The surge in hormones and social sensibilities seems to strike girls early and hard, often resulting in what I later learned to call "limerence"—infatuatory obsession, all-consuming passion defined by perseverating thoughts about the object of affection. In middle school, I recall it being almost obligatory to write some boy's name repeatedly in your spiral notebook or on the palm of your hand.

Most of my friends did; I settled for scissoring Randy Pellman's photo out of the sixth-grade yearbook and keeping it under my pillow.

Then one day in seventh grade, my friend Adelle came to school with her forearm bandaged. Naturally, we were all curious. She stayed coy and mysterious about it until recess, when she peeled off the dressing enough to show Bridgette and me her injury: the name Jason, carved into her skin, in capital letters an inch high. She swore us to secrecy, knowing we wouldn't, couldn't, abide.

We were appalled and delighted. In fact, we were a little jealous of such high passions—to Adelle's gratification. She hadn't used a knife, but had broken off the clip of a ballpoint pen and scraped its jagged metal edge over the letters again and again until they bled. She kept scraping even then, she claimed. The act proved the seriousness and permanence of her feelings for Jason, an oblivious thirteen-year-old the rest of us deemed "dorky." The scabs fell away after a week, but the name glowed in faint, pale scars for months. There was something appealing about the pain it must have caused, a willing martyrdom that proved her devotion and struck us as somehow noble. She was hung up on Jason for the entire semester, talking about him until even Brid and I started avoiding her.

I learned more about the subject years later, as an undergraduate at the University of Chicago, when we covered obsessional love disorder in one of my abnormal psychology courses. We called it by the acronym OLD. The term is a convenient catchall that describes the syndrome, but it's not a legitimate category in the *Diagnostic and Statistical Manual.* Medically, OLD arises from a stew of other dysfunctions: borderline personality disorder and obsessive-compulsive disorder, possibly with roots in infantile attachment disorders. Obsessional jealousy is one of its more obvious and dangerous manifestations.

It can make people do appalling things. Back in ab psych, our most lurid case study was that of Burt Pugach and Linda Riss, a story that made the national news in 1959 and, astonishingly, again in 1974.

When they began their affair, Burt was a successful New York lawyer of thirty-two, and Linda was just twenty-one. She was good-looking, vivacious, and single; he was unremarkable in appearance and, unbeknownst to her, had a wife and a daughter. He doted on her, but when she discovered he was married, she broke off their relationship. A determined sort, he forged divorce papers, showed them to her, and continued to "court" her. Eventually, she discovered the ruse, broke it off decisively, and reported his stalking to the New York police. Before long, she started a relationship with another man.

When Burt heard of her engagement to the new lover, he hired three thugs to attack her in a singularly sadistic way—by throwing lye in her face. The caustic liquid burned away one eye and severely damaged the other. Linda suffered disfiguring burns to the skin of her once-beautiful face and was functionally blind for the rest of her life.

It made the national news because it was such an affront, such a perversion of the tenderness and protectiveness we associate with romantic emotion.

What was a person in the grip of obsessional love capable of? The answer Pugach provided: Anything.

The police caught up with Burt, and he was quickly convicted. He ended up serving fourteen years in jail, but Linda's damage was permanent. No longer a beauty, traumatized, she became withdrawn, depressed, housebound. She tried dating, but was always rejected when she took off her head scarf and dark glasses to reveal her terrible scars.

How could the tender sentiments of affection and desire become so twisted that they could incite someone to inflict pain, disfigurement, or even death upon the object of their supposed "love"? Back at the University of Chicago, our professor challenged us with provocative questions: Surely, the perpetrator would have to be a psychopath, right?

Of course! we agreed. "He deserved the death penalty!" one of my classmates blurted. That begat a heated discussion and digression. Professor Thurman listened and served as provocateur, holding in reserve a surprise she had for us.

Remembering it, I couldn't help thinking of the daisy chain of love and murder, of Lance Burton and Fecteau and his wife, of Irene, of all the spouses who endure abuse and, through love or need or insecurity, then forgive. And have to live through it all again

Laurel's story seemed to be a case study in its own right, the kinked saga of not one but two such obsessional loves: Tony's for Laurel, Penny's for Tony. Laurel had tried to free herself, as Linda Riss had, but—even if Tony wasn't her murderer—had been too enmeshed and had failed. There it was again, I thought, love and murder, or at least love and horrific cruelty, twining together in cause and effect and cause again. Really, it was a Möbius strip. You can place your fingers opposite each other on a Möbius strip and call one side love and the other hate, but trace one finger around the loop and it will encounter the other. It's all the same side.

To cap off the unit on obsessional love, Professor Thurman had us watch *Fatal Attraction,* which had been a huge box-office hit a decade earlier. Glenn Close putting that bunny to boil on the stove in her former lover's home—yes, that stayed with us. We cast sideways glances at our current flames or hopefuls for days afterward.

With Conn still at work, I did some online research on generalities, then on case studies that might reveal something. There were dozens: cases of murder, imprisonment, disfigurement, torture. In Kansas, a man imprisoned his beloved in a dog kennel for some weeks, then ran her over with his car when she managed to escape, killing her. In Oregon, a woman castrated her straying boyfriend and saved his parts in a mason jar, thus "owning" him forever.

My hands started shaking after a few minutes. This kind of thing doesn't sit well with me. Conn thinks of me as a nice person, and at bottom maybe I am. But this stuff sparks an ugly burn in me.

I tried to get a grip on my emotions by resorting to an academic and clinical approach. I cataloged the elements of OLD, writing down key characteristics. It was all online, nothing much new since that ab psych class twenty years ago.

The obsessed, in idealizing their loved ones, inadvertently objectify them. They become "things"—possessions to be claimed, owned, jealously guarded. As Burt Pugach told Linda Riss, "If I can't have you, no one else will. And when I get finished with you, no one else will want you." From the little I knew about her, Penny seemed to fit this construct perfectly.

Another is the deluded belief that the other person reciprocates this feeling. When they deny it, the obsessed person often develops complex rationales: She's only holding back because she's insecure about expressing her true feelings and just needs my "encouragement." Or he's afraid of hurting his current wife and just needs me to help stiffen his spine enough to ditch her. Again, Penny to a T, and probably Tony.

Also, in their consuming preoccupation with the "loved" one, the obsessed person tends to lose empathy for or disengage from even their closest friends and family. I didn't know enough about Penny to say, but Tony seemed a good example, given his neglect of Irene and their children.

Did Laughlin fit into this framework? Had he become obsessed with Laurel—would that contribute to his motivational complex, beyond a desire to silence her? Aside from his objectification of his prey, I didn't think OLD symptoms correlated with his other deviant sociosexual traits. I settled for writing his name with a question mark after it.

More recent literature tended to embrace a neurological assessment. Functional MRIs of people in extreme states of limerence showed increased activity in the ventral tegmental area of the brain, indicative of high production of dopamine, the neurotransmitter associated with reward and gratification. Another key area was the insular cortex, associated with compassion, empathy, interpersonal experience—and, not surprisingly, anxiety.

Its permutations can be surprising. Professor Thurman, after we'd vented on how crazy Burt Pugach was, told us the astonishing punch line she'd been holding back.

Turns out Pugach kept in touch with Linda during his fourteen years in prison. When he got out, he proposed to her, she assented, and they married in 1974. They even wrote a book about it, *A Very Different Love Story,* published in 1976. They lived together in apparent happiness for twenty-some years, often appearing in public, Linda smiling beneath her huge dark glasses and the folds of her head scarf. In 1997, at the age of seventy, Burt had an affair with another woman—and again demonstrated obsessive, controlling urges—but Linda forgave him. I read later that they stayed together until her death in 2013, at seventy-five. Of natural causes.

When Professor Thurman told us this, we were absolutely gobsmacked.

"So, what does this tell us about human nature?" she asked, baiting us. "What should we conclude about the psychology of love? Of violence?"

We scratched our heads, baffled.

"No answers? No conclusions?" she prodded, laughing. "Well, me neither!" She was a terrific teacher, inspiring in all of us a desire to probe human behavior until we could answer some of these questions.

Pondering it now, my head spun again, and I lost all mooring in what, exactly, the human animal is. Penny, Tony, Laurel—who could truly plumb those depths, tease apart their layered motives, chart those dynamics?

I shut off the computer and took myself outside to a bright July afternoon, where the world made a little more sense.

I went for a jog up the falls road, pushing myself in an effort to burn off the discomfort that had come over me. Sure enough, the silver sliver of the falls, sending its plume of cold mist down the cleft, worked its elemental magic. I inhaled it deeply and tried to exhale every trace of Burt Pugach. As I was coming back, feeling better, my phone rang, and I was pleased to see that it was Conn. He was just finishing up work and suggested I meet him in Montpelier for dinner out.

Montpelier isn't a big town, but it boasts a robust restaurant culture. In summer, a dozen cafés and restaurants put out tables on sidewalks or take over parking spaces in the street. I spotted Conn at a table outside of Kismet, talking on his cell phone. I was struck by him, as always: a well-made man, easy in his frame, wearing that rusticized business casual outfit of sport jacket, slacks, and hiking boots.

To my surprise, he stood up when he saw me.

"Welles," he said. "Wants me to swing by Laurel's house. Let's go. We can come back for dinner after."

"You sure he'll be happy to see me?"

Conn chuckled grimly. "I don't give a shit. I need you to protect me from his lapdog. Give me a psych profile on her."

# CHAPTER 31

# CELINE

It took us half an hour to drive to Laurel's place, a few miles outside Waterbury. I told Conn about my visit from Mason and Katy, and reminded him to give Mace a call soon. Moving on to Penny, I gave him an overview of the literature on obsessive love disorder, the saga of Pugach and Riss, and the limitless cruelty OLD could incite.

All he could do was shake his head, appalled.

Then Laughlin: I mentioned the penchant for sexual predators to seek souvenirs, and told him Mason's story of the gas station owner with the camera in the bathroom. It was something we might want to consider when poking around Laughlin's life.

Conn didn't know what Welles wanted, but he was glad for an opportunity to learn what they'd found during the day's search. We both felt optimistic that some of our questions would finally be answered by Laurel's papers.

"And I'm serious about Selanski," Conn said. "She deliberately pushes my buttons, pushes the limits every time I see her. I've had it. If they don't want you there, tough luck, they don't have to see me, either."

"Did you talk to Ricky about writing an exposé on Laughlin?"

"I sure did. As I expected, she was a bit worried about conflict of interest. But I twisted her arm and promised I'd be a good boy. She gave me the green light. I'm legit."

"Is it time to mention Laughlin to Welles?"

"If he plays nice, maybe."

Conn's affect since I met him at the restaurant had struck me as un-characteristically curt or tough—determined, even a bit smug. Having a legitimate excuse to probe events at Martinson's had given him a better hand to play. Thinking about it, I decided that taking an active role in solving his sister's murder could potentially have therapeutic benefit. But his pugilistic tone made me uneasy.

"On the warpath, are we?" I asked.

"Damn straight. About time."

"Well," I said, "I'm glad I'm here to referee."

Maple Meadow seemed like a pleasant neighborhood, better maintained than many mobile-home parks I'd seen. Laurel's place was a double-wide in a tree-shaded yard bordered by hedges. Whatever I'd expected, I didn't anticipate the relative calm—we saw only two cars on the street near her driveway, a State Police cruiser and an unmarked sedan. No yellow tape, crime scene vans, or white-suited figures: The forensics people had apparently finished their work.

Welles came out of the house, looking dour, as we walked into the driveway. "Ms. Gabrielli, I don't recall inviting you here," he said.

"She's my witness," Conn told him. "I wanted her professional as-sessment of Selanski's attitude. Which I'm taking zero of today, Welles."

Welles's eyes flicked between the two of us. "Your outlook, Mr. Whitman—"

"Is going to be a problem? Here's the real problem: It's twenty-nine days since my sister disappeared. Did you find anything useful today, or do you just want me here to yank my chain?"

Selanski appeared at the door of Laurel's house, but Welles waved her back. She frowned, but turned and went back inside.

Welles pondered his options a little longer, but he must have taken the measure of Conn and apparently decided getting his back hairs up wouldn't be helpful. Beckoning us to follow, he stepped to a picnic table near a nylon-covered Quonset shed. When he sat, it was with the weariness of a man who'd had a long day.

"I've spoken to Detective Selanski," he said. "We have no reason to consider you a suspect. She has been instructed to be more courteous and understanding. We need to talk. Would you be up for her joining us, or would we all just get into a pissing contest?"

Conn shrugged an assent. As he and I took seats, Welles went to the door and called in for Selanski.

I had only met Welles twice, Selanski just once, but to my eye they looked tired and disappointed. We nodded curt greetings to Selanski as she sat next to Welles, opposite Conn and me. A little fleet of kids on bicycles floated past the driveway, heads turning our way.

"I can't sugarcoat the fact that it's been a frustrating day," Welles began. "We had a full search team here, assisted by people from the forensics lab. We brought in a canine unit, too. House, yard, shed."

"Cutting to the chase," Selanski said, "we didn't get much. Our best finds were fingerprints. Lots of them, various individuals. We expedited comparisons on AFIS and got only one known match—Tony Shapiro. No surprise there."

"I'm most interested in the papers," Conn said. "I gotta deal with those girls. Did you find anything that—"

"That's why we wanted to talk to you tonight," Welles said. "Her file cabinets were empty."

"Like *nada*," Selanski elaborated. "Either your sister never saved a receipt or her income tax forms or bank statements or pay stubs, not one, in her entire effin' *life*—not to mention her kids' birth certificates or vaccination records—or somebody took her papers."

Conn rocked with that, drew a hand across his brow. "Were the file cabinets jimmied?"

"No indication of it. We had a VSP locksmith do the honors today."

"Anything else missing?"

"Yeah, the nice bike in the shed," Selanski bit off.

They were all reading a great deal into this turn of events, but aside from sharing their disappointment, I didn't feel I was seeing the whole picture.

"Can I ask what this suggests to you?" I ventured. Under the table, my hand found Conn's.

"Somebody wants to hide something," Welles said. "The computer and the bike could have been stolen just for their cash value—personally, I doubt it—but not the papers. There must have been material in there that someone didn't want us to see. Something incriminating."

I squeezed Conn's hand, hoping he got the message: *Laughlin?*

"And it makes it harder to picture Penny McKenzie as the perpetrator," Selanski said. "I mean, she might have killed them, your proverbial crime of passion. But why would she give two shits about Laurel's papers? And when would she have come? She's been dead for a week."

"How'd somebody get inside?"

Welles began, "We examined every window and door. There's no sign of forced entry."

Selanski finished for him: "Suggesting that someone had keys. For the door and for the file cabinets. Where would they get the keys? Most likely from your sister's pocket."

Conn was still reeling. "So . . . where does that leave you? I mean, what's left for you to go on?"

"The various fingerprints could turn out to have value, if we can match them to someone. We'll request a warrant to look at your sister's cell phone records."

Selanski snorted. "Yeah—if and when we can even find who her provider was! I mean, who? Verizon, AT&T, Sprint, half a dozen others serve this region. In police parlance, the whole thing is a big pain in the ass."

"As her next of kin, I assume I have some responsibility to deal with her estate. Should I start paying her bills? And her kids—do I have any rights or guardianship responsibilities? I don't know anything about this process."

Welles was trying to find anything optimistic. "If she filed any legal papers, they'll be on record at the county courthouse."

"I have a will," Conn said, shaking his head. "It's in my file cabinet at home. Downloaded a template from online. Never filed it anywhere."

"But she had kids to think of, Conn," I said. "She might have been more disciplined about legal formalities."

"As for her financial obligations," Selanski said, "it's nearing the end of the month. She may get bills in the mail. Hopefully we'll be able to determine her cell service, credit accounts, and so on."

Her gaze went past Conn and me, and we turned. Some kids had collected at the end of the driveway, a couple with soccer balls in hand. They stared at us unabashedly.

"You kids *scat!*" Selanski shouted. She clapped her hands at them, one sharp *whack!* They scattered quickly.

Conn cracked a little grin at that. Maybe Selanski's personality had its uses after all.

The three of us stayed sitting, Welles rubbing his brow and saying nothing. This was turning into an avalanche for him. I wished I could comfort him somehow.

But Conn—after a few stunned moments, the gears had started turning in his head. He took out his phone and began pecking at it. When I leaned over, I saw that he had pulled up the Vermont Agency of Commerce website. He scrolled and tapped some more until his screen showed the Mobile Home Park Registry.

Selanski watched him for a moment, then rubbed her hands together and said brightly, "So! Got sumpin' for us?"

Conn actually smiled at her. "Yes. Have you checked her mailbox? She went camping around the end of June—you'd think her monthly bills would be in there."

We had passed Maple Meadow's post boxes as we drove in, a metal bank of about thirty unit-numbered lock boxes mounted at the entrance, where the rural mail carrier could easily access them.

"Well, there are legal issues to opening her box," Welles said. "Technically, mailboxes are federal property. We'll need the postmaster's permission and a copy of the master key."

One more scroll on his phone screen, and Conn stood up abruptly. "Looks like we're in luck. Maple Meadow has a resident manager. I'm going down there. She might have a master key."

Welles started to object—legal concerns.

Conn interrupted him. "Captain Welles, you're a good man. But I need to deal with this property and figure out a future for her kids. The manager probably has a master key. Small towns up here, nobody plays strictly by the rules—she's got to deal with tenants vanishing and leaving no rent or forwarding address. If she does, I'm going to open Laurel's box and look at her mail. You can come and observe, attest to the chain of custody, or you can arrest me in the act. It's really that simple. For all any of us knows, I *am* her designated executor, so it's not even illegal. If at some point it turns out to be a problem, I'll stipulate that I did it on my own and that you tried to prevent me. But we're up shit crick unless we can get some piece of paper and figure out what's going on."

Before Welles could answer, Conn strode to the end of the driveway, then turned left. I hurried to catch up with him.

Three houses down, he turned in at number 12, another double-wide in a well-maintained lot. He rang the doorbell and we waited for half a minute. The resident manager was a tidy woman in her fifties, wearing an apron over jeans and a white blouse. From the smell of chopped onions, I assumed she was starting to cook dinner. She opened the screen door to look us up and down, face neutral.

"Are you Paula Jefferson?" Conn asked. "Resident manager?"

"That would be me. What can I do for you?"

"I'm Conn Whitman—" Conn began.

"Oh, of course! My husband and I read your columns. They're our favorite."

"Well, I'm flattered—thank you! But I'm not here in a professional capacity, Paula. I am Trudy Carlson's brother. This is Celine Gabrielli, head of the school district's guidance department. We're over at her house now with the State Police, working on how to deal with her affairs and what to do with her kids."

Paula made a sympathetic face and leaned out of her doorway to peer down the street, where the back end of the State Police cruiser was just visible. "Yes, I saw the crime scene people earlier. I'm so sorry about Trudy. So sad for her and the kids. She's been a good neighbor."

"We were just discussing the investigation with Captain Welles and Detective Selanski? And we realized that her lot rent is probably overdue."

"Well, yes, it is. Of course, we completely understand—"

"So we were hoping you had a master key for the mailboxes. We could get her mail and I'll see to the rent check."

She hesitated, but not for long. "Yes. But I can't just hand it to you. I'll go with you." She disappeared inside and came back moments later with a key on a big wooden tag.

We walked back to the front of the main drive. Welles, looking harried, and Selanski with her tiny cynical grin, waited at the end of Laurel's driveway. Conn introduced them, and then the five of us made a small parade to the metal cluster mailbox.

Paula unlocked the master panel and swung it aside to reveal all the cubbyholes. Conn put on a pair of latex gloves Selanski handed him, then took out a small handful of envelopes and fliers. He passed them to Selanski, who put them into a plastic evidence bag. Paula re-locked the panel, we thanked her, and then we dawdled at the box as she headed back to her house.

"Doesn't look like a month's worth of mail," Conn commented. "She sent the kids to camp on June 23, went camping on the twenty-fifth or so. There should bills from the first week of July. Also, Laurel subscribed to at least three periodicals—*The Week*, *National Geographic Kids*, and *Outside*. The most recent issues in the house are last month's—where are the July editions?"

Welles gave him an appraising look. He'd underestimated Conn's observational skills.

"The earliest postmark here is July 16," Selanski said. "Suggesting that somebody got in here and emptied this box sometime prior to that date and after Trudy, Laurel, went missing."

Turning back toward Laurel's house, she swung the bag of mail like a kid with a sack of Halloween candy. "Who, if I may ask, the fuck?" she said to herself. "Oh my goo'ness gracious!"

We reconvened at the picnic table. Under the table, Conn gripped my hand tightly, and he turned to me, a question in his eyes. I nodded.

"Can I . . . ?" Conn asked, gesturing at the mail.

"What are you thinking you'll find in there?" Welles asked.

"For starters, if her Maple Meadow rent bill is in there, I need to pay it."

"And . . . ?" Selanski said teasingly. She sensed Conn had something to spill.

"I'd love to find a letter or a bill from a lawyer or legal-aid organization."

"Why would you expect that?"

They waited as Conn put his thoughts in order. "I have an idea who might have wanted to take her papers," he said.

That got their attention.

He started strategically, explaining that he had an assignment from the *Herald* to look into alleged systematic sexual harassment and assault at a regional outlet of a major chain store. Though he did not know the physical, anatomical details yet, he had corroborated victims' claims through interviews with store staff.

Welles was impatient with the long warm-up. "And this has what to do with Trudy Carlson?"

Conn finally gave them the crucial details: "As it happens, the store in question is Martinson's, and the perpetrator is David Laughlin, the store manager and my sister's boss. Laurel was preparing some kind of legal action against him. She interviewed her coworkers and former staff, preparing to pursue some kind of civil or criminal remedy. From what I've heard, she had enough material to sink David Laughlin's ship. He'd want to stop her."

"How long have you known about this?" Welles's eyes and voice were dead flat. "When were you thinking you might share this information with us?"

"I got this assignment yesterday, Captain. I then interviewed two Martinson's staff about twenty-four hours ago. I was planning to call you, but you beat me to it. I'm telling you now because the theft of

Laurel's papers and computer and mail sure as shit looks like something Laughlin might do. And sure as shit reinforces the idea that he had a motive for killing her."

Welles wasn't letting it go that easily. "I was explicit with you, Whitman, that you'd have consequences—"

"I've compromised nothing. These women are scared to death for their jobs and their marriages, and for their sake I've been very careful. He is a skilled, experienced manipulator who seeks leverage and uses it cleverly and cruelly. I am working on assignment from the publisher of the *Richfield Herald*, a respected independent daily newspaper. And I have just passed on everything I know so far."

Selanski turned to Welles. "What're we gonna do with this guy?"

We sat there, stalemated. Welles and Selanski were furious at Conn for his freelancing, but he was right, it was highly unlikely he had compromised their investigation in any way. And, yes, he was acting as a dutiful member of the Fourth Estate. He had also just opened up what had been looking like a badly stalled investigation.

After a moment, Selanski broke a sardonic chuckle. "Well, all I can say is, A, fuck me. And B, I gotta have a smoke."

She stood, found her vaping apparatus, and fired it up. Welles glared at us as Selanski went to pace back and forth at the far end of the yard, blowing gouts of steam into the air like an old-fashioned locomotive.

In retrospect, I see that evening changed the dynamic between Conn, Welles, and Selanski. Welles couldn't deny that Conn's eyes and deductive powers were astute, a valuable resource. His knowledge of how things worked, even his bullheadedness, made him an asset. And Selanski—Conn and I came to appreciate her style that day. She seemed to reciprocate, to the extent that she later opened some doors for Conn.

Somehow, a tacit understanding emerged: that Conn, and even his shrink fiancée, would be allowed a greater role in the investigation. We'd all trust one another a little more. Conn and I would have access to more information from their forensic findings, and they'd gain a pair of investigators chasing down details that the Major Crime Unit simply didn't have the manpower for.

The mail in the box led us nowhere—fundraising solicitations from environmental organizations, high-speed internet service offers, the new tag for her car's license plate.

Still, Conn and I felt a little better as we drove home. We laughed as we both admitted to getting a kick out of Selanski. And the deliberate removal of evidence was a "dog in the night-time" clue: The absence itself was highly suggestive of motive.

We felt as if we'd finally made progress, taken the first steps on the road to solving the many riddles surrounding Laurel's, Trudy's, fate. In this we were right—but it was hardly what we anticipated. Perhaps our new sense of license led us astray. We'd learned at once too much and too little. We gained a sense of our own powers that we didn't deserve, hubris that blinded us to much that should have been obvious.

# CHAPTER 32

# CONN

Mace came out to greet me with a wan smile. I had brought my rifle, a Ruger .22, to supplement the small arsenal I knew he had, mostly left over from his father's firearm collection. It's awkward to hug someone when you're carrying a long gun, but we managed it and then went inside. Mace had taken a few guns from the safe and arrayed them on the dining table with some boxes of ammo. I looked them over as he went to make a pot of coffee.

I took my time loading cartridges into the Ruger's magazine and thought about what I'd done earlier in the day. I had come away from our session with Welles and Selanski frustrated but feeling somewhat wiser.

I had also made a point of establishing trust with Paula, Maple Meadow's resident manager. Before coming to the Kings' camp, I went back to her with a check for Laurel's lot rent, then handed her a forwarding notice for her to put in Laurel's mailbox. I'd picked up a form at the PO and filled it out with a signature so illegible that it could be anybody's. The address I gave was my own, on Whimsy Falls Road. Paula didn't blink. We went out to the box together, found nothing new in it, and I watched her put it in for the mail delivery person to find. I figured this was better than pestering her every day for the key, or fighting with Welles over legal niceties. My sister was dead, her bills needed to be paid. And in this neck of the woods, small towns still worked this way: Common sense and practicality prevailed.

My date with Mace was long overdue. According to Celine, he had
been staying mostly out here at his family's camp in an attempt to spare
his wife and kids his disarray. I sympathized because I'd done the same
thing—hiding from the world—after my return from Washington.

When he'd finally returned my phone calls, we arranged to get together to do some target practice, drink a few beers, and talk. Celine had
offered some suggestions on how to reassure him and maybe coax him
back into the fold. Also, I figured that, given that he was still on leave,
he was out of the loop on the investigation. I planned to catch him up
on what we had learned, see if I could pick his brain.

"King Ranch," as we called it, was deep in the Northeast Kingdom
woods. The property had been in the family for generations—two hundred remote acres, with a cabin and barnlike garage perched near the
shore of a pond. It was the kind of place you couldn't buy today, very
private—the Kings owned both sides of most of the pond, and there
were only two other camps on the water, out of view around a spit of
woodland. The forest was deeply shadowed by pines and cedars, the
pond shallow and thick with water lilies. The Kings' wooden dock extended fifteen feet over the water, and they kept a little aluminum skiff
on the bank that we took out to fish for pike and pickerel.

I'd never met Mace's grandfather, but his father, Warren King, had
made good use of the place. I spent a lot of time out there as a kid, and
Laurel had come occasionally, too. The cabin was built of rough-sawn
boards, low-ceilinged but bigger than my father's log cabin, with a living
room, separate kitchen, utility rooms, and two sleeping rooms with bunk
beds. Warren King had been an avid hunter and fisherman, and a few
deer heads and stuffed pike, scary big, still stared down from the walls.

Later in life, Mr. King had taken up restoring antique cars and had
built the little barn to serve as his workshop. There was always an old
Studebaker or Edsel in there, undergoing Warren's loving restoration.
It was generous of him to let Mace and me work on our cars and motorcycles in there.

Mr. King had also set up a target range back in the woods, plowing
up a shoulder-high berm of earth and building two firing benches and

some target mounts. I put holes in my first tin can back there, and target practice was one of our staple activities when I visited. My shooting was never great—Laurel had better aim—but I had fun with it nonetheless.

Warren King had served in Vietnam, and had retained a military manner and a buzz cut. I found him intimidating, but he was always patient as he taught us to clean fish or shoot, and he gave us expert tutelage in car repair. His parenting was what my folks disapprovingly called "old school"—he'd take a belt to Mace now and then—but he had only once shown anger when I was around.

One weekend in high school, Mace and I had the place to ourselves, and we invited some friends out. We got puking drunk, whooping it up and leaving beer cans and tire ruts in the yard. Mr. King gave Mace and me a tough-love lecture and made us spend a grueling day cleaning up and regrading the lawn and nearby woods with shovels and rakes. Both lecture and shovels raised blisters, which we well deserved.

Looking back, I realized that it had been, still was, a very "male" environment—the hunting trophies, the guns, the rugged interior, the car repairs. Mrs. King was a smart and capable woman, but she seemed cast as the subservient wife and mother more typical of 1950s TV than 1980s female norms. That didn't prevent me from scarfing down the heaps of scrambled eggs she served up, or the cherry pies she baked for us.

The place hadn't changed much since those days: still an antique round oak table in the center of the L-shaped living-dining room, still a couple of sagging rattan armchairs, a rocker, a buffet with curios on it. Used paper targets were still tacked to a section of wall, shooters' names scribbled on them, souvenirs of exceptional sessions at the range. Warren King had been the best back then, of course, but recent targets suggested that Jody and Marshall had the sharpest eyes in the family. Other newer additions were drawings by Katy and Marshall—flowers and cars, respectively—photos of Jody on her Yamaha in midair or popping wheelies at motocross events, and a newspaper clipping with a photo showing Mace on the job, helping kids out of an overturned school bus and looking pretty heroic.

Mace had brought out a couple of his father's deer rifles, a 30-30

Winchester lever-action and a Springfield 30-06, classics with good scopes that Warren had meticulously bench-sighted long ago. Just "for shits and giggles," as Mace put it, he also set out an old .45-caliber cowboy six-shooter, with belt and holster. We checked their chambers and action as we warmed our bellies with coffee.

"So, Mace—uh, shooting's okay? I mean, after the thing at Big Lots?"

"Well, yeah. But I didn't fire. And I figured I'd better get back on that horse or stop carrying a sidearm." He grimaced as he took a sip of the scalding coffee. "I thought of going fishing, but then, you had your underwater thing, I worried—"

"Nah. I've been swimming same as usual. No PTSD. That I can't handle anyway."

He nodded. "How's Celine?"

"She's doing well—summer vacation. Sends you her love." I flashed back to Peacham Pond and couldn't help confiding: "I am so head over heels, Mace. She is . . . I don't know where to start. We've even mentioned marriage."

"About time. I'm happy for you." But his eyes wandered, and he looked lost again, anything but happy. I knew he was thinking about the places love leads, remembering Laurel, no doubt worrying about Jody.

"How about we do some shooting?" I suggested.

We gathered up the gear, slung rifle straps over shoulders, and carried ammo and targets. Mace brought a pack of paper targets, but he also had a couple of shopping bags full of beer cans, a perennial favorite. There were a lot of cans—given how much weight Mace had lost, I wondered if he consumed calories in any other form.

We followed a faint path through the pines for a hundred yards. Back in the clearing, we set down our equipment on the shooting benches, then headed out to arrange cans and paper targets on heavy wooden mounts and straw bales set up at the berm.

To warm up, I opted to start with my own gun. Mace loaded the

Winchester, and then we put on headphones. My Ruger made a cap-gun *pop!* compared to the percussion of Mace's 30-30, which hit the side of my head like a slap. My beer can stayed put, Mace's flung itself up the dirt berm.

"It's my scope," I told him. "Needs calibrating."

"Yuh-huh." Mace flicked me a skeptical grin.

We emptied and reloaded and emptied again, and I began flipping cans, too. The gunpowder smell filled the clearing and smoke-ghosts sifted away through the trees. After a while we opted for a break and took off our headphones.

"Time to make some new targets," Mace quipped. He'd brought a full six-pack of Budweiser tall boys along with the empties.

We popped our tops and lounged on the benches. The silence in the pine woods seemed cottony in the aftermath of the 30-30. I sipped, Mace quaffed thirstily.

"So, we saw Welles and Selanski yesterday," I said.

"Anything new?"

"They did a thorough search of her house and grounds. Didn't find anything important, they say. But some things had been taken from the house, with pretty big implications."

"Oh? Like what?"

"Her papers. I mean *everything*—bills, receipts, bank statements, any legal stuff. Her mailbox had been emptied at some point, too."

"What the fuck?"

"What indeed. I was hoping there'd be a will, or guardianship provisions for the girls. The foster family are okay people, but it's not a great situation. It would be helpful if I knew more about Laurel's wishes, but without papers, we're pretty well stymied."

"You tell them about the scumbag at Martinson's, what's his name . . . ?"

"Laughlin. Yes, and they perked their ears up. I'm not sure where they'll go with it, but Ricky Thurston gave me the green light to write an exposé of him—do some poking around anyway. Meaning Welles can't get too pissy about my asking questions."

Mason finished his beer, pried another from its collar. "I heard Irene Shapiro died. Did you know?"

"No." My shoulders sagged as a pang of sorrow hit me. I knew Celine would be heartbroken.

"It's a mess," he said. "Whole thing's this big . . . mess."

"You want to tell me where you're at?"

"Ah, it's just self-pitying lost-boy bullshit. I gotta get over it and get back to being a grown-up. Back to my family. My job."

I sipped some beer, waiting. A pair of crows flew over, the forest coming back to life now that the shooting had stopped for a while.

"But I mean, back at the house, you telling me about Celine? Feeling that way? Conn, promise me you'll never tell anyone, okay? Jody's the greatest, a wonderful woman who has put up with more fucking shit . . . I love her, I owe her. But that thing where you can't find the words? For me, that's how it was with Laurel."

"Mace. First love. It only happens once. Etches itself on your soul. You were kids. Everything good was going to happen, forever."

"I know. It's fucked up, is all."

I could have gotten psychological on him, explaining as Celine had that Laurel's death had triggered feelings and memories that were probably idealized, heightened by nostalgia, guilt, a sense of loss. But I figured I'd do better to keep things simple, keep silent and just listen.

"Thing is," Mace went on. "Where she was killed—her tent site?"

"What about it?"

"I was wondering about it? So I asked a guy I know at the state forensic lab. Turns out I was right, it was that place we used to go. Back in the day. Same place, above Pendleton Pond—with the ridge?"

I had wondered the same thing, and I did remember. As teenagers, Mason and I had camped out in dozens of random places, including a particularly fine spot not far from Pendleton Pond. It was a mile from a class-four dirt road, up a steep hill in thick woods. At the crest, a three-foot ridge of granite thrust out of the soil and ran about a hundred feet through the woods. It was a rare geological formation that created a little windbreak with a flat shelf just below, perfect for putting up a tent or just sleeping under the stars. A precipitous half mile down the far side was the rocky shore of the pond, a narrow cove good for swimming on hot days. There wasn't a path to the campsite, meaning you had to tangle your way up through trees and prickly low growth. We'd never encountered anyone else there, never even found a beer can or cigarette butt.

"A great place," I affirmed. "Very private."

"When you went off to grad school, Laurel and I used to go there. It was like our . . . honeymoon spot. I guess she still went there sometimes. Maybe all her memories of me weren't too bad."

"Oh, man, Mace. Of course they weren't."

"It's fucked up, you know? It was our special place. Set up the tent, go skinny-dipping in the lake, hike back up. Build a campfire against the granite, like a fireplace, cook dinner. Make love. Talk late into the night." His face was flushed, from beer or feeling. "And that's where she gets *killed*? How fucked up is that? It's these *ironies*, man, the fucking *ironies*. Whatever you loved, that's what comes back to hurt you?"

"Mace, you gotta let it go. You can't take life's ironies personally. Everybody gets their share."

"I know."

I felt a pang of sympathy for him. He looked worn, and there was an almost pleading expression in his eyes, begging for understanding.

"What can I do for you, Mace? When I came back from DC, my head so far up my ass, you really helped me. The food you brought me was the only thing I consumed besides bourbon. You said the right things. What can I do for you now?"

He appeared to ponder that, as if maybe he did have something specific to ask of me. But then he just nodded, clapped me on the thigh, forced a smile. "Just what you're doing, man. Just what you're doing."

I switched over to the Springfield, and we blew holes in more cans and paper targets. Even through headphones, I could hear our shots echoing off hillsides a mile or more away. My shoulder began to ache after

only a dozen shots. After a time we goofed with the old Colt, putting
on the belt and holster and practicing a quick draw. Neither of us hit
anything, but the attempt got us laughing.

Eventually we both knew we were done. We picked up our brass
and the mess of targets and headed back to the cabin. Inside, we laid
the guns on the big table, and Mace brought over a couple of rods,
some patches, solvent, and oil. As his father had drilled us, we began
cleaning the rifles.

"You up for talking about the investigation?" I asked. "Don't have
to. If it's uncomfortable."

"Why not? I can't promise any great inspirations, though."

"I'm thinking mainly of this asshole Laughlin. I mean, who else
would want to remove Laurel's papers, and her mail?"

"For the papers, he'd want to find her notes on her case against him,
keep them from anybody else's eyes. But why the mail?"

"I was thinking something from the lawyer. Papers to sign, a bill."

Mace shrugged. "Makes sense."

He was dividing his time between his fourth beer and the Springfield. He put a bore guide into the breech, then wet a patch with solvent,
attached it to the rod, and worked it through the barrel. This was good,
I thought, more like old times, when we could compare notes on life or
brainstorm or shoot the shit, intuitively following the other's thoughts.

"All we've got on Laughlin is a motive," I pointed out. "Could Welles
go into his house on the basis of his having a motive?"

Mason shook his head. "Can't get a warrant on motive alone. I
mean, how many people would have a 'motive' to kill me? I've gotten
people's licenses yanked, I've broken up domestic quarrels and taken violent spouses to jail. If I woke up dead one fine day, you couldn't just go
search the house of everyone who might have a 'motive.' Anyway, he'd
have to be a major dumbass to hang on to the papers. He'd've burned
'em long ago. Computer's burned, too, or sitting on the bottom of Lake
Champlain."

Frustrated, I thought about it as I worked on my Ruger, pushing
the scrap of rag through, savoring the volatile solvent smell.

"Celine did a criminal records search and came back with nothing. I can talk to more staff at Martinson's, but I doubt it would add much to what we already know. What else can I do?"

"Hey, don't ask me! You're the investigative wunderkind." Mace took a long swallow of beer and thoughtfully screwed the brush head onto his rod. "But the thing about records searches is, not every crook gets accused, let alone convicted. So, no record."

A good point. The absence of a formal record was no guarantee that Laughlin was innocent of prior misdeeds.

Mace went on: "Did Celine tell you about the thing we had a couple years ago, the gas station owner with a camera in the women's room?"

"Yes."

"She says something like that would be consistent with Laughlin. Compromise his victims. Give him coercive leverage after the fact."

"The gas station sounds like pure voyeurism. Our guy is more the hands-on type. He'd want the camera where he did his thing. Where would he put it?"

"Hm. Going into a bathroom with staff would get him noticed pretty quick. More likely it'd be his office, or some storeroom, some-place where he could close the door—" Mace stopped and looked at me sharply. "Why? What are you thinking?"

"Maybe I could get in there. See if I can find—"

"No way, Conn! Wandering around in the back rooms at Martinson's? Number one, you'd get caught at it. Number two, you'd compromise the evidentiary value of anything you found. Number three, if there *is* a camera in there, it'll record you coming to find it! Laughlin will know all about you. He'll cover his tracks, destroy evidence."

I thought back to my inept midnight visit to Laurel's house. Mason was right. Spying on Laughlin was a ridiculous idea. Even recruiting Gail Pelkey to seek out a camera wouldn't work because it would record her looking for it. Selanski's parable of the hunters was spot-on. And Laughlin had us stymied again.

"Yeah. Dumb idea. I'm just . . . frustrated."

We were quiet as we oiled the guns and gave them a final dry wipe.

Then we carried them to the safe and set them inside along with the ammo boxes. Mace shut the heavy door and spun the combination dial.

By the time he walked me out to my car, Mace had become reserved, his face going impassive: Mason King struggling to manage his feelings. I needed to head home, but I felt reluctant to leave him.

I stalled by taking a moment to appreciate his motorcycle again, contemplating the paint job, feeling that odd mental tickle. Then I made a detour to the dock to look over the pond, Mason tagging behind me. Dragonflies stitched back and forth over the lily pads, hunting mosquitos, and a hundred yards away at the bend, a heron stood motionless in the shallows, ghostly gray.

We had occasionally jumped off the end of the dock, but it really wasn't a place for swimming. The bottom was muck, the weeds too thick. Warren King had once shot a gigantic snapping turtle in there, and nobody relished the idea of swimming with creatures like that.

Now, the dock struck me as decrepit, its deck boards starting to rot, moss starting up on the posts. Next to it, the aluminum skiff was cradled on its trailer, its tiny Yamaha outboard cocked forward, oars on the bottom in a couple of inches of rainwater.

In fact, the whole place struck me as forlorn. Mason hadn't mowed the patch of grass that surrounded the camp, and the roofs of both cabin and garage sprouted green shoots growing from forest detritus gathered on the shingles. Like the man himself, King Ranch showed signs of neglect. I wondered what Mace busied himself with in his solitary days out here beside drinking.

"So—doing any fishing?" I asked.

"Went out a few days ago. It's getting pretty weedy, though. Didn't put a line in."

"Not to sound like I know shit, Mace, but I'm wondering if staying out here is good for you. Maybe it's time to come on back to civilization."

"I know. I'm about there."

"How about we have dinner at my place, you and Jody and the kids? Sometime in the next week or two?"

"Sounds good," he said expressionlessly.

I didn't know what else I could do for him, so I gave him another awkward hug and headed to my car.

# CHAPTER 33

# CONN

Not all crooks get caught or accused: Mace's comment stayed with me. The absence of a formal record on Laughlin didn't mean he had a spotless past. After I got back from King Ranch, I spent some hours on my computer, taking a second run at him. I found enough to warrant a drive to Manchester, New Hampshire, to meet with a detective from the city's Violent Crimes Unit.

The Local Moose Café proved to be as homey as its name suggested: an unpretentious place with a spacious wooden floor, barn-board trim, bright yellow chairs at widely spaced scattered tables, a chalkboard menu over the counter. I got there early and claimed a table in the corner, figuring Detective Frank Carter would want a private conversation. He had suggested the location. From my high-roller reporting days, I was familiar with such requests for a face-to-face: It's what you did when a topic was best not left to emails or the phone. And that we were meeting off the Manchester Police campus suggested he'd rather not have his colleagues see us talking.

In person, Frank Carter was older than I'd expected from his telephone voice, with a grizzle of close-cropped white hair above a brown face and short beard reminiscent of Morgan Freeman. I'd never met Carter, but I recognized him the moment he came through the door. There's a look to violent-crimes detectives: The sidearm in its shoulder holster certainly gives it away, but there's also something in the face that tells of a worldview in which resignation merges with determination. With him was a plump woman in her fifties, wearing a dark blazer over a purple blouse and carrying a briefcase. I flagged them from the table.

We shook hands as Carter introduced his companion as Detective Annette Larson, a colleague from the Manchester Police Violent Crimes Unit and designated investigator for its part-time cold-case unit.

"I really appreciate your meeting me," I said as they took seats opposite me. "I know this is coming out of left field."

"Normally, we wouldn't talk with a member of the press on something like this," Carter told me. "But I got a call from Detective Selanski, who we've worked with on a couple of interstate cases. Said I should give you the time of day, at least, and, if you're extra nice, the temperature. She characterized you as a sharp observer. Also as a lone wolf who could turn into a loose cannon."

That sounded like Selanski—in-your-face attitude, mixed metaphors. I pushed back a bit: "And how would you characterize her?"

They exchanged a glance.

"Uh, Marlene is quite a gal," Detective Larson hedged. "A very sharp detective."

"An acquired taste," Carter said, "but well worth the effort to acquire. And very, *very* good at catching bad guys."

I was grateful for their candor, and we all shared a grin.

I had taken a big chance, calling Selanski to let her know I wanted to talk to Carter. She had hesitated, chewing gum audibly as she thought about it. "Okay. I'll vouch for you. On one condition—I get the full monty when you get back. I mean fuckin' Xeroxes of your notes, tapes, whatever you get, everything. Clear?"

I made a lame quip about striptease, but she had already hung up.

My initial Web search on Laughlin had been cursory, but that first article gave me a starting place for a more thorough job. An hour of Googling didn't produce anything interesting, even when I used some Boolean operators to conduct more sophisticated searches and filtering. But the *Herald* maintained a LexisNexis subscription, which I figured might include more.

I made the rounds in the newsroom, gave Ricky a hug and a quick update, then went to my desk. A pile of pink memo slips and a topped-out telephone inbox awaited me, and I knew I'd have to spend some hours catching up. First, though, I went to Nexis, which includes a dossier search and analysis tool for media and journalism that I had often used to seek out executive and corporate information. I found Laughlin, made note of every company he'd worked for, then used various tools to search around the periphery of his career trajectory.

He'd spent some years in Manchester, in executive roles for major grocery chains. I didn't find sexual harassment lawsuits associated with his tenure or the companies, but I came across an obituary for a Cynthia Laughlin, wife of David Laughlin. The obit did not mention cause of death, other than that it was "unexpected and untimely." But armed with a date range, I found a short news article about it. Reading between the lines—"an investigation is ongoing"—I sensed that the police considered the death potentially suspicious. The article didn't imply that David Laughlin was suspected of anything, but my reporter's instincts felt that tug again, the fish tapping the lure.

From there I figured it was time to contact the Manchester Police. Manchester is New Hampshire's largest city, and their website revealed that they maintained a substantial criminal investigation team and were thus likely to have been the primary police agency conducting any investigation. I called Selanski, then was lucky enough to catch Detective Frank Carter of the Violent Crimes Unit and make this appointment.

We ordered coffee and pastries at the counter and brought them back to our table. I noted Carter's visual scan of the room, and was grateful that the mid-afternoon crowd was sparse. We could talk without being overheard.

Larson opened her briefcase, but only to take out a pad and pen. "First, a couple of conditions. Frank and I are kind of out on a limb here, because there's no official interest in David Laughlin. No case. No charges pending. Closed file. Our boss doesn't know we're here and doesn't need to know."

"Unless you tell us something that changes things," Carter said.

"So the conditions are, you can't write about this in your newspaper. You can't mention this meeting to anyone except to Captain Welles and Detective Selanski. With whom we'll communicate directly hereafter, if the situation warrants."

"See," Carter said, giving me a hard look, "we checked you out, Mr. Whitman. Your checkered past. So I'm gonna be clear with you. If you screw with us, you are a guy who's very vulnerable to getting screwed back."

"I got it." I met his gaze to show I meant it, and to show I wasn't intimidated.

Larson: "So, you show us yours and we'll show you ours. I got a basic outline from Frank, but why don't you tell me more about your interest in David Laughlin?"

I started with the sexual assaults, mentioning my interviews and emphasizing the premeditation and prior experience implied by Laughlin's selection, grooming, and extortion. Larson jotted notes, filling a page of her steno pad.

"And you stumbled onto this how?"

"He was my sister's boss at the grocery store. It turns out that my sister was collecting information for a lawsuit or criminal charges. There are maybe twelve, fifteen victims over a period of years. My sister went missing some weeks ago and is presumed dead—murdered. Her former boyfriend was a suspect until he was found stabbed to death. Now someone has stolen her computer and her personal papers, so there's no record of her project or where she might have gone with it. I want some deeper context on Laughlin."

I didn't say, *And I may have kicked her body while swimming and I'm full of grief and revulsion and rage,* but I knew they sensed my emotions.

They bobbed their heads, assessing the information. Carter bit his lips hard, Larson finished jotting and stabbed a period at the page.

"Well, you're a damn good investigator for having made the connection down here," Larson said. She swigged some coffee, then looked up at me with a touch of concern. "And now it's our turn. How're you with gory photos?"

"I've seen some. Managed it so far."

Carter cleared his throat. "This first part's mine because I was lead on Cynthia Laughlin's death. But let me say again that there is no open case, no charges, officially no crime." He waited until I nodded, then looked around the room to appraise our privacy again. "So, six years ago, around dinnertime, a 911 call. 'My wife's hurt! I think she fell down the stairs!' Nice suburban neighborhood, takes a few minutes for the ambulance to arrive. Four patrol officers also come, all routine with a severe injury or accidental death. David Laughlin is waiting outside, distraught. Just inside the front door, his wife is lying on the floor, legs still up on the bottom steps."

Larson opened her briefcase and took out a ring binder that she thumbed through to what must have been the initial scene photos. The first showed a spacious, well-appointed entry hall with a stairway along the left wall. A woman in a sleeveless summer dress lay with her head on the tiles of the entry. Her blond hair covered most of her face, but from what I could see she seemed to be in her thirties. Another photo from closer showed that the stairs came down to a landing, then turned left for just two steps to the floor. A short banister led to a sturdy newel-post on the landing, square in cross section.

A third photo of the woman's head showed a deep injury to her forehead, visible through a fan of hair, with very little blood.

"These were taken by the first police on the scene," Carter explained. "They had verified that she was dead but otherwise hadn't touched her or anything in the house. After seeing the wound, they called in the ME."

I tasted my coffee and realized I couldn't drink any. "What did Laughlin have to say about it?"

"He had just come home with their son, age eight. Laughlin says he came in the door, saw his wife, made his son stay outside. He called it in, sent his son over to a neighbor's house, then went to attend to her. He said he felt her neck, didn't find a pulse, but tried some mouth-to-mouth anyway. Then gave up."

"Okay."

"Anything strike you as amiss?" Larson put in.

I studied the photos. "Wouldn't he have pulled her off the stairs to try to resuscitate her? Elevate her head?"

"Our thoughts, too," Carter said. "Her dress, pulled discreetly over her legs? My first thought was 'staged.' She looked positioned to me. Also, the hair still over half her face, over the wound? Nobody checked that wound or did any mouth-to-mouth."

"Motherfucker!" I muttered. "Sorry."

Carter's mouth twitched, agreement with my reaction. "So, cutting to the chase. Our unit is brought in, I'm lead. We interview Laughlin, the pathologist does the autopsy, we've got a cause of death and a time of death. Cause is a single injury to her forehead, time is about when Laughlin left to get his kid from soccer practice."

Larson turned a few pages to reveal several photos taken on the pathologist's table. Cynthia's head had been shaved, and the wound showed stark against her bluish skin. It was an outrage on that smooth forehead, a deep purple dent, triangular, with three creases leading away from its penetrating center.

"The newel-post?" I guessed.

"You got it. One very hard impact. Death occurring almost instantly, thus the comparative absence of blood."

We all seemed to need a breather but nobody had an appetite for coffee. I hadn't taken any notes, but didn't need to. I'd remember this all too well.

Larson's brows had knitted and now she rubbed them with both hands. "You ever see the Netflix series *The Staircase*?"

"No. Saw the trailer, though. Guy claims his wife fell down the stairs, except there's blood up and down the walls, he tried to clean up before the police came. Injuries all over the wife's head, no weapon found."

Larson: "Right. So, this is the opposite of *The Staircase*. Well, sort of. No blood on the walls. One wound, from an obvious source. Laughlin's timeline is plausible."

"Okay, but my gut says it's fishy as hell," Carter went on. "I called it a possibly suspicious death. I brought in a forensic team, and they went over the staircase. The corner of the newel-post had blood on it and clearly matched the wound. We looked at the walls and upper banister with alternative light sources and fluorescing fingerprint powder. The banister lower down and the post, we used luminol on."

Larson opened a different folder and slid a couple of photos over to me. "It was August, a hot day, meaning that skin contact with any surface would leave a good amount of perspiration and skin oil. Here's the wall above the landing at the top of the stairs."

The stairs came down two steps from a second-floor hallway and turned left at another landing where the long flight began. The photo, taken in ultraviolet light, showed a heavily smudged area—handprints as well as a chaotic collage of larger, indeterminate shapes.

"You wouldn't be able to see this in normal light," Larson said. "Just a clean white wall."

"To me, it looked like a struggle had occurred at the top of the stairs," Carter said. "His handprints are there, hers as well. The bigger smudges are consistent with shoulders, forearms, elbows."

"Of course," Larson put in, "the kid's prints are there, too. It's a likely place to put your hand, or brush your shoulder, as you take the turn onto the long flight of stairs."

Carter got impatient. "But then there's the newel-post. Yeah, it's also a place people would place their hands, but given its location in the front hall it's also more likely to get wiped clean during normal house-cleaning. In fact, it was surprisingly clean and there was residue from a common spray-cleaning product. We hypothesize Mrs. Laughlin had wiped it down within the last few days. That was good luck for us. Show him that one, Annette."

Larson slid another photo over to me. This one, eerily dark, showed the whole square top of the newel-post and a length of banister rising to the left. There were many pale, luminescent smudges, but glowing bright on the banister and on the right side of the newel-post were two clear handprints.

Carter and Larson looked at me. I shrugged, waited.

"They're hers. We ran a dozen accident reconstruction scenarios—how she might have tripped, where she'd put her feet or hands, how she'd try to turn, and so on. Several are possible. But the one that fit best was, you'd put your hands there to resist when someone's trying to smash your face into the newel-post. You can see, they're very definite, crisp prints, suggesting hard pressure and sudden release, not a passing swipe."

Carter clenched his teeth after saying that, his head quivering with suppressed feeling. This case meant a lot to him.

I thought about it. I knew that police, for all their best efforts, were as prone to inadvertent prejudice as anyone. They can get a gut feeling and then succumb to confirmation bias as they go along, seeing only the evidence that corroborates their sense of things.

But, looking at the handprints, I could easily see a woman trying to hold herself away as someone standing behind her held her head with both hands and slammed it with horrible force against the corner of the post.

I passed the photos back to Larson. "So how'd it shake out?"

"Inconclusive. Inconclusive path report—a bit strange in terms of force and directionality, but not entirely inconsistent with an accidental fall. Same with the forensics from the stairs. Interviews with neighbors and friends suggested that they'd had marital difficulties—couple of friends said Cynthia thought he'd been messing around on the side. But no lawyers, no restraining orders, no divorce filings, no 911 calls, no funny life insurance. What's the motive? We took it as far as we could. The AG's office wouldn't press charges. Eventually, it was ruled an accidental death."

"It's not even a 'cold case'?" I asked Larson. "I thought maybe—"

"No. But." She took another file from her briefcase, brandished it, but didn't open it. "This one is."

Carter made an unhappy grin. "This is where it starts to look like the TV show."

"About a month before Cynthia Laughlin died, there was another suspicious death in that area. Vehicular homicide. Remember, this is six years ago now. Young woman, Jennifer Segal, just home from freshman year at college. She's riding her bike along the road, through a forested area between residential suburban neighborhoods. It's about nine p.m., it's pretty dark, but she's lived there most of her life, it's only a couple of miles from home, she's got lights on the bike. She's on her way back from a babysitting job. Hit hard by a car coming fast from behind. I mean *hard*. Her spine was broken on impact, and she was thrown twenty feet into a tree, fracturing her skull. Found later when her parents got worried and went looking."

"I take it this connects to Laughlin."

"Well, Jennifer had gone to high school in the area and was a popular babysitter, much in demand. She was working hard, planning to save money all summer to buy herself a car. She wasn't at the Laughlins' that night, but she had taken care of their boy several times over the years. Last time was a couple of weeks before."

"To be clear," Carter put in, "there was absolutely nothing connecting this girl's death to Laughlin." He seemed to feel obligated to repeat the disclaimers.

"Yeah," Larson said, "but he wasn't on anybody's radar then. She babysat for a dozen families. No reason to, say, take a look at the front of the Laughlin family's cars. At the time. I finally chased one of them down last year—a Land Rover he'd sold a few years ago. I looked it over. No sign of impact or body work, but that doesn't mean it didn't happen. A Land Rover, with that heavy grille across the front? Laughlin could have bought a new grille and replaced it himself."

"What's your theory? Why would he kill either of them?"

"Jennifer Segal was friggin' gorgeous. She was popular with the college boys and her social media postings show a sexy, flirtatious style. We think Laughlin made some moves on her, one night after babysitting maybe. She didn't like it. Maybe she said she was going to report him, maybe she talked to the wife. Maybe, even, the wife saw the Rover's grille or had some other reason to suspect Laughlin was the one who killed Jennifer. And she confronted him on it. Thus—" Larson touched her forehead, where the awful wound had been.

We went quiet for a while, toying with our undrunk coffees. There it was again, the weight—the soul burden that comes with contemplating unreasoning, violent acts. The sheer unfairness of murder. Larson's tale seemed to warrant a moment of silence.

"Lots of maybes," I noted.

"How true," Carter said dryly. "Thing is? You get all itchy when somebody comes on your radar for a suspicious death and other dead people show up nearby. Now Laughlin's up your way and people start showing up dead?"

I got it. "His inability to control his urges with his staff would be consistent with your theory about the babysitter. Did you talk to people at his workplace down here?"

Larson sucked her teeth. "Yes. But very carefully. Nothing accusatory. Mainly, just making space for somebody to talk if they had something to say. And nobody did. He was in administration, an office context, not a store, so not many coworkers to talk to."

"Guy's an exec, white collar. Clean living, a Little League coach. And we didn't have the forensics to put a sharp edge on the interviews." Carter frowned, pulled out his phone, tapped and scrolled. "I gotta get back to the shop," he said.

"He's been divorced a couple of times," I said quickly. "I can't get into the records—they're sealed. Can you? Maybe there'd be indications of—"

"Accusations don't mean anything in a divorce proceeding." The look Carter shot me was equal parts insulted and frustrated. "Yeah, I looked at his file from New Hampshire, back then, Detective Larson looked into his Vermont divorce. Nothing there for us. The usual. Other women—wow, the first guy in history to have a wandering eye! You think we didn't interview the wives? Said he was an unpleasant fellow. Nothing we could use."

Larson packed up her case files, latched her briefcase. We stood, and I brought our cups to the counter.

"So . . . what's next? Where can you go with this?"

"I'll stay in touch with Detective Selanski," Larson said. "But we don't have any information that'll help her. Just inferences. Jennifer Segal's case is theoretically open, but it is cold and I'm stumped for now. Laughlin—there is no case down here. If there's a way to move forward on his sexual assaults, that could open a door to other discoveries. Or, you hope he makes a mistake that gives you something solid."

Outside, we shook hands and went to our cars. I could tell they shared my mood: It had been an informative but ultimately unsatisfactory meeting. They backed out first, and Carter tossed me a wave and an unhappy smile as they pulled away. I had almost two hours of driving to think about it all. So many maybes. But so many coincidences, too.

Wait for Laughlin to make a mistake? What kind of mistake? If we had him pegged correctly, it could mean yet another dead person turning up in his vicinity.

# CHAPTER 34

# CONN

The mountains here break up larger weather patterns, so when a storm does get through their guard it's often violent and chaotic. The night I got back from Manchester, a bang-up thunderstorm blew in. I watched from the screen porch as the sky strobed, rain slashed, and my pine pole forest swayed and thrashed. The chimney moaned. Celine shared my love for dramatic weather, and I wished she hadn't opted to spend the night in town.

After a while, I went inside and lit candles in anticipation of a power outage. I was tired from four hours of driving, but energized by the storm, and was able to put thoughts of Laughlin aside and work on my next "Around Here" feature.

A proposed wind-power project in a nearby town had aroused a paroxysm of vehement feelings both pro and con. Six three-hundred-foot turbines, pretty as giant daisies in the computer-generated site renderings, would reduce carbon emissions, provide energy security, and increase tax revenues. But they would be installed on forested ridgelines that signified pride of place to many, require clear-cutting hundreds of acres of bear-habitat forest; at night the blinking red lights would be visible for miles.

A perfect recipe for community division—and for newspaper articles.

I consulted notes from my interviews and by ten o'clock I had a pretty good article that conveyed the combatants' understandable passion. Working title: "It's About the Future."

By the time I snuffed the candles, the storm had blown over the next ridgeline and the thunder subsided to distant cannon fire. I went up to bed, pondered calling Celine, then figured she could stand a break from me.

Hemingway had a dictum of writing for a fixed period of time each day, then utterly abandoning thoughts about the story for the evening. I envied people who could cut things so clean—I was of the gnawing type, mentally harrying my projects until they exhausted me or I made progress.

So it was as I lay under the slope of the rafters in the dark. I missed the drama of the storm and Celine's warmth next to me. I thought about Laughlin, but couldn't see a way to get more information about him.

If only we could find the materials Laurel had been compiling. But where were they? Mace was right: If Laughlin was the thief, he'd have burned Laurel's papers and destroyed her computer by now. That would leave us counting on her backing up documents on the cloud on some service we didn't know, an archive protected by passwords we didn't know. Or she might have given copies to a lawyer, whose name we didn't know and who would probably invoke client confidentiality if asked. I felt stalemated and could guess that Selanski and Welles felt the same.

My thoughts drifted. What came to mind was, of all things, Mace's motorcycle—his gas tank, that eagle against the sky, and the tingle or irritation it inflicted on me.

I have always given subconscious processes their due. Lying there, a mix of associations mingled and linked: Mace's gas tank, the whirling blades of the wind turbines, the storm I'd just witnessed, lightning-lit clouds churning above me. Spinning, the violent sky: yes.

On the very edge of sleep, it came to me as a visual image, not connected with time or place or even feeling: a motorcycle tank from my distant past.

It took me a while to place the memory. Becker, a friend from freshman year at Johnson State, was the one who provided pot to our circle of friends. Now an insurance broker, he was pretty wild back then. He enjoyed being the guy who subverted the dominant paradigm, and he liked dramatizing the probably minimal cloak-and-dagger required to buy a few baggies of weed at intervals. If asked where he got his stuff, he'd put on a paranoid face and intone, "He Who Has No Name in the Land."

I never particularly cared who his supplier was. But I went with him once to pick up his weed allotment from his mysterious contact. His car had conked out on the appointed day, and he asked to borrow mine. I refused because I half believed his self-dramatizations and didn't want my car involved in any greater crimes than a small-time marijuana pickup. So I said he could have the car on the condition that I'd drive. He reluctantly agreed. Becker directed us from dirt road to dirt road—for all I know, he deliberately took a convoluted route to confound me or imaginary followers—and finally onto a long private access road.

The seller lived in a 1950s-era single-wide aluminum-clad mobile home that even then sagged in the middle. It was set not far off the road, but its green paint had dulled with the years, and it was buried deep in saplings and untended brush, hard to see. Becker told me to park in the driveway and counseled me to stay in the car. He went around to the back of the trailer, out of view. They must have transacted business on a back porch or stoop, because I could hear their voices, if not their words—Becker's supplier spoke with the distinctive tones of the old Vermont accent, almost Irish. Farther down, the road was barred by a steel farm gate, bearing hand-lettered No Trespassing signs on it, the kind featuring guns and skulls on them. Vermont has always nurtured a good share of survivalist sentiment.

I wished I hadn't agreed to this and was only too willing to stay in the car. As I hunkered down, keeping a low profile, I found myself at eye level with the tank of a motorcycle on its side stand.

I had recently repainted my Honda's tank and was still in the stage of reflexively checking out every motorcycle I saw. I knew every make and model, and had been thinking that maybe I should trade up to a bigger bike. This was a beautifully customized, lean and trim Harley XLCH Sportster.

The whole tank had been expertly airbrushed as a turbulent, purple-black sky, with a stylized tornado prominently foregrounded. I admired it enviously until Becker returned with the weed.

Tank paint designs are like personal logos, statements of self. Somebody had paid for a high-end professional job on this one. It had to mean something.

Twenty-two years later, winds spinning in my drowsing brain, not yet connecting it to Laurel's long-ago lover and one of Selanski's prime suspects, it occurred to me: Tornado. 'Nado. Nadeau. Could it be?

On Friday morning, I emailed the wind farm article to Ricky, then called Selanski to tell her everything I'd learned from Carter and Larson. I told her I hadn't taken any notes and yes, this was as full as the monty got.

She was in a foul mood: "What Frank said—how you get 'itchy' when dead bodies start cropping up around somebody? Guy's a *poet*! Fuck."

When I asked her about how Laughlin's Manchester history might affect their investigation, she told me that she and Welles would give it some thought. And that sharing information about it would be on a need-to-know basis, and I wouldn't need to know.

So I asked her whether they had made any progress in tracking down Jesse Nadeau. She reminded me that there were thousands of Nadeaus in the state. He had no family connections that the MCU could find—the various Nadeaus they'd contacted claimed they'd never heard of him.

She said "chats" with his former "colleagues" at his most recent penitentiary didn't produce tips about where he'd planned to go upon release—not that they'd tell in any case. Selanski had looked at Richfield High School records and learned that he'd dropped out before graduating; the local address on file back then no longer existed because the building had burned down ten years ago.

"You know," she said, "people say it's too much sitting that gives you hemorrhoids? Truth is, it's this kind of shit. Not that I have them, because I do not."

"Sounds like you're not having the best day ever," I said.

"No, I'm not. And frankly, Whitman, you're kinda the cherry on top."

Coming from Selanski, I took that as an expression of affection. We signed off. Under the circumstances, I didn't mention my decades-old memory of a motorcycle gas tank.

I looked up John Becker Insurance and called him at his office. I hadn't spoken to him much since college, except to say hello if I encountered him on the street. No longer a raffish counterculture guerrilla, he'd acquired a folksy, affable style that I figured was useful for selling insurance. He knew my articles, but didn't appear to know about Trudy Carlson's murder or my connection to it. I didn't enlighten him.

"So," I said when we'd caught up, "'He Who Has No Name'— want to tell me who that was? I think I've figured it out."

He laughed. "If you're looking for weed, I haven't had a toke for like fifteen years."

"Me neither. No, I'm not."

"So what prompts this blast from the past? This for a story you're working on?"

"No comment."

He laughed again. "Nado. N-A-D-O as in tornado."

"That's what I figured. His motorcycle gave it away."

"Yeah, he liked to play the tough dude, had that sexy Harley. I guess it worked for the ladies anyway."

I winced, thinking of Laurel's time with him. "Any idea where he is?"

Becker hadn't seen him in twenty years. A year after my visit to the place, Becker got the sense that Nado was getting into hard drugs that he bought out of state, and the vibe out there got scary. Anyway, Becker was going to be graduating soon, was engaged to the daughter of a justice of the peace, needed to get serious about life. His pot-dealing days were over.

"Can you remember where the place was? I can't remember at all, except it was northeast from Johnson." I considered it unlikely that Nadeau still lived in that trailer, but he had gone to ground somewhere. His accent suggested he was local. If he'd retained contacts in the area, he might have returned.

It took Becker a while to recall and longer to describe the route. Back then, few rural roads were marked; you learned your way around by physical landmarks. He could name the state highways—from Johnson, he'd take 15 east to the road that led to North Wolcott, then head north and east on the dirt roads. He'd cross Route 14, then 16. After that it got complex and hazy in memory. I got the sense Nadeau's trailer was somewhere in the mostly roadless area northeast of Stannard.

I had unfolded a state map and tried to match roads with what Becker told me, without much luck. Landmarks? I had only driven it once, couldn't recall any. Becker remembered a dairy farm with a huge red barn, an old iron bridge at a river bend—neither were any help—and long stretches of uninhabited woodland.

"It was a private access road, though, right?" I asked. "There was a gate across it a few hundred yards down from the trailer. Lots of No Trespassing signs."

"Yeah, there was a mountain dude down there, the kind you don't mess with. Gun nut, sufficiency farmer. I figured Nado grew his stuff on his land. I think he was Nado's uncle or something."

I milked Becker for every detail he could recall, told him I owed him a favor, and got off. I had drawn a spiderweb of forking pencil lines that meant very little. But I found the idea of an uncle living nearby interesting. If Nadeau had gotten out of prison and wanted to go off the map, where better than a survivalist's redoubt?

Vermont has a strong tradition of respect for personal liberties. Most people don't know that while our Vermont forebears fought alongside their neighboring states against the British, they refused to join the original thirteen colonies. They didn't trust the other states and didn't join the US until 1791, fifteen years after the Declaration of Independence. With our rugged landscape, tough winters, muddy dirt roads, poor radio and cell reception, that independent, isolationist attitude has never died. The backwoods breed some hard, mistrustful people who can take you or leave you, and would sooner leave you.

When Celine points out that I have plenty of this contrarian, libertarian streak myself, I proudly admit, Fuck yes.

Still, they're difficult people to get to know, and they often have contentious relationships with neighbors and authorities. They tend to get into property-line disputes; they don't like paying taxes, having their cars inspected, or getting Social Security numbers or vaccinations for their kids. They'll grow what they want on their acres, they don't want federal inspectors checking the health of their cows, and they'll hunt deer in season or out. They argue that Vermont retains the right to secede, to create the Second Vermont Republic.

I had written a feature some years ago about this mixed-bag population of survivalist, secessionist, libertarian people. Some were young anarchists, some were sufficiency farmers, some focused on keeping a small environmental footprint and some on preparing for the coming apocalypse.

Working on the article had some tough moments, such as driving up to a remote cabin to be greeted by a big beard carrying a big shotgun. It broke the ice for me to compliment his Mossberg 12-gauge and ask what he had in it. "Bird shot, I'll take a load if you'll talk to me," I told the guy. "Buckshot, I'll keep driving." Fortunately, his sense of humor, another backwoods tradition, won out over other tendencies.

My journalism mentor at AU told me I should never throw away my notes, and I had taken this as gospel. I kept a score of file boxes stuffed with pages torn from notebooks, typed first drafts, newspaper clippings, photos, interview tapes, Xeroxes of encyclopedia entries, internet search screenshots, and court documents. Extensive notes are the compost that nurtures a good article, and, after publication, provide the paper trail that may be needed to verify your information.

My thought was that if Nadeau had a reclusive libertarian uncle, the man might have caused enough friction that he'd show up in the press at some point. Becker's directions gave me only a general area. But it should be enough.

My final article didn't include anyone named Nadeau or a profile of a survivalist type from that area. So I went to my notes. I had dug up information on fifteen individuals or groups, but had chosen only five to write about—those with views or lifestyles I considered representative of the breed. I finally found a good prospect for Nadeau's uncle in a Bennett Adams, whose fiefdom was somewhere out past Stannard, a township with a population of 207 and no paved roads within its borders.

Adams had had lots of tussles with the state and town, but I never interviewed him. He had been associated with the Second Vermont Republic movement in 2004, but later ran afoul of the group and stormed out of a meeting in 2007. SVR meeting minutes reported that he felt they were too much about airy-fairy theories; their commitment to the right to privacy, the Second Amendment, and freedom from taxation struck him as wishy-washy. Ultimately, I didn't feature him in my article because he wouldn't answer my phone calls, and anyway I had plenty of other interesting people to profile.

I tried to pin down an address via his phone service, but he no longer had a landline, and none of the online search services gave me a cell number for him. If he used phones at all—he might well not, given that there wouldn't be reception up there anyway—he used burners.

I used Google Earth to assist my search, referring back to the drawing I'd made from Becker's recollections. Northeast of Stannard, the visible roads run in an uneven ring about thirty miles in circumference, circling about seventy square miles of woods. With the heavy forest cover, satellite photos didn't show the smaller roads and private drives that branched off toward the center of the circle. You could only spot them from the ground.

Stannard had no downtown, no businesses. It did maintain a town hall and a part-time town clerk, who would have plot maps for tax purposes; Adams's address might show up there. But the office was open from eight until noon on Wednesdays only.

Today was Friday. It was a nice day for a drive. I had caught up with my work at the *Herald*. And I needed a swim—maybe it was time to explore the lakes and ponds up in the Northeast Kingdom. If my route took me to somewhere that looked like Bennett Adams's place, maybe I'd detour. I wasn't worried about making contact, if that happened. I'd done pretty well with his kind of people for the article. If he saw me, I'd pretend I was lost, or maybe I'd try to feel out what kind of guy he was—the bird shot or the buckshot type.

# CHAPTER 35

# CELINE

On Friday, Conn called to say he was heading up to the Northeast Kingdom to swim and to explore a possible location for Jesse Nadeau. I reminded him to be careful, and he assured me he would be.

I spent the afternoon at my own apartment, catching up with personal tasks. I cleaned my refrigerator—a mess, given how much time I spent at Conn's—and called my brother in California to compare notes on life, spouses, and careers. Then I called a couple of staff in the school system to check in on them and celebrate a summer of what had been, mostly, gorgeous weather.

My main errand was a casual visit to Jody King at the Richfield Farm and Garden store, where she worked as one of the managers. I timed it to arrive near closing time, on the off chance she'd want to chat after work. I had barely spoken to her at the police picnic, and some kind of contact seemed overdue. I was disturbed by Marshall's breaking the mirror and wondered if Jody might want a perspective from somebody like me.

Also, I was worried about her. My conversation with Mason, when he'd visited with Katy, suggested that she was wearying of the brooding, despondent husband.

Conn said the store used to be oriented toward actual farmers, but in recent years had begun catering more to home gardeners and pet owners: a greenhouse full of herb or vegetable starts, a main floor stacked with gardening tools along with sacks of grass seed, mulch, and pet food. The warehouse still held eighty-pound sacks of livestock grain, and in the yard out back you could still buy stock watering tanks and rolls of fencing wire. Plenty of heavy pickups still occupied the parking lot, but Vermont was changing, and the store was adapting.

In the old days, Jody probably would have been called "mannish," given her physical frame and body language. I knew the origins of her style: She was the sole daughter of farmer parents, and had grown up among three brothers. She had adopted their habit of walking with elbows out from her sides, striding purposefully if not gracefully, using her body with brusque efficiency to perform any task. She was handy with tools, good with a rifle, and for fun rode a dirt bike in regional motocross events.

For all this, I found her beautiful: shoulder-length hair of a lovely shade of gray, an angular face with disconcertingly direct hazel eyes, wide hips and narrow waist that offset her strong shoulders. At the store, she wore a sweatshirt, jeans, and a heavy denim apron, but I'd seen photos of her in her prom gown and wedding dress, and I could easily guess that she'd broken a few hearts when she was younger.

It was getting on closing time, and the parking lot was mostly empty, so I hoped Jody might have some moments between other customers to talk with me.

I was lucky to find her at the cash register when I came in. She tipped her chin in greeting as I grabbed a cart from beside the door.

"I should have called before," I said. "I wanted to tell you, that was a great party. It lived up to all the advance hype I got from Conn."

"The 'First Responder Fiesta'? Yeah, we try to show them a good time. You guys left before the real fun started." She was reloading the receipt-printer paper roll as we talked.

"Oh?"

"Well, the dancing. If you can call it that when half the dancers are loaded. Pretty funny. Those boys and girls can get pretty loose."

"I wish I'd seen that! But Conn was . . . having a tough day. So we headed home early."

Jody's expression darkened. "Can't blame him. The crowd was abuzz with talk about his sister. Probably made things awkward. I tried to act as normal as I could around him."

"He definitely appreciated that." I wasn't sure she knew the whole context of Conn's state of mind: whether Mason had told her about Conn's encounter in the reservoir, or the extent of his misery over his past failures with Laurel.

"Well, we're all gonna have to get back to normal sometime, right? Anyway, tell him thanks for going out to see Mace. He's back home, by the way. And on the job. Maybe Conn twisted his arm?"

"How is he?"

She gave an exasperated sigh as she clipped the printer cover shut over the new roll. "Honestly, Celine? Mace has gotta be the only guy I know who can feel guilty about *not* shooting someone!"

An older woman approached the register with a cart full of dog food and chew toys. They exchanged small talk as Jody scanned her purchases. Without thinking about it, I started bagging the small items. The woman's eyes went to my left hand, then flicked away, a familiar response.

She rolled her way out, and Jody checked her watch. "Coming up on closing time. What can I do you for?"

"Birdseed."

She left the register and beckoned me to follow. I pushed my cart behind her as we went back among the aisles, engulfed by the pungent smell of cedar chips and bagged stock feed wafting from the warehouse rooms.

"How's Marshall?" I ventured.

She looked back at me with a questioning frown. "Fine."

"Mace told me he broke a mirror. Been acting out a bit."

Jody faced forward again, the set of her shoulders suggesting irritation either at Marshall, or me, for asking. Or, maybe, at Mason for telling me about it.

"Allowance revoked until he's covered the cost of the mirror," she admitted. "He'll settle when all this high drama gets further behind us."

I assumed "high drama" meant Laurel's murder, Irene, Penny. "What's he doing this summer?"

"Soccer camp, job as lifeguard at the pool. Keeps him busy. Here we go."

We'd arrived at the birdseed aisle, a rainbow cornucopia of sacks of different sizes, hanging feeders, suet cages, and squirrel guards.

"This for out at Conn's?"

"Yes. Jody, I love the birds, but I don't know what the different kinds like to eat."

"Okay. So, these in here are pricey, but they've got the oilseeds that're best for wild birds. These over here are mostly corn, wheat, oats—cheaper." Moving on, she gestured to a pile of sacks featuring a vivid bluebird: "If you want to attract bug-eaters, get a brand containing mealworms."

As I pondered my multitude of choices, Jody's phone vibrated. She pulled it out and checked its screen impatiently.

"I gotta take this. Anyway, read the labels. My advice, go for the high oilseed counts."

She hurried off. I thought about the birds I'd seen at Conn's and realized that I knew only the brightly colored ones, the cardinals and jays, the robins. I read lists of ingredients and finally hefted a couple of twenty-pound bags into my cart, one with oilseeds and one with mealworms.

Another woman was working the register when I got there, but she told me I could catch up with Jody in the warehouse section. I went back to find her lifting bulk-wrapped boxes of canned cat food off a shipping pallet and stacking them onto a dolly.

"So, you want to grab a drink after work?" I asked. I knew it was a long shot.

"I don't know, Celine. I gotta get these things on the shelves before I go tonight." I must have looked disappointed, because she went on, "You could help, if you want. Go faster with two."

She stacked the plastic-bundled boxes shoulder high, then deftly tipped the dolly back and began wheeling it toward the front. At the cat aisle, she levered it upright, then used a utility knife to slit the heavy plastic on the top box. She yanked the transparent sheet off, and we began placing the cans where Jody indicated, rotating each so the Purina logo and cute cats faced the front of the shelf.

"I can see how this might get old pretty fast," I told her. She had loaded the dolly with six boxes of forty-eight cans each.

Her mouth tightened in a sardonic grin. "You could say that."

"So, I was thinking about you the other day," I began.

"Oh yeah?"

"I get these days when I'm hit hard with . . . stuff from when I was married to Richard. And after he died. I mean, I am totally, madly in love with Conn. But it still sneaks up on me sometimes? And I wish I handled it better. I wondered if you have times like that. How you manage it."

I was surprised at myself. I had been thinking to open an outlet for her confidences, and yet I sounded more like someone hungry for offering my own. Maybe I was.

"Your Richard died in a helicopter crash, right?"

"Yeah. Not how you'd expect a high-school English teacher to die. National Guard, weekender."

"Well, my husband loved the service and signed up again even though I asked him not to. Loved his Humvees and Bradleys and M2 50-cals. Boys and their fuckin' toys."

She gave me a quick sideways glance, as if checking on how I'd taken this rare flash of bitterness. I nodded.

"Mainly what I do is, I remind myself that a lot of other guys died, a lot of other wives have grief, and I'm not so special. And then I stuff it back in its drawer."

We finished the top box. Jody tossed the cardboard and loose plastic to the floor and then slashed open the next pack. Turkey-and-giblets flavor this time, the next shelf over.

Jody expertly slotted the cans into place, but I fumbled a bit, my missing fingers complicating things.

"But your kids," I had to ask, "surely you tell them about who their father was? I'd think—"

"If they ask, I say he was a good man who wanted to serve his country. And they should be proud. You've seen his photo, on our mantel." She turned away to slash open the next box. "But we pretty well never go there. Katy never even met him, Marshall only as a baby. And Mason is their father. Period."

She said the last decisively, and I understood why. It seemed hard, but ultimately it was true. And Jody didn't want diluted or ambivalent loyalties in their family. I could imagine the classic line from a defiant teenager, which Marshall was rapidly becoming: *You're not my real dad!* And did Mace ever have wavering loyalties toward this other man's kids? I doubted it, but in any case, neither attitude was going to get any traction in Jody's household.

"It was nice to see him with Katy the other day. She's such a lovely kid. It's so obvious how much they adore each other."

Jody kept at stacking cans. "What'd you guys talk about?"

"Well, the 'high drama,' a bit." Thinking of Irene, I felt again the wrenching pang of sorrow and guilt that had hit me when Conn told me she'd died.

I fumbled another can and realized I'd paused overlong. "Mainly, he talked about how he was sorry for imposing his state of mind on you. Mad at himself."

She nodded, more to herself than to me. "Yeah, Mace. A softie. Cards on the table, heart on his sleeve. Huh. And yet the guy can keep things to himself surprisingly well if he has to."

"Like what?"

She made a face of disapproval—of herself, I thought, saying too much. She tossed the empty box, slashed open the next, and we began stacking salmon pâté.

Not looking at me, she went on: "Celine. I appreciate what you're trying to do. Really. Yeah, we're under a little stress, and I guess it shows. But this isn't my bag? Girl talk, heart to heart? Nothing personal, but in my family, Mom and Dad didn't exactly encourage touchy-feely stuff. You sorta toughed things out, got them back on track. Didn't complain. Worked for them, works for me. We'll sort it out ourselves. Like I say, nothing personal. But."

That "but" was a period at the end of this discussion. I felt a little re-buffed, but I was hardly unfamiliar with this outlook. Our far-flung school district was still largely a farming community. Many of the parents I dealt with were like Jody's folks—people who stood on their own two feet, kept dirty family laundry out of view, and were suspicious of intrusion.

We worked side by side, saying little, until we got the last cans stacked. Jody pulled a trash bag out of her apron, and she stuffed the plastic into it as I stomped the cartons flat for recycling.

Jody rang me up, thanked me for coming by and for helping stack cans, and with a professional smile told me she had to close up now. I rolled the cart out of my car, loaded the bags into the backseat, and got in.

Through the glass door, I could see Jody and another staffer closing out the register and turning off the lights. I wondered if Jody had close female friends, and what they talked about. She wasn't always as reserved. The last time I'd seen her at the store, back in April, I'd found her hold-ing a tiny yellow chick to her chest while dozens of others pecked and toddled under the heat lamp in their cage. She stroked it and cooed to it as if it were a kitten.

I kicked myself for not being faster on my feet, with a better reply when she suggested Mace could keep things to himself if he had to. *Like what?* I wondered. But she had been clear about her boundaries, and I needed to respect them.

I had driven only about two blocks when the blat of sirens sounded behind me. In the rearview mirror, I saw a fire engine closing up quickly, lights ablaze, and I pulled to the curb. Behind it came another, then a couple of ambulance vans, then a stream of sheriff's and Richfield mu-nicipal police cars.

My phone buzzed, and I snatched it up.

"Celine?" It was Ricky Thurston, at the *Herald*.

"Ricky, hi!"

"Do you know where Conn is?"

The sirens had upped my pulse, but that's when my heart hit my throat. "Ricky, he, he went on a drive, up toward the Kingdom. I haven't heard from him."

"Well, I can't reach him. Out of range, I guess. We've got a major fire in downtown, and we need all the reportage we can get. Any idea how to reach him?"

"Ricky, if you can't get him, I can't."

"Okay. If you hear from him, tell him to get down here pronto."

The whooping, blatting panic parade had passed, but from the sound of it I could tell it had stopped somewhere not far away—downtown. I edged into a parking space and walked up Main to North, where I looked down and saw the myriad flashing lights. I smelled it then: burning. Half a block down, flames lashed out the windows of a building, vanished, lashed again. Above the fire engines and emergency vehicles, a cloud of murky smoke billowed and surged.

Before I moved to the area, Richfield had suffered a series of fires that reduced several downtown buildings to empty brick shells and stinking ashes. The cause was determined to be arson, committed by someone never caught. For five years, Conn told me, the business district had consisted of rows of fine old storefronts with jarring gaps between, framed by the blackened brick walls of adjoining buildings. The scorched smell pervaded downtown, he said, until a bunch of federal and philanthropic grants paid for reconstruction. They'd rebuilt the lovely nineteenth-century facades in the original style, and I wouldn't have known the difference if Conn hadn't told me.

I walked on and then stood with a few dozen others where a Richfield policeman stopped us. After a moment Jody appeared next to me, and spellbound, speechless, we watched the battle.

I learned a lot about fires that night. They don't burn steadily, and get extinguished steadily, until the good guys win. Actually, they flare explosively as critical temperature thresholds are achieved and suspended particles and gases ignite. The flames lunge out like the arms of a predatory creature snatching at prey.

Each flare brought a noise from Jody's chest: The men and women fighting it were mostly volunteers, and she knew every one of them.

More fire engines arrived as neighboring towns came to help: Montpelier, Barre, Northfield.

I saw Sarah, one of Conn's colleagues, among the onlookers, along with a *Herald* photographer. Ricky phoned me again, still looking for Conn, while we stood there horrified, mesmerized. I started to feel sick. Smoke, adrenaline, civic concern, I told myself. But where was Conn?

Arcs of water lifted from the street and into the gaping windows, and an aerial ladder began extending from the clutter of massive vehicles. Then some signal must have passed among the firefighters, because they pulled back suddenly. Seconds later, a section of the brick facade of the building gave way, collapsing straight down but then tumbling into the sidewalk and street in a wave of shattered masonry. With it came the carved granite slab proudly proclaiming the building as The Tennyson Block. It landed with an earthshaking thud and broke in half.

Onlookers gasped and groaned. Another dimension of fires, I realized: They steal place, they steal history, they bring loss and sorrow.

The hole gave the fire what it needed, and inside the flames gobbled air hungrily. I could only see the fire as an angry, voracious animal. But the gap also let in more water. The aerial ladder lobbed a heavy stream from above and soon a second rose and started bathing the next building over.

Again and again, people in the crowd repeated *I hope nobody's hurt. Do you think it's arson again? God, I hope nobody's hurt. Isn't that where Jennifer works?*

"I wish there was something I could do," Jody said. She was shifting, swinging her arms in frustration. She got out her phone, pecked, waited, shook it impatiently, put it away again. Then she spotted someone she knew, one of the Richfield police officers, a handsome, dark-haired man in his late twenties. She waved him over.

"Mark, have you seen Mason?"

"Yeah. He's redirecting traffic on the other side of town."

Jody's urgency subsided a notch. "Are they thinking it's arson?"

Mark said in a low voice, "Fire chief says there had to've been an accelerant, based on how fast it took over." He looked downcast. "Fuckin' A, you know? We just got the place rebuilt!"

Somebody called for him. He tossed a goodbye wave and went back to his duties.

"Nice to think Richfield has to burn every few years so some motherfucker can get his rocks off," Jody growled. Her lips set in a white line.

We watched for another half hour, until it looked like the worst was over. The monster inside surged with less conviction, then subsided to a sullen pulsing glow. More steam rose than smoke. A couple of engines pulled away, leaving the rest to the Richfield department.

It was starting to get dark by the time Jody said she had to get home, check on the kids, get dinner going.

We walked together back toward the farm store, coughing occasionally but not speaking. The air was full of the smell of old wood burning, with an acrid bite of plastic from carpeting, wiring, office equipment. Another overtone was sadness—a beloved landmark, gone from this little town. At my car, we hugged quickly, shared commiserating frowns, and then I watched her stride away. I tried calling Conn again, got his service, then started my car and drove out to his place.

# CHAPTER 36

# CELINE

I was surprised to find an unfamiliar car in Conn's driveway when I pulled up. It was a dark blue sedan, with the studiously unmarked look that gave it away as a police vehicle. It was starting to get dark, and I had tried to call Conn again, without success. Seeing this car, not his old Subaru, brought a tingle of adrenaline to my hands.

I parked and leaped out into air that smelled of burning, even here in our sweet woods, four miles from town. When the other car's door opened, it was Detective Selanski who got out.

"Ms. Gabrielli!" she called.

"What's going on?" I blurted.

She looked taken aback at my urgency. "Not much. I just now pulled in, hoping I'd catch your fiancé in the flesh. He's not answering his phone. Not for me, anyway."

"He went for a swim. Not sure when he'll be back." I walked past her to the door, trying to steady my nerves. The door wasn't locked—Conn seldom bothered. I opened it and turned to find that she'd trailed me onto the porch.

"He swims at *night*?"

"Evenings. Less boat traffic. He swims long distances." I flicked on an interior light, not sure how to respond to her presence. Curiosity won out: "Would you like to come in?"

"Sure!"

We went inside. I tossed my purse and turned on some more lamps. There was no indication that anything was amiss and no sign of Conn. Reflexively, I checked my phone for texts.

"What brings you out this way?" I asked.

She sucked her teeth. "I was hoping for a skull session with your guy, who seems pretty smart. And you, if you're up for it. Captain Welles has been tied up with another investigation, maybe you heard? Double murder up in Alburgh?"

"No. If I see or hear the word 'murder' nowadays, I tend to skip what comes next."

"Well, one of the victims is the daughter of a state senator. Welles wants to oversee that one personally. So he's busy and I thought I'd compare notes with you two."

We went to the kitchen and I turned on the lights over the counters. "Detective, I haven't eaten yet. Have you? Last I looked there was leftover penne with Italian sausage. I could make a salad."

Selanski came to the counter and sat on one of the stools. "I'm okay, thanks."

"Drink?"

"God yes!" she said with relief, then decorously corrected herself: "That is to say, 'Why, certainly—but only if you're having one.'"

"I am certainly having a glass of wine. I've just been watching downtown burn. It was scary and sad and I'm pretty tense."

"Yeah, you seem a little on edge."

I turned to look at her. She seemed utterly relaxed, meeting my eyes straight on. That kind of observation, prodding and provoking, came easily to her.

I took a bottle from the cabinet and rummaged to find the corkscrew. "Conn says you have a reputation for being a really good detective."

"Good at bullshit detecting at least. Where is the lad anyway? He's got you nervous. Not picking up for you, either, huh?"

She was smart, I had to concede, and had a habit of always coming at you. I uncorked the wine and poured us both deep glasses. I came around and sat on one of the stools, taking a lateral, non-confrontational conversational position even as I came into her space. I wanted to throw a little English back at her.

"You know," I said, "when we first met you? Frankly, we thought you were a nasty piece of work. Now I realize there's method to your approach. You like to throw people off balance, then observe their behavior. Grab that peek through the window."

She smiled, unruffled. "And in your trade, PhD from U of Chicago and all, you do the opposite. Put them at their ease, get 'em to let their guard down, then observe their behavior. Like right now! Doing a great job, too!"

We sat side by side and toasted to our methodologies. Yes, she was smart and did her homework, too. No doubt a good combination for detective work. She quaffed back a good slug, giving me license to do the same. I wondered about her personal life. Gay? Straight? The absence of signals told me only one thing clearly: a private person, her own person.

"Conn really is swimming," I told her. "Also doing some research. Up in the Kingdom. Yes, I wish he'd let me know where he is. It's just bad cell reception, I'm sure."

She nodded dubiously and quaffed again. I expected her to ask what he was researching, but she didn't.

"So, yeah, my colleague in the Fire Investigation Unit says it's definitely arson. Pretty scary. The building's gutted. But so far, they don't think anyone got badly hurt. First two floors are businesses, offices, everybody had left for the day. Upper floor was getting renovated, no residents."

"Conn says there was a spate of arsons downtown, some years ago."

"Before my time up this way, but yes. Richfield townies are crossing their fingers, hoping this isn't the start of another spree."

I heard a car rumble on the potholes in the road, and I turned quickly to look out the front windows. But the headlights passed on by. Selanski caught my reaction.

"So, I won't ask what 'research' our boyo is up to. But while we're waiting, I wonder if you had any perspectives you'd like to share. I suppose Conn told you about our feeble attempts to put the pieces together, and how they don't connect. The best link so far seems to be that guy Laughlin and the theft of Laurel's, Trudy's, papers. He's got a good reason to do that, and probably the best motive construct we've got for her murder. You have any others?"

I had only one: a crime of passion, derived from obsessional love. I told her what I knew about the psychology of OLD, the tale of Pugach and Riss, and the parallels with Tony and Laurel, Penny and Tony.

She shook her head at hearing Pugach's tale. "Does Laughlin fit in that, uh, mental universe anywhere?"

"I don't think so. The women at Martinson's—nobody implied he was particularly hung up on Laurel. He's a serial abuser, not an obsessional one. He needs fresh new proofs of his power, his control."

Selanski nodded, processing that. Then she gestured at the wine bottle. "Mind if I . . . ?"

"Please. I'll join you."

She poured. We clinked glasses again.

"Yeah, so over on the table by the door. A plastic bag with letters in it, a pair of latex gloves. Envelopes with forwarding stickers on them. Couldn't see, but—addressed to Trudy Carlson, I'll bet. Not to pry, but, hello? WTF?"

I was impressed by her quick eyes—she hadn't lingered at the door.

"Arrest Conn. He put in a forwarding notice at the post office for his dead sister. So he could pay her bills. He's got a contrarian streak. It's also common sense."

She poked her thumb over her shoulder at the bag of mail. "At least he's preserving possible trace evidence, yes? The gloves?"

"Yes."

She made a disgruntled, resigned noise, then turned her attention to her wineglass—fiddling, not drinking. "Anything interesting?"

"I haven't looked at it. Conn says not."

I heard another car trundling on the road, and I reflexively spun around again. To my relief, the windows lit up with headlights, a car turning into our driveway.

Selanski smiled to herself, eyes on the counter. "This is one of those moments when you wanna love him up and kill him at the same time, isn't it," she said.

I warmed the penne and made a big salad, and we ate at the dining table. Conn looked tired but good—he had put in five miles in Caspian Lake, he told us, didn't get our phone messages till he came ashore. He had talked to Ricky on the way home, and they'd developed a strategy for reporting on the fire. On-scene had been covered by others, but Conn would handle follow-up on the investigation by the State Police and the fire marshal's office. Full details would take several days to emerge as analysts probed the rubble and the Arson Unit did lab work.

A few glasses of wine didn't much change Selanski's affect. She stayed sardonic, astute, subtly observant. And provocative, if more gently so.

A person long accustomed to being herself, I decided. Maybe, I thought, if you pursued a profession long enough and with sufficient devotion, you became an embodiment of it. Individual personhood—did it sort of fade away, subsumed by your professional roles and duties? Conn often had to pull me up short on shrink mode: Had I become, first and foremost, a psychological problem-solver? And Conn, too: always the digger, the inquirer, the reporter.

Selanski cleared her plate and pushed it away. "That penne and salsiccia was splendid. Who's the chef? The woman with the Italian last name, or the guy who owns the house?"

Conn raised his hand.

"*Bravissimo*," Selanski told him. "You guys are definitely cool. So now help me out here."

We adjourned to the couch and soft chairs near the woodstove. It was too warm to light a fire, but Conn set some candle sconces burning. I wondered how his quest for Nadeau had gone, but knew he'd wouldn't bring it up with Selanski here.

"As I told your beautiful fiancée, Captain Welles is preoccupied with another homicide and is less available for this case. So, I'm hoping you'll help me think through, what would a journalist call it, the backbone of the story."

"Personally, I call it my through line. The theme, the sequence of cause and effect, that ties the details together."

"Yeah! So we've got bits and pieces and no through line. Celine has given me her view on a psychological through line, what did you call it . . . ?"

"Obsessional love disorder."

"Thus a crime of passion. But so many pieces don't fit that."

"Stolen papers, stolen computer. Stolen bicycle," Conn offered.

"And," Selanski said, "both male and female victims. Who killed whom first, and why both? Why would Laughlin kill Tony? So what do you brainiacs think of the idea of multiple perpetrators with multiple motives?"

Conn sighed. He yearned for closure, for certainty. "I'm listening."

"My thought was," Selanski went on, "you got Penny killing both her obsessive-love wannabe and his undeserving lover out of anger and jealousy. Not so bad, right? And you got Laughlin, who hears about Laurel's probable death. He seizes the opportunity. Goes into Laurel's house to steal her computer and papers, and later comes by to steal her mail. Stuff that incriminates him in something else entirely."

Conn and I thought it over.

"Sounds possible," I said. "But there was no sign of forced entry. Where would Laughlin get the house key if he didn't get it from Laurel?"

"The Martinson's women said Laughlin liked to rummage in their day lockers, right? Maybe he borrowed her house key and made a copy for himself."

Conn seemed skeptical. "He'd have to have done that well in advance of her murder. Before she went camping, anyway."

"Of course he did!" Selanski fired back. "You said he's a premeditator, the way he selects staff and chooses victims, then basically extorts them. He must have learned about your sister's project. He'd already intended to take her materials. It was coincidental, good luck for him, that she got killed."

"For all we know, he made copies of other women's keys, too," I suggested.

"Why would he?"

"Access to their private spaces would give him another proof of his power over them," I said. "Or, he has plans for some voyeuristic visits. Or some other leveraging motive."

"But what about the mail?" Conn put in. "I guess Laughlin could have borrowed that key, too, but it would be hard to get a copy made—hardware stores don't carry blanks for those post boxes."

Selanski stuck out her chest and put her thumbs under her lapels, a preening posture. "I think I figured that one out. Went back to her place and scouted around, just putting eyeballs on it again. To the left of her front door, there's a tiny little hook, like old ladies hang teacups from? With nothing on it. Person who stole the papers spotted the key, took it when he or she left."

Conn smiled at her. "Good eyeballs."

"Which would mean the killer, or the thief, was already thinking ahead," I said. "To something arriving in the mail."

"If it was Laughlin, his goal was to get rid of evidence of my sister's project. Maybe he worried that she'd contacted a lawyer, and he wanted to intercept mail from that lawyer."

Selanski pouted. "You'd think he'd worry about the risk of showing up to steal her mail. On the other hand, trust me, even smart crooks can be pretty dumb sometimes."

We were quiet for a moment, thinking it through. In the silence, we heard a motorcycle approach on our road, slowing for the potholes. Conn looked out the window with interest as its headlight appeared, flickering through the trees in front. My first thought was that Mason was coming by, and I wondered how he'd like meeting the Nazi lady detective. But the bike grumbled past and on into the night.

"Any other multiple-perpetrator scenarios come to mind?" Conn asked.

"If not Penny, Nadeau or some other unknown person killed your sister and Tony. And, again, totally separate story, Laughlin stole the stuff."

But there were more scenarios. We kept banging our heads against it: One person—Penny, Laughlin, Nadeau?—killed Laurel; another person killed Tony. No—blood from both of them was found on the knife. Or Tony did kill Laurel, and somebody caught up with him later and used the same knife to kill him. Who? And what about the third DNA sample found on the knife, from someone unknown?

Selanski suggested a technique that her people often used when they were stumped: visualize the crime scene, then build out, backward, from there. Reverse-engineer how it came to happen.

We gave it our best.

Laurel went out to camp in her tent, her beloved spot. Somebody—could be Laughlin, Penny, Nadeau, someone else—knew where she was going, or followed her there. Did that person intend, in advance, to kill her? Or did it unfold through a series of accidental escalations? In any case, they interacted, the person killed Laurel. For whatever reason, Tony showed up, either at the campsite or as the person dragged or carried her body down. Tony saw what had happened; the person had to kill Tony, too. The killer loaded the bodies into Tony's truck, took them away to dispose of them. Came back later to retrieve his or her vehicle. The days of hard rain that followed erased any useful tire tracks.

But how did the killer get back to that remote place to retrieve their vehicle? Did another person drive them? Where was Tony's truck now? And where was Laurel's body? Why wasn't it found at the stump dump, too? Why wouldn't somebody just leave the bodies up at the campsite, and, as Selanski put it, "vamoose"? Unless there was physical evidence on the bodies that somebody hoped to hide.

Or maybe Tony was killed first, and Laurel witnessed it—the collateral-damage theory. Or maybe Tony *did* kill Laurel, then was himself killed someplace else, not the campsite—the only blood found up there was Laurel's.

Or. Unless. Maybe. But. We hit uncertainties and contradictions wherever we turned.

Conn was tired, and this focus on his sister's death was wearing on him, the dead ends and ambiguities frustrating him. "It seems to me that more evidence is needed. Just . . . one more dot that we could connect. Down in Manchester, Detective Larson said our best bet might be to go after Laughlin's sex crimes, see if other evidence emerges."

"I'd love nothing more than to nail that fucker's ass," Selanski said. "I'd love to have an excuse to take a DNA sample from him, maybe he's the donor of our third sample on the knife. Maybe Tony's truck is in his goddamn garage! But right now, the only connection the MCU has is the fact that Laurel worked at his store and you telling *us* that somebody told *you* that he did bad sex things with his staff. Even to question him, we need more than hearsay about hearsay."

"What would be enough?"

No doubt anticipating Welles's disapproval, she gave Conn a slit-eyed gaze before answering. "Laurel's documentation of sex crimes would provide enough to bring him in for a talk about that. *That only*, I should emphasize. But from there, we could try to track down his whereabouts in the time frame of the murders. We could say, 'Hey, Dave, funny thing that Trudy's trying to bust you and she gets killed—know anything about that?' But motive isn't enough. We'd need forensic evidence to spook him. Catch him with inconsistencies."

"Did you run his—"

"Yep. Soon as I heard he'd been looked at for his wife's death. Carter's people printed him in Manchester, so his prints are on file. No, they don't match any of the unknowns we found at your sister's house."

We pondered that for a long moment, sharing disappointment and frustration. In the silence, I heard the rumble of a motorcycle again, this time returning past the house from uphill, again slowing to dodge potholes. In another moment, the bike revved as it accelerated onto the paved road, and soon the sound dwindled and vanished into the noises of the night woods. Conn's head tipped minutely as if he was tracking it.

"Anyway," I reminded them, "Laughlin would have destroyed the computer, her phone, the papers, long ago."

"Ayuh!" Selanski said, sour, miming the old New England accent. She checked her watch, stood, and stretched hugely. "Anyway," she said, "with *that* happy thought, I'm afraid my pumpkin has arrived. I gotta boogie. Thank you for an excellent dinner."

We saw her out and waved as her car pulled around the driveway and onto the town road. When Conn came back inside, fatigue was obvious in his face and posture.

"Good swim?" I asked.

"Beautiful. Cold, though. Takes it out of you, after a few hours."

"And your other mission?"

We went back to the couch, Conn slumping deep into the cushions. "I found what I was looking for. The place where that guy Nadeau used to live."

"And?"

He chuckled. "The trailer's kind of folded in half—big branch came down on top. I could hardly see it through the overgrown sumacs. The driveway's got blackberry canes growing in it now."

"Think he might have moved down the road? To his uncle's land?"

"Well, the gate is still there, blocking the way. I drove up to it, got out, looked around. I got a glimpse of a farmhouse, way up the hill, a couple of small barns. Still lots of bristly No Trespassing warnings, and the No Hunting signs on the trees along the road are dated just last year. Signature's illegible, but could be 'Adams.'"

"So, what's next?"

"My guess is that Bennett Adams is still living there. Doesn't mean Jesse Nadeau is there, doesn't mean Nadeau had anything to do with Laurel's death."

"Jody and I watched the fire," I told him. "It was . . . sad."

He scowled, sad and mad, a man who loved his hometown. "How is she?"

"Seemed good. Grateful to you for bringing Mace home."

"He's returned from the wild?"

"Yes. And back at work."

Conn nodded, pleased.

"She made an odd comment—said Mace seemed like a guy who put all his cards on the table, but he was also pretty good at keeping things to himself if he needed to."

"Hm. What do you think she meant?"

"I don't know. I asked, but she was fed up with my intruding. I don't blame her—I had been pushing it, I guess. She politely told me that when she grew up, her family was not into a lot of talking through things. And that the King family would handle this themselves, thank you."

Conn frowned and then rubbed his knotting forehead. "Well. For another time."

We put off the dishes until the morning. We snuffed the candles, turned off lights, and started upstairs. Halfway up, Conn turned around and went to lock the door.

Maybe it was this gesture, something he seldom bothered with, or maybe it was some aspect of his behavior, his tone. Tension, anxiety? Or maybe it was just the long day, the fire, my hours of worrying about where he was, landing on me. But the thought crossed my mind: *Was Conn good at keeping things to himself? What kind of things?*

# CHAPTER 37

# CONN

I was determined to do something special, to have some kind of adventure, with the girls—I couldn't stand the thought of sitting in Elaine Clarke's studiously bland living room, trying to make conversation while straining to avoid the fact of their mother's death. A natural death might have been manageable, but the preposterous outrage of *murder*—how do you talk about that with children? Old photos of Laurel and me, and reminiscences of our youth—we had done that. What they needed was to step back into life, the present, being kids. Their summer had been constrained by events, the Clarkes weren't outdoor enthusiasts, and Ben and Anderson struck me as unfortunate companions for these girls.

When I'd asked Vickie Landauer about taking them swimming or biking, she informed me that I wouldn't be able to see them outside the foster home, or unchaperoned, until the Department for Children and Families had done a background check on me. If I wanted to bring them to the cabin, they'd need to do a home visit first.

The background check made me nervous—I worried that my criminal conviction and disreputable history in DC would nix such visits. I warned Vickie that they'd find some funky stuff on me, but it was now thirteen years in the past and my record had been spotless since. She reassured me that the department would contextualize.

The home inspection went well. Celine helped me clean up the cabin, and she was there as Vickie and another DCF case worker took a look around. They knew of Celine in her professional role, and her presence, the fact that I had a fiancée, no doubt improved their confidence that I was an okay guy. We ended up on the screen porch, drinking iced tea, talking about the fire, and discussing our various jobs.

"Lovely porch!" Vickie said admiringly, looking out into my pine woods. "It wouldn't be hard to winterize, would it? Make another bedroom, put in bunk beds?"

I opened my mouth to answer but stumbled over it. Celine observed my reaction and had to stifle a laugh.

Saturday, I made a conscious effort to clear my mental desk of worries about the investigation and work and give myself over to having a good time with the girls.

They had suggested that we go to Burlington's North Beach, which I enthusiastically endorsed. North Beach is a mile of sand with Lake Champlain stretching blue and clean, out of sight to left and right, the Adirondacks majestic on the western shore, eight miles away. Saturday, it would be crowded, but I figured the busy human throng would also be refreshing for them.

I paid my respects to Mrs. Clarke and hustled the girls into the car. We had just started the drive when Maddie suggested another plan: "Could we go for a ride on the bike path instead?" Julie quickly seconded the thought: "We always go there with Mom."

Initially, I thought it was a great idea. The paved path runs along Champlain's shore bluffs for fourteen miles, the last three miles on a narrow causeway across open water, with thrilling views.

"We can do both," I reminded them. "Bike as long as we want, stop at any of the beaches if we feel like it."

But I had agreed before the full implications hit me. I soon learned that nobody had brought their bikes to the foster home, which meant a stop at Maple Meadow to retrieve them. As far as I knew, it would be their first return there since the DCF had taken them in. I didn't know the protocol for visits to their former home, or what its emotional effect might be. I thought about calling Vickie, but didn't want the girls to hear my consternation.

On the other hand, the DCF hadn't expressly forbidden it. Best to plunge on, I thought.

I opted to start by picking up my bike, a longer detour to Richfield. It was a good transitional step anyway, a way to anchor them in a happier past before the stop at Maple Meadow.

I used the opportunity to tell about my father's building the cabin when I was six and Laurel just four, and the fun we'd always had there. Back then, I told them, we thought of it as "out in the country," but in the decades since, other houses had been built along the road. "But I still see a bear in the backyard every now and then," I said.

Their faces quickened with interest as we pulled into the driveway. I caught a glimpse of the place through their eyes: a comely log cabin with a green metal roof, trees all around, flowers in beds and pots on the porch, round lawn table and four chairs. In front stood big silver maples; behind, the pine woods were in perpetual motion even on this relatively windless day.

"It's so pretty," Julie said.

We went inside, and they explored cautiously. At the bottom of the stairs, the photo gallery caught their interest. I joined them and pointed out who was who. They recognized their grandparents and their mother.

"And that's Mason, right?" Maddie said. "Mom's first husband?"

I was momentarily surprised, but then remembered that Laurel's gallery included a wedding photo of the two of them.

"Yes. And this is him, too." I pointed at Mace and me, age twelve, with our fish. "We were best friends. Still are, actually. He's a sheriff's deputy now."

Julie stroked her mother's face in one photo before moving on. In another moment, she found a photo of Celine that I'd placed on the bookshelf near the stairs. I had taken it on my cell phone and by chance caught one of those moments of special grace or light that seem to reveal the inner person—wind lifting her hair as she looked up at Whimsy Falls with a mix of curiosity and reverence. The fine, questing arch of those eyebrows.

"That's my girlfriend," I told them. "My fiancée, I mean. I told you about her, right? Her name is Celine."

"'Fiancée' means you're going to marry her?" Julie asked.

"Yes," I said.

They nodded, filing the fact away. Then it was time for us to go.

I attached the bike rack to the car, strapped on my old bike, and we headed for the more difficult stop.

I pulled over at the entrance to Maple Meadow, overcome by misgivings. Celine would know what to do—why had I thought it better to do this on my own? In the backseat, the girls had gone quiet, and the faces in the rearview mirror were apprehensive.

"Have you been back home since, since when you got back from camp?"

"No," Maddie said.

"Are you sure you're okay with it now?"

They checked up on each other.

"I miss our house," Julie said. Maddie nodded.

I still couldn't drive on. I put the car in park and twisted around to face them. "Girls. I don't know anything about being an uncle. I want to take good care of you, but I don't know how I'm supposed to? I need you to tell me."

We sat there for a full minute as the girls looked out the windows at their old neighborhood. From out of view down a side street, we heard kids' voices, laughing and shouting as they played.

"We should get the bikes," Maddie said.

So we did. I pulled into the driveway, and we all got out. Somebody had mowed the lawn, I was glad to see—probably the resident manager, keeping up appearances.

We went to the shed and I unzipped the door. The girls came warily inside, looking around. Julie went to her bike, toed up the kickstand, and rolled it through the door as I held the flap.

"Where's Mom's bike?" Maddie asked.

"I think it was stolen," I said.

Maddie grabbed her bike and jerked it around, frowning. "She didn't want it anyway."

"Oh? Why did she buy it then?"

"She didn't. Somebody gave it to her. She didn't want him to give it to her, but her old bike got broken. She said the one he gave her was really expensive, and he wasn't really her friend, like he was trying to make her have to be his friend."

I'd been warned not to interrogate them, but I desperately wanted to know more about this man. "What was his name?"

"I don't know. She didn't want us to meet him." Maddie's face had set hard, fighting some emotion I couldn't interpret. Primarily disapproval of this guy, I thought. Or of my probing. Or maybe just the pain of remembering. She started to roll her bike out.

"Maddie, wait. Can you tell me anything about this man, anything at all?"

"No! She said she was done with that period of her life! She wasn't going to be seeing guys like that anymore. That's why she didn't even want to have the same name anymore!"

I let her pass, then zipped up behind her.

But we weren't done with the hard stuff yet. Julie pointed out that Mom always made them wear helmets when they rode bikes.

"Where are the helmets?"

"In the kitchen closet," she said.

My shoulders slumped. "Girls, I don't have a key!"

"I still have mine," Julie told me. She rolled her bike to the car, propped it, went to dig in her backpack. She came back and handed me the key.

They looked frightened as we went up the stairs, as if something scary lurked inside. I unlocked the door and went in first. The girls followed after a hesitation. It was as I'd last seen it, except mustier and now dusted gray with fingerprint powder on every surface. And more forlorn: The soul of a family had lived here, and it was evaporating away, becoming a ghost.

Holding hands, the girls went briefly into every room, as if confirming that their mother was nowhere to be found.

I had never felt so out of my depth in my life. Not even standing in front of the judge in Washington, drowning in shame, confessing my sins and awaiting my punishment.

*Who did this?!* I wanted to scream. *Who took her away?!*

I trailed behind them. At their mother's bedroom, they hovered uncertainly just inside the door, then quickly retreated. When we got to the kitchen, Maddie opened a narrow closet and took two helmets off their hooks. She handed one to her sister: red with black dots, a ladybug. Julie was pale and shaky, on the verge of tears. The kitchen smelled foul, no doubt rot smell seeping from the refrigerator.

"Is there anything else you'd like to bring?" I asked.

Obediently, they went to their bedroom, looked around at the vestiges of their former life, and selected a few items. A pony. A crystal. A purple ballpoint pen.

"And now we'd better get going," I told them. "We still have a half-hour drive."

Their bikes were small. I put Maddie's on the bike rack with mine and lashed Julie's to the roof rack with bungees. Visiting the house had left all three of us stunned—we didn't say much on the drive up.

We parked near the public boathouse downtown, put in a few miles dodging rollerbladers and other bikers on the path, then stopped at Leddy Park for a swim. It's a narrow beach, with water that stays shallow for a hundred yards out over a smooth, sandy bottom. My nieces had been here with their mother, they said, and they sloshed and waded far out. Two skinny little girls among all the other people, somehow out of place, playing uncertainly, just trailing their fingers over the surface. I went out with them, cruised around near them in thigh-deep water.

They mainly watched other kids goofing, most with parents, as if trying to discover what they should be doing. I watched, too. You're supposed to play crocodile and chase them, right? Or they're supposed to ride your back as you swim or scramble along the bottom, right? Or you dive and pretend you're a shark and surprise them by pinching their bottoms. Or you put them up on your shoulders and then throw them off.

None of it was possible. A dreary epiphany: So much of our horseplay involves pretend menace, pretend combat, pretend danger. I couldn't enact it with these girls.

After a while I half-swam, half-crawled fifty feet away and just observed them. Something differentiated them from the other kids splashing all around, as if they were in full color and everyone else filtered, backgrounded. What was it? I wondered. Just the sadness evident in their lackluster attempts to play? No. There were lines connecting them to me, I saw. Only to me, among all those people. Invisible lines of belonging. Of blood belonging and a debt of caring.

We idled in the water for an hour. A line of towering cumulus clouds began moving our way from across the lake, pushing ahead of it a high layer of haze that gradually dimmed the sun. Eventually it was time to get back on our bikes, get pedaling. Time to head back to the foster home.

I unloaded their bikes under a threatening sky, then checked in with Mrs. Clarke as the girls waited at the car for the obligatory hugs. I drove back toward Richfield feeling jumbled inside, churned up. Halfway back, just as it began to rain, I realized I hadn't returned the house key to Julie. I thought about turning around, but decided I'd keep it—she sure wouldn't be using it. And somebody had to go in there and clean out the refrigerator, vacuum, wipe up fingerprint powder, air things out. Start thinking about what to do with Laurel's possessions.

Had our goodbye hugs been more sincere, more trusting? I thought maybe so, a small increment of closeness and duration, but I couldn't be sure. Maybe it was just wishful thinking.

# CHAPTER 38

# CELINE

We had rain on Saturday night, followed on Sunday by sweltering heat that brought up stupefying humidity. Conn had to do some catch-up work at the *Herald,* so I spent an enjoyable low-key day by myself at his cabin. With every window and door open, the light summer breezes stirred the hot air inside. I worked in the garden and then caught up with some reading, sitting in the swing bench Conn had hung in the screen porch. It was the coolest place to be. Outside, the pines moved gently. I thought about Conn and his nieces, their trip to the lake, and my thoughts led nowhere except hurt for all three.

Conn came home at five, dripping sweat. He found me on the porch and sat next to me on the swing. He pushed us rocking back and forth as we kissed.

"I like your outfit," he commented.

"Well, dress for success, I always say." I was wearing the smallest cotton shift I owned, hitched up high, with not much on underneath it.

"Success at . . . ?"

"Use your imagination."

We kissed again, longer. When I stroked his back, my hand came away wet.

He laughed when I showed him. "I was thinking of going for a swim. How about we both use our imaginations later, when it's cooled off a bit?"

I pouted, but knew he was right—even on the porch, the heat of our bodies against each other was too much. I told him it sounded like a plan.

I followed him into the house as he got his suit and towel. He asked me if I wanted to come with him to Molly's Falls Pond, but I declined, figuring I'd stay home and cook dinner for once.

I read and daydreamed on the porch until the light started to fade, then did a few chores. I took the bags of birdseed out of my car and lugged them to the shed, then went to the garden to harvest some greens for dinner—a salad, I figured, cold grilled chicken sliced on top. Inside, I turned on some lights and was at the sink, washing lettuce, when I heard a motorcycle rumble up in front and shut down.

It would be good to see Mason, I thought. Jody and I hadn't managed the chat I'd hoped to have, but I had been worrying about Mace and Marshall. I wanted an update on how things were going. Maybe I'd learn more about whether Mason kept certain things to himself, as Jody had suggested, and could do something to help him unload.

He pounded on the screen door.

"Come on in!" I shouted.

I heard the spring stretch and the door slap shut as I cranked the salad spinner. When I turned to greet Mason, I saw a stranger.

He was tall, well over six feet, wide with muscle in his shoulders, wearing a black T-shirt, black jeans over narrow hard hips, motorcycle boots. He had an angular face and black hair pulled back into a ponytail, and I guessed he had Native American blood in his ancestry. The bridge of his nose was knuckled with white, deformed cartilage that spoke of broken noses. His forearms were tattooed with images of wings and wheels. His dark eyes moved up and down my body.

Reflexively I tugged my shift down, feeling naked. Thoughts scattering, I couldn't remember where I'd left my cell phone.

I'd lost my breath, but managed to blurt, "Can I help you?"

"I'm looking for Conn Whitman."

"He'll be back any minute." Actually, he wouldn't. It was now eight o'clock. At best he'd just be getting back to shore, with an hour's drive home.

Jesse Nadeau stepped farther into the room, up to the counter. "Mind if I wait in here?"

"I know who you are."

"Well, the pleasure is not mutual. Who are you?"

"Celine. I'm Conn's fiancée. What do you want, Jesse?"

He blew out a breath and half sat on one of the stools, eyes scanning the room, me, the counters, me. "Celine, you gotta relax, okay? I'm not going to hurt you." His eyes met mine. "I know, I've got the prison vibe. And you're not wearing much and my eyes go places. Sorry. I'll work on that."

"How about if you go outside and wait."

He scanned the room again. "So you can call the police? No. How about I stay here and you stay right there and we get to know each other. Until Conn comes and we talk."

"I'm going to pick up a knife," I told him. "To cut vegetables."

He twitched his shoulders, a shrug.

Before I picked up the knife, I took Conn's big denim cooking apron off its hook and put it on.

He watched me as I tied it around my waist. "So what you know about me is, maybe I killed Laurel, or Trudy as I hear she's called now. But I didn't. Cut somebody once, but I've never killed anybody."

"Nice to know."

He grinned, corners of his mouth sharp in his cheeks. Everything about him was sharp—his cheekbones, his nose, his eyebrows, his flicking eyes.

"You known Conn a long time?"

"Three years."

"How about Laurel?"

"I never met her. She and Conn didn't see each other much. They'd been estranged for a long time."

He nodded—that was no surprise to him. "What do you do for work, Celine?"

"I'm a psychologist. I work for the school district. How about you?"

"Doing logging for my uncle, otherwise not much. I picked up some machining skills at North Lake. Hoped to get a job at that, but I came back and landed in this clusterfuck about Laurel. So I have to keep my head down. My employment prospects are not so good."

*Normalize,* I thought. *Keep him talking.*

"North Lake?" I remembered I was holding a knife, so I started slicing carrots. It proved hard to do while keeping my eyes mostly on Nadeau.

"Town of Baldwin, Michigan. Where Vermont subcontracts for prison 'beds,' as they like to call the cages. Last four years."

I nodded.

"Celine, I see some pictures on the wall over there. I can tell a couple of them are Laurel. If I walk over there to look at them, could you just stay where you are? And not run off? Because then you'd freak me out and stuff."

"I'll stay here."

He got up and strode to the bottom of the stairs. I got a shock when I saw that he had a sheath knife hanging from his belt. He checked to see that I'd stayed put, then leaned to scrutinize the photos.

"So that's what she looked like as a girl? Cute kid. And that's her and her shitbag husband. She showed me a picture of him. Told me some stories about the fucker."

I almost told him I knew Mason, that he was a good friend, then thought better of it.

Nadeau touched Laurel's face and then came back to the kitchen counter. This time he stayed standing, leaning on the counter with both elbows, chin on his fists, rocking forward and back with nervous energy. In addition to winged wheels, his forearms bore tattoos in zigzag stripes—an attempt at a Native American motif.

Out on the porch, my cell phone rang. I'd left it on the arm of the swing bench. It rang five times, then stopped as the answering service cut in.

"'Conn'll be back any minute,'" he quoted. His sharp grin came and went.

"He will."

"'Come on in,'" Nadeau quoted. "Who were you expecting?"

The phone rang again with unsettling insistence, then went silent. Conn often called twice in a row if I didn't pick up the first time, a way of signaling that the call wasn't just a telemarketer.

I finished the carrots. Scallions next. I wanted to keep the knife in my hand and moving. "Why are you here, Jesse?" *Say his name often*, I thought.

"Well, if it was to do something shitty to you, wouldn't I have done it by now? You're the psychologist, you figure it out. Go ahead, ask me about my mom."

"Was that you who drove past here on Friday night?"

"Good ears! Yeah, I would have stopped in then, but I saw the unmarked cop car in the driveway. Those little chrome hubcaps really give it away. Dumb fucks!" He chuckled, watching me closely as I picked up the bunched scallions, fumbled, and dropped them. "Jesus, you really are scared shitless! Chill, girl!"

I held up my left hand, my half-hand, an explanation other than nerves. Or was I hoping to arouse his sympathy?

His eyebrows went up over eyes that softened slightly. Injury, scarring, was something he understood.

I turned my attention to the scallions.

"So, what kind of guy is Conn?"

I thought about it for a moment. "He's a wonderful man. He's a superb reporter, partly because he's compassionate toward the people he writes about. He *listens* to them."

"Oh yeah? Well, Laurel was ripshit with him. He was this hotshot in DC who didn't give crap about his underachieving sister when her life fell apart." He shook his head, incredulous. "Good listener, my ass!"

"He was going through his own bad period. Job problems, divorce. Drugs."

Nadeau mimed playing a violin, face a mask of bogus sorrow. "My heart bleeds. Some of us got twelve years' hard time for our bad period. He got *what*?"

"He blames himself every day! If she'd lived, he'd be making it up to her."

He put down the violin, put his hands back on his chin, rocking faster now, frowning. Energy was coiled in him, but it had turned inward, his thoughts burning.

*Normalize,* I told myself. Normal actions, predictable movements. *Defuse. No surprises.* "Are you going to get jumpy if I go to the refrigerator for a tomato?"

"I'm not jumpy. You are. Go ahead."

I fetched a big tomato we'd bought at the farmers' market, but didn't start on it. Instead, I faced Nadeau, knife in hand, hand on hip. *Get him talking.*

"Why's it matter so much now, Jesse?"

He was about to answer when the light in the room changed. We both turned to see the front windows go bright with headlights from a car turning into the drive. My relief was quickly followed by increased tension. My heart started pounding. How would it go down? Conn would see the motorcycle, maybe figure who it was, come in hot-wired. Jesse was already keyed up, and my efforts to talk him into a calmer state, my de-escalating body language, had only served to arouse his anger.

But the lights stopped, then panned away. Somebody using our driveway to turn around. It happened every so often. A neighbor down the road forgot to get the milk, so—back to the grocery store. The windows went dark again and the car trundled away toward the paved road.

"Just somebody turning around," I said. *Or Conn, seeing the motorcycle, deducing who it was, deciding on a strategic approach of some kind, or Selanski, or—*

"Maybe." He stepped quickly to the door, peered out, looked back to check on me. I didn't move.

He sidled to the window and waited, looking outside, then approached the counter again with quick lithe steps. This time he stopped at the opening to the kitchen, three feet from me. He was vibrating with nervous energy. *Drugs?* I thought. No—the car coming and going had alarmed him.

"Put down the knife," he said.

I hesitated.

"Do it." He scratched his side, hitching his T-shirt just enough to reveal the handle of his sheath knife. He loomed at the end of the counter, prison-muscled arms banding with tension.

I set the knife on the counter.

"Now take off the apron."

"Jesse, please, what—"

"*Take. Off. The. Apron.*"

I undid the waist strap, slid the neck strap over my head. Dropped it to my ankles. Stood there shaking in my tiny summer shift and bare legs and bare feet. Waited as he looked my body up and down.

"Now, I'm real big and you're little and you're hardly wearing anything, right? And I've got a knife and you don't, right?" When I couldn't speak, he said again, "*Right?*"

"Yes."

"Is this what shrinks call a power inequity, or some psychobabble crap? Somebody's more vulnerable, somebody's less."

"Something. Yes."

His chest heaved once, convulsively, a sob or a tension spasm.

"You getting this? Anything? What am I trying to do here?"

"Trying to get me to listen to you."

His face showed a tiny release at that—relief, I think. He turned his head around to check the front windows again, then snapped his eyes back to me.

"You ask why's it matter now? Why's it *matter?* Because I gotta start a *life*, and I can't because somebody thinks I killed a woman I knew twelve years ago, never saw again. I'm gonna hit the road now. Tell Conn I gotta talk to him. But tell him not to talk to the cops and not to come out to my uncle's place. I'm not there, okay? I'm not anywhere. And Ben is old and cranky as a rattlesnake and could make a mistake we'd all regret if he sees Conn there again. I'll come by here another time."

He went quickly to the door, stopped. "You'll tell him, right? 'Cause I can disappear again. And come back again, right?"

I nodded.

The door slapped shut, the motorcycle cranked to life. Nadeau sped out of the driveway and his engine rumbled, then roared away.

I went to the door and locked it. Then I changed into some sturdy, concealing clothes. Then I did my best to calm down, my habit or meditation, resorting to a rational, professional, process. What had I observed? What did I believe was the truth of the person who was Jesse Nadeau?

How much of our encounter, in how much detail, should I tell Conn? Everything, I decided, except that last part about our relative vulnerability. Conn might not see it as I came to, a show of dominance intended to demonstrate his lack of violent intent—a prelude to surrender. A convincing plea for understanding.

# CHAPTER 39
# CONN

I came home to find Celine wearing jeans and shoes and one of my heavy denim work shirts. When she told me what had happened, my first response was a burst of glandular protective rage, followed by amazement at her self-control. What astonished me most was that she had inspected her encounter with Jesse Nadeau and made an evaluation of his intentions. She said she thought he was being truthful—a man trying to start his life again and unable to do so because he was a murder suspect.

I wondered what would have happened if I'd been at the cabin. Would my presence have escalated things? I wasn't sure I trusted myself, my judgment in such things.

"I'm sorry I was so late," I told her. "I won't do it again."

We held each other, her body vibrating with tiny tremors that took a long time to fade.

I was angry at myself. I should have left earlier, come back sooner. More, maybe I should have anticipated Nadeau's visit.

Not keeping secrets, just for Celine's peace of mind, I hadn't told her about one detail of my trip to Stannard. When I'd driven up to Bennett Adams's gate to look for signs of habitation, I'd seen plenty of recent tire marks in the dirt road, including some motorcycle tracks.

Not a big thing, lots of people have bikes. But later, when we were talking to Selanski and heard the motorcycle pass, I wondered if there was a connection. Motorcycling gets into your blood, and Nadeau had no doubt hungered for that feeling of freedom during his years in prison. The bike wouldn't be registered in his name, or Selanski would have known, nor would it be the same Harley XLCH I'd seen decades ago. But once a Harley rider, always a Harley rider. V-twin engines have an uneven beat to them, immediately identifiable if you know your bikes. The bike that drove past the cabin had that rough Harley putter.

But there was no way Nadeau could have followed me home. I'd headed from the deep woods above Stannard to Greensboro, ten miles away, parked, swum for two hours, then driven over forty miles on two-lane roads coming home. I would have noticed a motorcycle tailing me.

So how had he found my house?

The big question was whether to tell Selanski and Welles about Nadeau. I was inclined to, but it was a decision I wanted Celine to make.

"Would you feel safer if we told them? That's all that matters to me."

"Oh, Conn. What would they do? Go out to Adams's place? He wouldn't let them on the property. Then what, Ruby Ridge Two? Anyway, I believed Jesse when he said he wouldn't be there."

Celine stayed thoughtful as we washed the dishes. I let her process the question. Finally she said, "It was scary, Conn. But I don't believe he wanted to hurt me. He . . . gave me evidence of this. Maybe I'll regret it, but I say, let's give that man a chance. Let him come back and talk to you, figure out what's on his mind. Then decide."

Still, I was torn. Rationally, I couldn't see a motivation for Nadeau to hurt me, or Celine, even if he had killed Laurel—his best bet would have been to stay invisible. But rationality is for reasonable people. I didn't know who Nadeau was. Whoever he'd been when Laurel was seeing him, his years in penitentiaries could have changed him. Bitterness or rage could drive him to irrational acts.

"You're sure?" I asked again. I nudged her cell phone, on the counter.

Celine nodded, more decisively now. "Yes."

We opted to drag the mattress down to the screen porch, sleep where the small night breezes could cool us. We let go of our earlier amorous plans. We barely touched—too hot, too much in the way just now.

Keyed up, I tracked the night sounds around us, every tick and rustle and sigh, until I lost consciousness.

Monday, I followed Celine's car to her apartment in town. She was ambivalent about "fleeing" the cabin, but I told her it would ease my mind. I had a lot of work to do and wanted to make sure she wasn't in danger. I trusted her judgment about Jesse Nadeau only to a degree—I needed to meet the guy myself.

I gave her a kiss that I hoped would last the day, then I went on to the *Herald*. The shop: As on Sunday, I cherished the quiet air of industry in the newsroom, the muffled chiming of phones, even the sharp scent of hot printer toner and coffee burning on the bottom of the carafes. I'd missed it.

There was plenty of local news to be got up for Tuesday's edition, what with the fire and the murder of a state senator's daughter. I conferred with Sarah, who had done most of the reporting on the fire. She brought me up to date on what was known, gave me a list of contacts she'd developed, including the building's owner and the owners of the shops and businesses on the first two floors. They would figure in my follow-up reporting, along with news of the arson investigation by the State Police Fire Unit and the fire marshal.

Back at my own cubicle, I made calls and wrote some copy. When I felt reasonably caught up with my obligations, I called Ricky, who was out of state at a convention. It was coming up on the two weeks of part-time I'd promised her. I knew my absence was putting additional workload on my colleagues, but I was still neck deep in Laurel's murder. I told Ricky that I still didn't know what "the duration" was, emotionally or logistically, and needed to extend the current arrangement for another two weeks. She had no choice but to assent, which she did gracefully.

"I'm gonna win a Pulitzer for this paper," I told her. "So help me. I'm gonna do it for you, Ricky."

She laughed wryly, affectionately. The grown-up. Putting on her

Irish accent: "Heard that before, Con-nor. Said it meself a few times. But thanks."

But my mood faltered when I spoke to Will Patchen, chief of the Richfield Police Department, one of six contacts I was pursuing about the fire. I had talked with him hundreds of times in the last ten years, but not since Mace and Jody's cop picnic.

"Hey, Conn," he said. His voice was both weary and caffeinated.

"Will. Long weekend, I guess."

"It has been that, yes. No rest for the wicked."

"You know why I'm calling. I wanted to talk to you first, then I'll talk the Fire Investigation people. What's the latest?"

"So you haven't heard?" His tone told me it was bad news.

My heart did a dive. Will Patchen was a good man, policing a modern, often contentious community, trying to run a department that was dutifully trying to balance circumspection and transparency in a completely porous information environment.

"We found a body in the rubble, Conn. It's now a homicide investigation, too."

"What happened?"

"This morning the demo team was removing a fall of bricks from the back wall? And they found human remains."

"Oh, man. Any idea who?"

"Not for sure. But I'm guessing it was Artie. He liked to snooze in the vestibules back there."

Artie was a well-known, mostly homeless boozer who frequented downtown. His begging and sometimes uninhibited behavior had been a subject of citizen complaint for fifteen years, but he was also a pretty nice guy, a good listener, funny, not one to judge anyone else. I had even considered writing a piece on him: How a somewhat crazy, indigent alcoholic had become part of our town's identity and was even treasured by some. In his younger, more socially integrated but wilder years, he'd been known as "Party Artie," alternatively spelled "Party 'earty."

"I won't name the corpse until it's certain. What's the status of the identification effort?"

Will said it was in the pathologist's hands and would require close analysis of the remains. The corpse's face was unrecognizable.

As for how the fire started, the arsonist used an accelerant, apparently igniting it just after the last person had left the building, around 5:50. For more details I'd have to talk to the others on my list.

I thanked Will, wished him fortitude, and rang off.

Typically, suspicious fires are investigated jointly by the Vermont State Police Fire Investigation Unit and the Department of Public Safety's Division of Fire Safety. The process of exploring a fire's cause, point of ignition, and progress through a building is an exacting science, complicated by dangers investigators face at the scene. Materials were likely still smoldering, there could be gas pipes or containers of volatile substances in the rubble. Badly damaged structures can drop upper-floor members on investigators, masonry walls cracked by heat sometimes collapse without warning. Investigations often move slowly as rubble is removed and structures dismantled to assure safety for the guys in the white suits.

Now that it was deemed a homicide, the investigation would take on more complexity, involving other departments.

I got through to Emmett Ellerson, the Fire Unit's lead investigator assigned to the fire, who told me he was at the scene and invited me to meet him there. I drove to downtown, but parked a couple of blocks away to avoid the congestion I knew would surround the site. Sure enough, one lane of North Street was closed at mid-block, and municipal police and sheriff's deputies directed traffic. The sidewalk was closed off with yellow plastic-mesh fences. I spotted Mason half a block away, using hand gestures to direct cars to a detour. I waved but he didn't see me.

The Tennyson Block had been a charming example of mid-nineteenth-century urban architecture. Now, the street-level storefronts were blasted, the tall, upper-story window frames were vacant and scorched, and one side of its brick facade had collapsed. The gaps revealed blackened timbers hanging in the empty shell, above a floor heaped with sopping, stinking ash and rubble. The roof was entirely gone. The acrid smell—charred wood and burned plastic—was harsh in my throat.

Emmett came out through the gaping front door, wearing a white suit. He pulled down his respirator and shook my hand. We stood in inky wet that oozed from the rubble and turned to gaze back at the building. From our perspective, I could see right through the storefront windows to the rear, where a backhoe worked to remove fallen masonry.

"I won't keep you long. I know you've got a lot on your hands."

"It's a shitter, Conn. I always liked this building. Total loss, now. And old Artie—pretty sad."

"Sounds like everybody's sure it's him."

"Yeah. The body's charred, but it's his size and Will Patchen says he took his naps on the stoops or in the vestibules back there. Nobody has seen him, and nobody else has been reported as missing. So."

I got out my notebook and jotted a few lines. Emmett went through what they knew so far. On Saturday, they had taken rubble samples to the State Forensics Lab and had identified the accelerant: a mix of gasoline and kerosene.

"Gasoline ignites quickly but goes out just as quick," Emmett explained. "Kerosene sustains the burn longer, gets the structure going."

"Does the accelerant say anything about motive, in your experience?"

Emmett shrugged. "Smart choice if you really want to destroy the place. Implies purpose, intent. Not just a thrill fire."

They hadn't completed mapping the fire's path, but Emmett guessed it started at the back of the building. A lot of accelerant had been used, judging from the speed it took over the building, the thoroughness and relative uniformity of the burn.

I asked who would be liaising on the homicide, and he named a detective from the MCU that I didn't know, Philip Osterman. He was around the back of the building right now.

"Hey, Emmett," a white-suited figure called. The person beckoned for him to come back inside.

"Gotta go," Emmett said.

I wished him luck. Then I walked down the block and cut through an alley to the parking lot behind the buildings. A large area near the Tennyson Block was closed off with mesh fencing, inside which the backhoe moaned as it engaged a bucket of rubble. I watched as it rotated and dumped the mess on the asphalt, where workers spread it using shovels, inspecting each piece as they went. The building had had two rear doors, one of which was still intact. The other was now a shallow crater surrounded by a ring of rubble and a line of police tape. Inside the ring, a uniformed State Police officer and man in plainclothes conferred.

I introduced myself, showed my press ID, asked if I could talk briefly.

Detective Osterman had white-blond hair and pale skin that made him seem younger than he likely was, probably early thirties. We went over the basics: The demolition crew had just begun removing rubble when they found the body. State Police crime scene techs had extricated it and combed through the nearby debris looking for anything informative. The best they'd gotten was a couple of empty beer cans found with the corpse, burned and barely identifiable as Pabst Blue Ribbon. The body had been taken in for a postmortem. Results were pending, but the cause of death was probably either smoke inhalation, burning, or crushing. There was no ID on the body, not much to indicate who it was—male, smallish, bad teeth. Age uncertain, but bone analysis would pin it down. The ME had made a preliminary guess of mid- to late fifties. Artie's age.

"Will Patchen thinks it's probably Artie. What can your people do to verify identity?"

"Good question. We'll have the body's DNA, but who can we match it to? I don't know if Artie's prints are on file somewhere, but in any case I don't think the body has enough prints left to compare. I doubt Artie ever went to a dentist, but we'll put out a call to see if we can match dental work. And we'll search for relatives we might get a DNA sample from."

I took notes, gave him my card, and asked that he send me the language for a call to relatives; I'd make sure my articles included it.

I put in a few more calls, got answering services, then went back to the *Herald* to write up what I'd gotten. Deadlines: We'd need final copy for Tuesday's edition soon.

I did my job, but Nadeau's eventual reappearance loomed over me. When—tonight? A week from now? Would we hear him? Would he knock? Would he choose to surprise us? I hoped we'd made the right decision about him.

A tune was stuck in my head, and it took me a while to identify its weird, apocalyptic menace: Phil Collins's "In the Air Tonight."

It was coming. It just wasn't what we thought.

# CHAPTER 40

# CELINE

I wanted to be there.

Though I trusted Conn utterly, I'd seen the protective, possessive reflex surge in him when I told him about Nadeau's visit. And, as I'd observed when he was gearing up to meet Welles and Selanski, he was becoming more confrontational when dealing with anything related to his sister's fate—impatient and quicker to anger. Would he get physical? Would Nadeau? Conn was incredibly fit, but Jesse Nadeau was bigger, heavier, and surely more accustomed to combat. I sincerely believed my presence would calm both men, reduce the chance of a volatile exchange.

I also felt that I had connected with Nadeau. He had something to tell, or to ask, that we should hear. His pending reappearance cast a dark, tense feeling over the day, but the final distillation of my feelings was sympathy.

How do you prepare for such a visit?

That evening, Conn and I didn't talk much, partly because we were *listening*. As the sunlight faded and we turned on the lamps, a sense of siege set in. We locked the front door. We stayed up late, waiting, then decided to sleep on the porch again. This time it was a strategic choice: We would hear everything, and we would not be where an intruder with hostile intent would expect us.

Conn debated bringing his rifle to the porch, then decided it would risk an escalation if Nadeau availed himself of one of his uncle's guns. He did load the magazine, but left the gun leaning behind the bedroom door upstairs. We opted to sleep in our clothes. We brought flashlights with us, turned out the house lights, and lay there in the dark, waiting, listening.

It must have been well after midnight when we both startled awake. A wrong noise in the night—a crash and scrape, nearby. We sat up and waited and it came again—*clank, scrape, thump.* From around the front of the house.

"What the fuck?" Conn whispered. He stood quickly. He picked up his big flashlight but didn't turn it on.

The breeze still carried whiffs of burning, and all I could think of was arson.

We opened the screen door carefully, quietly, still not using our lights. Creeping around the corner of the cabin, passing the garden, we heard a clatter and more scraping and dragging. At the front corner, we could hear that the sounds came from the shed. Yes: The roll-up door was open, and we could see someone move inside it, dark on dark.

Conn flicked on his light, and we were shocked to see two green eyes, reflecting bright against a black mass. A bear. Its shadow loomed huge behind it as it startled and turned toward us.

"*Hey, hey! Shoo!*" Conn shouted.

The bear hustled away into the darkness, footfalls crackling off into the woods. We went up to the door to find that the shed was a mess, with both bags of birdseed disemboweled and spread out on the floor, rakes fallen, a stack of Conn's maple syrup buckets toppled.

"My fault," I panted. "I put the birdseed in there but didn't pull down the door."

"The joys and hazards of rural living," Conn said. He tugged the door down and swung the latch over.

We cut the lights and stood in the blue dark, our hearts pounding.

"Beautiful creature," Conn whispered.

"He was *massive!*"

"Actually, probably only a two-year-old. Big enough, though."

We sat at the lawn table for a moment, just catching our breath,

chuckling at how tightly wound we were. Part of me was simply thrilled at
having seen my first wild bear, and so close. We waited for several minutes,
calming by degrees, then went back around the cabin and into the porch.

We got onto the mattress and lay there. It was surely after one a.m.,
maybe later, and my tension began to slip away as I thought: *No Jesse
Nadeau tonight, I guess.*

That's when someone cleared his throat, just through the screen
not four feet away.

"Surprise," Jesse Nadeau said, invisible in the dark.

Conn stood up quickly, a single lithe movement. "Nadeau."

"Conn Whitman."

"What's the plan, Jesse?"

"Just talk. I've been watching. Wanted to make sure you didn't have
some kind of a trap for me. Police or something."

"No trap, Jesse," I said. "Just us."

"Gonna invite me in?"

"Sure," Conn said. He turned on his flashlight, went to the screen
door, slid the bolt, stepped back.

A subtle shadow moved behind the screen, and then the door
opened. Jesse Nadeau paused in the doorway, wincing until Conn lowered the beam to the floor. The three of us stood in the strange light for
a moment, then I went into the house. I turned on a couple of lamps.

"After you, man," Conn said. *Strategic,* I thought: *not turning his
back on Nadeau.*

Nadeau came in, dressed the same as he was before, all black. Behind
him, Conn turned off his flashlight but kept it in his hands, a heavy
four-battery light with a barrel as long as his forearm.

Nadeau took in the room, quick eyes searching for danger, for tricks,
traps. He looked at me, dressed in jeans and checked shirt, and his sharp
grin flickered.

"I like your PJs. Ready for action, huh?"

"I didn't hear your bike come up," Conn said.

"Yeah, well. Borrowed a pickup. Parked and walked the last half mile. Celine seemed to hear me, last time, but *you,* I don't you know for shit. So I figured I'd case things out for a while."

Conn sat at the dining table and gestured for Jesse to join him. "Still driving that sexy XLCH?"

Nadeau stayed standing. "How'd you know about that?"

"Remember that guy Becker, long time ago—bought pot from you? I came to your place with him once, back when I was in college. The tornado on your bike—super paint job. I never knew your name, just put it together a few days ago. N-A-D-O. I rode, too, and I envied that tank for years. Stuck in my head."

"So much for staying under the radar, huh? No. Different bike. No fancy paint." Nadeau's mouth creased, that sharp-cornered grin.

Conn was doing an amazing job, I thought, establishing common ground.

"Want to have a seat, Jesse?"

Nadeau took a turn in the room, that coiled energy not letting him go. "You got anything I could eat? I been roughing it. Could use a bite."

I went to the kitchen, rummaged in the refrigerator. "Boiled eggs okay? I can make some toast."

"Sounds great. Appreciate it."

I set out a bowl with three eggs in it and put some bread in the toaster. "Orange juice? Milk?"

Nadeau came to the counter and at last sat lightly on a stool. "OJ'd be good," he told me. Turning to Conn, he said, "You've got a great lady here. She's smart and she listens. You could put down that flashlight."

Conn set it upright on the dining table, still near to hand, a compromise.

Nobody spoke as Nadeau cracked an egg and peeled it quickly. He put it whole into his mouth, chewed twice, swallowed. All three of us startled when the toaster chunked. Nadeau peeled a second egg as I buttered the bread and brought it over.

"How'd you know who I am? Where I live?" Conn asked.

Nadeau folded a piece of toast, bit off half of it, hardly chewed it. "My uncle. Paranoid as shit. Keeps game cameras in the woods, at the gate? He showed me the video of you driving up and looking around. Who the fuck? he asks. I didn't tell him I recognized you."

"How did you?"

"Your sister. She showed me newspaper photos, her bad-boy brother up to his ass in trouble. I saw you on TV one time, some talk show, saying how sorry you were!"

"But how did you find this house? Nobody trailed me back from Stannard!"

"Been here before. You had just come back. We drove past, Laurel told me you'd moved in here. Told me you'd bought her out of the cabin, thirty thousand bucks. She said, 'This is where I got the money, Jesse! My asshole brother bankrolled us.'"

Conn looked stunned. I could tell he was searching his memory, searching his conscience.

Nadeau cracked the last egg and devoured it, watching Conn.

"I'm not getting all of this," Conn told him, "but yes, I bought her out. Pop died, left it to both of us. I wanted to keep the place, she wanted money. I had enough saved. We got it appraised, split the value equally."

"I believe you. She never complained about the split."

"So why was I the asshole brother? I mean, I know I was. But—specifically?"

Nadeau drained a tumbler of orange juice. "How much time you got? That could take all night."

Conn palmed his eyes. "Jesse, I am feeling like shit about my sister. For so many reasons. Is telling me how I'm an asshole why you're here?"

Nadeau looked at him speculatively, looked over at me with that same expression—one of wondering where to go from here.

"Actually, maybe. Mainly I'm here because I didn't kill your sister, but I'm a suspect. I need to get out from under it, man, I need to get a start. I can only think of two reasons anybody'd accuse me of it. One is, I just get out of the pen, and somebody kills your sister. Timing is suspicious. Right?"

"Right."

"And the other is, she's the one who sent me up, so I get out and I'm gonna take revenge for twelve years in shitland."

"That's what the police think, yes."

"Problem is, it's not true. She didn't send me up. So where's my motive?"

"Jesse, she testified about your transporting and dealing. That's a fact."

"Yep, it is. It was also a plea deal. She and the lawyers and me talked about it. We figured I'd take it all, why have both of us go down? The lawyers said we were both looking at seven to ten years. So at the hearing, she testified against me and I pled guilty to get the rap entirely off her. The state saves the money of a trial, the prosecution is grateful. She stays out, I get a shorter stretch."

"Why would *she* have gone to jail?"

"Remember the thirty thou you paid her? Laurel came up with the idea. Make a big purchase, a one-time deal, clear a hundred thou, be all set. I had a connection, she put up the buy money. We were partners."

Conn shook his head. "So my sister made you do it? I should believe you why? Because you were what, a saint?"

"No, I was a fucked-up loser and she was not far behind, trust me. She didn't make me do it, we were in it together. With my record, my ass was cooked anyway, no point in her going to jail. We figured she'd get off if she testified, just an innocent girl, pregnant, I'd plead and get a reduced sentence—just six years. And that's what happened. We kept in touch the first year. The lawyer should be able to confirm how it went."

Conn sagged. "Pregnant. Whose?"

"She said mine."

"You said you got six years, but you were in for twelve. Why?"

Remembering, Nadeau stayed surprisingly calm. "I'm part Indian, right? Guess what, lots of race rage in the penal institutions. So Tonto got a lot of shit and didn't have the cavalry to back him up. So finally, I had to cut a guy. No, he didn't die. But I got another six-pack. They transferred me to keep me alive."

Listening to him, watching his face—hard, resigned, used to tough stuff—I couldn't imagine this recital being a lie. It wasn't a script, didn't seem practiced or forced. He didn't strike me as subtle enough to pull off a facade of injured innocence.

"When you were in jail, you kept in touch?" I asked.

"Yeah, I just said. Telephone for a while. She wrote me letters a couple times."

"Were you hoping to . . . get together again? After you got out?"

Jesse snorted, derisively. "Sorta kinda. Six years is a long time to ask somebody to wait. But there was gonna be a baby, so maybe."

"What happened?"

"She lost it. Said it was a miscarriage, but how would I know? A year after that, she says she's shacking up with this other guy, gonna get married. I'm like, okay, I don't blame you. I'm a long time gone. We weren't exactly Romeo and Juliet."

Nadeau was too hard to be sad about it. It was too long ago, and long accepted. His life had not left much room for sentimentality.

"That was Billy Carlson?" Conn asked. "The guy she married."

"Carlson, yeah."

"Jesse, you want something else to eat? I can—"

"No, I'm good."

I came around the counter, passed Nadeau's looming, lounging frame, and sat across from Conn at the dining table. From the way Conn looked at me, I could see he was getting lost in this. He believed Nadeau, too. But the revelation of Laurel's pregnancy and the court process—all of which an attentive brother should have known—was overwhelming him. Here came the guilt and shame and self-condemnation again.

"So, Jesse, what do you think we can do for you? How can we help get you off the hook?"

He looked uncertain, as if his thoughts hadn't taken him that far yet.

"You're in touch with the cops, right, victim's family stuff? Look up the case from back then. Find the lawyer. I'm out in the boonies, man, no phone or internet, afraid to be seen in town, I can't do this shit myself! You talk to them."

"The police will still want to talk to you."

"Talking, I'm okay with. Arresting or shooting me on sight, not so much. You talking to them first would chill out that first contact."

Conn's face was stiff with a barely concealed, pained wince, as if he had a headache. But he rallied, organizing his thoughts. "First question they'll ask is your whereabouts on or around June 25. And if you have an alibi."

Nadeau chuckled. "Oh, I have a great alibi. An old crank uncle who's getting pretty gonzo upstairs, lots of cred with his neighbors, you bet. If he remembers, he'll say I was out on his back forty skidding logs. Which is true."

"Okay. What was your lawyer's name? Back then?"

"Public defender, Black gal, young. Eunice Williams."

Conn went to the desk and came back with a notepad and pen. He jotted the lawyer's name.

"She still with the public defender's office?"

"No clue."

"What will we learn by talking to her?"

Jesse seemed to have considered this. "Couple of things. One, Laurel and me were on good terms, she was grateful. Said she loved me. You can see she felt bad about me taking the whole thing."

"She say anything about that in her letters?"

"Yeah. But she had to be careful about writing down anything about the pleas."

"You keep any of the letters?"

Nadeau's mouth smiled, but not his eyes. "Shit gets lost, twelve years."

Conn bobbed his head, jotted, glanced at me. Nadeau watched him closely, more curious than wary.

"So, Jesse. Can you tell me, was Laurel into coke? Is that part of why you two bought into it? You could sample your own wares?"

"Coke? No, man. Coke was yesterday by then. Oxy."

"So, she, did she . . . ?"

"Oh yeah." Nadeau watched Conn react. "You really were out of touch, weren't you. You didn't know squat about her. And your sweet lady here says you're such *gooooood* listener."

"I'm trying to mend my ways," Conn said dryly.

"What a great guy."

Conn took that like a slap and clearly wanted to push back at Nadeau. "And did you have anything to do with her taste for oxy? Because you were selling pot twenty years ago, and Becker tells me you started selling serious stuff somewhere back then, so—"

"Hey, she was into it before we ever met! Got a prescription, got hooked. Classic on-ramp."

"What, she had surgery, or . . . ?"

Nadeau was getting worked up. His leg started to jiggle, and then his chest gave one of those convulsive clenches I'd seen before. He stood up, strode through the room, flexing his shoulders, swinging his arms as if trying to fling off excess nervous energy.

"This is where you get to hear what an asshole you were," Nadeau said. "I mean, I heard her, man, I *heard* her on the phone, telling you about how her husband had beaten up on her. And you did fuck-all. 'He'd never do that!' is what you said. 'You're stoned, you don't know what you're talking about!'"

Conn looked stunned, confused. "You mean Carlson?"

The pressure in Nadeau was gaining momentum. His long legs carried him randomly through the cabin, boots hacking the floor. "Man, I did a lot of shit, but I never beat up on a woman. Look at the hearing record! They're trying to understand why she's turning me in. 'Did Mr. Nadeau ever strike you or otherwise act violently toward you?' Laurel says, 'No. Never.' Look it up!"

Nadeau stopped at the stairwell and looked at photos of Laurel. "Carlson? That was after my time. This guy, this fucker!" he shouted. He slapped Mason's face, sending their wedding photo flying.

# CHAPTER 41

# CONN

So there it was: What's true? What's "truth"?

Nadeau was big and wore a *don't fuck with me* aura that he'd probably begun cultivating long before his years in jail. But he struck me as honest—he was seeking only one thing: relief from his continuing imprisonment at his uncle's fortress farm. He didn't ask for sympathy, didn't threaten, didn't try to finesse. He was a man come to grips with himself during a long period of privation, impatient with sentimentality and vulnerability and excuses.

I tried to remain impartial. I told him I was willing to believe him, and that I'd check with his lawyer from back then. If she confirmed his story, I'd tell the lead investigator. I told him he should initiate contact with Selanski, and I wrote out her number and gave it to him. But he took it with a look of contempt, and I doubted he'd use it.

Eventually he left us, slipping out through the screen porch and overland through the woods to wherever he'd parked his borrowed truck. But before he went he painted a picture of Mason, of Laurel in the aftermath of her marriage to Mason, that staggered Celine and me.

He had challenged us: *Why do you think she'd go with a guy like me?* I didn't suggest *Because you gave her the fix she needed!* Instead, I just bounced the question back at him: *Why?*

His answer was essentially, *Because she needed big and dangerous and unpredictable enough to give that fucking husband second thoughts about ever touching her again.*

Did she say how she got onto oxy? *Oh, yeah. Two front teeth punched out of her head by your buddy. We spent four grand of your money getting implants to replace the bridge she'd gotten.*

After he left, I badly wanted to talk to Celine: *What's your take on him? Is he telling the truth?*

She was moving around the room distractedly, plumping pillows on the couch, little tasks that kept her from looking at me. "Conn, I am way too tired for this now. I can't deal with it objectively. Another time."

I took it as a rebuff—she was disgusted with me after hearing just how thoroughly I'd ignored Laurel. I hadn't known about her pregnancy, her miscarriage, her front teeth: pretty outrageous inattention.

That is, if we believed everything Nadeau said.

We dragged the mattress back upstairs and went to bed. Celine was asleep, or pretended to be, instantly. But I couldn't join her. I realized I hadn't gotten a phone number for Nadeau and castigated myself for carelessness. Unless he called Selanski, I figured we'd get another surprise visit from Nadeau sometime soon.

Then I lay sleepless as all the bad ghosts came back.

Estelle D'Ambrosio said I'd find Laurel between my ears. I had started inspecting my memory, running the magnifying glass along the years when we'd lost touch, when I'd lost her. Then the daily realities of the police investigation, the forensics, the successive discoveries, had overtaken us. I hadn't kept up the process.

After Nadeau left, I lay next to Celine, twisting in the sheets, sweating from self-hatred and tension, thoughts buzzing and swarming. Did Laurel call me in DC? Many times. It wasn't always about disaster, not at first anyway. Later, when she and Mason were having a hard time, they both called, blaming each other for screwing up the marriage.

It was not long after I'd started living apart from my wife. They always made bookend accusations, always escalating: *He did this! She did that!* Did Laurel tell me Mason hit her? Yes, and he told me she was screwing somebody else and taking drugs.

He said, she said. I was five hundred miles away and couldn't verify. My sister, my best friend. How could I take sides?

Now, fifteen years later, I couldn't recall the details of those calls. I'd been busy, preoccupied, at first with my bottle-rocket rush to the top, then with the tangles and messes of my fall.

I did remember a particular night when I got calls from both of them. At the time, I was a moth getting very close to the flame, nearing the end of my journalistic crusade against Senator X, which in retrospect had turned into a status, sex, and drugs joyride for me by then. I was at a posh bar in Foggy Bottom, K's, a popular watering place for politicos, sycophants, climbers and hangers-on, wannabe cognoscenti, and clever guys like me.

It's hard to convey now what a rush I got from being there. I felt *in,* and in the know. I was a spy on an important top-secret mission. I had prizes in my resume and powder in my pocket, and people liked me. I hadn't met Silk yet, but there were other women in the senator's escort circle, and I was sitting with three of them and a creepy little guy, not their pimp but a peripheral weasel who claimed to know things. The stools were tall, the table clear glass, so I was never out of view of long legs in short dresses, and I liked that.

The night was going well—I was making inroads with the women, circling in on Senator X. The jazz over the speakers was seductively hip. The warm amber lighting, sliced by leaves of potted palms and punctuated by sparkles from bottles and fluted glasses and earrings, got me higher than the coke we slipped away at intervals to snort. The sheer *urbanity* of it was a drug for a country boy.

My phone rings. I'm deep in conversation at that round glass table, and I shouldn't pick up, but I glance and see it's my sister. Reflexively I take the call. I plug my other ear against music and chatter so I can hear better. She's distraught. Something about Mason: Conn, you have to do something! Can't you do something?

Okay, calm down, calm down. What's going on.

I've told you this! He hits me! I've tried to talk to him, I've tried to settle him down, I've told him I love him, nothing works!

There's something slurred or lispy in her speech, as if she's drunk or high.

You stoned, Laurel?

I am. So are you, sounds like.

I feel a sweet touch on my thigh, and through the tabletop I see a gold-nailed, graceful hand placed lightly there. I look up to see, what was her name, Glory? gazing at me with a sly grin.

Okay. So your husband is hitting you. I'm five hundred miles away. Call the goddamn police.

She sounds like she's crying. Conn, don't you get it? He *is* the police! I have called. It all goes away. His brothers in blue don't want to hear it!

That beautiful hand is making small, slow circles on my thigh— teasingly, mockingly. The others at the table are silent and looking at me with the same amused, slightly embarrassed expression. It's déclassé to do this in public, I'm losing my cred.

Okay, so, Laurel, listen, I'm in a meeting. I can't do this right now. I'll call him, okay? Hear his side of it, too.

That outrages her. God damn you! she says, then something I can't make out, what with her slurry speech and the background noise at my end.

Talk to you tomorrow, I say. I love you, I add as an afterthought.

Later, I got a similar call from Mace. He got about the same treatment from me as Laurel did.

Remembering that night, I cringed inwardly as I wondered: Did she have that slurred lisp because her front teeth had been knocked out?

But—Mason? I'd known him all my life! By then, he'd been at the sheriff's for four or five years. And now, he was a pillar of the community, a good father and husband, a trusted friend who had never let me down.

Nadeau hadn't seen anything, I told myself, he was reporting secondhand. Laurel told him the same stuff she'd told me. True, not true? It was only half the story in any case.

Still, I had seldom spent time with Mason and Laurel since they'd married, I'd never seen the dynamic in their household. I could believe they'd had very different expectations of what married life was supposed to look like. Mason had been raised in a "traditional" household, where his father's word was law, where the belt was used on Mace's backside, where the mother did her duty and knew to keep her head down and opinions to herself.

Laurel could never have become Mrs. King—she'd been raised in a progressive home, taught to be assertive and confident, to say what she meant, to challenge people she disagreed with. She was smart and between her native verbal skills and ironic outlook, her tongue could be laceratingly sharp. Maybe Mason felt he needed to bring her into line—that's the reflex he'd have learned from his father.

And if what he said was true, that she was sleeping around, I could see that he might slip up. Not that violence was acceptable, not at all—but wasn't it a fairly predictable response to infidelity?

But that was a chicken-or-the-egg question. Celine had once told me about a couple who had gotten into an escalating mutual punishment cycle that took a toll on their kids. The husband beat up on the wife. The wife slept with other men. The husband said he hit her because she'd slept with other men, the wife said she slept with other men because the husband had hit her. Celine had used some psychological jargon for the dynamic, reciprocal cost-infliction, but it added up to tit for tat.

Which came first for Laurel and Mason? Whose version of "truth" was true?

Celine and I drank coffee at the kitchen counter on Tuesday morning. She had dark smudges under her eyes from lack of sleep, and I'm sure I looked worse.

"I told you I was a shit back then," I said. "I never tried to white-wash it. Did I?"

"No, you didn't."

"So why're you so distant?"

"I don't mean to be distant. I'm just processing." Her eyes met mine over her coffee cup, unreadable. "I guess it's different, hearing it more . . . blow by blow."

"I *did* neglect her. I beat myself up every day—you know this! Not to make excuses, but I *was* legitimately busy in a very consuming, very demanding job, and I was a long distance away. And I had loyalty to both of them, I couldn't just take her word on—"

"But it looks as if you kind of ended up on Mason's side."

She watched me think about that. Now her eyes conveyed a firm message: *This is something you have to consider.*

"I don't know if that's true. It's more that, by the time I got back here, it was kind of moot. They were divorced. She had a boyfriend, then married Carlson, then had some more sleazy guys when he left. Mason was this upright guy, sheriff's deputy, clean living, and my sister was really . . . I mean, you'd have to have seen it. Let's just say she was not the most together or credible person. It was easier to reconnect with Mason. I suppose Laurel could have seen it as my taking his side, or implicit acceptance of his hitting her. If he did."

She bobbed her head, taking it in. Understanding, but still holding back. Letting me listen to myself. I drank my coffee, grateful for the burn.

"Would beating up Laurel be consistent with your sense of Mason?" she asked.

I had pondered that during my hours of tossing and turning. "Not entirely inconsistent," I admitted. "His family culture was old-fashioned, male-centric. He could get physical, I've told you about a couple of times."

"How about in grade school? Playground fights?"

"God yes! This was back in the eighties. More farmers and loggers than lawyers and financial advisers, once upon a time. Read *Tom Sawyer*—fighting was just part of a boy's social vocabulary."

"You, too?"

"Absolutely."

"As often as Mason?"

"Well, no. But his father, his upbringing—'Stand tall! Never back down!' That kind of thing. It, uh, invited challenge."

Celine got up and went to rinse her cup in the sink, then started on last night's dishes. Over her shoulder, she said, "When Mace was here with Katy, he told me something like, 'back when Laurel and I were married, I did some things.' Implicitly, bad things. He didn't explain. But his emotional distress seems to center on contrition. Guilt. I think that's consistent with his having beaten her up back then. He's blaming himself, indirectly, for her death."

"Yes. As I am." I came around the counter to stand next to her. "Will you forgive me?"

"More to the point, will you forgive yourself?" She sidled against me, hip to hip, hands still working in the sink. "Don't worry. This has just given me a lot to think about. But you're still my favorite loon."

It didn't take long to track down Eunice Williams, Nadeau's lawyer for his drug-transporting conviction. She had moved on from the Public Defender's office and was now a partner in a small private firm, Dawson, Williams, and Randall, based in Montpelier. I was lucky enough to get through to her, and she kindly made time for me at eleven o'clock.

Their office was on the second floor of one of State Street's fine brick buildings, two blocks from the Statehouse. The wooden stairs creaked, but the lobby and hallways were beautifully renovated, retaining the glowing wooden wainscotting and crisp, crimped-metal ceilings.

Eunice Williams was in her midforties, the dark brown skin of her face formed around smile lines, her hair smartly coiffed. We shook hands across her desk and I took a seat. Tall, Victorian-era windows looked out on State Street, letting in light from the sky and the sound of traffic.

"So—Jesse Nadeau. That's a name I haven't heard in a while! You got me interested, Mr. Whitman. This for an article, or . . . ?"

"No. This is entirely personal. Jesse asked me to talk to you so you could confirm his version of his arrest and conviction."

"Which was . . . ?"

"That he and Laurel were equally involved in moving the drugs, but that you and her lawyer helped work out an arrangement where she agreed to testify to avoid jail time and he pleaded guilty. That they both wanted that result, it wasn't a hostile accusation on her part."

"That's correct. We worked it out together. I thought it was the best outcome, under the circumstances. She was younger, female, and pregnant—credibly innocent, lots of sympathy factor there. He'd had some prior run-ins with the law and had that biker look. Not so good, no way would he get off, so his best bet was the sincere contrition and guilty-plea route. Six years for him only was better than seven or eight for both of them." She cocked her head, puzzled. "Why has this come up? Why did he contact you?"

"Have you been following the murder investigation of Trudy Carlson?"

"No. I mean, I'm vaguely aware of it, but I don't have time to keep up."

"Trudy Carlson is Laurel Whitman."

"Whoa! So she's your . . ."

"Sister."

"I am so sorry!" Her face buckled with sympathy.

"Thank you." I nodded, gave it the necessary pause. "The reason Jesse contacted me is that he got out of the pen three months ago. He's considered a suspect in my sister's murder, and he wants my help to set the record straight. He—"

"Wait, what? Hang on! He pleaded, got six years. Should have been out six years ago!"

"He got into trouble inside, hurt somebody. Got six more."

She thrust out her lower lip. "Too bad. I mean, he was a tough dude, it's not surprising. I worried about him, all the race shit that goes on, how many Native Americans are gonna be there to back him up. But you always hope for the best, maybe they'll come out all right. Like that."

"Ms. Williams, do you by any chance have a copy of the hearing transcript?"

"I could get one. You could, too. It'd be in the Judiciary's records, you can fill out a transcript request online. Might take a while, though." My disappointment must have shown, because she grinned. "But I spent ten years as a public defender, and I've still got some good pals at the Washington County judiciary, over in Barre. Let's see if my magic wand still works."

She made a call, spoke familiarly with someone at the other end. Holding her phone with her shoulder, she put on reading glasses and began tapping her computer keyboard. She found the date and docket number of Jesse's hearing and read it out. After a moment, her eyes told me she was pleased. She said a warm thanks and gave the receiver a kiss.

She hung up and turned back to me, smiling broadly. "Still works! Marge is the court administrator, and she pulled up the transcript. She said she'd send it right over." Turning back to her computer screen, she said, "And it . . . should . . . be . . . right . . . *here.*" She scrolled and tapped, and a printer came to life on a side desk.

Eunice stapled together the sheaf of papers and handed it to me. "If you see Jesse again, tell him I said hello and wish him good luck. Same to you, Mr. Whitman. You hang in there."

Every reporter has days when nothing works, no one answers the phone, leads dead-end, you can't find the document you're looking for, the number you wrote down isn't right. Then there are the exceptions, when things go like clockwork. Today was one of those: I'd spent barely fifteen minutes with Eunice Williams and had gotten everything I needed.

I took the transcript down to my car and read it. Jesse had been telling the truth. The tone of Laurel's testimony was clearly not antagonistic, not frightened. No, Jesse had never hurt or threatened her. She was testifying against him for his own good, she said, to get him away from the drugs and bad associations—presumably, the good-girl narrative the lawyers and Jesse and she had come up with.

I tucked the papers into my briefcase and called Selanski.

# CHAPTER 42

# CELINE

In retrospect, I can see that Nadeau's visit was a turning point. Events picked up speed and urgency. If we were off balance before, we were more so after—more driven, too.

After Conn left on Tuesday, I went out to the shed to clean up the mess the bear had left. I swept up the birdseed and used the loaded dustpan to refill the feeders around the property—*duh*, I scolded myself—hung straight down from high branches for the sole purpose of keeping them away from bears. I reassembled the bags as well as I could and sealed them up with duct tape, stacked the sap buckets, put the shed in order. Lesson learned, I made sure to roll the door down when I was done.

Had some distance crept between Conn and me? A little. Nadeau's tale had brought home to me the true degree of Conn's neglect, and how strung out he'd been on his cocktail of chemical and social highs in DC. He'd never misrepresented himself, not at all, but he'd never spelled out the details.

And Mason: I couldn't help but believe Nadeau, and I wasn't sure I could ever regain my prior sense of Mace without the taint of this association. A man who had hit his wife hard enough to knock out her teeth.

What did any of this imply about the two men I knew today, so many years later? On one hand, I was susceptible to our age-old, instinctive sense that people have a "fundamental" character or nature, unchanging. On the other, I believed that people *do* change, they *can* achieve better balance, they *can* mend their ways. My profession and the values that guided my life were based on that premise.

At the very least, Nadeau's revelations made me understand the intensity of the guilt both men felt. Now I got it.

I was still out in the yard when the Postal Service car—just a Jeep with jerry-rigged right-hand drive and blue flashers tacked on top—rolled up to the mailbox at the end of the driveway. I waved to the carrier and then, as Conn had reminded me, went inside to get the plastic bag and gloves, in case anything had arrived for Laurel.

Among the miscellany addressed to Conn, I found one letter with a forwarding label on it. It was addressed to Gertrude Carlson, and the sender was the Law Firm of Cyrus Morgan Vandermeer. We had been hoping something would come from a lawyer, so that alone made my heart jump. But the address was what really got to me: 127 North Street, Richfield, Vermont.

That was the Tennyson Block. Destroyed by the fire.

I called Conn and found that he was meeting with Selanski at the State Police barracks. When I told him about the letter, he conferred with Selanski and asked me if I was up for a drive to Waterbury. She wanted to see it, too.

I parked next to Conn's Subaru in the barracks' parking lot and went into the three-story, mostly brick complex. Inside, an officer led me to a small meeting room with a metal table, four chairs, and not much else except a badly neglected potted fern and a window with a view of the parking lot.

Selanski sat with her chair tipped against the wall, feet on one corner of the table, scowling.

"I sure hope you got something good for me," she said. She was clearly in a foul mood.

"I don't know. I didn't open it." I set the bag of mail, including the new letter, on the table.

Selanski thunked her chair legs down, sighed heavily, and left the room. Conn watched her go with a tiny grin. She reappeared with a pair of nitrile gloves and a silver letter opener. Then she sat and tapped the handle of the letter opener against her front teeth for a while, keeping us waiting.

"So, before we look at the mail, has Conn told you about his morning's discoveries?"

"No."

"Please jump in if I've missed something," Selanski said. "To summarize, Nadeau came to your place last night. He knew where you lived because he'd been there before, with your sister, thirteen years ago. He's been living out in his uncle's woods, ass end of nowhere, and has heard we're looking for him. He told you he and Laurel were both into the drug-transport thing, that in fact she bankrolled the big buy with money she got for her share of your father's cabin. That jibes with the money, and the timeline, right, when you came back from your *Hindenburg* act and moved into the cabin?"

"Yes."

"He says Laurel's testimony was agreed upon, part of a plea deal facilitated by their attorneys. No hard feelings, yada yada. He comes back after twelve years upriver, discovers he's a murder suspect. Tells you he can't start his life until it's cleared up. So you, Conn, do your due diligence and go meet his lawyer. Who confirms everything. The deal got Laurel off the hook and him a reduced sentence. The hearing transcript bears out the absence of hostility and you can read the plea deal in or between the lines, at your pleasure." She slapped at a sheaf of papers of the table.

"That's about it, yes."

"Which pretty well puts the kibosh on Nadeau as a suspect, unless we find some forensic evidence. Motive was all we had for him."

I had to speak up: "I know subjective impressions don't carry much weight in a murder investigation. But from what I saw of Nadeau, I believe him when he says he didn't kill Laurel. It's not consistent with his frame of mind. He's just not in that . . . headspace. Just my two cents."

"Two cents and the cost of a PhD, huh? I hope you told him I want to see him anyway."

"Of course," Conn said.

"Got a number for him?"

"No."

"Give him my number?"

"As a matter of fact, I did."

"Well, hallelujah! So next time you all get together for a social occasion, ask him to use it, would you? Thank you very much. Now, let's see what the US mails have for us."

I pushed the bag over to her. "The one on top."

Selanski pulled on her gloves and carefully slit the envelope. Her eyebrows went up as she read it out loud: "'Dear Client, we at Cyrus Morgan Vandermeer are writing to inform all our esteemed clients that we will be closed for an indeterminate period due to the devastating fire at our offices in Richfield. We will be making personal contact with you at the earliest possible time. Please rest assured that we will do everything in our power so see that your legal interests are being served. If you have questions, or if you urgently need legal services and would like to find other counsel, please call et cetera et cetera. Thank you for your patience and understanding. Sincerely, yada yada.'"

She slapped the letter down and we all just looked at one another.

"So—how're we going to get this motherfucker?" Selanski growled.

She meant Laughlin. It just couldn't be coincidence that this arson fire burned out the very law office Laurel was presumably consulting on legal actions against him.

Conn was the first to speak: "Well, surely the lawyers backed up their files to the cloud, right?"

Selanski shrugged, not so confident. "Or an external drive that got cooked along with everything else."

"How many hoops do you think we'd have jump through to get access to her files?" Conn asked. "Presuming they survived the fire?"

"Could be a whole circus of warrants and probates and hoops and garters, lastly through a hogshead of real fire," Selanski said grimly. "Or not. Maybe you can do your 'trust me, I'm a good ol' local boy' routine and finesse cutting some corners again." Selanski gave Conn a look, all vinegar.

Selanski's phone buzzed on the table and she swept it up impatiently. "*Did* I say I was not to be disturbed? I did? Really? *Very* good!" She slapped at her screen to disconnect and glared at us as if we were the offending caller.

"What's the status of the arson investigation?" I asked.

"Murder investigation," Selanski corrected. "My buddies over at Arson are kinda bummed because the heat was intense, the roof and upper floors collapsed, and there's not much evidence on the arsonist. Best they got is the remains of two five-gallon plastic fuel jugs, but they look like two big shit pies, they're melted flat and burned and won't have fingerprints."

"What about Artie?" Conn asked. "Was it Artie?"

"Still working on it, but the pathologist says the bones show aging consistent with Artie, and no one has seen Artie since the fire."

Conn nodded, then raised a finger and hazarded, "I had a thought."

"Well, praise the Lord for small mercies."

The corners of Conn's mouth twitched in another suppressed grin. "The women at Martinson's. One of them, Gail Pelkey, knew my sister pretty well. I was thinking of talking with her again. She's a section manager, no doubt reviews staff time sheets? She might be able to check and see if Laughlin took time off around the date of Laurel's death. Or tell us if he was in the store last Friday between, say, five and six."

Selanski wasn't impressed, but shrugged in acquiescence. "Why not? Even if he was AWOL at those times, it won't prove anything. But it can't hurt to know."

Selanski's phone vibrated again and skated toward the edge of the table. She caught it with a catlike gesture, put it to her ear. Whatever the issue was, she rolled her eyes as she listened. "What'd I say? What did I say? That's right. So it's on you, and don't ask me because I'm busy."

She clicked off, frowning. "Can't get good help these days."

Then she looked at us as if surprised we were still there and made a shooing gesture with her hand.

"Carry on, carry on," she ordered impatiently.

Outside, Conn and I leaned against our cars, knees almost touching. Thin clouds had covered the sky, suggesting a front was moving in.

"Selanski's not having a great day," Conn said.

"You're smitten with her, admit it."

"I am. Totally. You know what I really love? It took me a while to pin it down—her self-satirizing thing. So deadpan. With such panache."

It was good to see his grin flicker on his tired face. It was a fractured grin, though, rueful and full of concern. He had a lot on his mind.

"I guess she had some hopes pinned on Nadeau."

"Yeah, and I threw ice water on it."

"Did you two talk about other leads? The people she went camping with, or the anonymous tips they were getting?"

"No. I should have asked. But my guess is that if they're working those angles, they're not panning out. Selanski was hot on Nadeau. I think Laughlin is everybody's new fave."

That was the sense I got, too.

"So, Celine—what's your plan for today? Want to spend an hour or two with your beloved?"

"Probably."

He explained: Laurel's house was starting to stink and needed cleaning. We were up in Waterbury anyway, might as well see to it.

We caravanned to Maple Meadow and parked in the driveway of Laurel's double-wide. The day had darkened further, and the radio said rain was coming. When we went inside, especially in the weakening daylight, the place seemed forlorn. It wasn't just the scent of rotting food

and mildew, or the gray-powdered surfaces—Conn was right, it was as
if the life force or esprit that had animated it was draining away. It was
no longer anyone's home.

This was just a cleaning visit. Eventually, we'd need to liquidate the
place and store or sell Laurel's belongings, but there would have to be
a probate process first, allowing Conn to become estate administrator.

We opened all the windows, then started in the kitchen, attacking the
refrigerator first. Everything went into plastic trash bags we found under
the sink, and I took the bags to the bin outside as they filled. Conn began
scouring the interior, passing me wire shelves and plastic drawers, which
I washed in the sink. The agreeable scent of bleach cut through the stink.

Conn and I were a good team, needing few words to coordinate.
When we finished the fridge, I wiped up fingerprint powder as he vac-
uumed. I began mopping the linoleum as he moved on to vacuum the
carpet in the living room. Then I went to the bedrooms, stripped the
beds, and started a load going in the washing machine. Everything was
musty, fingerprint powder was everywhere. The bathroom was too small
for both of us to work in it, so while Conn scrubbed the fixtures I returned to the living room to water the plants, dust windowsills, and do
some general tidying.

Then I sat on the couch. In the absence of mildew and food-rot
smell, with the storm-front breeze starting to flow though, I discovered that it was actually a nicely put-together room. The furniture was
inexpensive, but all the elements for a good ambience were there, that
ineffable proportion of wood to fabric, wall to window, plants, paint-
ings, books on shelves, pretty things. Laurel had had good taste.

After a while I went to the bookshelf, sat down cross-legged, and
scanned the titles. I assumed Welles's team had opened every book to
search for contraband or cash or papers, so I wasn't looking for "clues."
I was just curious about Laurel, and bookshelves are pretty reliable por-
traits of personality.

This was a mixed collection. There were quite a few little-kids' books
here, with most of the classic titles in evidence: *Goodnight Moon, Char-
lotte's Web, The House at Pooh Corner,* and there were more in the girls'

room, geared toward young adult readers. Laurel's outdoor enthusiasms were evident in trail guides to hikes and climbs, and manuals for identifying animal tracks, insects, trees, and flowers. Her fiction collection was eclectic, ranging from literary bestsellers to mysteries and a few romances—not unlike my own tastes.

There were about twenty titles related to personal development, offering a DIY approach to psychology, fitness, parenting, nutrition, and meditation. A home-repair guide. A few volumes on history and archaeology, some biographies, a couple of memoirs. It was a bookshelf accumulated by someone with a wide range of interests, who did a fair amount of reading.

*Hello, Laurel,* I thought.

Conn was whistling tunelessly to himself in the bathroom. I pulled a few volumes at random, scanned them, slotted them back. Then one particular title caught my interest: *Winning Women and Comeback Queens.* The subtitle explained that it was a collection of biographies of inspiring women throughout history. I hadn't read it, but I vaguely remembered the title from some years ago, a minor bestseller. I'd noticed it because I sometimes recommended reading material to challenged moms coping with divorce and troubled kids.

Laurel had made a remarkable comeback. It wasn't surprising that she'd bought books of this kind, seeking inspiration from other women who had struggled. Out of curiosity, I opened it and scanned the table of contents.

Dozens of women were profiled in short biographies—suffragettes, abolitionists, scientists, warriors, nurses, athletes, authors, philanthropists, entertainers. The theme was that of resilience, overcoming hardship, bouncing back to victory. Most of them were familiar—Eleanor Roosevelt, Sojourner Truth, Marie Curie, Harriet Tubman, Joan of Arc, Florence Nightingale. Some were less known—Hildegard von Bingen, Boadicea.

One name struck me, and I inadvertently exclaimed "Huh!"

"What?" Conn called.

"Come take a look!"

He came to sit next to me as I put my finger on an entry in the table of contents: Gertrude Ederle.

"Gertrude. Think there's a connection?"

Comeback queens: Laurel—Gertrude—had read this book and at the least had taken solace and strength from their examples. Maybe she'd decided that she was going to *be* one of these women.

The folded corner of the first page of Gertrude Ederle's chapter confirmed our conclusion. Conn and I read the six-page profile to discover that she was an American athlete from the 1920s. In 1925, she attempted to become the first woman to swim the English Channel—and failed. But then, overcoming both public skepticism and her own doubts, she tried again in 1926. She not only succeeded, but she set the record for the fastest Channel swim ever—two *hours* faster than the fastest man. Her record held for twenty-five years.

"So, comebacks," I said. "Gertrude Ederle got brave, failed miserably, took a lot of flak, then came back to absolutely kick ass. First woman to make it, and her record lasted for *twenty-five years*? That's what your sister had in mind for herself, Conn! To the extent that she'd take that old-fashioned, ungraceful name. A daily reminder of her commitment."

Conn made a miserable noise. I knew what he was thinking: *And somebody killed that rising spirit, that phoenix of a woman.*

"I think I gotta quit for today," he told me. His voice had gone hoarse. "I'm gonna finish up in the bathroom and let's head out, yeah?"

But he didn't stand. As I closed the book, we spotted an inscription in ballpoint pen on the inside cover page:

*To Laurel, the winningest, comebackest woman I know, with absolute faith that there's much more to come. Stay the course!*
                                                        *—Katherine*

It was dated March 17, four years ago.

"Who is Katherine?" I asked. "Could she be our missing mentor, or sponsor, or therapist?"

We looked through every book related to self-empowerment without finding any more notes from Katherine. At last, feeling claustrophobic and frustrated, we went out to sit at the picnic table. The clouds had thickened further, and the breeze brought the smell of rain.

"March 17 is her birthday," Conn told me.

"So—this Katherine gave her the book as a birthday present. She had some background with Laurel, enough to recognize where she was at, psychologically—a threshold. Laurel followed up with a determined symbolic rebirth as Gertrude."

Conn just nodded, holding my hand, staring into nowhere. I waited for him.

"Lots of work to be done," he said after a time. "And I need to talk to Mace. I mean, I don't know how to sort out what Nadeau told us. I can't just let it go, but I don't know the starting place for that conversation. I don't know the goal of that conversation."

Yes, that was a tall order. I was trying to think of suggestions when the rain began, pattering on the vinyl cover of the shed, the roof of the house, the maple leaves above us. Wind started to make a rushing sound in the trees on the nearby hills, crescendoing. We went inside to close the windows, then locked up and took our separate cars back to Richfield.

My thoughts? I was thinking of Conn's amusement at Selanski's dudgeon, his fleeting grins. When I'd first met him, I'd been charmed by his grins and smiles—whole face, almost childlike, honest. But now only half his face smiled, an ironic, wistful lift of one cheek, while the other side remained resigned and joyless. At the realization, my chest clenched. *My dearest man!* I thought. *I want to see you smile again, all the way, your beautiful full smile.*

The rain hit suddenly, windshield blearing, and even with the wipers on high they could barely slap it away.

# CHAPTER 43

# CONN

I tried calling Mason first thing Wednesday, still unclear what I wanted to say to him or what I hoped for in return. When I let myself feel anything, my shoulders bunched, my hands clenched into fists. My last visit with Maddie and Julie, and our expedition to Laurel's house—my anger at the outrage of her murder was growing. My frustration, too.

His cell rang and went to the answering service. I left a simple message: "Hey, Mace. Give me a call when you can."

Celine had some school-related work to do and was planning to look through her resource guide for anyone named Katherine. If Katherine was the mentor or therapist who had helped Laurel, she might know something of use to the investigation. On the other hand, the inscription was dated four years ago—had Laurel stayed in touch with her? Katherine might know nothing of her more recent circumstances.

But it was a good bet she would know more about Mason and Laurel's marriage and its aftermath. And my role, or absence of one, in her life. Neither of which I looked forward to hearing about.

My next call was to Selanski, who said she could meet me at my friggin' convenience, she had absolutely nothing better to do. Then I called Gail Pelkey.

"Hey, Conn," she said. "I've been hoping you'd call." She had a nice phone voice, low and warm and full of implicit trust.

"Is this an okay moment to talk?" I assumed she was at Martinson's.

"Perfect. I'm out front taking a cigarette break. Which I'm cutting back on, by the way. Inspired by your sister."

I told her my errand and asked if she would have time to swing by the State Police barracks. She said she could spare a half hour during her lunch break, at noon.

That left me a few hours to kill. Not enough for a swim, but enough to put in some time at the *Herald*. I drove to the office and did my best to triage my workload. I caught up with the news feeds and office gossip, and learned that the re-vote on the school budgets had passed. It pleased me to think of Celine encountering this news when she went to her office today.

The most recent State Police press release about the murder of the state senator's daughter said they were pursuing all leads and invited anyone with information to contact the tip line. Its carefully crafted ambiguity told me that Welles wasn't making much progress. The Fire Unit had not released any new forensic details on the fire. Laurel's murder had faded entirely away.

Thirty-six-unit low-income housing project proposed for Randolph, neighborhood residents protest. Discount clothing store to open on the Richfield strip, downtown merchants object. Dog-leash laws to get stricter enforcement, dog owners complain.

Small-town life, and democracy, in action. Ordinarily, I'd take some pleasure in our town's perpetual contention and chafing, but I was too preoccupied with my own internal churning. I dashed off a couple of short articles, flipped them to editorial.

My last errand before driving to the State Police HQ was to call Cyrus Morgan Vandermeer, Laurel's lawyers. I got their answering service and left a short message, giving them my personal number and my line at the *Herald*.

We met in Welles's office. Captain Welles was there, uniform crisp as ever but face more weathered than I'd seen him, and his close-shaved chin was marred by a razor nick. He managed a quick perfunctory smile and handshake, then sat back behind his desk.

Gail and Selanski were already at the meeting table, Selanski in her blazer, notepad at the ready, Gail wearing her Martinson's store tunic, looking tense. For hellos, Gail and I exchanged smiles, and I touched her shoulder as I sat down.

"We've just been introducing ourselves," Selanski told me. "Captain Welles had a little time, and he was kind enough to join us."

I took a chair and let Selanski lead the conversation.

"So, Ms. Pelkey," she said, "has Mr. Whitman told you anything about our investigation into Trudy Carlson's murder?"

"No. We talked about Mr. Laughlin's sexual, um, abuse of the staff, and Trudy's work on a lawsuit against him. He didn't have to explain that it might be related to Trudy's murder, that it could be a motive. I told Conn I could see the guy doing whatever it took to cover his ass."

"'Conn,'" Welles quoted. "So you two know each other pretty well? First-name basis?"

Gail looked puzzled. "No. We've met one time. His sister called him Conn, so—" Then her brow crinkled and I could see that she was absorbing his implication. "You know, Mr. Welles, I work all day in a place that's full of sexual harassment and insinuations and little fucking comments. Don't expect me to put up with it here!"

Welles didn't flinch and he said nothing.

Gail stood up awkwardly and glared at Welles's impassive face. "Unless we're clear on that, I'm leaving. Had it up to here. Ball's in your court, big guy."

Selanski cleared her throat and gave her boss a dead-eye look.

Welles said, "I sincerely apologize. I meant no implication or disparagement."

Gail sat back down, not fully satisfied, breathing hard. It had taken a lot of courage to confront a uniformed, authoritative guy in his own domain.

"Now that we've cleared the air," Selanski said, businesslike, "we'd like to ask you some questions and possibly a favor. First though, we need to be assured that our discussion today will remain strictly confidential."

"Of course."

"With that understanding, I can tell you that we are considering Mr. Laughlin a person of interest in the murder of Trudy Carlson. We have several reasons, Trudy's dossier as well as other details that we're not at liberty to discuss at this time."

"I understand."

"We do not have enough information on Mr. Laughlin, insufficient probable cause, to question him or get a search warrant for his home or workplace. However, we may be able to investigate him more fully if we have a little more information."

"Or exclude him, to be clear," Welles put in.

"Okay . . ." Gail looked to me, puzzled.

"It was my idea," I told her. "We know, within a day or two, when my sister was murdered. It would have required some time for the murderer to drive to the area of her campsite, hike up the hill, kill her and another person, and dispose of the bodies."

"And relocate and conceal Anthony Shapiro's truck," Welles added.

"So we wonder where your boss was on June 24 or 25," Selanski finished for me. "Take any time off? And did he look any different when he came to work—extra tense, or tired, maybe cuts or bruises?"

Gail thought about it, shook her head. "Honestly, I can't remember. I'm sorry. But time off—I can check the time sheets in the files. Laughlin has to punch in and out like anyone else. I have to review my staff's times, so can access them."

"That would be great," Selanski said. "As long as you don't put yourself at risk in some way."

"I don't think I would. Not just by checking time sheets."

Selanski lifted her chin toward me, and I took the cue.

"And there's another date," I told her. "And time of day. Last Friday, between, say, five and six p.m."

"That one, I do know. He took a half day off. He said he had to take his son to a doctor's appointment."

Selanski and Welles exchanged a glance. Selanski jotted notes to herself.

"Thank you, Ms. Pelkey," Selanski said. "Now I have some questions that might be difficult. They involve specific sexual behaviors. Are you up for answering them? Would you be more comfortable speaking without men present?"

Gail shifted uneasily in her chair, eyes on the tabletop. "I'm not going to tell you much in any case. Might as well go ahead."

"Can you give us any sense of Laughlin's specific actions with you or any of the other staff? Physical acts? This is important because at some point sexual behavior becomes a criminal act, which we can pursue. Again, I do not want you to answer if you are uncomfortable with this question."

"My case is different. It's not necessarily indicative. Because I accepted and reciprocated at first."

"Can you explain?"

Gail looked at me, ashamed but, as before, squaring her shoulders and facing into it. "His initial approach to me was flattering comments about my appearance, then casual physical contact. He had just come on the job. I was single and lonely, and I didn't know anything about, you know, whether he was married or not. I guess I preferred to assume he wasn't. I found him sort of attractive. Later, he told me he was getting divorced. I thought there were possibilities."

"Okay."

"So when he started touching me more, um, intimately, I was seeing it as, you know, a relationship progressing. I sure didn't know it was, like his . . . habit. His MO."

"At the store only? Or—"

"At the store at first. Later, at my place. When the kids were at school or with their dad."

Selanski nodded.

Gail gulped a few breaths. "And I'm not going into specifics about that."

"That's fine. We don't—"

"Then one time I saw him in his office. The door was open just a little, he didn't notice. He was with . . . a girl at the store. A fairly new hire. She was facing the wall, hands kind of braced on the wall. And he had his hand under her skirt from behind. I couldn't really see her face, but . . . the sides of her cheeks were bunched up . . ."

Selanski took a couple of deep, slow breaths, giving it time, watching Gail closely. Welles remained gray and impassive, but his eyes were now half lidded, with a glint that would cut glass.

"Did you confront him about it?"

"I said something later. He just said I should mind my own business, she wanted it just like I had wanted it. And I should watch my own ass because he could cost me custody of my children."

Selanski took some time to regroup. "Thank you. Now, this is very difficult, and I'm sorry we have to go here. At the time you and he were seeing each other, was Trudy Carlson working there?"

"Yes. She had started not so long before he came on."

"And do you think he was assaulting her as well?"

"I'm not sure. Probably yes. Because not long after, she started quietly talking to everybody about what they'd experienced. I told her about myself, but nobody else said anything at first, it took her a long time to win their trust. Some of them left or were fired. I told her what I knew, but I knew my take on it was fucking *compromised* by it being consensual. Some of the time anyway."

"I take it you stopped seeing him, but he kept making unwelcome physical contact with you?"

"Do we have to do this?"

"Only if you're okay with it. I mean that, Ms. Pelkey."

"Then yes, he did, and no, I'm not telling you anything about it. I'm going to throw up."

I hated to say anything, but I felt it was a detail that needed to be addressed. "Gail, serial sex abusers often try to obtain 'souvenirs' such as compromising photos or videos. Do you think Laughlin might do that?"

Her eyes went to the corner of the room as if trying to remember, but I suspected she was thinking back to her times with him at her apartment. I wondered: Did he bring a camera? Did he script and direct the encounter? She actually did look nauseous.

At last she muttered quietly, "I don't know."

We waited in silence for a time, and then Gail startled us all by saying "Oh fuck!"

She jumped to her feet and quickly gathered up her purse. "I've got to get back! My lunch break is almost over. I don't want to have to explain anything to Laughlin." At the door, without turning back, she said, "I'll look into the time sheets."

Welles and Selanski and I sat. I would have liked to walk Gail out, to thank and comfort her, but didn't want to reinforce Welles's suspicions. Or Selanski's—always observant, she had noted our hello smiles and my hand lightly touching Gail's shoulder.

Welles was the first to speak. "Marlene. I am tired, I'm getting frustrated, and I'm slipping up. If you have future contact with Ms. Pelkey, please reiterate my apologies to her."

"Will do, boss." Comforting him.

"Did we learn anything today?" Welles asked.

"She witnessed an assault in Laughlin's office," I said. "If he does do the souvenirs thing, that's where a camera would be."

Selanski jotted, looked up again. "Noted. But we're still miles away from the murders or any excuse to question him or look at his office. What else have we got?"

"I've left a message with the law firm," I said. "If Laurel's files were backed up off-site, that could give us something."

I looked over to Welles, worried that he would take exception to my involvement and ready to challenge him. But he didn't. Maybe he figured that, as her surviving sib, I'd have a better chance of getting access to the papers without weeks of legal red tape. Or maybe he was getting desperate enough to let me forge on my own way.

Welles made an unhappy face. "What about the fire? Any chance of linking it to Laughlin? Aside from motive."

"Sorry, boss. The Fire Unit folks aren't optimistic. I've got Dennis

Manring looking at gas stations to see if anyone remembers a customer filling a tank of gas and a tank of kerosene. Maybe some video on that. But the arsonist could have bought them at any of hundreds of gas stations—that's weeks of legwork." She blew out a long breath. "But we're keepin' on keepin' on."

It had been four days since my last swim, and I was feeling it. Physically, this meant an actual ache in my shoulders and the back of my legs from lack of use. Mentally: a head like a musty attic, stale, no ability to concentrate, to make decisions, to see anything clearly.

I was in Waterbury, so after I left I opted to swim in the reservoir there—a terrific lake, seven miles long, clean. Midday, midweek, I figured there wouldn't be much boat traffic to worry about, though I did have some concern for snags after yesterday's downpour.

I drove five miles from the State Police barracks to the nearest of the public beaches, got my suit and towel from the backseat, and changed in the men's bathroom. Waded in like any other beachgoer, but slipped under the buoys and headed out into the open water.

For about ten minutes I swam hard, like a machine, until I realized I was trying to punish or purge myself. Not so good. So I quit the slicing crawl and spent five minutes striving instead for grace, diving in deep arcs and feeling the water's gentle pressure as a caress. *Thank you*, I told it. I went down until my ears hurt, then made the yawn reflex at the top of my throat to equalize pressure. Down farther until the surface was a distant silver shimmer over a vast dim realm and my lungs started to complain. Then rising in the same curve and bursting into the welcome air just in time.

Gather breath, do it again, deeper still. Arc and soar.

Better. The lake felt almost like a unified living thing, a massive being enveloping me. It could be benign, often was, but it was powerful and set hard rules, too. I'd tried to explain this sensibility to Celine once: *Lakes are little gods*, I said. *Local gods.*

I dove and rose until I felt I'd switched channels and was ready to swim again. This time I began a slower crawl, paced, rhythmic in the way dancing is. At about three miles, I began to tire. Regretfully I reversed and headed back toward the beach. An hour later, I stumped and sloshed ashore just at the right moment—more would have been too much, less not enough. No snags at all, no alarms.

*You can still have a perfect swim*, I thought. *Maybe there's hope for you after all.*

# CHAPTER 44

# CONN

Swimming again. I am far out, changing strokes often, keeping eyes open above and below the surface. The scent of water—mineral, slightly fishy, vegetative, atmospheric—lingers in my sinuses. I'm taking it easy, swimming lazily, but after a little while the fear of snags creeps up on me. We'd had that hard rain, that's right, the feeder streams would have caught fallen branches and dragged them into the lake. Wary, I keep my eyes wide open underwater.

As I continue, the sky becomes overcast, the daylight congealing, not penetrating the lake. The view below me becomes increasingly obscure and the depths become gradually more shadowed and mysterious. Something frightening in them. Or something unclean.

I realize I am in the Richfield Reservoir, with its silty, olive-tinted water. The water is too warm, body-temperature, unrefreshing, and tastes of decay. What am I doing here? I told myself I'd never swim here again! Looking down, my shadow raying away in the silty haze, I'm hit by a wave of vertigo as if I'm perched on a high ledge and could fall. I need to get out of this water but the only way is to swim back, a long distance. How have I come so far?

I look above the water to orient myself, but my eyes are bleary, the light is blurred by a sullen glowing mist and there are no shores, no landmarks. Which way is land? I tread water, turning to scout for clues to the nearest shore. Maybe there's a darker band above the water this way. Or no, this way.

And my shoulders are tired, I've swum too far, my legs feel heavy and unresponsive. What was I thinking? Why did I swim so far in this awful water? My body is leaden, gravity is pulling me. The opaque depths are sucking me down and I don't have the strength to resist, I can't catch my breath, I can't get enough air.

I'm struggling to keep my head above the surface, and then my foot strikes it, the yielding thing, the bulbous thing. Terrified, I look below and it's right there, not spinning away but bobbing and shuddering right below me, murky blue-white, bulging with grotesque shapes hidden within the shroud. I stroke away but my foot is stuck, it's snared in a rope, wrapped, snarled, binding me to the thing.

I kick at it with the other foot, feel the yield of bloated flesh, but it still clings to me. I pry at the ropes with the toes of my other foot. Nothing yields, I have to draw breath. I convulse hugely to get my mouth above the surface, I gulp in the decay-scented air. The thing won't let go.

I take a huge breath and bend and reach down my trapped leg with both hands, sliding down my thigh and then down my calf to the ankle. My fingers pick at the ropy tangle and it feels hard, bony, it's actually fingers, hard clenching fingers, two hands, gripping my ankle. As I yank and pry, they shift suddenly to clamp my wrists, too, and I'm locked into this position, bent double like the thing in the shroud.

I scream underwater, bubbles explode from my mouth as I blow out the last of my air. I arch my back as hard as I can, wrenching backward away from the thing and its grip and I smash something solid with my head.

I open my eyes and it's dark. There's no milky luminous fog, just enough light to recognize the wall and ceiling of my bedroom at the cabin, reassuringly solid. I've smashed my head against the headboard.

The rafters and the white slanted ceiling brighten suddenly and now the room has shape and size. The light over the stairs has come on.

"Conn? Are you all right?"

Footsteps, and there's Celine coming up, emerging full in herself at the top of the steps, beautiful, concerned.

"Wow, Conn, you were moaning and groaning! What was that thump?"

"A dream," I say. "Had a bad dream."

Her face moves with sympathy. "Dinner's ready. Whenever you are." She turns and descends and now I've found myself in space and time: coming home, glad to find Celine there. Talking briefly, feeling a pleasant drowsiness, opting for a nap.

How had that fine swim, my well-earned fatigue, metastasized into such a horrible dream? The ropes around my ankle, binding me to the blue-white bundle: Yes, that object in the reservoir was still holding me, couldn't be pushed away. It was staying with me. It had to have been my sister, murdered, then wrapped and tied and submerged there. What else could it have been? And if it was, why didn't Welles and his people find it when they searched? Anchor, rope, tent fly, Tony Shapiro's shrunken body in the rubble. There was a pattern or design here, one that had tormented me before, but that I still couldn't decipher.

# CHAPTER 45

# CELINE

Conn emerged from his dream badly rattled. He told me he'd been swimming and had again kicked the swollen thing, this time tangling in the ropes that bound it. The ropes felt like fingers.

Its origins and implications were so obvious that we didn't explore it. It was best to let the horror fade away, bring him back to solid ground with the small distractions of domestic life. I lit some candles, set out the Caesar salad I'd put together, and told him about my day.

It had been a good one for me, given the news that the school budget had passed in the re-vote. At school, I caught up with paperwork that would finalize contracts waiting on the result, then called various colleagues to share congratulations. We wouldn't have to go through that again—not for another couple of years anyway. I'd had to let go one of our guidance staff from Little Falls Middle School, but she was nearing retirement and had volunteered to take the axe if cuts were needed.

I looked at the blotter calendar I kept on my desk. August 2—already? Another ten days of semi-vacation, and I'd be back here full-time, preparing for the fall semester. My regret was tempered by affection for my office, for the shining corridors and bright classrooms, that indescribable school smell, my chats with maintenance staff on the way in. Things orderly and normal.

*Winning Women and Comeback Queens*: Laurel, Trudy, had made an astonishing recovery from a long, troubled period. A disciplined recovery. Conn had bootstrapped himself, but in my experience this was rare—sustained transformation tends to happen when an individual has an inspiring role model. More, an *invested* role model, someone who actually, personally, cares about their recovery and sticks with its inevitable ups and downs.

Katherine who?

I searched our current referral database for therapists, psychiatrists, and drug and alcohol counselors, but didn't find any Katherines. Of course, the book's inscription was over four years old. Katherine could have retired or died or moved to Alaska.

We updated our referral list yearly, as new people were certified or came into the area and as others left the field or moved. We also backed up all documents to a cloud-based service, so prior editions of our referral list should exist somewhere in cyberspace. I went into the archive, found the directory from four years ago, and was thrilled to find a Katherine Charlebois. Her listing told me that she kept an office in Montpelier, had an MS in social work, and specialized in individual and couples counseling.

I tried the phone number and was told that it was no longer in service, so I followed up with an email, giving her my number at school as well as my personal phone. Impatient with the prospect of waiting for a return call, I googled the name and found a number of entries for her. Photos showed a woman in her late sixties, plump, with a benevolent smile and a soft cloud of white hair around her head.

While I was browsing, my inbox chimed, and I clicked quickly over to it. My email had bounced back.

Searching further, I found an obituary for Katherine Charlebois from last year. She had died of unspecified natural causes at sixty-nine.

My morale flagged, but I decided I had no proof this Katherine was the right one, and I should keep searching. When I pulled up the directory from five years ago, I discovered an additional Katherine who seemed to have promise.

Katherine Krantz had an impressive resume that included a PsyD, Columbia's version of a PhD, in clinical psychology. Her specialties included both drug and alcohol addiction and PTSD—a good combination for Trudy, I thought. I called the listed number and spoke briefly to a stranger who had no idea who or where Katherine Krantz was. I sent an email to the address listed, then went back to Google to learn more about her.

Photos showed a woman of about fifty who vaguely reminded me of Jody King—measuring eyes in an angular face with a determined set to jaw and brow. She was deeply tanned, with short hair, black but streaked with gray. Apparently she was a hiker and environmentalist as well as a therapist, and had written a book about the rejuvenating power of outdoor adventures—*Spirit Treks*, published seven years ago.

We hadn't seen that book in Laurel's shelves, but I went to Amazon to learn more about it. The author photo showed the same woman: fifties, angular face, and a level gaze. Apparently the book's theme was the psychological and spiritual benefits of solo wilderness experiences—especially for women. That convinced me that I had the right person, the woman who had inspired and guided Laurel. But where was she? The author bio said only that she lived in Vermont, or at least had as of seven years ago.

I searched Facebook and LinkedIn and found dozens of women of the same name. None of them were this person or a likely alternative candidate for Trudy's mentor. Maybe she had changed her name, or married and taken on her spouse's last name.

No one else was in the guidance office—still out savoring the last days of vacation—but I hazarded a call to Dot Lansing, my administrative assistant, who occupied the desk in my outer office during the school term. We called her Redoubtable Dot because she was a long-serving employee—a true stalwart. After thirty years with the district, she also served as the wetware memory of our department, a reliable source for names and details otherwise forgotten. Her devotion was such that I was pretty sure she'd pick up, even though I was intruding on her vacation time.

I called her home landline, left a message on her machine, and then called her cell. When she answered, I was pleased until she told me she and her husband were about to launch their kayaks.

She cut off my apologies with a laugh. "Not a problem, Celine. You know me! What's up?"

"Institutional memory needed."

"Got it on me here somewhere, I think. Ask away."

I told her I was looking for Katherine Krantz, who had been in our referral directory as of five years ago but of whom I could no longer find a trace. I described her face, in case the name didn't ring a bell.

"One more second, hon," she said, and I realized she was talking to her husband. I pictured them in some idyllic spot, kayaks half in the water, paddles in hand.

"I don't know, Celine. Krantz, vaguely familiar. Into outdoorsy things, I think. Um. This for a D and A referral?"

"Yep." *D and A* was shorthand for drugs and alcohol.

"If I'm thinking of the right person, I'm pretty sure she worked with the veterans hospital in Springfield quite a bit. Also vet organizations up our way. Boys coming home with injuries and PTSD, get on the opioid track, can't get off. Right, and she was also into, what . . . Native American healing, or Wiccan, or something a bit off the mainstream. Your predecessor thought she was maybe a little . . . *much* for troubled school kids and mommies and daddies."

Dot told me she had no idea where she'd gone or why she'd left the practice. I thanked her, wished her a good voyage, and disconnected. My inbox chimed, announcing that the email I'd sent Katherine had bounced back.

"Actually," I told Conn, "I almost called you. 'What would intrepid re-porter Conn Whitman do?' I'd ask."

He shrugged and swallowed a mouthful of salad. "No hard method. Just ferret around the edges. Work off of what you do know."

"Well, that's what I figured. So I made some calls to vets' organiza-tions, but the handful who remembered her didn't know where she'd gone."

"She may not be the right person in any case," he reminded me.

I made a telepathic face. "My inner voice is telling me she is."

Conn's grin moved up one side of his face, and my heart panged.

"Anyway, that's as far as I got," I said. "I had to start setting up district staff meetings and confabs with principals and local prevention organizations. Then I wanted to come home and, frankly, see my sweet patootie. My main squeeze."

"For which I am very grateful." He gave me a sincere, but still incomplete, smile.

We ate without talking for a while, just listening to the evening birds' liquid calls in the woods.

"Oh, and there's something else we should discuss," I said, remembering.

"Uh-oh."

"Laurel—shouldn't we call her Trudy now? She decided that's who she was going to be. Seems to me we should respect that."

"Yes. I'll try anyway. Might take a while for me."

So, Trudy it was, when we remembered: Trudy as in Gertrude Ederle, whose Channel swim ranked as one of history's greatest sports achievements—her record lasted twenty-five years, rivaling Babe Ruth's home run record for durability. I had looked up the origins of the name and discovered it meant "spear of strength."

Laurel, Trudy, had been aiming high.

On Thursday, I had some more chores to do at school, so I left the cabin early. But once I settled at my desk, I alternated school duties with continuing efforts to find Katherine.

I'd done mountains of research in my time, but not this kind. In college, I had sought out peer-reviewed studies recommended by professors. I consulted established experts in their various fields, and I read books considered foundational for my field. If secondary sources didn't provide answers, I used their citations to seek out primary sources. I considered myself a skilled investigator.

But this was different. There were no experts to consult, no clinical literature nicely cataloged in any library. I didn't think Katherine Krantz was dead—I'd dug deep into the Web and state death records and found no notice of her death. She had no social media presence, no recent publications, no business listing or personal phone number in any directory. I even conducted a criminal records search with no luck. She must have changed her name, or had gone off grid in some way. Where? Why?

I called a dozen colleagues in the counseling field, but again, few remembered her and no one knew where she had gone. Thinking to pick up more cues as to her interests or where her life path might have led, I ordered her book to see if I could find clues there. It would take a few days to arrive.

There was a Wiccan group in Vermont—I'd seen posters for herbal healing trainings and retreats on the co-op's bulletin board. And there were various contacts for the Abenaki tribe, Vermont's original residents. They held celebrations, ceremonies, and traditional healing events at intervals throughout the year. But if she was into Native American healing, she might have made contact with any of hundreds of regional or national organizations.

I made calls, sent emails, and got few replies. My hope began to fade.

Finally, feeling some trepidation, I dialed Mason's number. My discomfort was due to a dissonance in my sense of him, to knowing things about him I couldn't yet mention. At some point, I would, Conn would, talk to him about what we'd heard from Nadeau. It would be rugged emotional terrain without a road map.

Still, when I conjured Mason in my mind's eye, what I saw was his carefully checking the chinstrap of Katy's helmet just before they rode off on his motorcycle. A little girl and a big bear of a man with eyes full of care and tenderness.

I was a little surprised when he picked up. He immediately apologized for not yet returning Conn's call. He'd been spending time out at the camp again, "catching some summer while we've got it." Right now, he was again doing traffic management at a highway construction zone. I could hear the whoosh of passing cars at his end.

I didn't tell him about seeing Nadeau, but I caught him up on our pursuit of Laughlin—the letter from her lawyer whose office had been conveniently destroyed in the Tennyson Block fire.

"All right!" Mason said.

Then I explained that I had figured out who Laurel's addiction counselor had been—at least, as of four years ago. I wanted to talk to her in the hope that they'd stayed in touch, maybe learn something about the purported new boyfriend, or other details that would assist the investigation. Maybe even something about Laughlin. But I couldn't find contact information for her—could he run a lookup for a driver's license and car registration?

Mason readily agreed, said he'd get to it when he could. I thanked him, we chatted briefly about Jody and the kids, and then he got a call over the radio that needed his attention.

I closed the line, wondering if he had noticed anything different about my tone—the reserve I just couldn't overcome. It occurred to me that he seemed reserved, too—something pat or neutral about his conversation, his voice, almost as if I were some stranger.

At that point I was out of ideas. *Time for patience*, I told myself. Maybe some of my calls and emails would get answered and maybe I'd learn something that would maybe lead to Katherine who would maybe tell us something useful.

The string of uncertainties made me grumpy. Patience was probably not my strong suit, I decided.

# CHAPTER 46

# CONN

I got Gail's call not long after Celine left for school. She was taking a break in the form of a stroll past the other storefronts at the Martinson's shopping center.

"I feel crappy about that meeting with Selanski and Welles," I told her. "I would have walked out with you, but I didn't want, uh—"

"'To give the wrong impression'? Welcome to my world, Conn. Fucking tightrope of possible wrong impressions. I got pissed at Welles, but frankly I'm glad I did. And I'm pretty used to it." It was nice to hear her chuckle—half a growl.

"Well, we're gonna do something about it," I told her.

"On that score—I looked at the time sheets."

"And?"

"Well, you have to understand how it works. The store's open fourteen hours a day, seven days a week. Doors open at eight, but Laughlin and first-shift staff get here at seven. Nobody can work a hundred-some hours a week, so there are two assistant managers who take over when he leaves. Sometimes they switch with him for first shift, and all three trade off so the weekends are covered. It can be pretty fluid, depending on everybody's needs."

"Okay."

"So we maintain staffing calendars for coming weeks—who's going to be on vacation, or trading shifts, whatever. Trudy's camping trip was on there for weeks in advance."

"Got it." *Making it easy for him to make plans*, I thought.

"Everybody punches the time clock with a personal identity code, and a computer collates the data on a spreadsheet for payroll and for supervisory oversight—like, 'Jeez, that prick Jason skipped out on two shifts this week!' So I looked at the sheets. Long story short, Laughlin wasn't here on June 24 or June 25. The assistant managers took his shifts."

I felt a surge of satisfaction: *One more nail in your coffin, fuckhead.* I must have made a sound, because Gail laughed out loud.

"Right?" she said, pleased. "Right?"

"Did he say where he was going to be, where he was?"

"Timesheet says 'personal day.'"

"Too bad. 'Doctor' or 'conference,' something we could disprove, would have been nice."

"Yeah. But it's a start. And by the way, I took screenshots of the time sheets in case they magically go missing or get altered. I can send them to you. Or should I send them to Detective Selanski?"

My phone told me I was getting a call from someone else—Selanski's number. I asked Gail to send the photos to Selanski and copy me, and that I had to take the call.

Before she closed the circuit, I said, "You're pretty cool, Gail. Just so you know where I'm coming from." It felt good to compliment her.

"Thank you, Conn. You, too."

Selanski said she was in Richfield with a colleague and wanted to talk. I suggested meeting them at the Daily Grind in downtown, then brushed my teeth and put on some semi-civilized clothes. When I got there, I realized that it was probably not the best location: Its front windows looked across the street to the sorrowful gap where the Tennyson Block had been. The entire structure had been removed, leaving bare the brick walls of the buildings on either side. Dump trucks came and went. Backhoes front and back were filling in the basement hole with rock and gravel, moaning and clanking, a safety measure until rebuilding had been approved and funded.

Selanski was already inside, at a corner table with a tall man wearing a State Police uniform shirt and regulation trousers. The Daily Grind had a budget-conscious, vinyl-dominated ambience, but was famous for its artfully roasted beans, so though it was just mid-morning, a steady stream of customers came in for coffee and pastries. The construction noise turned out to be an asset, a background hubbub that would make it hard for others to overhear us.

Selanski sliced a little *hi ya* wave. "This is Dennis Manring, who's been doing some great work for the investigation. Wants to become a D, little does he know, poor sap. Manring, this is Connor Whitman, ace reporter."

Manring stood to shake my hand. He had dark brown skin, a close-shaven scalp, a firm grip, and a uniform shirt as sharply creased as one of Welles's. "Pleased to meet you, sir," he said.

"Norwich grad? Cadet Corps?" I asked.

"How'd you know?"

"Nobody but a former cadet would call me 'sir'!" I gestured at my rumpled clothes, unshaven face.

They laughed at that. Norwich University, a half hour from Richfield, was a well-regarded private military academy. It wasn't a hard guess: I had often visited the campus to report on one story or another, and every uniformed student had opened doors for me and called me "sir."

I sat facing the front windows, where I could see the backhoes laboring.

"So," Selanski told Manring, "Whitman is a stubborn sumbitch and has wormed his way into our confidence. He's now sort of a mascot for the team. I tell him about 80 percent of what we know and my guess is he does about the same." She gave me a speculative squint, then corrected herself: "Oh, make that seventy percent."

Manring bobbed his head, putting it together: Selanski was teaching him the ropes, the proverbial intangibles of homicide investigation—including managing people like me.

"Got Gail's photos," Selanski told me. She put her fist out for me to bump with my own.

I was glad to see her in a good mood again, and told her so.

"Well, I've got some nice show-and-tell today. But first, I'd like Detective-to-be Manring to catch you up on his progress. He's been doing a lot of legwork, chasing down all kinds of loose threads."

Manring made a self-deprecating shrug. "It's not really much. First thing was, I was assigned to running down anonymous tips that came in. We got hundreds in the early days, so there was a backlog from the start, took time to catch up. One tip was from a young-sounding male, who said Anthony Shapiro told him he was going to see Trudy when she was out camping."

"In itself, not a biggie," Selanski put in. "Tony was on our radar just from his association with her. But."

"The tip was logged before Mr. Shapiro's body was found. What made it interesting was that the caller clearly knew him. He said Mr. Shapiro was planning to plead with your sister to get back together with him. Tony told the anonymous caller that she agreed to meet him out at her favorite campsite, so he was pretty happy. Apparently Mr. Shapiro had gone to the site previously, and he thought it meant his, uh, plea would be well received."

*No, Tony,* I thought, *she was planning to let you down, decisively but in a nice way.*

We startled as a resounding *clang!* came from across the street. We looked to see the tailgate of a dump truck bounce again as its bed lowered.

"Just about jumped out of my skin!" Selanski griped.

Manring explained that he had traced the number to an athletic shoe store in Burlington, had gone to interview staff there. When he walked in, there were no staff visible, no one at the register. Only two were on duty, and they were back in the storeroom, trying to find shoes for customers. Manring walked up to the register desk, where he found the phone. Next to the phone: a Post-it note that read "Dial 9 for outside line."

"The staff told me they didn't know any Anthony Shapiro. My guess is our anonymous caller just came up, used their phone, and departed."

I didn't see the importance of this. Selanski must have noted my puzzled look.

"What I'm getting out of it is a better sense of the scene of the crime. Tony knew where the campsite was and had his hopes up, which to my mind increases the likelihood he was killed out there around the same time Trudy was."

I thought back to our attempts to visualize the sequence of events at the campsite. Somebody came up, killed Laurel—Trudy, I scolded myself—for whatever reason. Tony arrived as the murder was taking place, or shortly afterward, and was killed as well. Tony's truck would have been good for transporting the bodies. It must have had his boat's anchor and rope in it, suggesting to the killer a convenient means of disposal for Laurel at least.

Visualizing it brought up a nagging question. "Can I ask something that's been bothering me?"

"Shoot," Selanski said.

"Given the missing tent fly, the thing I kicked in the water, the anchor and rope, it looks like someone wrapped my sister's body and brought it down. But why bother? The campsite's a mile from the road, a lot of effort to bring a body down. And they put themselves at risk of discovery. Why not leave everything where it was and just get out of there?"

"That's been pestering me, too," Manring said. "I came up with two possible reasons. One is psychological—some killers are ashamed of their act and want to hide the evidence of it. To symbolically bury the crime itself. Bury the guilt."

"He's been acing his criminology courses," Selanski told me. Her dry tone couldn't disguise her pride in her protégé.

"The other possibility is that there was evidence on the bodies—or at least on Trudy's."

"Like . . . ?"

"I'm sorry, Mr. Whitman, but, uh, semen would be a possibility."

They gave me compassionate looks as I thought of Laurel's being raped before she was killed.

"Or blood," Selanski added. "Maybe that third-party blood on the knife was from an injury the killer got during the struggle. And some of his blood got on Laurel's body. He wanted to hide the fact."

Manring: "The removal of the bodies suggests that the perpetrator was taking precautions to avoid identification. Also, DNA degrades rapidly in water. Your sister's probable immersion could suggest they had some knowledge of forensic science."

I took a menu from the clip, feeling like I should at least pretend we were going to buy something. The others did likewise, but nobody looked at them. Across the street, the backhoes scraped and lifted and swung, reached and dumped.

"Okay. We are bumming this man out, Manring. Sorry, Whitman. But I wanted you here today because there's some really good news."

"That would be nice. Thanks." I meant it. I increasingly trusted Selanski's motives and liked her quirky style. I'd been impressed by her calm and authority during our meeting with Gail Pelkey.

Manring cleared his throat, gave a questioning look to Selanski.

"You go," she said, "and I'll put the cherry on top."

"I was assigned to help verify the identity of the corpse found over there," Manring said, tipping his head toward the backhoes. "It turns out Arthur Shindell, Artie, occasionally slept at a couple of overnight shelters provided by church groups. He was fairly regular at Bethany Church, on Spring Street—so much so that he had a favorite bed. In winter, the shelters fill up every night, but in summer the homeless population has other options, so Artie had his choice of beds. The beds there have old, steel-tube head- and footboards, covered in an enamel paint that's perfect for receiving fingerprints. His bed frame gave us dozens of prints of the same individual. We dusted them and are certain the latents we got belonged to the man people knew as Artie."

"And we got a match!" Selanski said.

"I thought the body was too badly burned—no prints."

"Oh, it was," she crowed. "But we recovered some beer cans with the body, right? Pabst Blue Ribbon, those twenty-four-ounce big boys. The two with the body were crisped pretty clean, just the barest residue of paint. But we found a third can, also PBR, same size. It was under a dumpster about fourteen feet from the vestibule where Artie was found. Unscathed. And covered in prints that matched the prints from Artie's favorite bed."

I nodded, glad we'd achieved almost certain identification of the corpse in the fire, sad that Artie had met his end that way. But Selanski was grinning from ear to ear, wringing her hands with suppressed glee.

I got the message. "So now I guess we're ready for the cherry on top?"

"There were other prints on the can, Whitman. Which belong to David Laughlin."

In an instant, I caught a measure of Selanski's excitement. It wasn't a feeling of satisfaction, but a rush of toxic anger and hate. A gust of nervous energy derived from a bad mix of adrenaline and pent-up tension and hunger for retribution. I pictured him coming to burn the lawyers' offices and finding Artie in one of the rear doorways. Not wanting witnesses, he provided Artie with enough beer to knock him out, or at least enough to cloud his memory. Left him to guzzle, came back when he knew he'd be plastered. Did he care if Artie also burned to death?

"Does that give you enough to bring him in for questioning?" I asked.

"Sure. Enough for a conversation about a beer can, which would lead to, 'Yeah, I bought a few cans and left them in the car while I ran some errands. Somebody must have stolen them from my backseat.' And then, knowing he was on our radar, he'd go home and destroy any other evidence he might have."

"Sounds like you're still one piece short of a search warrant," I said.

"We're working on it," Manring said. "I've been going to gas stations asking about purchases of kerosene and gasoline. A few of them still have video from last week, but mainly I'm talking to cashiers. If Laughlin bought the accelerants, he'd have been smart enough not to use his credit card. To pay in cash, he'd have to fill up the cans outside, then go inside to pay. Somebody might recognize him or remember his car."

"Manring has been to twenty-three gas stations, working out from Richfield. Within an hour's drive, you've got another, what . . . ?"

"Uh, sixty-two. And if you put Waterbury at the center of the circle, where Laughlin lives, you include all of Chittenden County, maybe another hundred."

The math was imposing enough to quash Selanski's ebullience. We sat there with the machines laboring across the street, and her face told me her mood had morphed into one like mine—angry and deadly serious.

"Thing is, crooks think they're clever," Selanski growled. "So I make up my mind to out-clever them. They can be patient, watching and waiting, so I'm gonna out-patient them. They think they've been thorough in considering all the angles? Covering all their tracks? I'm gonna out-thorough them. They think they can hunker down and wait for it all to go away? I'm gonna outlast 'em. *Bet on it.*"

Across the street, the machines ground on, and we just listened to them for half a minute.

"And you write that down, Manring!" Selanski commanded. "That's fucking holy writ!"

# CHAPTER 47

# CONN

After leaving Selanski and Manring, I went over to the *Herald* to answer calls, put to bed some small news items, and flail away at an uninspired "Around Here" draft. I couldn't concentrate. The investigation had changed tempo as the noose tightened around Laughlin. Every time my phone light flashed, my pulse jumped in the hope that it would be Laurel's lawyer, at last returning my calls, or Selanski, with some breaking news.

True, Laughlin would invent reasonable explanations for why a beer can with his fingerprints on it was found at the scene of a fatal arson fire. But the string of coincidences implicating him was stretching toward statistical improbability: that the fire was set on an afternoon he had taken off work, that the fire gutted the office of the lawyers who were helping my murdered sister develop a ruinous case against him. Somebody had stolen Laurel's papers, apparently using her keys to get inside her house and file cabinets. He had taken personal leave on the day Laurel was murdered. All of this in the shadow of the Manchester murders.

But it was all inference at this point, suggestive coincidence. Would we ever have enough evidence to nail him?

When the phone flashed, an unfamiliar number on the display, I snatched it up.

"Conn?"

"Yes."

"This is Cy."

"Uh—"

"Cyrus Vandermeer. I am, was, your sister's lawyer. Also her boy-friend? Back in middle school?"

Small town. This was "Cy," as she'd called her first love, the nerdy gawky kid whose last name I'd never bothered to learn.

"Of course! Cy! Thanks for calling."

He apologized for taking so long to get back to me. I told him I completely understood, asked if we could meet at his earliest opportunity. He proposed a bag lunch at his temporary office downtown.

Cy had turned out better than I'd have predicted from his earlier years. He was taller now, and his scarecrow build had filled out. The short beard he'd grown couldn't hide his receding chin or prominent Adam's apple, but it lent him a touch of maturity and masculine authority.

His second-floor office was sparsely furnished and had a hastily assembled feel. An all-in-one printer and other office basics occupied folding tables against the walls, along with four cheap filing cabinets. His massive oak desk had the scuffed, bruised look of a Goodwill artifact. Behind it, no doubt replacing a cluster of framed diplomas, he had taped up photos of Abraham Lincoln, Martin Luther King Jr., Gandhi, John F. Kennedy.

He must have noticed my looking around. "It's just me," he explained sheepishly. "Morgan is my middle name. My wife and I figured I'd sound like a bigger firm, with, you know, three names on the letterhead. Though Susie sometimes works as my paralegal." He gestured to a framed photo on his desk: a plump, smiling woman in her thirties.

We shook hands across the desk and I took the folding chair in front of it.

"I am so sorry about your sister," he said sincerely.

"Thank you. And I'm sorry about your office. It must be quite a challenge to get your practice back together."

"Well, it is that. I'm probably going to lose half my clients, just too much on my plate every day to give them the attention they need. Insurance'll cover the short-term losses, but only so far. Long-term— who knows?"

He spread the wax paper of his sandwich, lifted the top to inspect it, and closed it again, apparently satisfied. I set out my falafel wrap but didn't open it.

"Cy, I've been reporting on the aftermath of the fire, but that's not why I'm here. Or not directly anyway. I need to talk to you about my sister. I understand she was a client of yours."

His eyes darted up to mine, wary. "You her executor? There are issues of client privilege here."

"I'm her next of kin, so I have to deal with her house and kids. Actually, I was hoping you could tell me about her will or other survivorship provisions."

"She didn't leave a will?" He took a huge bite that left him with a dab of mayonnaise in his beard. "With kids and all, I told her she really should draw one up. Told her she should just download a free template from the Web, fill in the blanks."

"She may have. But her papers were stolen from her house after she was murdered. Somebody was stealing her mail for a while, too. Somebody very concerned about documents she may have had."

I held his eyes, hoping he'd get it.

He frowned, stopped chewing, then sat back as the ramifications hit him. "Uh, I hope this isn't going where I think it is. Like, there's a connection between her papers at home and the fire here."

"I'm afraid that's where we're at. Sorry. I've been working with the State Police. We know about her boss at Martinson's, the evidence of sexual misconduct she was compiling. I have spoken to several of her coworkers."

"Wow. So . . . you're thinking maybe *I* was the target of the arsonist? Her files? And it's the guy, what's his name, the manager? He's, like, covering his tracks?"

"David Laughlin. Correct—that's the theory. As yet unproven."

His eyes were wide. He'd be asking himself about the rules governing client confidentiality privilege after death, and how much he should tell me. I hoped he would also be wondering if he could still be at risk from Laughlin.

I had anticipated this and had done some homework to help persuade him. "Cy, I'm going to say two things. First, one of the women he sexually assaulted said, verbatim, 'I can see him doing *anything* to save his ass.'"

"Yeah, I read that in Trudy's interview notes, too." His Adam's apple bobbed. "Oh. I see. Great. Just great."

"Second, about privilege. Vermont Rules of Professional Conduct, Section 1.6(b)(1), are explicit that a lawyer *can* reveal information relating to a client if the lawyer believes it's necessary to prevent a criminal act that's likely to result in somebody's death or bodily harm. My sister is dead. Tony Shapiro is dead. Artie Shindell is dead. How many are we gonna let this *fucker* kill?"

I'd lost traction on that last curve and started to skid dangerously, practically shouting my final sentence. "Sorry about that, Cy. I'm feeling pretty bad about my sister. I'm heartbroken. But there's a lot of . . . anger that comes up."

He raised two hands, warding or calming me. "Okay, okay. I'm sold. And I don't blame you."

When I asked him about Laurel's case file, he told me he didn't use online backup because his cloud archive had been hacked some years before. Instead, he had backed up files on a separate hard drive. It had been destroyed in the fire, but fortunately he also maintained separate CD backups for each client, which he kept in a safe at his home.

She had brought the case to him three months ago, not sure what to do with it. Her materials provided detailed accusations by eight women, including herself, as well as the names of another three she thought would join a lawsuit if they felt safe enough. They discussed whether it was just a suit against Laughlin, personally, or whether Martinson's might be liable for turning a blind eye to his conduct. Laurel had also asked whether this should be class action or a civil suit, or whether they could file criminal charges, too.

"None of this is my specialty, I told her I'd have to look it all up."
Cy stared at his fingers, thinking back, and winced as if something hurt.
"I did some work on it. Martinson's, I looked at their corporate records,
hard, in several states, and couldn't find indications of habitual or systematic tolerance of sexual misconduct. On the class-action thing, I
told her it was dubious."

"How come?"

"The laws are complex, there are gray zones up the ass, excuse my
French. There are four main considerations—numerosity, commonal-
ity, typicality, and adequacy. 'Numerosity' is how big the 'class' is. Some
courts think this has to be at least forty plaintiffs. I decided we'd be weak
there. Uh, 'typicality' is how similar the alleged crimes or injuries are, and
in this instance there's enough variation—some of the parties admitted
to having consensual relations—that it might be a tough sell. So, that's
two strikes against a class action. Then there's a criterion called 'superiority.' Basically, the superiority clause means you go after a class action
only if it is demonstrably superior to other legal remedies."

I was impressed, and grateful that he'd done this work. "So . . ."

"I told her that, in my opinion, the class-action route wasn't the best.
But maybe we could swing a consolidated litigation, where a number
of plaintiffs' suits are presented at one trial."

"So you went to preparing a civil suit?"

"Conn, uh, I didn't get as far as I'd have liked." Now he looked really
miserable. "It was . . . She, she came to me because we'd kept in touch
over the years, she felt she could trust me. And because she didn't have
any money. She asked for pro bono, and I said yes. But I'm basically
a one-man band here, there's only so much time I can give. Plus, even
before the fire, I was super preoccupied. My wife was pregnant and then
two weeks ago she gave birth—a son."

"Congratulations, Cy!"

"Thanks. But, see, I got a little behind on your sister's suit. Then I
hear she's missing, then dead."

He spread his hands and looked at me with a truly woeful expression. Another person who let Laurel down, another plea for forgiveness.

"Not your fault. How could anyone have known?"

We commiserated silently, sandwiches forgotten.

"Your sister," he began shyly, "she was a really sweet person. When we were . . . you know. She was twice as smart as me and twice as good-looking, but she was always kind, even when she broke up with me. How could somebody kill a person like that?"

He'd asked the world, not just me, and no reasonable answer came to mind.

"So, Cy. Can you give me a copy of her notes? Or could you provide one to the State Police? Or do we need some probate process or court order for that?"

He nodded, made an unhappy grin. "Under the circumstances, as you said, I think 1.6(b)(1) gives me leeway. A defensible excuse, anyway. I'll send the files if you give me a contact at the State Police. But I gotta tell you, I've read it all, and I can't think of anything in there that'll show him as a killer."

"Maybe not. But the lead detective, Selanski, is hoping Laurel's materials will give her a reason to interview him or probable cause to search his home. Go after the sex crimes, maybe find something implicating him in the murders."

I jotted Selanski's email and phone number on one of my own business cards, and slid it across to Cy.

He picked it up, read it, then distractedly picked its edges with his long fingers. Clearly, he was getting a case of nerves—the thought that Laughlin had killed, had burned down his office, was growing on him.

"I guess I should get that file to her right away, huh?"

"That'd be good." I was buoyed by the thought that this could be the "one last piece" needed to get a search warrant and pin Laughlin to the wall.

"Maybe I'll finish my lunch at home," Cy said. "Get that file sent off first."

He checked his watch, rolled up his sandwich, and began gathering papers from separate stacks on the desk. He looked at his own shaking fingers. "Jesus, I'm kind of freaked out. That guy, he needs to get put away! But even for the sex crimes—Conn, with Laurel, uh, Trudy, dead, there's no plaintiff! Laughlin could just walk away from it all."

"Unless one of the other women steps up. I'm going to look into that." I was thinking of Gail Pelkey. Would she be willing? She had a lot at risk, but I couldn't see her as a person who would let something like this pass.

Cy closed his laptop and packed it into its case. I pocketed my untouched falafel wrap, thanked him, and made my way to the door.

But he brought me up short. "Given all that's happened, I thought maybe you were going to ask me about the other thing."

"What other thing?"

He hesitated. "Last time I met with her, like two weeks before she went missing, she asked me about a restraining order."

The back of my neck tingled as I went back to his desk. "'Restraining order.'"

"I figured you'd know all about it. Uh, the problem, the guy."

Suddenly the blood began pounding in my temples. Dizzy, I gripped the edge of the desk. "I don't know about it."

"She didn't tell me much. Actually, she said she was asking on a friend's behalf. I wasn't sure I believed that. You gotta understand, clients are often reluctant to talk about, uh, embarrassing things at first. Sometimes they claim it's not about them, it's about 'a friend.' Usually I take this at face value, play along, and later they admit it's themselves, you know?"

"So what was the issue for this supposed friend?"

"It was a nuanced problem with a guy who was, I guess you'd say, 'overly fond' of the friend. And wouldn't take 'no' for an answer. He was putting pressure on her and she wanted it to stop but wasn't sure what to do about it. Is this about Laughlin? I asked. But your sister said no, this was a guy who would wait for the friend outside work, come by her house uninvited. She thought maybe he followed her sometimes, but she wasn't sure. Laurel, Trudy, wanted to know what happens when you take out a restraining order."

"Okay . . ."

"And I tell her, there's restraining orders and there's restraining orders. Is it an RFA situation, or—"

"What's an 'RFA'?"

"Relief from Abuse. Basically, it's a restraining order on someone you currently have an intimate relationship with or have had a relationship with in the past. As opposed to a stranger."

The heat from my temples spread to my forearms, and I could feel adrenaline start to tingle in my hands. "What was 'nuanced'?"

He looked downright miserable, as if he'd failed Laurel and the world yet again. "The friend, I mean maybe it *was* about a friend, didn't want to get the guy in trouble. But if it was Laurel, she was that way, maybe she was too compassionate . . ."

"Could have been talking about Anthony Shapiro? Tony?"

He shook his head. "She never said his name. Wouldn't tell me much of anything about him. I explained the basics on the statutes, but she didn't know if the friend would want to pursue it or not."

"Tell me more about 'nuanced.'"

"Well, he had a family, he had a job. He'd lose both if she took out the order. The friend thought maybe she was overreacting, maybe she would just talk to him one more time."

"What'd you say?" Tony, I wondered, or the supposed new boyfriend?

"I ask if he'd said or done anything to threaten her, and Laurel says, 'No.' I wanted to be really clear on this, so I keep at her, but she's adamant he hasn't been threatening. But she still seems to me, like, pretty worried. Nervous. So, I'm still playing along with her, I ask if the friend is afraid of him, and she says, 'Well, maybe.' I ask why. She says she thinks he might have deliberately wrecked her bicycle."

"What?!"

"Again, she wasn't sure. For a while, the friend was riding her bike to work? She'd lock it to a post on the side of Martinson's, near the receiving dock. One afternoon she comes out and it had somehow slid down the pole and somebody had driven over it. Totaled it."

"Why'd she think—"

"Because this guy, when he hears about it, buys her a new bike. Like, the next day. Expensive one, too. She wondered if he'd set it all up so he could be, like, her savior, her benefactor. She'd 'owe' him. Like that."

My head was spinning. "Jesus, Cy, that suggests a pretty scary level of premeditation—"

"That's what I told her! She says the friend can't be sure that's what happened, but it left her a little nervous. So I say, 'If you're, if *she's* afraid of him, or he's disrupting her normal life or other relationships, *at all*, go to the police! Tell them, let him take the consequences.'"

"And she said . . . ?"

"Said she'd tell the friend about it. She wasn't sure if technically it should be an RFA or not, which I didn't get, because he either was or was not a relative or somebody she'd been with. She just kept saying that for this guy, a restraining order would be disastrous."

*Nadeau?* I wondered. Maybe he lied to us when he said he hadn't been in contact with Laurel. Maybe he had a wife and kids from before he got together with Laurel? I didn't know if Nadeau was on some kind of probation, but a restraining order would be disastrous for any ex-con. Her confusion about whether it should be a Relief from Abuse order could be a matter of how long ago they'd had a relationship.

"Did I fuck up?" Cy asked miserably. "Should I have contacted somebody? I mean, it was all so up in the air, my wife was almost due. And then the baby came, and then the fire, and . . ." He seemed on the verge of tears. "I should have, shouldn't I? Called somebody?"

I was still stunned, grasping at straws. It had to be Nadeau, I thought. "Did she suggest he had a criminal history?"

"No, just the opposite! She said the guy was in law enforcement himself. It would definitely not fly with his department. Honestly, she, I mean I guess it probably was Laurel, she seemed more concerned for him than for herself!"

# CHAPTER 48

# CELINE

I was alone at Conn's, working outside, when an unfamiliar truck rattled down the road and pulled into the driveway. It was a big, beat-up flatbed that looked like a farm truck. Jesse Nadeau was behind the wheel.

It was Friday, and Conn had gone to the *Herald* offices. I quelled my unease as Jesse got out, dressed as always in black. He looked around, stretched, rolled a kink out of his neck. I was holding a steel-tined garden rake and must have looked defensive because he made a bitter twitch of a smile.

"You afraid of me again?" he asked. As before, his hyper-alert body language had triggered the same in me.

I set the head of the rake on the grass, dialing it down one notch. "Any reason I should be?"

"Nope."

"Okay. What can I do for you, Jesse?"

"Did your husband get in touch with my lawyer?"

"He did. And he had her send a transcript of your hearing to the State Police. It bears out your story. They still want to talk with you, though."

He looked minutely relieved. "Maybe you could give them a call. On my behalf."

"You have Detective Selanski's number, don't you? You can call them yourself, set up a time to meet."

He cracked his knuckles, then tipped his chin toward the lawn table. "Mind if I sit down?"

"Go ahead. You want something to drink? I'm pretty thirsty myself. I've got lemonade." I was thirsty, but mainly I wanted to get my cell phone, which I'd left on the kitchen counter.

I went inside but kept my eyes on him through the windows. Sitting at the lawn table, he moved his head in a deliberate way as if conducting a methodical scan of the cabin, yard, and near woods. I felt for him— his habitual vigilance told me a lot about how he'd lived.

I found my phone and checked for messages, hoping Mason had called or texted with news about Katherine Krantz: Nothing. I got a couple of glasses and a carton of lemonade, and went out to rejoin Nadeau, feeling a little better with the phone in my pocket.

I found him leaning back in his chair with hands clasped behind his head, trying to look relaxed but displaying his upper arm muscles intimidatingly.

"Celine. I'm keyed up like a wolverine. I haven't had a conversation with anybody outside the criminal justice system in years except my bat-shit crazy uncle. If I make you nervous, guess what, you make *me* nervous. I have not talked much with women. Don't know how anymore."

"You're doing a fine job," I told him. I poured two glasses from the carton and went on: "It's just that nervousness begets nervousness, it can spiral up. You and I don't have to do that here."

"It's easy for people to take me the wrong way. Especially cops. What I'm getting to is asking you a favor. Call them for me. Set up a meet."

I thought about it. "I can do that."

"And be there. When I meet them." His gaze told me this was important for him.

Selanski told me that by chance she was in Richfield on some other business. When I explained that Nadeau was reluctant to present himself to any police agency, and wanted me there, she said she'd have a few minutes to come by Conn's place.

"Sounds like a wild one," she said. "Uneasy in confined spaces?"

"Well, he's had some experience with them. I guess it leaves an impression."

Selanski told me it would be another half hour before she could get to the cabin. Watching me as I talked to her, Nadeau really did seem like a feral animal, suspicious of every movement and word.

When I disconnected, he asked, "What kind of guy is this detective? Gonna try to macho me, or more finesse me?"

"She's a female. She is pretty hard-nosed. But she also has wicked sense of humor, if that's any help. Kind of quirky. I think you can trust her."

He didn't seem reassured.

We finished our drinks and sat as the trees around the yard moved gently in undetectable breezes. The midday sun mottled the lawn in a shifting mosaic. It was a serene scene, but waiting made the tension rise again. I didn't want to sit there trying to make conversation with him.

"Jesse, I'm starting up my real job soon, and there's yard work to be done. You're welcome to sit here and get nervous, or you could help me. If you want. It might take your mind off worrying."

So that's what we did. I weeded the front flower gardens and tasked him with loading the garden cart with bark mulch from a pile near the shed and bringing it to the beds. He effortlessly lifted and levered the cart, then shoveled mulch where I told him to. His muscles were formidable, his tension palpable, and yet in some ways he seemed like a child—uncertain, eager to please. To prove himself capable of being normal.

We were still working when Selanski turned into the driveway in her unmarked car. She parked next to Nadeau's truck and got out as Nadeau visibly tightened up. The other door opened and a tall, dark-skinned man got out, wearing a crisp State Trooper's uniform shirt and slacks. Nadeau eyes went to the gun in the trooper's holster and laid his shovel on the ground.

Selanski approached Nadeau without hesitation, but the trooper stayed back, alert, at the back of the car twenty feet away. It was a strategic position.

"Jesse Nadeau," Selanski said, looking him up and down.

"That's right."

"You've been on my mind for some time now, Mr. Nadeau. I'm glad I get to meet the real deal at last. My associate there is Trooper Dennis Manring—Ms. Gabrielli, maybe Conn mentioned him to you? He's doing some work on this case and I thought you two should clap eyes on each other."

"Pleased to meet you, ma'am," Manring called. He glanced my way only briefly. He was watching Nadeau.

"Mr. Nadeau, I read your hearing transcript, and I just now was talking to your lawyer. I got the general drift, okay? I have a few questions for you, but for now we are no longer considering you a person of interest in our investigation of Ms. Carlson's death. *Provided*," she added sternly, "provided you do the alphabet thing."

"Alphabet thing?"

"Mind your p's and q's from here on in. Also dot your i's and cross your t's."

Nadeau moved his head forward and back—not saying yes, just trying to take in Selanski. He turned to me and asked, "This the sense-of-humor thing you told me about?"

"Uh, hard to tell," I told him. "I wouldn't count on it."

"Good advice," Selanski said. "Now, Trooper Manring and I are in a bit of a yank, time-wise. So let's have a nice chat and we'll be out of your hair. What time we got, Manring?"

"Twelve minutes until we have to hit the road, ma'am."

We all sat at the lawn table. I was astonished at Selanski—her self-possession, the way her unpredictable style could actually defuse tension, if only by baffling people. Manring kept his hands well away from his gun and Nadeau kept his hands and forearms on the table.

Selanski went over the basics with him, reviewing his history with Laurel, the oxycodone purchase and transport, the plea deal, the reasons for his extended sentence. After a few minutes, she put her chin on her chest and pursed her lips, thinking something through.

"Okay. Manring?"

"Five minutes. We should pack it in soon, ma'am."

Selanski turned to me. "Ms. Gabrielli, I could use some time alone with Mr. Nadeau. A couple little issues that might be sensitive. Trooper Manring, probably you should go get the stuff from the car."

She turned her attention back to Nadeau, eyes blade-sharp.

I felt dismissed, but out of my depth. I tagged behind Manring to the car and stood there as he opened trunk and took out a small case that contained nitrile gloves and two vials with swab caps—a saliva DNA sampling kit. Back at the table, I could see that Jesse was getting animated as he answered Selanski's questions.

"He seems to trust you pretty well," Manring said.

"Yes. I don't know why, but yes."

"I've got to ask him for a DNA sample. As a stabilizing presence, I'd like you to encourage him to acquiesce without resistance. You think it'll be a problem? Because Selanski and Welles . . . man, they got to have all the pieces in order. And I don't relish the thought of trying to subdue this guy."

He flashed me a smile.

"He won't object. He'll put on a defiant posture, but he's not stupid. He knows you and Detective Selanski are rescuing him."

He bobbed his head and looked away from me to call across the driveway: "Ma'am! We are at two minutes and counting!"

She was zeroed in on Nadeau and barely turned to flash a thumbs-up.

"Dare I ask what the big 'yank' is about?"

Manring cracked a grin. "She told me you'd ask. And authorized me to tell you, under strict confidentiality advisement. We're searching David Laughlin's residence and office. We got Ms. Carlson's sex-abuse files from her lawyer. Some pretty ugly stuff in there. Along with that beer can, it was enough to get the warrants."

I followed him as he hurried across the driveway and approached Jesse Nadeau. Manring made a very formal announcement of his request, Jesse stood up quickly, a defiant reflex, but then caught my eye. I nodded. Manring repeated that it was "for elimination purposes," and did the swabbing.

As Selanski watched the procedure, I saw that her affect had changed again: face gone unreadable, eyes flat. I wasn't sure if it were something Nadeau had said or just the impending search. I had to assume the sudden appearance of the State Police would come as an unpleasant surprise to Laughlin and make for some tense moments.

Manring screwed the tops on the vials, slipped them into a plastic evidence bag, and thanked Nadeau. They started back toward their car, but Selanski abruptly spun on her heel, finger raised in that *one more thing,* professorial way.

To my surprise, she walked right up to Nadeau. At about five-three, she was almost a foot shorter, so she had to crane her neck to look him in the face.

She put one palm on his chest, causing him to flinch minutely. "Jesse, you done good today. Now it's time for you to come in from the cold. That thing you got, you know what I'm talking about, it'll wear off if you just rub up against regular people and fly straight long enough. It's gonna take a couple years, so you gotta be patient with yourself and the rest of us. Just stick with it. Hear me? You come in from the cold now." She patted his chest and turned away again.

Nadeau and I watched them go, speechless. Selanski's car threw gravel as she peeled out of the driveway.

I walked Nadeau back to his truck. When I asked him what they'd talked about, he said Selanski said to keep it under his hat for now.

"Teacher said." The corners of his lips sharpened, his version of a smile, as he made a zippering motion across them. Clearly, relief was starting to percolate through him. "I gotta mind my p's and q's."

# CHAPTER 49

# CELINE

"Conn," I said. "What's eating at you?"

We were on our way to see Katherine Krantz, halfway through the hour-long drive, and Conn had kept mostly silent. As I drove, I told him about Nadeau's "coming in from the cold" and the search warrants on Laughlin, thinking it would cheer him. But he kept his face to the window, jaw muscles tense, just watching the forested slopes slide by.

"Nothing," he answered.

"Ah. That." To me, "nothing" is the most blatant dodge.

"Sorry, sweet Celine. It's just wear and tear. Metal fatigue."

He had come home from the *Herald* to tell me he'd located Katherine Krantz. He had asked Will Patchen to run a motor-vehicle lookup, and Will had come back with truck registration and driver's license information, an address if not a phone number.

I was pleased. I hadn't yet heard back from Mason, and was curious to meet Katherine for a number of reasons. We couldn't call her, so we decided to drop in unannounced.

Conn checked his watch and mustered to the task at hand. "So what's our agenda with her? What do we hope to learn?"

"Personally, I'd like to know how she inspired such a remarkable change in your sister."

"So—mostly professional curiosity on your part."

"Well, not entirely."

"What else?"

"Conn, I'm sorry, but I really want more perspective on Laurel and Mason. Because if what Nadeau said is true, and we want to stay friends with him, we'll need to sort it out with him. And I don't have a clue how to do that. Maybe Katherine will know more."

He nodded. "Like, did my sister talk about getting beat up? Did Mason really punch her teeth out? Was that how she got into opioids? That kind of thing would come up as part of a talk process for addiction counseling, right?"

"Definitely."

"And we want to know if they stayed in touch after she wrote that book inscription. Does Katherine know anything about more recent developments in her life? Like the new boyfriend."

"Yes," I said. "Although that may be kind of moot. Given that Laughlin is probably about to get arrested."

The thought plunged Conn into morose introspection again. I drove without intruding, missing my charming, funny, talkative companion terribly. After a while, I thought I deduced what had begotten his mood: Katherine Krantz no doubt had also heard tales about how Laurel's full-of-himself journalist brother had neglected her, had abandoned her, for so long. Conn didn't need another reminder.

She took the news of Laurel's death like a boxer taking a hard punch—recoiling, then eyes tearing and puffing. For a moment she seemed stunned, at a loss. We were standing in the vestibule of the Upaya-Kaushalya Zen Center's main building, a modern post-and-beam entry largely devoid of the Tibetan or Japanese trappings I associated with Buddhism. She wiped her eyes, took a few breaths, and then walked past us to open the front door.

"Let's take a walk. It's better to be outside for . . . things like this."

We followed her out to the circular driveway that fronted the lodge-like main building. A series of barns and paddocks around the drive explained the sign hung below the Upaya-Kaushalya mailbox: *Finest Morgans.* Apparently the center supported itself in part by raising and selling Vermont's native-bred horse. In nearby pastures, the big, muscular creatures grazed contentedly, and the air was full of the sweet scent of grass and manure.

Katherine wore a green canvas shirt and jeans tucked into tall rubber boots. In person, I found that she did indeed resemble Jody, at least superficially: tall, slim, an angular face below dark hair in a functional cut. But her movements were more intentional and graceful, and the lines of her face, though certainly resolute, told of compassion more than pragmatism. If Conn expected harsh judgments, I didn't think he'd find them here.

"I'm sorry to have brought such awful news to such a beautiful place," Conn said. "I'd have called if I'd had a number."

Katherine shook her head. "Not the first patient I've lost. Just . . . Laurel was important to me. She'd made such a transformation. She inspired some of the changes I made in my own life." She gestured around at the broad pastures, the split-rail fences, the peaceful horses here and there. "I needed to give the human world a wider berth, I guess you could say. She showed me that. It was starting to overwhelm me."

I sensed understatement. I knew she had worked with injured veterans for over thirty years, even at the Springfield VA hospital, where they still cared for Korean War survivors.

Katherine gave Conn an appraising look. "But you didn't come here just to tell me. What is it you want?"

"To learn more about my sister. You probably knew we'd been estranged for some time."

"Yes. But last I heard from her, she was planning to reconnect. Optimistic about it. I'd have thought—" She glanced at Conn and cut herself short. "Ah. I'm sorry."

Katherine told us she needed a running start to get to it: context.

She had worked primarily with veterans. Pain was a constant in the lives of her patients, and so was opiate addiction. Most suffered from emotional pain as much as physical pain. Maybe they'd lost friends in one war or another, and they blamed themselves because they'd made a mistake in checking equipment or they hadn't been heroic enough in battle. Or maybe they had simply survived when their buddies hadn't. Once home, they felt ashamed of cowering when a plane flew over, losing their jobs, or hurting their spouses or kids. If you rake yourself over the coals with guilt and shame and loss, that's pain, and you'll do almost anything to make it go away.

Some blamed others for their pain—the Army, the government, Veterans Affairs, the enemy, inattentive wives, disrespectful kids, an uncomprehending civilian society. Katherine discovered that guilt and blame were essentially the same thing. Even blaming someone else injured her patients, too—if the whole world has done bad by you, you live in a shitty world with no hope. A pain-filled place.

Over years, she developed a therapy based on forgiveness of self and others. Her therapeutic goal was to help patients forgive themselves, but for many that was impossible. Paradoxically, she found that they had a better chance of succeeding if they forgave someone else first. As she put it, her patients had to practice the surgery on others, as it were, to learn from their own actions how to excise self-blame, guilt, and shame.

"From the start, Laurel had a lot of blame to sort out—at first, mainly others. For example, she blamed her first husband—Mason, right?—for his physical violence, and the injuries that got her started on drugs. She blamed you, Conn, for 'making' her marry Mason—he was your good friend, right?—and for not doing something about his abuse later."

Conn started to speak, but she cut him off. "And she had some hard self-blame to face into. She blamed herself for not helping you deal with your father when he was dying—she knew it was hard on you and probably affected how you felt toward her. She felt bad about how her life choices were affecting her daughters. You name it, she hurt for it."

Conn walked stiffly, expressionless, just taking it in.

"I told her building her personhood on blame was just weakness. An excuse to keep failing. So then we worked on forgiveness. I encouraged

her to find forgiveness for all of it, find another means to get rid of the
pain besides a drug. Conn—you were so easy! She loved you and forgave
you. Mason was much harder. She had to remember what his father was
like, the expectations there. Mason was an only child because his mother
couldn't bear any more children after two deeply disappointing miscar-
riages. Some of his violence derived from the example of his father in their
household. Some derived from frustration at their inability to conceive and
his guilt over not providing the big family his parents had hoped for. He
blamed Laurel for that. Or wanted to. She had herself checked out, medically. He refused. Yet she loved him and she believed he truly loved her."

A van came toward us down the long driveway, with the
Upaya-Kaushalya logo on the side. The scattered horses turned their
heads to watch it, curious. Inside, men and women chattered and
laughed, then waved and smiled as they saw us. They headed on past
us to the main building.

I was watching Conn. Laurel's "easy" forgiveness should have been
balm for him: I'd have expected his face, his shoulders, to show some
release. But he had been brooding as much as listening.

"Can you forgive too much?" he asked.

She looked at him closely. "It's a tough question. What prompts it?"

"Somebody murdered my sister. Who was rising like a *phoenix*! I
am bitter and I am sad and I am outraged. Am I supposed to forgive
the murderer?"

Katherine bobbed her head as she thought about how to answer.
"That's not something I can tell you. It's up to you. You know what the
name of this place means—Upaya-Kaushalya? It's a concept of practice
based on individuals using their own methods or techniques to grow
spiritually, as best meets the needs of the situation. The world is unpredictable, so sometimes you need to improvise how you respond. It
may not be the 'truest' or 'best' practice in some abstract or absolute
way, but it may still be what's needed at any given moment, better than
some inflexible dogma. If that sounds loosey-goosey, trust me, it's not
an easy way out. It means you must constantly decide what's the right
path to take."

"Sounds like that puts us right back where we already are," Conn said darkly.

"Being 'where we are' is precisely the goal," Katherine said, unruffled.

Conn wanted to drive on the way back, to give his hands something to do. I didn't mind; I wanted to think about our meeting with Katherine.

Forgiveness as a medical therapy, not a religious tenet: She must have been among the first. In the last fifteen years, more and more clinical studies had shown a positive correlation between a patient's ability to forgive and their mental and physical health, in recovery of any kind. Self-forgiveness would certainly be crucial for Conn. I made a mental note to talk with my staff about its applications in our school district's guidance offices.

We'd been disappointed when Katherine told us she hadn't heard from Laurel for several years and knew nothing of her circumstances. She was moved to hear about her name change. Maybe the importance of forgiveness was the best thing we'd gained. Blame and forgiveness— two sides of the same coin. Or sword! Yes, I decided, like the Möbius band of love and murder.

I didn't know what we'd learned about Mason, though, what would help Conn connect with a man who had done so much to harm his sister. Nor had we learned of any new boyfriend, or recent circumstance that might lead to Trudy's murderer. Hopefully, that was soon to be resolved by other means.

I was musing along these lines when my cell phone buzzed, signaling the arrival of a text. I thumbed the screen to find a message from Mason.

> Did the DMV lookup on Katherine Krantz. No license, no registration, no moving violations on file. Last license renewal 10 yrs ago at old address you gave me. Sorry. Wish I could be more help. Mace

I must have made a noise of surprise, because Conn glanced over. "What?" he asked.

"Oh. Nothing." I put the phone away.

Conn nodded, still preoccupied, hearing the weakest of dodges, leaving me to sort it out.

Mace must have made a keyboarding mistake, I thought. Or he didn't find time to do it and didn't see the importance of it. Or, most likely, the same thing that plagued Conn: He simply didn't want us to learn any more unsavory details about his past with Laurel. That had to be it.

# CHAPTER 50

# CONN

I was churning with conflicting emotions and opposing rational inferences. Mason was a good guy! My best friend! No, Mason was a violent man who had sent my sister careening into a life of drugs and lousy choices.

Had he also murdered my sister?

I tried to maintain the outlook of an objective reporter, considering material evidence for one or another viewpoint. Laurel's asking about a restraining order against someone in law enforcement, the crushed bicycle, the physical abuse long ago—it was bad, but it didn't add up to murder.

On the other hand, there was an inexplicable hole in the pattern of events: my midnight call to Mason, the discovery of the anchor and rope but the absence of a body in Richfield Reservoir. Between call and search was a thirty-hour window when someone must have removed the body, and Mason was the only person who knew about my encounter.

But—*Mason*? Surely there was another explanation!

My inability to decide was killing me. And what should I do? Forgiveness was a wonderful idea. I got it. I agreed. But I wanted to annihilate my sister's murderer. I thought back to Lance Burton, who took justice into his own hands. Could I do what he had done? At times I felt I probably could. But Burton *knew* Fecteau was a danger to his family and the community—Burton had evidence to support this in so many prior emergency calls, in bruises and blood.

By comparison, I had mostly supposition. When does glandular certainty conquer rational doubt? Answer: Only when the chemicals of anger and arousal get the upper hand. I resolved not to let that happen.

Why wasn't Mason calling me back?

On Saturday, I tried to find distraction in the mundane errands of daily life. Celine's reminder that fall was approaching triggered a casual review of preparedness. Firewood: I inventoried my woodpiles and determined I'd need to get up at least three more cords. While I was at it, I checked the two hundred-pound propane tanks I used for the kitchen stove, standing against the cabin wall under a little canopy I'd built. They were battered and filmed with rust—my father had bought them long before I'd taken over the place. Like him, I'd never bothered setting up delivery from the gas company, just took the tanks in to Seeley's Steel & Welding to get them refilled.

It was a good thing I checked. One was empty, the other almost, so I disconnected them and half rolled, half carried them to the Subaru. I tipped them into the car, then put splits of firewood against them to keep them from rolling.

I also needed to visit Bronson's Auto Yard to see if I could find a used AC unit for my old Subaru. Bronson's was just half a mile from Seeley's, so I figured I'd do both on the same swing. Both were open only until noon on Saturdays, so I'd need to keep old Norm Seeley's gabbing under control.

At any other time, I would have relished the excuse to visit Seeley's, a cluster of steel buildings in a big asphalt lot halfway to Northfield. The stock warehouse was the size of an airplane hangar and stacked with steel bars, tubes, I-beams, sheets, lengths of rebar, welding rods. A pair of rails up near the roof carried a gargantuan rolling hoist that the guys who worked there operated with admirable finesse.

My destination was the gas house, an open-sided steel structure where Seeley kept big tanks of propane, oxygen, and acetylene, along with scores of smaller tanks like mine.

Norm Seeley met me at the front. He was pushing seventy-five, I figured, but pushing it well: losing hair but not humor, his muscles going stringy but still strong. We shook hands. He peered into the Subaru, then went inside and came back with a heavy-duty dolly. We loaded one of my tanks onto it and started back into the building.

"You know, I could get arrested for this," he commented amiably.

"For what?"

"Fillin' these for you. These tanks are date-stamped when they're manufactured. See that there? They're supposed to get decommissioned after expiry date, and yours are ten years over. I believe I filled these same tanks for your dad!"

We'd had this conversation every couple of years. "But they're in fine shape, Norm! I mean, a bit of rust, but I keep them on a cement pad, keep a roof over them—"

"Oh, I know. But they could be corrodin' from inside—condensation." Norm rolled the dolly up to the filler tank, stood it, and bent to inspect the lower end of my tank. He found a small hammer on a nearby workbench and tapped experimentally around the bottom.

"Sounds fine, though." He gave me a wink. "I'll do it this once."

He affixed the filler hose, opened the valve, and we listened to the hiss as propane charged my tank. I caught a whiff of gas odorant, like garlic.

"And you're lucky, Conn," Norm said, killing time. "Your buddy Mason, he come in for refills for his weldin' setup, a few weeks back, and I told him 'No way.'"

"Oh?"

"Those oxy and acetylene tanks of his—same ones his father used! I told him, 'I ain't refillin' those tanks. If you've got a weldin' project going, it's time to invest in new equipment. Regulators, hoses, you shouldn't trust 'em for stuff as flammable as that, not that old.' His hoses were crackin' just from old age, kinda like me. Thank the good Lord, he switched 'em out without a fight. Huh! Back in the day, his dad was a hard man to disagree with!"

Norm chuckled, remembering. True, Warren King could be assertive, formidably so.

I didn't know what Mace might be welding, and once again I realized how long it had been since we'd spent time together, or talked
about anything besides Laurel's murder. Maybe he was teaching Marshall some metalworking, a good father-son experience.

Norm and I rolled my filled tank out to the car, unloaded the second,
and went back inside. Norm affixed the filler hose and we waited as the
gauge needle rose.

"Yeah, old Warren King, he used to fix them old antique cars. Loved
seein' 'em in the Fourth of July parade. Mason take that up, too?"

"Nah. Mace and I used to fix our cars in Mr. King's garage, but Mace
isn't into it. He's got plenty on his plate—kids, sheriff, and all. No time."

Norm nodded, understanding. Three kids of his own, five grand-
kids last I'd heard.

We loaded the second tank and propped both of them carefully. I
paid up, thanked him, and headed over to Bronson's auto scrapyard.

I always got a kick out of Bronson's, too, but of a different sort. The buildings were ramshackle and grimy, and the men who worked there were a
good match for their environment. Inside those long, rusted sheet-steel
fences, it was the Wild West, the old Vermont outback.

The office stood on its own, a falling-down wooden shack with a
truck scale directly in front. Across from it, a huge, battered steel building
held the workshops, where crews dismantled cars and pickups, pulling
off any parts with resale value before sending the hulks to the crusher.
Another nearby steel shed served as the warehouse, stacked to the rafters with salvaged parts. Beyond it lay long avenues of junked vehicles,
sumacs and weeds growing between, random parts strewn haphazardly.

When Mace and I were teenagers, they'd let us go back in there with
our own tools, inspect the wrecks, and yank a water pump or brake
drum for our cars. Nowadays, they either had your part on a shelf in

the warehouse, or they'd put you on a list and call you if they could find one in their acres of wrecks. "Insurance reasons," Hill Bronson griped.

I pulled up at the office, went in, found nobody there. But there was plenty of action across the way, four wide-open bays with people at work on pickups and cars. I shielded my eyes from the nuclear sear of an arc welder in one of the bays, where a helmeted man was cutting loose some component from the back end of a pickup. I spotted Hill Bronson in the next bay over, working with another man under the hood of a station wagon. He was called "Hill" because he was a giant, tall as well as round, the size of guy who put a kink in your neck if you talked to him up close.

Not a conversationalist like old Seeley, he put down his tools and squinted at me with impatience. I apologized for butting in, told him what I wanted. Hill had an encyclopedic knowledge of what was on his shelves and in his lot.

"Got a couple dozen Outbacks in the yard. Leave your number and I'll call you if any of the ACs are good."

He knew me from past visits, but I gave him a business card anyway. He pocketed it in his grease-stained coveralls, spat a stream of tobacco juice, and went back to work. I skirted a spray of welding sparks and went back to my car.

I drove home with a little blind spot floating in my field of vision, from an accidental glimpse of the welding arc. Along with it, a hornet took up buzzing in my head: Mason, buying welding gases.

A thought occurred to me, and it rapidly metastasized into a horrible certainty.

# CHAPTER 51

# CONN

I called Mason, got his answering service again, then drove over to his house. I couldn't live within my skin.

I didn't have a clear idea of what I was going to say or what I expected from him. To the extent I could sort out a single emotion from the chaos of rage, sorrow, confusion, fear, loss, and sense of betrayal, I was above all hoping he would set me straight. He'd face into hurting Laurel in the distant past, explain some extenuating circumstances, show sincerest contrition. He'd show me that my worst suspicions were groundless, everything was in my mind, a matter of coincidence or supposition.

I latched onto that one hard, and added to my list worrying about the repercussions of my suspicions—whether our friendship could survive.

There were no cars in the Kings' driveway, and the open garage doors showed it was empty except for the two motorcycles. But Marshall was on the blacktop shooting hoops. When I pulled up and waved, he took a break long enough to say hello—a lanky kid of that difficult age of when their limbs lengthen and eyes get guarded around adults. He told me his parents weren't home. He wasn't sure when they'd be back, but he'd let them know I came by.

Looking past him into the garage, I could tell from the spotless concrete floor and tidy interior that no welding projects were in progress.

So I drove to Mason's camp. King Ranch was an hour away, and I had a vague hope that the drive would settle me, that I'd decide on an agenda or a strategy, or that my phone would ring and it would be Mason and we'd arrange to meet somewhere. But none of that happened before the service gave out and I pulled into the Kings' driveway.

A quarter mile in, the cabin came into view. No truck in the turn-around, no lights on inside. I pulled up to the front porch and got out into the late-afternoon light, shadowed here by the big pines. The trees absorbed sound, leaving it quiet except for the barely audible shimmer of insects over the pond and occasional bird calls deep in the woods.

I went up the steps and knocked, then tried the door handle: locked, of course. I didn't bother try to force it. Warren King had built the place well. Up this way a remote camp, unoccupied for long stretches, needed to be impervious to thieves and vandals. I sat on the front steps, wondering where Mason might be, worrying that he'd show up, hoping that he would.

I swatted mosquitos for a few minutes, then got up and walked around, trying to shed the intolerable tension. In Mason's absence, my most pressing mission was to check out the garage, but I feared what I might find. Stalling, I went to the dock to look over the expanse of lily pads. No heron today. I realized that for all the fun we'd had out here, I'd never actually liked this spot—the shallow water, the marshy humidity that rose from the water and lingered in the little clearing and the pine forest all around.

The atmosphere seemed especially oppressive in the absence of upkeep. Back in the day, Warren King had run a tight ship, maintaining a patch of grass around the buildings, trimming boughs from trees near the cabin, putting fresh gravel on the drive each summer, painting the window frames and porch pillars. To brighten things up, Mrs. King put out flower boxes and had planted hollyhocks and rosebushes, now long gone.

Yet even when we were kids, despite the agreeable distractions of shooting and fishing, I'd never found the place inviting. The interior was too dark, the ceiling too low, Mason's father too large a presence. The glass-eyed stares of the animals on the walls creeped me out.

I knelt on the dock and reached my hand into the water: lukewarm, as I'd suspected. It was a natural pond, locked in by land, with minimal inflow. Mucky bottom—if your buddy unexpectedly shoved you in, you often came up with a leech or two.

I got up to inspect the skiff, which was in the water, tethered to the dock. The bottom was dry now. Leading away from shore, a wandering trail of displacement in the lily pads indicated that Mason had been taking the boat out recently.

If my conclusions were correct, he'd have used the little aluminum boat to recover my sister's body from Richfield Reservoir after my midnight call. It would have required several hours and quite an effort: driving out here from town, hitching up the trailer and towing the skiff to the reservoir's boat launch, backing down the ramp in the pitch dark, steering the boat out and northward a couple of hundred yards to the narrows. He'd have needed some long pole to poke around underwater until he located the body, and then some tool to cut through the rope—a telescoping pruning saw, I figured, such as I used for trimming branches around my cabin. The hard part would have been hoisting the bloated, waterlogged body over the gunnel. But Mace was a big guy, with enough weight to counterbalance it. Once he had it aboard, he'd have just left it in the boat as he pulled the trailer back out here.

Was she in the pond now? Probably, I thought. Just retie the shroud, make sure to put holes in it to let gases out and crayfish in, add some more weight to make sure it stayed down forever. At its deepest point, the pond was only about fifteen feet, but it never fluctuated and no one ever had cause to come into this arm of it. I had never seen another boat on it, not even when I was a kid.

Still no sign of Mason. Reluctantly I walked past the cabin and over to the small barn Warren King had built for his car restoration hobby, forty feet away and deeper in the woods. It was newer than the cabin, with a big roll-up door in the gable end that faced the driveway. Mr. King had kept valuable tools and cars in here, so he'd built it with security in mind. Thick board-and-batten siding rose fifteen feet to the eave, and the rolling garage door was an industrial weight with a built-in lock supplemented by a heavy chain and padlock. The sides had a few windows, but they were small and Warren King had set them high on the wall, where they'd bring in light but would prohibit would-be thieves from peering through from ground level.

On the side opposite the cabin, where the pines grew close, there were two narrow windows, sills just above my reach. I walked around the building, tried the steel man-door at the rear with no expectation of success, then scouted the back of the house and woods for inspiration on how I might climb high enough to look into the windows. The light was dimming as the sun dropped lower, its rays filtering at a low slant through miles of pine forest.

No ladders. But in the woods I found a couple of fallen pine limbs, fairly straight and nine feet long, that might substitute. I dragged them around to one of the forest-side windows, then spent some minutes breaking off their smaller branches, leaving stubs to step on. When I propped them up side by side against the wall, they made a serviceable stepladder. I needed to gain only four or five feet.

It was hard to keep them positioned, but I made my way up and at last stood on two awkward stilts with my head just above the windowsill. The glass was dusty and it was darker inside than out, but by putting my face against the glass and sheltering my eyes from the evening light I could see inside.

It was a narrow room, long enough for three cars, rising from a concrete floor to trusses that supported the roof. The steel-topped workbenches still lined the walls, and the chain hoist and pulley that Warren had hung from the trusses still dangled in the middle.

Beneath it was what I feared I'd see. A big shape, partly covered with a tarp: Tony Shapiro's truck. The back end had been stripped of the body panels and bed, right down to the dirty steel beams of the chassis, the naked drive shaft and transaxle. Mason hadn't gotten to the front yet. The drape of canvas over the cab told me that Tony's truck had extended mirrors, helpful when towing a boat.

I had been expecting this, had girded myself against this moment, but the sight stunned me. Abruptly I felt as if I was dreaming again, my worst nightmare manifesting. *This cannot be true.* My mind raced, trying to find alternative explanations: *It's not Tony's truck, it's some project of Mason's, he's converting some old beater into a flatbed for some reason.*

The oxyacetylene tanks stood on their dolly just inside the roll-up door, alongside a pile of sheet-metal sections—the corrugated steel floor of the truck's bed. He had sheared them into manageable sizes. Given the recent trail in the lily pads on the pond, I could guess where the tailgate and rear fenders and sidewall sections were. Now I knew what Mason had been spending his time on during his sojourns out here, instead of doing the repairs the place needed. He'd been cutting Tony's truck into pieces and dumping them in the pond, where they'd rust away to nothing in a few years.

The branches started to slide away from one another and I couldn't hold them together anymore. One foot slipped off its stub, and I barely had time to leap free of the collapsing rig. I had just landed when I heard the approach of a vehicle on the driveway.

# CHAPTER 52

# CELINE

Selanski's sudden appearance late Saturday afternoon surprised me. She was alone this time, and looked harried and speedy as she got out of her car and approached me. I had just finished another round of yard work and was fighting off my rising worry by reading through the lawnmower owner's manual to figure out why it ran so unevenly. I was compulsively checking my cell phone, hoping Conn would answer my calls to him.

"*Buongiorno*, Signora Gabrielli," she called.

"*Ciao*," I said. "I thought you'd be in on the searches of Laughlin's place."

"I was. But lately I keep having to chase down some tricky little issues in your town, too. Conn here?"

"No, sorry. I'm not sure where he is. I know he went to pick up propane for the kitchen stove, because the tanks are missing. But I was gone for most of the day myself. Anything I can help you with?"

Selanski didn't answer. She fired up her e-cigarette and inhaled mightily. "These things bother you?" she said, choke-voiced, as she exhaled.

"A little—"

"Then I'll keep my distance." She stayed fifteen feet away, blowing clouds of clove-scented steam that eddied off into the woods.

"Conn isn't answering my calls," she said.

"I doubt he's dodging you. We're both eager to hear what's happening with the searches. Want me to try?"

"Sure."

I tapped Conn's name on my phone, waited, got his answering service again. I left another short message.

"Let me try Mace," I told Selanski. "Conn's been trying to get to together with him, maybe they connected."

I got Mason's answering service, too, then disconnected and gave Selanski an apologetic shrug.

She had stopped her catlike patrolling. "'Mace' would be Deputy Mason King? Trudy's ex? Conn's old buddy?"

"Yes."

"So where might they be, if they're hanging out?"

Her intensity was unsettling. "Can you tell me what this is about? You seem—"

"No. It's a Conn thing this time. Deputy King live here in Richfield? They have a favorite bar, or . . . ?"

"Mason and his family live over on Ridge Avenue. I doubt they'd be there. Bars—possibly, but neither one is a big bar type."

Selanski quenched her vape and slipped it into her blazer pocket. She came to grip the back of one of the chairs and put a sharp eye on me. "Why do you say they wouldn't be at the King house?"

I felt suddenly I'd said too much. Selanski would always catch subtle omissions or dissonances.

"Conn had some personal issues to talk with him about. Not something they'd want to get into around Mason's wife or kids."

"And you're gonna be loyal and not tell me because it's none of my business and it's private."

"Well, frankly—"

"Like he wants to talk to Mason about beating up on his sister back in the day. Figure out how to deal with that. 'Cause, yeah, that's messy."

"I take it you got that from Jesse Nadeau?"

"As I bet you did."

Selanski's phone buzzed, and she hurried over to the driveway to take the call, her back to me. I couldn't hear much of what she said, except "Good, good," and "Too bad. Stay on it. Keep me informed."

She returned to the table and took her stand behind the chair again. "You'll be happy to know Laughlin is officially nailed on the sex stuff. Laurel's materials suggested we'd find souvenirs, that's what gave us the warrant. First we found a concealed camera in his office at Martinson's. Now we've found his video collection at his house."

"That's terrific!"

"Yeah, it is. We also found a collection of keys. We're thinking he stole keys from his victims at work, copied them, and used them to creep their houses. Or jerked off just thinking about his power to do so. Or whatever these nutjobs do. Presumably how he got into Laurel's house to steal her papers."

"Anything linking him to Laurel's murder?"

"Short answer, no comment, I've said too much to a civilian already. Shorter answer, no. But we can probably get him for killing Artie Shindell. And you're gonna have to keep this to yourself, Ms. Gabrielli. Like, *seriously*, because Welles will crucify me if he hears I've told you anything."

"You know you can trust me!"

"Sure. So since I can trust you so much, I can trust you to tell me where fucking Conn is, right? He out following his nose again, instead of his brain, or—"

"Honestly, I don't know! I'd say swimming, or maybe he went out to Mason's camp. There's no cell service out there, that's probably why—"

"And where's this camp?"

I told her it was over an hour away, out past Lyndonville—a big piece of really remote land, in the King family for generations. I said I'd only been there twice and couldn't give accurate directions.

She was walking away before I finished. I watched her pull out and realized I was trembling. I wanted to call Conn, call Mace, call Jody, somebody. *What's going on?* I'd ask. But then I wondered who could I trust. Maybe at this point Selanski was the only one.

# CHAPTER 53

# CONN

I came around the corner of the garage just as Mason brought the grill of his pickup against the back of my Subaru with a quiet crunch. He kept his foot on the gas as his much heavier vehicle pushed my car until its bumper nudged the floor of the porch. He gave it a couple more revs, then turned off the truck and climbed out. His choice of parking arrangements told me a lot about his intentions.

He was still in his deputy's uniform, gold star pinned to a black utility vest with pouches for traffic flares and extra magazines for his Glock and whatever else they kept in there, sheriff's patches bright on the shoulders of his shirt. His boots were well shined beneath creased slacks, and his gun sat high in his belt holster.

"I was afraid I'd find you here," he said.

"I was just leaving. How about you back off your truck."

"Nobody's leaving. Why were you snooping around the garage?"

"Just let me out of here, Mason. I didn't see anything. I don't know anything."

"Any like what thing?" His big face was flushed but his cheeks were held as stiff as two pork chops. When I veered and started toward the driveway, he moved laterally to block me, hand on his gun. I stopped, fifteen feet away.

"What're you going to do, Mace? Kill me, too?"

"Let's just you and me talk for a while, Conn. Talk about what happened. I know, I can't expect forgiveness. Maybe understanding? So maybe I won't have to kill you?"

"You can't get away with it. Celine knows I'm here."

His cheeks crimped in a quick, bitter grin. "No, she doesn't. I stopped at your place on my way, looking for you. She had no idea where you were. I told her I'd give you a call. She was pleased I was making an effort. 'You guys need to talk.'"

He must have seen me eyeing the edge of the woods, looking for the best route around him, because he drew his Glock. He leveled it in two hands, pointed just to the left of my stomach.

"Nobody will hear the shots," he reminded me. "And your car can disappear, too."

"So you're really going to do this."

"You just gotta go into the house now, Conn."

"No."

He raised the gun and fired, close enough that I felt the hot wind of percussion on my face. The shot rang flat, sucked up by the pines. I didn't move.

"I don't know why you gotta be such an asshole," Mason said. "Why couldn't you have just left it alone? What the fuck, Conn? Doesn't thirty-five years of friendship mean anything to you?"

"It did."

"Let's go into the house now. Maybe you think you know everything, but you're wrong. I can fill you in."

That got to me a little. Every reporter knows there are always stories within stories. Maybe there was some exoneration or explanation I hadn't thought of. And my judgment had become erratic, maybe I'd overlooked something, my anger at my sister's murder was interfering with my objectivity. I didn't think he wanted me inside to make killing me easier—in fact, it would make a mess that would take some cleaning up, that would leave evidence. Out here, just hose the blood into the soil, rake over some fallen pine needles. Anchor me well with some part from Tony's truck and drop me in the pond. Take the car into the garage and cut it up, too. No one had any reason to come here, to sus-pect Mason of anything.

I turned to face the house. "It's locked," I said.

Something clinked on the steps to the porch and I saw the keys appear.

"You go on ahead," Mason said.

I took up the keys and approached the door. Behind me, I heard Ma-son's heavy tread on the steps. I decided I'd open the door, leap inside, slam it shut and slip the dead bolt behind me. Then what? I didn't know, but it would give me some momentary advantage. I couldn't get at the guns in the safe, but I'd hear him coming through the front or back door, and I'd be waiting to hit him with a chair. Or I'd head out the other way and sprint into the woods.

The moment the lock turned, my head seemed to shatter, lightning exploded behind my eyes. The blow drove me forward through the door and onto the floor. My mind stuttered, blackness rushing in. I forced my eyes open but they didn't work, the dark interior was gyrating, shapeless and confusing. I rolled onto my side and heard more than saw Mason step inside and shut the door behind him.

"Known you too long, Conn. Know how your mind works. Get up."

When he switched on the overhead light, I saw that he held a tele-scoping baton. My scalp tickled as blood seeped into my hair.

"Come on, big guy. Up. Pull your shit together." He prodded my chest with his boot.

I lurched upright, lost my balance, caught myself.

"Over there," he said. He gestured to one of the ancient wicker chairs. I stumbled toward it and fell into the embrace of its basketlike arms.

"You think this whole thing isn't breaking my heart?" Mason said. "You think I've been faking it about your sister, how shitty I've been feeling?"

He looked at me expectantly, but I was still too concussed to answer. He waited, then snapped the baton shut and returned it to its belt hol-ster. He sat heavily in the chair opposite me, gun pointed at me again. Only a little coffee table separated us, nothing on it but an empty beer can and a vase of dried flowers.

I managed to get my lips working again. "I don't know anything about you, Mace."

"Sure you do. She was the love of my life, Conn. Like I said, Jody's great, but she's never touched me where Laurel did. Inside."

"Which explains why you knocked her teeth out."

He looked startled. "Where'd you get that little tidbit?"

"Reliable sources."

He shook his head, despairing of me. "You know, Conn, your narcissism isn't your best feature. Always the smarter one, a step ahead. Always the higher achiever. So very verbal. Can you imagine how tiring that gets for us mere mortals? Let me tell you, it got old twenty, thirty years ago! And I gotta say, your sister had some of the same mannerisms."

"Poor boy."

"Keep it up, shithead. You're not a step ahead now. I'm not a happy camper, I'm feeling all, like, volatile. Making me mad is not a great plan."

I was thinking: How would Celine handle this? She would let him spill his guts, she'd sift his emotions for whatever leverage she might find. Seem sympathetic, avoid judgment. Let him drop his guard, then seize the advantage.

"You were going to give me the 'context' on why you killed my sister. How it was justified, right? I'm waiting, Mace. I'm all ears."

He looked at me searchingly, as if deciding how to answer. Blood trickled down my neck and spread into my shirt collar. The windows of the cabin had gone dim and tinged with orange as the sun began to set.

"Your sister was not easy to live with. She had a lot of opinions and she wouldn't ever stand down. My dad rode my ass, told me to keep her in line. Every now and again, that's the advice I took. 'A firm hand.'"

I lost it: "You ever try taking a firm hand with your dad? Tell him where he could stuff it?" Immediately, I regretted saying it. Celine would have accepted the statement, used his emotional drift to lead him to a point where she could maneuver him. But as my head recovered, my rage began building.

"Shut up, Conn. You have no idea. No clue."

"So you killed my sister because . . . she had her own opinions? Or because you were afraid to tell Warren to get his beak out of your business?"

His gun exploded, the flare coming right at me. My ears went cottony, but behind me I heard a delayed tinkle of broken glass. He must have hit a mirror on the wall.

"I just told you I wasn't in the mood for any shit. Didn't I?"

I gestured at the gun. "This is your idea of 'having a talk'?"

He just glowered. When he didn't say anything, I prompted him: "And then there was the thing of having kids."

Again he looked surprised. "What thing?"

"Come on, Mace. You were shooting blanks. And blaming her for not conceiving."

His face was impassive, a slab, but reddening. "Who the fuck you been talking to?" Before I could speak, he answered for me: "Let me guess—her therapist or guru or whatever, Katherine Krantz. Well, yeah, there was that. Ever have somebody impugn your balls, Conn? Tell you your sperm doesn't swim right or whatever? Probably not, studly dude like you, perfect track record and all, but *man*, that is not a nice thing to tell a guy. On the basis of no evidence."

"But she was right."

"Yeah, turns out she was, but she couldn't have known. It didn't go down easy, Conn! Get into an argument about whose turn it is to do the fucking dishes, and she makes these comments, has to bring *that* into it? So one night I lost it. A two-second slip of control. I admit it, I regret it. But I'll tell you what, it worked! She dropped that line pretty quick."

He tried to look smug, but it just made him look ill. More than anything else, he was susceptible to shame and guilt. How to leverage it?

"So then she fucks this guy, some lowlife peckerwood. And how'd I find out about it? A buddy of mine at the sheriff's sees them coming out of his house together. That's no *fun*, Conn, everybody has to know your wife's sleeping around? Your self-esteem, your workplace status, they kind of take a *hit*, Conn. So when we're tossing blame around, buddy, remember—"

"Was this before you made a habit of beating up on her, or—"

"I never made a fucking *habit* of any fucking thing! What, you never slipped up? Conn Whitman, he never had momentary lapses of judgment or control! Talk about glass houses!"

I should have absorbed that, banked it and finessed him with it somehow. But I was barely anchored myself, and something occurred to me. "You know what, Mace? Think about this before you answer. If you were a woman like Laurel, and you knew your husband, who you dearly loved, had a problem, and just wouldn't admit it, what would you do?"

"I give up. What?"

"You might try to get pregnant by somebody else. To give your husband what he wanted, a family. To make home life tolerable again."

He opened his mouth to come back at me, but he shut it again as the idea resonated. His eyes told me his mind was spinning back, thinking about the sequence of ruptures in their relationship. Waves of hurt hit him.

But it resolved in a look of disbelief and scorn. "Man, that is downright *Shakespearean*! The impotent king's dutiful, virtuous queen sleeps with the help on the sly to preserve harmony in the castle and continue the royal lineage. It's a great theme. And a dubious inference on your part."

He was breathing hard, emotion getting the better of him. By now my head had mostly cleared. Maybe the best solution was to bait him into recollection, focus him internally, on images of the past. Get him distracted and then make a move. He was bigger and heavier than me, but I was faster, fitter, more agile. He was hunkered deep between the arms of the sagging wicker chair, gun in hand but encumbered by his vest and belt.

"How'd you fall in love with her again? You're the so-called new boyfriend, right?"

"That was a mistaken perception, because she always told me 'no.' But I didn't mind the States thinking that way. I reinforced it with some anonymous calls to the tip line. But I didn't fall in love with her 'again.' I was *still* in love with her. Encountered her by chance at Martinson's, behind the bakery counter. One look and I could see she had gotten her shit together. God, she looked *gorgeous*, Conn. Fuck me, I walk out and suddenly my world has gone hollow, I'm incomplete. My marriage to Jody was suddenly, like, a fantasy. Good, loyal, hardworking wife, two great kids? An illusion. A *hallucination*. I waited in the parking lot and talked to her when she got off shift."

"And how'd she react? Seeing you?"

"She was nice. Cordial. Told me she had turned over a new leaf, was into fitness stuff, had two kids. She was glad to see me looking well. Jesus God, just talking to her, her *accepting* me, after all the shit that happened? It was like *sunshine* washing over me." The fervor in his eyes showed how powerful that moment was, how important it was that I understood.

I could easily imagine his self-blame metastasizing over the years. And here's this reborn Laurel, Trudy, my phoenix sister, determined to be a balanced, integrated human being, being kind. Yes, forgiving—and wanting some kind of reconciliation with her own past, as we all do, never imagining how Mason was seeing it, never intending it to go anywhere. Relinquishing blame as a crutch, including self-blame. The foundation of her recovery.

How ecstatic that absolution must have felt to him! Mason taking her kindness the wrong way. All the nostalgia, the idealization of their early years, suddenly imagining what could have been. The normal muddle and frustration of real married life, real kids and their real problems, so tedious and messy compared to this streamlined, shining ideal.

I felt a pang of sorrow. My dearest friend. A hardworking man, earnest, striving to be "good," a good citizen, yet always a little lost and lonely, incomplete, prone to the midnight ache and doubt. Suddenly finding a strong bright line in his soul, long abandoned. Of course he'd strive for it, that fantasy ideal. *The poor, sad, deluded bastard*, I thought. He filled his chair, so big, so full of his own failings and contradictions, such a good friend for so long.

I fought off the sentiment. "But you *murdered* her. How did that fit in with all that glory, all the reconciliation, letting go of your shame and guilt? How'd all that good stuff end up with her *dead*? And Tony Shapiro? That's the part I don't get."

This made him uncomfortable. He rearranged himself in the chair, hitched one shoulder. His eyes strayed briefly, but he kept the gun trained at my chest as he figured out what to say. When his eyes returned to my face, they were hard, strange to me—the way he'd looked at Captain Welles when we were in Laurel's shed.

"Why don't you tell me how it went, Conn? Because you seem to have it all figured out. And you're so very good with words."

"What's the point? You're going to kill me whatever I say."

"I never said I was going to kill you—you said it. Go on. Tell me the whole story."

When I started talking, I was surprised at how fully formed my sense of it was. The narrative had been coalescing in my mind for weeks, a shape emerging out of the mist, but I had been denying it, suppressing it. *Not my best dearest oldest friend Mason.*

"She was beautiful and all the good things could maybe come true. So you stopped by Martinson's now and again. She was always kind, willing to spend some time with you. She talked about how forgiveness is the root of healing. You learned she was single. Maybe Jody was in one of those distant phases wives get into. Jody, always a bit too practical, while Laurel, she had this . . . lyrical thing about her. You figured you'd eventually persuade Laurel, make her remember the old dream, too. You'd connect again and it would be blissful and you'd tell Jody you wanted a divorce. That would be rocky, but worth it."

He shrugged, stuck out his chin. "Not bad." He gestured with his gun for me to continue.

"You wanted to show her you understood her new fitness thing, her outdoorsy thing. You wanted to give her something, so you ran over her bike and bought her that nice Trek. You brought it to her house, surprised her with it. She told you no, but you insisted, maybe you just drove off and left it there. But then I pointed it out as anomalous to Captain Welles, out in the shed, so you had to steal it. Otherwise we'd trace its purchase, figure out who bought it. Or it would have your fingerprints on it. I suppose it's in the pond now?"

"I wanted her to know that I totally *got* her changes! I *supported*—"

"But she kept telling you 'no.' Why didn't you listen?"

"You know how women are! They want to hold all the cards. She said 'no' but I could see she didn't mean it. She emphasized 'forgiveness' too many times, she was too gentle and sweet and apologetic about that 'no,' trust me. She was tipping my way, man!"

"You saw what you wanted to see."

He didn't like that attitude. "Such a superior mind! Wow, you coulda been a somebody! I'll bet Celine would say something nicer and more like the truth. Which is that, when your hope burns so bright, its light fills every corner of you, burns away the shadow of every doubt. I was wrong, I can admit that. But don't try to *strip my soul of poetry*, you fucking prig! Don't turn my, like, *prayers* into shit!"

He took another shot at the far wall, not near me but convincing enough about his mindset. I refused to flinch, but then another shot ripped through the rattan back of my chair three inches from my head, and I reflexively jerked away. That gratified him.

I brushed chips of reed off my lap and waited until I figured both our ears had recovered.

"So one day you go to Martinson's and she's not there. And you ask somebody where she is, and they say she took a few days off to go camping."

He chuckled grimly. "Yeah—and I'm thinking, *I know where she went!* That she went to our old campsite—how else could I see it but as an *invitation*? A special, super-private place where we could discover each other again. Right? I mean, I didn't know for sure that's where she'd gone until I rode out and saw her car there."

"Rode out. You were on your motorcycle. And when you saw her car, your heart took wing, as they say. Everything is going just as you hoped, your dreams are about to come true. But then you hurry up the hill, she's surprised to see you. Not happily surprised."

His face went stiffer, eyes more hooded. The gun had drifted as memory seized him, but now he re-centered it on my chest.

I went on, wanting to defy the authority of that gun: "At first you thought she was being playful—like, a tease, an inside joke, just between the two of you. Like back in the day. But she keeps at it, tells you to leave, don't come around her anymore. That kinda pissed you off, I suppose."

Mason was breathing harder but said nothing. In my mind I could see it all perfectly: Mason stoned on soaring hope and desire, brought down hard.

"You come up and you're bursting inside, but she says go away. So, what, you try to hug her, kiss her, remind her why you're there. And she shoves you away. You tell her to take it easy, but she says it again, 'Just go away! What are you thinking?' It takes you a minute to figure out she means it, but then you tell her, 'Okay, I'll go, but let's just be together just this one more time, like a, a sacrament, to honor what we had.' *Please*, you say."

Mason's skin was turning pink. I didn't want to say what came next, but I couldn't stop. At some point he would either shoot me or he'd become so distraught I could make my move. I thought back to Celine's description of the self-delusion that comes with obsessional love.

"You're thinking, She's just not getting it, how important this is, how *huge* this is. If she can just *feel* what you're feeling, she'll get it. You're sure she feels it, too, she's just not admitting it to herself. So you try to kiss her again and she backs away and you grab her arm and then she's got her knife in her hand. And you're just not having that *shit*, right? She led you on, she can goddamn well give something back. Some fucking token, right?"

He didn't answer. His eyes were baleful and mournful in equal measure.

With just the ceiling light on, the cabin was dim and dreary, silent except for Mace's panting. Faintly, outside, I heard the evening birds flute their last songs of the day.

"You try to get the knife away from her, she fights back, she's much stronger than you anticipated. It gets out of hand. Somehow you end up stabbing her. Then you come to your senses. But it's too late. Did you rape her before or after she was dead?"

Mason's gun exploded in his hand, the flare coming at me, the powder stippling my face. Rattan chips littered my shoulder.

"*Don't you fucking talk like that.* How could you even *think* a thing like that?"

"Because afterward you wrapped her in the tent fly and brought her down the hill. Why go through all the effort unless there was DNA evidence on her body? Why not just leave her there?"

The question seemed to confuse him. His eyes searched the coffee table, the floor, for an answer. "I wasn't rational! You're talking like I'm some, some genius super-criminal, figuring out the angles. But I was practically blacking out, I couldn't breathe, I couldn't think straight. I couldn't stand to see her lying there. First I covered her up with the fly, and then I realized I'd have left fingerprints all over the damn thing. I'm winging it, Conn, I'm feeling shittier than I've ever felt in my life. So I roll her up in the fly and tie it with the tent's guylines. I figure I'll take her down to Pendleton Pond, put some rocks in the wrapper, sink her. I start down there to re-connoiter, make sure there's nobody on the cove, and halfway down I see these fucking woodchucks in their pontoon boat, big party going on. So instead I bring her down the other way, figuring I'd put her in her car and drive her out here, bury her or something. I just dragged her, it's so steep, the fly makes it like a sled, it's easy. But what you're not getting is how I was *feeling,* okay, because if you think I'm enjoying this moment, you're wrong. It was the worst, ever. All I'm thinking is, 'Jesus, God—Jody and the kids, they can't know, I can't get caught, they need a husband and a dad.'"

He was heaving with sobs but was too tight to let them out, just convulsing as if starting to throw up. Maybe he was.

"I believe you." I did. I did believe he had been in a state of utter misery and terror and self-loathing. His confusion would have been abso-lute. The enormity of it would have been crashing down, crushing him.

"So we get down to the road, I'm thinking I'll unwrap her and find her car keys, put her in her car. Take her somewhere. Come back in my truck, pick up the bike later. Rain was forecast. If nobody found out for a few days, there'd be no trace of my tire tracks. All I was thinking about was Jody and the kids. Our reputation in the community, our livelihoods! When you have kids, the whole thing changes, Conn, something you wouldn't know *jack* about. I realized how crazy I'd been. It was about the kids!"

I believed him. I bit back the hatred I felt for his weakness, his lack of self-control. He was looking at me pleadingly, willing me to under-stand, sympathize. Did he really think I would forgive him, or I'd sign on to help protect the kids and pretend we'd never had this conversa-tion? Maybe he did.

"But just then Tony Shapiro pulled up in his truck," I prompted.

"What the fuck was he doing there? What the *fuck*? I'm getting near the road, dragging what is obviously a corpse. I've got blood on my shirt, and here comes that little prick, starting up the hill. He takes one look and his eyes go wide. I'd put her knife in my belt so I could cut ropes and tie things. I was on that fucker in a second! I didn't feel a goddamned thing, I *hated* the wimpy little prick. What was he doing there? Had she arranged to meet him up there? Our special place?"

"So then you had a truck. You put the bodies in it. His boat's anchor and rope were in there and so you decided to drown Laurel somewhere after all. But why Richfield Reservoir? Why not out here?"

"Yeah, well, my luck was not running so good, was it? It was late afternoon by then. I got two dead bodies in an open truck bed. I can't go driving around in daylight! So I hid out until after dark. I figured I'd drive out here, stay on the back roads. But then I'm coming along 16A, by then it's the only way out here without forty miles of detours, and I see bright lights way up ahead. It's like ten o'clock, I'm thinking, 'What the fuck.' Turns out they're doing night repairs! Got light towers up, the road's lit up like a film set. Backhoes, guys in orange vests, guy with a sign funneling traffic into one lane. No way they wouldn't see."

"So you turn back. Laurel's already wrapped and ready to sink, plus Tony conveniently left his anchor and rope in the truck bed. You pass the footpath to the cliffs at the narrows, get an inspiration. Just tie her up good. You remember it's super-deep there. You pull over, drag her to the top of the cliff. Come back, get the anchor and rope. Double her over, put some stones in—"

"I don't want to talk about this part."

"Then, just a couple miles back, there's the stump dump. Drive up to the masonry dump area, carry Tony back in a ways, cover him with stones and gravel. Heavy rain is forecast. It'll be weeks before anyone finds him, maybe months. Maybe never, if you're lucky. Then you remember the knife. So you wipe off your prints and take it uphill and bury it, too."

"Shut up now."

"You gotta talk about all of it, Mace—"

His gun flared again, burning my cheeks with powder residue. I could barely make out his words in the deafness afterward.

"What *matters*, Conn, is talking about the emotional side of this. You think anybody wanted to kill anybody? That's not who I am. But it *happened*. And now I am permanently fucked up inside, but *I gotta cope*!"

"And I'm supposed to feel sorry for you." I was thinking: *It didn't "happen." You* did *it*.

He just stared—the glazed look of an emotionally exhausted man. We looked at each other, and the fact is I did feel sorry for him. I felt sorry for myself, too. Mason had been part of my foundation, sometimes the steadiest thing in my life. It was like every bone in my body was out of its socket, the basic mechanics of me were all undone.

"And then you went back to get your motorcycle? Or did you do that the next night?"

Again, he looked taken aback. He shook his head as if trying to clear it, trying to come back from the emotional whirlpool of that night to the logistics of it.

"No. It was in the truck. Tony, he had a plank in the truck. I drove the bike up. What's it matter?"

"Not much. Not now."

I slumped in my chair, stretched my legs out in front of me as if overcome by hopelessness, feet under the coffee table. The body language of defeat, surrender. I think Mason had truly hoped to talk me into understanding, seeing it his way, and through an ultimate act of loyalty, into saying nothing about this. But his face had slowly settled into an expression of deep regret as he realized it wasn't happening. That he really would have to kill me now.

That's when I kicked upward with all my strength, both feet lifting the coffee table and flipping it into Mason's face. I was out of my chair before it even hit him. His gun went off, and I assumed he shoved the table off him, but I didn't see it because I was at the door. I got a glimpse of him struggling to get out of the deep chair as I flung it open and went through.

# CHAPTER 54

# CONN

It was nearly full dark outside. I leaped down the stairs and ran past our bumper-locked vehicles, thinking to cut into the woods where the turn-around narrowed. But Mason appeared at the door and I instinctively swerved to put the vehicles between us. I was running toward the pond, not the woods. It took Mason a few seconds to move laterally on the porch where he could get a shot at me. By then I was halfway to the water.

His first shot wasn't close, but then I heard another and I saw a pine branch twitch to my right. I couldn't pause to think, I couldn't turn toward the woods and show him lateral exposure. Instead I hunched and ran right off the end of the dock and into the water. I hit flat, then stood in the chest-deep water to pull off my shoes. Behind me, I heard Mason grunt as he jumped off the near end of the porch and landed hard.

I swam straight out, tangling in weeds. I had to lift my head too high to draw breath above the cursed lily pads. Ahead was the dim expanse of the pond, misting over, behind came Mason, trying to get an angle for another shot.

I dove. In clear water, with a good lungful of air, I could swim fifty yards underwater, but not here. I was swimming through weed stems and was already short of oxygen from my sprint. Mason would see the lilies moving and place his shots accordingly.

I put in maybe twenty feet, struggling through clinging plant

matter, before I had to come up for air. I rolled before I hit the surface
to expose as little of my head as possible and was able to grab a breath.
Then I was under again, thinking only *distance, distance.* The underwater light changed suddenly as a luminous green ceiling appeared above
me. Mason must have paused on the dock to turn on his flashlight, and
hadn't noticed the lilies moving until too late to shoot. I frog-kicked
and used a breaststroke with my arms to part the ropy weeds in front
of me. Twenty feet farther out, I cut hard to the left to avoid leaving
a predictable path.

When I came up for air, I heard the crank of the skiff's little motor.
It was an opportunity to grab more air, swim some strokes at the surface. *Puhrr, puhrr. Puhrr, puhrr.* Then another hard yank and the engine
started up. I heard him rev it and then I went under again. The metallic
whine of the motor filled my ears.

I was less than a hundred feet from the dock. Another two hundred,
and the weeds would thin, making swimming easier. I knew I couldn't
get that far before he caught up with me. What then? If I headed to
shore, the mucky shallows would mire me as I floundered out, I'd be
a sitting duck. On the other hand, Mason was at the back of the boat,
steering it and controlling the throttle. The bow would ride high, hard
to see over, and he'd need two hands to hold the flashlight and the gun.
He'd have to stop to shoot.

I came up again, just my face above the surface, sucking three deep
breaths, as the boat closed in. When he was twenty feet away, I dove
down again. The skiff slowed, and Mason panned his light over the surface for signs of me. For now the wake would be spreading, disturbing
the lilies all around, making my movements harder to track. But my only
shelter would be the sides of the boat itself. If I could surface silently,
right against the hull, exhale with as little noise as possible, he'd have a
hard time pinpointing my location. He was no doubt in an adrenalized
rage by now, hands as unsteady as his judgment.

The shadow of the hull loomed closer and then it was above me.
Mason put the motor in neutral. I rose and placed my hands against
the aluminum so I could sense his movements. What would I do in his

shoes? I'd wait, standing so as to be able to see close to the hull, flashlight and gun held the way police are taught to, ready to fire at the first clue.

When I felt the boat shift toward the starboard and saw the light panning to that side, I came up under the port gunnel, treading water as I exhaled and brought in another precious measure of air. Mason panned the light in a full circle over the lily pads, but couldn't see my head, just five feet from his own. I held myself as motionless as I could and still stay at the surface.

"You sure you want to be down there, Conn? Never know what you might bump into. *Who* you might bump into. Scary thought, huh?"

I sank again, found a different spot, came up slowly. I was dying to gulp air but had to ease each breath out and in again.

"I know where you are, Conn," he said. "Smart guy like you has figured out the tactics. But I'm standing here and I have all the air I want. You're treading water or underwater and at some point you'll get tired. You make one move away from the boat and I've got you."

Suddenly the boat rocked as Mason leaned to my side. I went directly under the hull, waited, then thought to come up where the bow overhang created a longer shadow. I'd feel the boat's pitch change if he came forward.

He was talking again or still when I surfaced, quiet as a turtle.

"You think I won't shoot through the hull? I will. One small hole in this hull, I'll make it back to shore before it becomes a problem. But one small hole in you—you're fucked."

He must have seen something move among the lily pads, because he shot into the water a few feet from the boat. I was thinking about how many bullets he had spent, about what generation of Glock he had. I'd interviewed some police official a few years ago, asked about standard-issue law enforcement weapons. Was it a 17? That would be seventeen rounds in the standard magazine. He had fired six or seven times. Or was it more? I had lost track. In any case, it didn't matter: He still wore his sheriff's vest, no doubt with another magazine in it. He wouldn't run out of ammo.

The boat swayed, then went steadier, suggesting he had sat down.

The light still came and went on the surface of the pond, an erratic lighthouse beam. I kept treading water in the longer shadow of the bow, unable to breathe fully. He was *listening* for me now.

"This is the shits, isn't it. You and me, out here. Who would have pictured this thirty years ago? Hell, five years ago, two years ago! Pretty sad."

He waited, maybe hoping he'd bait me into answering.

"You were inspiring to me, Conn. The guy who was going places. I knew I couldn't keep up with you, but what I *could* do, what I *did* do, was be solid, steady, a good friend, a public servant. I've *saved lives*, Conn—you ever do that? I don't think so! I'll tell you, it's a good thing to do. When you add somebody up, shouldn't you put that on the scale, too? I mean, does it seem right that only the mistakes count, at the end of the day?"

That question had always confused me. In fact, Mace and I had talked about it, in more than one of our midnight conversations, camping out, the starfield inviting big thoughts. I wondered if he was deliberately reminding me of our ambivalence. On one hand, Hitler was supposedly nice to his dogs—did that counterbalance the Holocaust? No. On the other hand, some teenager takes care of his single mom and younger sibs, picks up litter, works hard at school, and then one night drives while drunk and kills somebody.

How should the scales tilt?

"I was hoping you and I could decide that tonight. I really was. Because I've mostly been a very good boy. Laurel and Tony weren't perfect, by the way. But no, nobody should have, like, ended their chance to become better people, right? I agree. But add in the fact that I have a wife and two kids, don't you have to ask where's the ultimate moral benefit? What's the fair price for, like, a very short time of stupidity, and lots of dashed hopes and dreams, against being a good man? And who would really pay? I'd go to jail, that'd suck, but Jody and the kids, they'd have *what*? A lifetime of shame, poverty? No dad, all kinds of screwed-up Freudian shit? And they didn't do anything!"

I wondered what he expected. Laurel had kids, also. So did Tony. Was I supposed to swim out where he could shoot me? Mason's whining only added to my rage.

"This is *tragic*, Conn! This is just tragic. You and me? This is break-ing my fucking heart, so help me. How the fuck did we get here?" He was half sobbing now.

Abruptly, the boat shoved backward in the water as he lunged toward the bow. I dove quickly under the center and heard the metallic *tew!* of a bullet through water. He'd put his hand over the gunnel and fired into the space where I'd been only an instant before.

I hadn't taken a full breath. As if pissed that I wasn't there, Mason angled a couple more shots from the bow, hoping he'd get lucky.

I surfaced at the stern, trying not to gasp, head next to the puttering motor. Mason must have figured that's where I'd go, because a second later he was there, shooting down, a spray of shots at different angles.

I came up on the starboard side, out of breath. I must have made too much noise inhaling, because he was right there, another shot that shocked the water near my leg.

I came up under the bow again, now seriously oxygen-deprived.

"Connor. Give it up, man. I've got two magazines and all the air I need. I can do this all night. I'm getting better at this, and you're getting tired."

He had me figured pretty well, because suddenly a hole appeared six inches from my face. He'd shot through the hull just above the water line.

I came up on the far side to find the light subtly changed. Mason's flashlight panned, but a steadier beam lit the surface. I heard Mason's breathing above me and readied for another dive.

A shot thumped the air, but it wasn't from his gun.

The boat rocked as Mason flipped over the gunnel into the water. The splash sent the boat away from us. He tried to reach the retreating hull but couldn't catch it. His flashlight sank, its beam angling up from ten feet below, giving his face and the boat an eerie green tinge. Then he was flailing, trying to stay afloat in his boots and vest and slacks. I had no idea what had happened, but the boat cast a shadow around us from some light on the shore.

Mason's head went under and he came up coughing. "Fuck, that hurt. Fuck! Conn! Where are you?"

I was there. I was shoving the boat farther away from him. When

I dipped my head underwater, I saw in the green glow that both his hands were empty. A wisp of darkness curled into the water from his shoulder. He'd been hit.

I came up for air just out of his reach. A flailing, clinging man can drown even an experienced lifeguard. And I didn't feel much like a lifeguard.

"Whitman!" a voice shouted from the dock. Water in my ears, I couldn't tell who it was. Then: "Whitman, you goddamn dumbass!" And I knew it was Selanski.

Mace heard her, too, even floundering and sputtering.

"I can't stay up," he coughed. "Ticked my shoulder. Arm's not working right."

"You want me to *save* you?" I paddled backward as he moved toward me, the instinct to clutch and cling overpowering him.

He coughed, went under, struggled up again. "Right. I get that."

I treaded water, in agony. The boat's motor puttered quietly on. Selanski shouted from the dock.

"Do what's right, Conn," Mason spluttered.

"What's that?"

His mouth went under again. Beneath him, his boots flurried, useless. When he came up he was gasping, desperate, starting to suffocate. Lily pad leaves and stems draped his head.

"There's no way back from this, is there?" Mason said.

Over on the dock, Selanski was swearing. "Whitman! Goddamn it, answer me!"

"Conn. You've always had my back, man. I can count on you, yeah? You'll do what's right, yeah?" He was trying to stay up, but one arm wasn't working well. The poor light made his face indistinct but he seemed to be looking at me, eyes sending a message. Then he went under again. When he came up, his weak paddling had rotated him in the water. His back was almost to me. A great big back, bloated with his sodden vest.

I put my arms around him and I held him.

"I got your back, man," I told him. "I got your back."

I tightly held my dearest friend until he stopped moving.

# CHAPTER 55

# CELINE

I got to the hospital before Conn did and spent ten minutes pacing in the emergency ward waiting room among other frightened people. My heart pounded every time EMTs pushed gurneys through from the ambulance bays. At last the far doors opened and Conn walked in, followed by a pair of Vermont State Troopers. He looked bedraggled, and he had a bandage wrapped around his leg over his jeans.

When I hugged him, he smelled of water and mud, and his shirt was moist. I couldn't let him go. We stood there for a long time, holding each other as the troopers talked to the woman at the admitting desk and gave her some paperwork. It was eleven o'clock and I still had no idea what was going on.

An hour earlier I'd been pacing the floor at the cabin, approaching panic. It was two hours past sunset, and I'd had no word from Conn since I'd left the house in the morning. *It's not really so strange*, I told myself after Selanski had left. *He'll be back any minute, he just went for a long swim. Lake Memphremagog, or someplace farther away than usual. His phone is out of juice, that's all.*

I didn't believe it. Something was amiss. Conn had been too reserved yesterday and last night, and I sensed he had learned something he wasn't telling me. And Selanski had known something when she'd swung by. She was *onto* something.

After Selanski left, I had called Mason again, got no answer, then called Jody. She told me Mace had been on sheriff's duty today and she had expected him home much earlier. Her clipped, tight tone sounded curt or disapproving, but I knew it was because she was worried, too. She didn't know where either man was. She said she'd call me if she heard from them.

*Swimming. Phone out of juice. Here any minute.*

I was still chanting that mantra when the phone rang, an unfamiliar number on the readout. It was Conn. Road noise told me he was calling from a car.

"Celine—first, I love you. I am fine, really, I'm not hurt at all. I'm borrowing Trooper Rodriguez's personal phone. We just got reception again. Selanski insisted I go to the hospital. I would've been happy to drive myself, but the Subaru is 'evidence' and they have to hang onto it for a while. These guys are great, I asked them to take me to Richfield Hospital instead of Saint Johnsbury so it'd be closer to home. I'd love it if you wanted to meet me there in another forty minutes or so."

He asked me to bring a change of clothes. Said he loved me again. That he was fine. His stilted, rambling speech told me he was in shock. When I asked him what was going on, he just said it was a long story, he'd rather tell me in person.

I let go of Conn so he could shake hands with Rodriguez and the other trooper as they left, and then I sat with him as he registered at the admitting desk. He couldn't remember his Social Security number, and it took him a long time to fumble his insurance card out of his wet wallet. Clearly, a man exhausted and in shock.

The irony of emergency rooms: You get there in a big hurry but then sit around for a long time, at the triage nurse's discretion. I took some comfort from the fact that Conn's injury didn't warrant fast attention. We sat in a curtained carrel for half an hour before a doctor arrived.

It gave him time to tell the story. The disappearance of the thing he'd kicked in the reservoir had nagged him from the start. Why would the killer move Laurel's body? Only the fear of someone finding it would drive them to take the risk. And the only person who knew about it was Mason, after Conn called him, who had indeed called Captain Welles the next day—but had two nights and a day to retrieve the body. The same was true of Laurel's stolen bicycle—again, Mason had heard him point it out to Welles, had known the police would look into it, and had stolen it so it couldn't be traced. Mason, able to head him off at each turn.

Conn just didn't want to believe it, he didn't want to tell me about it because it seemed too crazy and he didn't want suspicions to pollute my relationship with Mason. But then Laurel's lawyer said she'd asked about a restraining order against someone in law enforcement. And he discovered that Mason had bought welding gas recently, suggesting what had happened to Tony Shapiro's truck and why Mason was spending so much time out at King Ranch.

"Why didn't you tell anybody!" I asked. "Why did you just go out there on your own, if you thought Mason was a murderer?"

"I wanted him to tell me it wasn't true. It was all in my head, and my friend really was a good guy and I hadn't lost him forever." Conn slumped on the edge of the bed, drained in so many ways. "I felt I *owed* him a chance to explain. Isn't that the dumbest shit ever?"

An orderly pulled the curtain to put his head in. "Sorry it's taking so long, Mr. Whitman. The ER's a popular spot on Saturday nights, unfortunately. Dr. Corcoran will be here soon as he can."

When the curtain swung shut, Conn recounted what Mace had told him in the cabin: a shifting array of rationalizations, emotional justifications, paradoxed values, philosophical excuses. Accusation, denial, remorse: layer upon layer of competing feelings. To me, the only constant was that he was an out-of-control man who had killed two people and wouldn't hesitate to kill another.

Conn's narrative got more disjointed when he told me what happened out on the pond, but my anger rose as he described Mason's continuing to argue his case, to plead, to finesse, to bully, even as he was shooting at Conn.

"He was suffering, Celine. He was crying even as he was shooting at me. 'This is just tragic, Conn. This is just fucking tragic.' And it is."

Selanski had called for support, and an hour after Conn made it to shore Welles and others began to arrive. Selanski and Welles sat on the front porch to debrief him, waiting for an aquatic unit to arrive. Manring and some others broke into the garage and found Tony Shapiro's truck. They expected to find Laurel's body in the pond when dive teams went out in the morning.

In the dim porch light, it was a while before anybody noticed the little rip in the thigh of Conn's jeans and the blood seeping into the wet denim. When at last an EMT took a look, she found a shallow furrow drilled by one of Mason's bullets. Conn said it didn't hurt, he hadn't noticed it at all.

It had been that close, I thought. Mason wasn't being demonstrative, dramatizing, trying to prove a point. He was trying to kill Conn. The thought made me feel dizzy, sick. What would have happened if Selanski hadn't arrived?

"How did Selanski start considering Mason a suspect?" I asked. "I thought everybody was sure it was Laughlin."

"Basically, she got there the same way I did. The pattern had been nagging her from the start. The thing I kicked had to have been Laurel's body. But where had it gone? Why would the killer risk exposure by retrieving the body unless he was afraid it would be found if he left it there? There was that window of time, from when I called Mason until the police began the reservoir search. And only one person knew about my encounter."

The orderly came back with a bottle of water, which Conn uncapped and quickly drained.

"But even Selanski couldn't quite get there," Conn continued. "Mason King, longtime sheriff's deputy, family man, well respected in the law enforcement community? Couldn't be. Except then Nadeau tells her about Mason's violence when he was married to Laurel. That got her dander up. The clincher came when Trooper Manring came up with something. Apparently, I'd gotten Welles curious about the bicycle, too.

All the while Manring's looking for Laughlin's purchase of gas and kerosene, he was going to bicycle stores, too. He knew the brand, if not the
model, and the color. When he went to a store, he'd show the staff photos
of Laughlin, Shapiro, and Nadeau. Did any of these buy a fairly expensive red Trek in the last couple months? No luck. But he and Selanski had
been talking about the puzzle of the body's disappearance, Mason as the
only one who could have taken the opportunity. Yesterday, he thought
to show them a photo of Mason, from the sheriff's website. And one of
the clerks recognized him as the buyer. Selanski followed up with a quick
visit to Cy Vandermeer, that's why she was in Richfield today, to see if I
had missed anything when I talked to him. Making sure she had every
detail straight. Vandermeer mentioned the restraining order."

We sat beneath the buzzing fluorescents for another ten minutes,
holding hands but not saying much. There was so much I wanted to ask
him, but he was running out of steam. Tonight was not the moment.
Maybe there'd never be the right moment. When I let myself feel, I felt
outrage at Mason for trying to take this man from me. I breathed and
thought of Katherine Krantz and inwardly chanted, *Forgive*. Breathe.
*Forgive*. Breathe.

Dr. Corcoran had the clear complexion, white eyes and teeth, of a man
who lived right and stayed fit. He'd brought the admitting papers with
him, including the State Police statement the troopers had left. His eyebrows went up as he read through it.

"Long night, huh?" he said sympathetically.

He bathed the wound, numbed it locally, and put in six tidy stitches.
His biggest concern was sepsis, given the murky pond water. He dashed
off a prescription for antibiotics, handed Conn a printout about wound
care, wished us well, and hurried off.

I helped Conn into the clean clothes I had brought, and we left the
hospital. Conn fell asleep in the car and I had to rouse him when we got
to the cabin. Still, he insisted on a shower before going to bed. I taped

a plastic kitchen trash bag over his bandage and helped him scrub, then toweled him off and led him upstairs. Throughout, he was docile and obedient as a big dog getting its bath.

His gunshot wound really wasn't anything much. Inside, though— that's where the real damage had been done.

# CHAPTER 56

# CONN

"I have a story to tell you," Selanski said, "and it's probably not gonna be one you want to hear."

"Oh, look, Detective, I—"

"I know, I know! You have been through the *mill*, Whitman. You've had a lot of unpleasant surprises and you've done a yeoman's job of making this case happen for us. But you can get this from me, or you can hear it from somebody else in a less congenial environment."

She gestured at the restaurant we were sitting in—agreeably stylish but not ostentatious, elegant but relaxed. A candle fluttered at the center of each table. Nicely dressed people, mostly couples, sat comfortably at the tables, talking, toasting, eating, laughing. In the far corner, the hump of a wood-burning pizza oven rose to a chimney above a glowing hearth of coals.

Selanski herself looked slightly done up, a dressier blazer and slacks. As I had approached her table, I noted that she wore low heels, small stud earrings, and no shoulder holster. She hadn't dressed for me, but for the place, as I had: same jacket, but a clean shirt and khakis instead of jeans. I seldom got to Burlington, a big metropolis by Richfield standards, or went to places like this.

"In my professional life," I told her, "I start calling people by their first names after a while. Helps build trust that leads to a better interview. Mind if I call you Marlene?"

"Call me whatever. I'll call you Whitman."

A waiter came—young kid, barely old enough to serve alcohol—wearing black pants and black, buttoned shirt. He started to introduce himself, but Selanski held up her hand.

"We're here to spend some money and we'll give you a good tip. But only if you kinda stay out of our hair. I don't want to know your name any more than you want to know mine. Let's start with a bottle of this Chianti." She pointed to a line on the wine list.

Chris, or David, or Justin had enough experience to nod appreciatively and vanish.

Selanski grinned as she watched him go. "He'll get over it. Give him something to bitch about in the salad-prep area."

"You've been a waitress, sounds like."

"I've been everything, Whitman." She shook out her linen napkin and put it on her lap. "So. I hear you've been laying low since our long night out at, what'd you call it, 'King Ranch.'"

"You hear from whom?"

"Gal named Celine Gabrielli."

"Well, she'd know."

I had taken a two-week leave from the *Herald*. Devotees of "Around Here" would just have to miss a few installments. Ricky, bless her, would have to fire me or hire somebody or whatever small newspaper publishers did. Eight days had passed since that night out at King Ranch, and I wasn't sure I was doing all that much recovering. The bullet wound had never hurt, and now all I felt was some itching and a slight hitch when I walked. The other stuff was more difficult, and I didn't think I had a handle on it yet.

Mainly I was reeling from the loss of my best friend. He wasn't just dead—he had retroactively excised himself from me, had *redacted* himself from my life, leaving a furrow going back decades. It would need time to heal. Who was this guy? Who had he been all along? Killing my sister. Doing his best to kill me. How deep can betrayal get?

Where did that leave me now?

I'd spent the last eight days doing about what I'd done when I came back from Washington: hiding out and regrouping. The difference this time was that I wasn't drinking and that I had a loving, unflagging, wise companion to keep me steady.

Dear Celine: She did not ever push it. She could easily have gone into therapeutic overdrive, but she knew me too well. If I came out of this, it would be by my own devices or not at all. Nobody knew the whole story—not even me, really. My recall was chaotic, images were superimposed and juxtaposed in memory. Selanski and Welles had debriefed me in detail that night and a couple more times in the following days, going over my talk with Mason before I'd kicked the table over, and everything he'd said while trying to shoot me. Meanwhile, they had conducted a thorough, days-long forensic investigation of King Ranch: the cabin, the garage, the pond, the nearby woods. They surely knew everything. Except what was in my head. Except what had happened in the water.

So what was Selanski on about?

She had watched me go internal for, I'd guess, a full two minutes. Being watched by Marlene Selanski is an experience unto itself. I roused only when the waiter reappeared with our bottle of Chianti. He displayed the label and pulled the cork and was about to do the ritual of pouring a splash and awaiting approval, but Selanski held up a hand.

"Thanks, kiddo," she told him. "I'll take it from here."

Good kid. He said nothing, just smiled and left the bottle for Selanski to pour.

"Well," she said, "here's to a successful solution to multiple murders in a lovely rural community that doesn't need that kind of shit to disturb its serenity. Also to the arrest of a serial sexual predator turned arsonist and murderer. Our streets are safe, the bad guys got their just desserts. Right?"

I had started to raise my glass, but she hadn't picked hers up.

"Except," she said.

"Oh man—"

"Sorry, Whitman. Celine says you haven't gone to the *Herald*. She says you unplugged the radio, don't read the newspaper. She says you work around your place and swim and don't talk to anybody, hardly even to her."

"I'm trying to pull myself together. I need the world to back off for a little while, that's all."

She bobbed her head, accepting but letting me know it wouldn't be that easy. What frightened me most was the sympathy in her eyes. By this time, I had great respect for her—more, a kind of affection you get when you've been in the trenches with a person and seen them in some tough situations. This wasn't a look I'd seen before.

"So you're out of the loop, I get that, I get why. But it can't last forever, and tonight I have the fun job of bringing you up to speed." She tasted her wine, nodded approvingly. "This is on me, by the way. Expense account, have a ball."

I looked at my glass and realized it was empty. I had drained it without noticing. It was the first alcohol I'd had in over a week—I was wary—and it was hitting me fast.

"You're starting to freak me out. Please get on with it."

"So, that night I get to the camp and there's your buddy's truck jammed up against your Subaru. The vehicular body language doesn't bode well, right? And then I hear a gunshot from out on that mudhole pond. I go onto the dock, shine the light out, and I see Deputy King shouting and muttering and shooting down at the lily pads. I'm reasonably sure it's Whitman in the water. I pop King in the shoulder and he goes over."

"I was there, remember?"

"Oh, I do remember. Except for what's happening during the two–three minutes I'm shining my flashlight out there, hollering and wondering what the fuck. There's the little boat and I can tell there's something going on behind it, where I can't see. Ripples and splashes, voices, coughing. And I am ripshit with myself for not popping the guy center-mass."

"You saved my life!"

"You bet I did! Thank you and you're welcome. And then you come around the boat and paddle to shore, but your buddy, he doesn't put in an appearance. I make another reasonable assumption."

The waiter appeared again, pad at the ready, but Selanski held up her hand. "Another few minutes," she said. "Like twenty."

When he'd gone, she refilled our glasses and looked down at the table as if framing her thoughts.

"You're in shock, I do the necessary, help arrives. Welles and I interview you. We take apart the place, it all jibes, we get teams out to retrieve King's body and the boat, go through the cabin. And everything you said, he said, checks out. Shapiro's truck in the garage, sections of it in the pond. And that fucking bike! And your sister's body. Sorry, Whitman. I won't go into that."

I nodded my appreciation. I had declined to identify the body. Over a month in the water, I doubt I could have. A DNA match and dental records confirmed it was Laurel.

"But you know Welles and me, this is a crime scene and we gotta do our thing. Our *whole* thing. We take that truck to the forensics lab. We *dissect* that cabin, I mean who knows what's been going on here? We're takin' care of business."

"You're getting me ready for . . . what?"

"So yeah. We got fingerprints all over the cabin, and we want to know whose they are. I mean, maybe Mason King's got connections to Tony Shapiro's druggie friends, or your sister's prints will freakin' show up, who knows? Lots of surprises in this line of work, my motto is 'no stone unturned.' Mason's prints and yours, we recognize. But we got lots that we don't, so for elimination purposes we get prints from Jody and the kids—probably the prints are theirs, all the times they've been out there over the years. Just takin' care of business, right?"

She was frowning by now. She poured more wine into our glasses, shook the almost empty bottle, and turned to scowl toward the kitchen.

"You told the kid to get lost," I reminded her.

"Right. So, Whitman, sorry about this, Jody King's prints make our computers go *bing!* Not in the AFIS database, to our knowledge she's never been printed before. They match some of the unknowns we pulled from your sister's house."

I just sat. I had no thoughts.

"Aaaand then there's the awkward thing of asking her for a DNA sample. This was a few days ago. She's pissed at us, who wouldn't be? Grieving widow, kids in shock, all the rest of her woes. But what's she gonna do? And what kind of match do we get for her DNA?"

I just looked at her.

"You got it—that third sample on the knife. The mystery protoplasm. We'd been surprised that it wasn't Laughlin's and bitterly disappointed when it proved not to be Mason's. It was Jody's blood."

"You can't really be thinking—"

"Well, we had speculated that the killer left DNA on Trudy's body, maybe you-know-what, maybe blood from an injury sustained during the fight. So Manring checked every hospital within a sixty-mile radius. No suspicious slashing injuries reported in the time when your sister was killed. But an inspection of Jody's forearm shows a fairly recent cut. It's just a scar, but obviously it'd been stitched up tight with clumsy sutures. First she says it's from way back, but that doesn't wash at all, it's too recent. Then she says, oh right, she cut herself at the feed store and she sewed herself shut. She and her dad used to sew up cows that stepped in barb wire and such. They've got basic vet supplies at the store, why bother with a trip to the hospital?"

I opened my mouth to say something, but forgot what it was. An image flashed into memory: at the cop picnic, the elastic compression brace Jody wore on her arm, covering her biceps, elbow, and half her forearm.

"We couldn't match her DNA with blood on Trudy's body—too much time in the water, too degraded. But meanwhile, we've been working on those corrugated plates from the bed of Tony Shapiro's truck. Mason was cutting the thing up but, he hadn't sunk those out in the pond yet. Down at the lab, they go over them with, fuck, chemicals I can't pronounce and alternate light sources. And lookie here, what's this waffle-pattern residue? Clear as shit in the right light. Somebody says, that's a tire track—motorcycle. Hm, okay, Mason has a motorcycle, and he told you he rolled it up into the truck when he made his getaway. Except he's got this big road bike, linear tread pattern, weighs five hundred fifty pounds, I looked it up. But Jody was into motocross, I saw the photos of her at the camp and at the Kings' house, doing jumps and popping wheelies. She has this skinny little dirt bike, 125 cc, big knobby tires for cross country and hill climbs and all that fun stuff. A *lot* easier to get into a pickup—just pop a wheelie, get the front wheel onto the tailgate, lever it from there. Her bike's tires match the waffle print on the truck bed panels."

I was silent as I remembered. Mason had stumbled a little when I'd asked what he'd done with his motorcycle after killing Laurel and Tony. He'd told me he put the Triumph in the truck—Tony had a plank in there, he said, he drove it up. But in the back of my mind, it had registered: The Triumph and Mason together would weigh close to eight hundred pounds, that would have to be quite a plank. The two of us had a hard time getting his bike onto my little trailer, with a much lower bed than a pickup and a pair of two-by-tens for a plank.

Selanski let me digest it before she went on. "And there were traces of blood on those truck bed plates. They hadn't been in the water, right? Somebody had worked hard to wipe it up, but we're pretty good with that shit. We find Tony's blood and another trace whose donor you probably already guessed."

I didn't have to ask about motive. Mason had fallen in love with Laurel again—no, he'd insist, *still*. At some point, Jody somehow got wind of it. She'd gone to Laurel's house to confront her, leaving her fingerprints here and there. Laurel had assured her there was nothing going on, Jody had backed off. But some time later, something else triggered her concern. Maybe she followed Mason and he led her to Martinson's. Or she learned about the expensive bicycle purchase. She had lost one husband, no way she was going to lose another. She was going to give her kids a normal family, two parents. No matter what.

"So," Selanski went on, "Jody gets it into her head that she's gonna have it out with Laurel once and for all. She goes to Martinson's, asks for her. This kid who works in the bakery section confirms he told some woman that she'd gone camping. Jody guesses where, maybe she and Mason had camped there sometimes. So she goes up, things get out of hand. After that, it all goes down basically as we visualized it, as Mason told it, Tony Shapiro stumbling into it at the end. Except it's Jody and not Mason doing the killing and dragging and throwing Laurel off the cliff."

I finished my glass of wine and Selanski poured the remainder of the bottle into it.

"I don't know if I'm going to have much of an appetite," I told her.

"You want me to order another bottle?"

"No. Thanks."

The gentle hubbub of the restaurant was surrealistically remote, the way sounds in the air go strange when you put your head under the water. Waitstaff came and went, customers greeted one another. Laughter from the bar. At the far end of the room, the chrome kitchen doors flashed as they swung. Selanski was better at waiting than I'd have expected.

After a while, I asked, "So where's it at? With Jody?"

"We took her in today."

"What about the kids?"

"Jody's got brothers and cousins up the wazoo all over the state. They'll go to an uncle in Morrisville for now."

I nodded. Glad it wasn't some stranger care arrangement.

Selanski sat with her chin resting on her fists, observing me.

I was thinking about duplicity. How long had he maintained his facade, lied to me? "Any thoughts on when Mason learned about this? I mean, did she tell him about it right away, or did he put it together in bits and pieces?"

"Dunno. My money's on the night you called him about kicking the thing in the reservoir. She'd have known he'd have no choice but to call us, because if he wouldn't, you would. She couldn't let him do that without getting the body out of there first. My guess is, they had a *very* tough conversation after you hung up. And that they had to work together to move your sister that night."

The kids, I was thinking, it would have come down to the kids. Jody, the pragmatist. Jody, the mama bear. *What's done is done, Mace. Yes, it was bad, it was a mistake, it got out of hand, but it's done, it's the past. Now we have to look to the future.*

So many shadings. All the shifting motives. What we intend, what we actually do. Did Jody go up there planning to kill Laurel? To scare her? To have a heart-to-heart talk? Who knows what exactly happened? Only Jody. Who knows what she told Mason? *She attacked me, I had to defend myself!* Or, *It's your fault as much as it is mine!* That one would get to him. The shadings, the gray zones.

There's Mason; it's the middle of the night. He's stunned, appalled, but Jody explains, exonerates herself as much as she can. And ultimately, what matters is what happens now. *It is about the kids. It's about us. It's about the future.*

And what does Mason feel? Maybe he feels some relief—his obsession, his frustration, it's all been resolved by events beyond his control. Maybe he does feel culpable—he let that crazy deluded love run away with him, and look where it led. Possibly he even feels a twinge of satisfaction—Laurel sort of got what was coming to her, for refusing him. Or, as he might have been persuaded to see it, for leading him on.

I didn't know. I had no idea. I had no insight into human nature or psychology at all. Least of all Mason's.

"Yeah, makes your head spin, doesn't it?" Selanski said. "Times like this, I gotta ask myself why I got into this line of work. But I'm used to it. You're not. I'm no psychologist like your girlfriend, but I suspect you've got some serious shit kicking around in your head."

I grunted affirmation.

"Now here's the thing. I couldn't see what was going on on the other side of that boat, right? I mean, I winged Mason King, and he fell in. And you're in there, probably getting winded with so much time underwater, so much adrenaline going. And he falls in, he's fully dressed, even has boots on. One arm is maybe not working so well. And he's been shooting at you for a while. He almost got you at least once."

More than once, I was thinking. He'd shot through the hull just a few inches from my head.

Selanski looked side to side and leaned forward, lowering her voice. "You know what? His magazine held seventeen rounds and there were only two left when we fished the gun out of the pond. So if it was me in the water, I would *not* be charitably inclined toward the guy. Maybe you're not sure if he still has the gun in his hand. He's floundering, not much of a swimmer, weighed down by his clothes and boots and equipment. What're you going to do, *save* the fucker?"

"What do you want from me? Where are we trying—"

"What do I want *from* you?" she snarled. Her eyes were falcon's eyes. "Nothing. You're a good guy, Whitman. Man of conscience. I don't know what happened behind that boat, but I hate the thought of you giving yourself shit forever and ever. Maybe you're thinking, 'Fuck, poor Mason *martyred* himself for his family! Did a great job of confessing, made it seem so real, taking it all on himself and keeping Jody out of it. How noble.'"

I didn't answer. She was reading me perfectly.

"What I'd like is for you to accept that it was a real hairy situation, and that *justice sometimes gets served raw*. Fifteen shots? If it was me out there with him, I'd've said, 'Have a fuckin' *bite!*'"

She caught her breath, then snarled again, "Fifteen shots!" Her voice dripped contempt.

Yes, there was that. I felt that, when we were in the cabin, when we were in the water. I felt it still. But I really couldn't say what I did, thrashing and tangling in the weeds. I held him, yes. Did I hold him up? Down? Was I comforting him, saving him, killing him? Can you do all three at once?

"In the water," I mumbled. "He asked me to do what was right."

"Yeah? What do you think he meant?"

That was the question.

Selanski scanned the restaurant and spotted our waiter. When she saw that she'd caught his eye, she made a gesture at our empty bottle: *Another.* Then she turned her fierce gaze back to me.

"I humbly suggest that you did just what he asked," she said, not humbly at all.

# EPILOGUE

# CELINE

Summer wound down and fall infiltrated the hills and valleys: warm days, chilly nights, stains of rust and yellow appearing in the leaves. I began full work weeks at school and was grateful for the reassuring routine and daily sense of small accomplishments. After two weeks off, Conn returned to the *Herald* and it seemed to help restore him. As he came back toward himself, our time together became more enjoyable again. I had no desire to spend time at my apartment, and it was good to be with him every evening when our workdays were done.

We slowly resumed our lovely version of courtship, but, as at the beginning, we were patient and somewhat wary. Conn, for all that he's skilled with words, with observing and speaking nuanced things, didn't want to talk about Trudy or Mason or Jody. He claimed he couldn't think about them yet.

I didn't believe that, but I didn't mind, either, because I didn't know what I'd say to him. He wasn't a patient or a client, and nothing I'd learned in school seemed to apply to this situation very well. Yes, murder puts you up against a lot that nothing else can prepare you for. I couldn't find any therapeutic axiom better than what Selanski told Nadeau: *That thing you got, it'll go away if you rub up against regular people, fly right long enough. Just be patient with yourself and the rest of us.* Something like that.

Patience—an underrated virtue, an under-practiced art. Katherine

Krantz had untied one knot when she told Conn how easy it was for his sister to forgive him. But it would take a while to percolate through his psyche. Nadeau faced the same challenge. We didn't hear from him, but I thought about him sometimes, wondering if he was still a wolverine, wary around humankind, or whether he was letting his freedom sink in, ease away his hypervigilance. I hoped so.

The sexual assault trial of David Laughlin began, and though he hired some expensive lawyers, it wasn't going his way. Gail Pelkey took over where Trudy had left off, persuading his other victims to testify against him. Despite a flurry of defense objections, the court agreed to let the multiple plaintiffs proceed in a consolidated litigation, all testifying at the same trial, and to admit the video evidence seized from his home.

"He's going down!" Selanski crowed when she called to update us.

In the end, six women filed civil lawsuits. Jocelyn Macey didn't join in. She had deposed on video for his criminal trial, but wouldn't appear in court, and she wanted nothing to do with the civil trial. She didn't seek damages. She and her fiancé had wedding plans and wanted to stay focused on life's good things.

Good advice, I thought.

Laughlin's trial for the murder of Artie Shindell would be next. Trooper Manring finally found the gas station that sold him the accelerants used in the fire, and traffic cams at a couple of Burlington intersections showed his silver Ford Taurus coming and going only a few blocks away, Laughlin's face visible in the windshield. Still, Selanski fretted that the murder case might give the prosecution some trouble in court—the defense could chip away at too many details. She'd show up to testify, but it was no longer her baby—the Attorney General's office had excellent investigators to follow through on it.

But Jody. Oh, Jody. Conn wouldn't read or listen to any news about her upcoming trial. Selanski thought that Jody was doing herself a disservice by taking the Fifth too often, denying evidence, claiming prosecutorial bias and misconduct. Cops and prosecutors both recognize this pattern as fancy footwork in the face of the obvious.

One night when I couldn't sleep, I lay there next to Conn and thought about Jody. She was a strong, practical, get-things-done woman. Never a complainer or a whiner, never playing the victim. She had fallen in love with a newcomer to the area, a Black man, and had defied her father's doubts about the marriage. Her husband had previously served in the Marines and after the horrors of the first battle of Fallujah had re-upped. He was killed in Iraq in 2006, leaving his farm-girl wife at home with a one-year-old son and an as-yet unborn daughter.

And so Mama Bear was born.

No wonder Conn couldn't listen to the daily developments in the prosecution of Jody King. They weren't little, or local, or passing. For him they were vast, universal, foundational, rooted in contexts rooted in contexts without end. Regional histories and family histories and the accidental histories of each individual. Right, wrong, truth, falsehood. Priorities. Urgencies. Fears. Losses.

We talked a little about Mason and his willingness to take the blame for murdering Trudy and Tony. Conn was particularly troubled by Mason's duplicity—his ability to talk with us while concealing the facts of the murders. It struck him as utterly at odds with the man he'd known.

But I didn't see it quite the same way. Mason's misery had been authentic, and he had been candid with Conn and me about his feelings for Trudy and his sorrow at her death; all he'd had to do to stay camouflaged was to frame its outward manifestations with the right explanations. And while Irene Shapiro's shooting of Penny McKenzie really did traumatize him, it also provided him with another layer of emotional camouflage. That is, we could rationalize his reserve, or any out-of-character behavior, as resultant from that trauma and misplaced guilt.

Finally, there was family pride and Jody and the kids to protect. And Jody to school him and remind him and script him.

What Conn and I did not, ever, talk about was exactly what happened in the water, with Mason wounded and beginning to drown—drowning being the official cause of death. I'm not sure he himself knew. Did he enact Lance Burton's role—terminating a dangerous man who had just confessed to murdering two people, who had shot at him fifteen times, who very well could be a menace to the village? Did he help Mason drown, or let him drown, as a mercy? According to Selanski, Mason had seemed to ask for that, at the end. Or maybe Conn simply fought back to preserve his own life—and won that fight.

I don't know. I don't need to know. I am content to let it remain Conn's to sort out, his Upaya-Kaushalya moment. His challenge of self-forgiveness.

I am a psychologist. Healing is my supposed profession, and non-judgment is central to my practice. I've never physically injured anybody and have no desire to do so. But when I think of Mason shooting at Conn, I basically come down where Selanski did. My blood boils. Maybe I'll need to look at that someday, but in all truth it doesn't bother me that much and I am in no hurry.

Conn's changes are tectonic in scope, though. If he gets deep with me—not often—he gets abstract, or inarticulate: Who're you going to hate? Who should you blame? Who can you forgive? How much should you forgive? This twining of love and murder, lies and devotion and betrayal and loyalty—what's it all about? His hands make fraught, tangling gestures when he talks about it.

He talks about how absolute determination seems like a virtue— look at the example of his sister, and of Katherine Krantz!—until you consider the other places it can lead a person, like where it took Jody and Irene. And Mason.

Adopting a local saying, I caution him against getting his chain wrapped around his own axle. That makes him smile, a little.

Conn began the probate process needed to deal with Trudy's house and belongings, and eventually to have a say in his nieces' future. It would take a while, he was informed: red tape.

We went to see the girls and, according to Conn, had a good time.

For me, it was tense. They seemed wary, watchful, and needy, and I didn't know how to act around them except in a professional way that would make any smart kid's alarm bells go off: *bogus!* But he swore they took to me and were more relaxed than he'd ever seen them. He gave me credit for this—undeserved, because I mostly just went with the flow and tried to avoid getting cute.

Then we had them over to the cabin for a glorious late September afternoon, and they did indeed seem to have a good time. Conn enlisted them in a project—to hang a tire swing—and they took to it with good will. After untold attempts to get a rope over a promising high branch—throwing a string attached to a rock, even trying to shoot arrows over with an improvised bow—they succeeded. Cheers all around. The way it works is, you run up the strong rope after the string, bring the end down to make a slip knot, then run it back up again. Simple, in concept but new to this Chicago girl. We all had some terrific swings, especially with Conn giving us mighty pushes that sent us up higher than the cabin eave, right into the branches. The girls and I swung Conn with equal vehemence though less success, altitude-wise.

A couple of days later, I came home to find Conn in the screen porch with a tape measure, kneeling as he jotted on a legal pad. We had several choices, he told me as he showed me the diagram he'd drawn. With insulation, glass windows, and a few amenities, the porch would make a decent bedroom for two, either with a bunk bed in one big room, or with two smaller subdivisions for individual beds. Or, he said, flipping the page to a second-floor plan he'd sketched, they could live in the new addition he'd build against the west wall, and I could take over the renovated porch as my home office and personal space. Or vice versa.

I hadn't spent a night at my own apartment for over a month, he pointed out, no sense in spending money on rent for a place I never used, especially when the money would cover the loan payments on the renovations here.

He must have noticed that I was a bit taken aback—we hadn't discussed any of this—because he said, "Just putting it out there, sweet cheeks." Throwing that one back at me with a flash of eyes and a grin.

His grin was still cracked, coming up on only half his face while the other side stayed mostly ironic and rueful. But it was less pronounced and I was worrying less.

Somehow, that tape measure was what did it for me. Silly, I know. But surely that's the way to go—to take the measure of a future. Put the tangly and unquantifiable stuff aside for a bit, even just for a bit. Plan a good space to live in, something tangible and real. Mark out the shape of it with due deliberation, get the proportions right, and then make it happen with earnest goodwill. Best anybody can do. Periods of endings should be seized as periods of beginnings.

"Not a bad idea," I told him. "I'll toss it around and have my people get back to you. Soon."

# ACKNOWLEDGMENTS

The author is deeply indebted to many people for their contributions to *The Body Below*. Readers should know that any factual errors occurring in the text are entirely my own excesses of license or just idiocy, and not the fault of my expert advisers! Sincerest thanks are due to:

Captain Scott Dunlap, head of the Major Crime Unit, Vermont State Police, who endured my interrogations with good grace and filled me in on VSP administration, procedure, and various complex legal details.

Brenda Gooley, operations director for the Family Services Division, Vermont Department for Children and Families, who gave generously of her time to help me understand foster care, adoption, and the nuances of state custodianship in Vermont.

Richard I. Rubin, attorney, of Rubin, Kidney, Myer, and Vincent, who provided real-deal legal advice (and unwavering support for the arts and artists over many years).

Major (retired) Tim McAuliffe, former head of the New York State Police Forensic Investigation Center, whose terrific education in all things homicide-related has stood me in good stead for so many years.

All the good folks at Blackstone: Josie Woodbridge, editorial director, for her enthusiasm and elegance; Madeline Hopkins, for her editorial expertise and admirable patience; Alenka Linaschke, for designing this book's stunning cover; and Rick Bleiweiss, head of new business development, for so much support and inspiration.

And of course Stella Hovis, my darling companion and chief facilitator for all my novels and, really, most everything I do.

The characters in this book are entirely fictional—with three exceptions. Burt Pugach and Linda Riss were real people whose story provides a challenging example of obsessive love and its disturbing permutations. More inspiringly, Gertrude Ederle is also a real historical person. When she swam the English Channel in 1926, she was not only the first woman to succeed; her time of fourteen hours, thirty-nine minutes set a record that remained unbeaten by anyone, male or female, for twenty-five years. She went on to win Olympic medals and set twenty-nine more world records, some of which endured for eighty-one years! Her dominance in her sport is comparable only to that of the world's very greatest athletes, such as Babe Ruth, Wilt Chamberlain, Martina Navratilova, Michael Phelps, and Serena Williams, and her fascinating story is well worth remembering. For an introduction, the author recommends *Young Woman and the Sea: How Trudy Ederle Conquered the English Channel and Inspired the World*, by Glenn Stout.